W9-BEU-844

WITHDRAWN

WITHDRAWN

HAVE YOURSELF A BEARY LITTLE MURDER

MEG MACY

WHEELER PUBLISHING

A part of Gale, a Cengage Company

GALE
A Cengage Company

Farmington Hills, Mich • San Francisco • New York • Waterville, Maine
Meriden, Conn • Mason, Ohio • Chicago

Copyright © 2019 by Meg Macy.
Wheeler Publishing, a part of Gale, a Cengage Company.

ALL RIGHTS RESERVED
This book is a work of fiction. Names, characters, places, and incidents either are products of the author's imagination or are used fictitiously.
Wheeler Publishing Large Print Cozy Mystery.
The text of this Large Print edition is unabridged.
Other aspects of the book may vary from the original edition.
Set in 16 pt. Plantin.

LIBRARY OF CONGRESS CIP DATA ON FILE.
CATALOGUING IN PUBLICATION FOR THIS BOOK
IS AVAILABLE FROM THE LIBRARY OF CONGRESS

ISBN-13: 978-1-4328-7028-7 (softcover alk. paper)

Published in 2019 by arrangement with Kensington Books, an imprint of Kensington Publishing Corp.

Printed in the United States of America
1 2 3 4 5 6 7 23 22 21 20 19

To my fuzzy hubs,
a teddy bear at heart,
my Sweet Pea for impeccable timing,
being born at Christmastime,
and to Mom, who always made
the holidays so special.

ACKNOWLEDGMENTS

Huge thanks to Wendy McCurdy, my wonderful editor, who brainstormed with me at Malice Domestic about this "Santa Bear" book, in a noisy restaurant — but she never seemed in a rush. Thanks also to Norma Perez-Hernandez at Kensington for her enthusiastic support; Paula Reedy and the hard-working copyediting department; John Scognamiglio for the title help; and the art department for this wonderful cover. Such a delight!

Special thanks to my childhood friend Laura McGee for letting me borrow and read all her Happy Hollister books, and for buying my first Trixie Belden book as a birthday present. That led me to collect the rest of the series (scraping up my allowance, week by week), and a lifelong love of mysteries. That's why I write them. I love seeing my books on the shelf!

I also want to thank my longtime friend

Sharon (and writing partner for D. E. Ireland), who gave me a great plot tip; to my Sweet Pea as first reader; my sisters for their support; my "tea time" friends for much needed breaks. And my enthusiastic readers and fans for sending me photos of their beloved teddies, plus cards and other surprises. Mwah!

It's too bad we're not all teddy bears.
More stuffing would only make us cuter
and cuddlier.
Richelle E. Goodrich,
Making Wishes

CHAPTER 1

"Santa Bear, Santa Bear, we're gonna see Santa Bear!"

The two kids' singsong chant made me laugh. I noted how both the little girl and boy in matching red jackets and striped stocking hats hugged their well-worn teddy bears close. "All his elves will be there, too," I said. "Have a wonderful time tonight!"

The Silver Hollow Annual Tree Lighting and Festival of Lights Parade was one of the highlights of the town's holiday season. Two dozen slim artificial evergreen trees stood among the Village Green oaks, maples, ash, and elm trees, most bereft of their leaves. Several shops had decorated the festive trees. Mary's Flower Shop used silk poinsettias, while Fresh Grounds hung huge inedible cookies on theirs. We'd ordered silver-sequined plastic teddy bears for our Silver Bear Shop & Factory tree. I had a devil of a time fastening the oversized bears between the white light strands and blue velvet ribbon bows.

The parents, who flanked their kids, herded them toward the big red tent on the lawn past the courthouse. "Merry Christmas," the mother said. "Have fun tonight."

"Same to you. Stay warm!"

I shivered in the cold breeze, which swept over the crowd swarming on Roosevelt Street. A decent crowd for almost midweek, too. Dusk would come soon, although the village clock had only struck four fifteen. The early December sun had been veiled behind a bank of gray clouds for most of the day. I'd left Aunt Eve in charge of the Silver Bear Shop, which remained open due to the crowd coming to see the tree lighting and village parade. People from all around Southeast Michigan came in to take advantage of last-minute Christmas shopping.

My mother was talked into taking over the event's committee chair job a month ago, a huge commitment. Dad and I had helped with half a dozen projects to prepare for the event, but that didn't take a load off Mom's stress level. Everyone in my family noticed how cranky she'd been lately. That was bound to end after today. We hoped.

I stopped to chat with my cousin Matt and his adorable girls, standing with other friends who'd brought their kids for the parade. Family groups planted chairs and blankets at the street's curb alongside the hotel, the courthouse, and the Village Green. They had a hard time corralling their excited children. One little boy dropped a bag of marbles, which rolled every which way. Cara and Celia joined in grabbing them up, laughing and giggling.

"I want to keep this one —"

"No, Celia, they're Tommy's marbles," Matt said. "Give it back."

One woman hailed me. "Ms. Silverman? We bought my son a teddy bear for his birthday at your shop. Back in September. My husband didn't realize that Sawyer left it outside in the backyard. Unfortunately, when he mowed the lawn, he didn't see the bear."

"No problem! Bring it in any time. If we can't repair it, we'll replace it."

"Thank you so much."

"We guarantee our bears, whether they've been torn up by dogs, cats, or even a gator. Yes, one little girl on vacation in Florida left hers on the lanai of their rental condo. Needless to say, the alligator may have thought it was a tasty snack."

"Oh, my. A friend of mine bought a bear, not one of yours, and her son was playing hide and seek. He put his wet bear in the oven, hoping it would dry. I guess she didn't realize it when she started making cookies and preheated the oven."

I nodded. "Oh, yes, we've seen it all. Every week we receive a bear or two that needs a 'hospital visit.' We don't mind repairing any of our bears."

"Do you offer a teddy bear clinic?" the woman asked. "To help kids get over their fear of visiting the doctor or a hospital, I mean."

"No, but it's a great idea," I said. "I'll have to consult our calendar and add that to our events next spring. Have a wonderful time at the parade."

They headed off toward Main Street. I spied Emily Abbott, whose long black hair, streaked with red and green, looked festive compared to her Goth-style makeup, leather pants, and a matching jacket studded with chains and zippers. Lace mitts covered her hands but left her black-gelled nails sharpened to points in full display. She had to be cold, though, given the way she jumped up and down to get warm. Her cheeks were reddened from the wind, too.

"Hey, Sasha!" She weaved her way through a group of teens to join me. "Congrats on winning that Teddy Bear Keepsake contest last month. Your aunt was telling me about how your shop's been entering, like, forever, but never won before."

I had to laugh. "Aunt Eve exaggerated. We only submitted for five years, but yes. We're thrilled that our Beary Potter Keepsake wizard bear was chosen. It's such an honor."

"Beary Potter? That's so cool!"

"We're using 'The Magic of Christmas' for our promotion," I explained with a smile. "It's a special six-inch tan bear wearing a black robe, a maroon and gold scarf, plus those round glasses. And of course, he'll carry a wand."

"I can't wait to buy one."

"We sent off the first five hundred," I said, "but the orders keep pouring in. The cutoff date is this Saturday, so make sure you order one. We'll be swamped getting them produced before the Holiday Open House. I hear you're working a part-time holiday job."

"At the Magpie's Nest, yeah," Emily said with pride. "I'd better run or I'll be late. I'm covering the shop while Maggie rides her float in the parade tonight. She told me five o'clock, but I wanted to get there early due to the crowds."

"Great seeing you. I'm heading over to check on our float now."

15

We parted ways, Emily scurrying toward Main Street while I race-walked up Kermit, past Ham Heaven, the Silver Scoop Ice Cream Shoppe — closed for winter — and the Pretty in Pink bakery. The Quick Mix Factory loomed ahead, with its triple towers and boxy building. The floats had yet to line up in order in the huge parking lot. Amy Evans, who usually ran the village events, had been called out of town on a family emergency; her mom required extensive care, so Mayor Bloom urged my mother to take over the job. All the councilmen and business owners in Silver Hollow had been relieved.

I had to admit Mom had a flair for organization. After a lengthy committee meeting to introduce herself and check on progress, she'd accelerated plans and encouraged progress. Everything was now on track for a huge success.

A crowd of teens, dressed as elves in felt hats, green shirts, and patterned red pajama pants played hacky sack, joked, and laughed around Santa Bear's elaborate plush red sleigh. Its gold-painted runners sparkled even without the lights turned on; black leather straps held the sleigh in place on a trailer covered with cotton batting to resemble snow. The eight fiberglass reindeer, however, had yet to be installed on the curving track ahead of the sleigh. Several men swarmed around the float, including the newly re-elected mayor, Cal Bloom.

A sudden boom startled me, followed by a flare of bright fireworks that lit up the sky over the nearby residential streets. "Kids today," the mayor complained. "Why do they have to set off those big shells?"

One worker snorted his displeasure. "Ever since the governor passed that law, they shoot them off whenever they can. No matter how expensive."

"I know, I know. It's all about money." Bloom's booming voice echoed in my ears as well. "Legislators don't give a fig if the rowdies disturb the peace. I swear it's a scheme to fill state coffers. And the noise doesn't help traumatized vets like poor Jack Cullen."

"Don't forget the poor dogs," I said under my breath.

The New Year's Eve and Fourth of July fireworks took place at the village park, close enough for Rosie to wear her special Velcro shirt. It helped a little to calm her nerves, but I still had to crate her. My sister's cat always hid under the basement stairs. Both Maddie and I had been so busy lately, we'd been neglecting our pets. Onyx had been leaving little "presents" in my sister's closet to express her disapproval.

At least Rosie had the decency to do her business outside.

"Looks like you're having trouble getting the float ready. Never had trouble before." Cal Bloom glared at the youngest worker, who ignored him. "That row of lights is crooked —"

My mother suddenly materialized and grabbed the mayor's arm. "Now, Cal, let them do their work in peace. Help me and Sasha rearrange things over here." She tugged him toward our Silver Bears in Toyland float. "Look at these, all stuffed in willy-nilly. The kids won't see the silver bears at all unless we put them in the forefront."

Cal nodded. "Sure, sure. I don't mind helping."

"And then you can head off to get into your Santa Bear costume. It wouldn't do for the parade mascot to be late! Sasha, what is it?"

I gestured to the glittery cotton batting that covered the trailer around the huge toy box. "We should have replaced all this last year. It's dingy, to say the least."

Mom nodded. "Too late now, but I'll have your father take care of it for next year."

18

I grabbed a large brown bear and wedged it between two small dolls. Mom rearranged him to dangle out of the toy box, whose curving canopy was outlined with white miniature lights. Mr. Silver, our biggest bear, sat on the float's edge beside the box. Dad had also added newer details this year, including red and white candy canes, green lollipops, and small evergreen trees frosted with artificial snow. We'd kept the old white bear-shaped sign at the back. Red letters spelled out our shop's name, although Maddie had repainted it last week.

"Judith! There you are," Barbara Davison said, hurrying over to our float. "I need — Oh, Cal, it's good to see you. How's Alison?"

The mayor shrugged. "Fine, fine. I hardly ever see my wife, even though I bought her all new furniture to make her happy. She's always too busy taking care of her mother."

"I don't know why. Silver Birches has a sterling reputation for care, and Alison ought to trust them. Both my parents were far better off there than at home."

Barbara was Mom's closest friend in town, and lived in the house that matched our shop prior to all the renovations my father did. She resembled Martha Stewart, with a quiet demeanor, blond pageboy hairstyle,

19

and an easy smile. She always wore designer clothing. The wool Burberry coat with its cashmere checkered scarf must have set her back a cool thousand. Barbara turned to Mom, looking concerned.

"Can you please check my niece's float? I don't know what she was thinking, really. Her shop is so new, after all. She ought to have spent more time and effort to make it look halfway presentable. Cissy always did a wonderful float."

"I thought Maggie was going to use the same one with a new sign."

"My daughter called this morning and said Maggie ripped everything off and redid the whole thing. It's a mess." Barbara shook her head. "See if you can talk to her."

Mom didn't look pleased at that, however. Could it be that bad? I was tempted to give an opinion, but figured they'd ignore it. Maggie Davison had taken over Cissy's Time Turner shop and transformed it into the Magpie's Nest, which displayed collectibles and unique items for restaurant décor; she'd kept most of Cissy's vintage items to sell, however. That seemed decent of her. Maggie was a free spirit, the exact opposite of her meticulous cousin. Cissy had planned her Valentine's Day wedding down to the minute, and it was no doubt costing a fortune.

I walked faster, passing the Winter Wonderland float sponsored by Bloom's Funeral Home, with fake deer, an ice pond, and evergreen trees dusted with glittering snowflakes. The local coffee shop and bakery, Fresh Grounds, had a fabulously decorated gingerbread house and a huge coffee cup on their float. Wendy Clark, glue gun in hand, attached the last few gumdrops on the huge Gingerbread House float. The local bank's float held a working carousel. Each brightly painted horse or zoo animal had big red bows around their necks, and lights looped between them and around the top.

Two men checked the wires and started it spinning. "Have a Holly Jolly Christmas," sung by Burl Ives, rang in the air while the carousel animals jogged up and down for several minutes. Another man unplugged it.

"Works now."

"Yeah, must have been that loose wire at the top . . ."

I walked on, wondering why Cissy would care about Maggie's float. "You'd think she'd be too busy planning the wedding," I said aloud, although no one was close by to hear me.

I'd visited the Magpie's Nest shop on its

opening day, a week after Halloween, and was amazed at the visual feast for the eyes. The shelves and tables displayed hand-painted folk art, copper molds and other vintage kitchen utensils, old typewriters, horseshoes and duck decoys, old suitcases, clocks, tools, piggy banks, shutters, mechanical toys, and metal animals of all kinds. Anyone who hated clutter would loathe stepping beyond the threshold.

Like Cissy. Not that the Time Turner shop had ever been perfect. She'd displayed her items haphazardly as well, although her jewelry counters had been neat. I caught sight of Cissy haranguing her cousin Maggie, whose wild corkscrew red hair blew around her face.

"That's a royal mess! You wouldn't dare put that thing in the parade —"

"My float is totally moxie. And it's all mine, so buzz off."

Gus Antonini, Cissy's fiancé, muscled his way toward the two women. "Aw, come on, Maggie. At least take off that big Grinch."

"No. It's staying, along with everything else."

I stopped cold after spying Maggie's float, with its manger scene, palm trees, camels, and a winged Santa pig. An angel blowing a trumpet looked puny beside the huge, furry

Grinch in his red and white suit. A white Christmas tree with multi-color oversized bulbs stood beside the green figure. More bulbs crisscrossed overhead in a latticework frame that topped the float. Gnomes painted red and green lined the float's edge, too.

"Come on, Cissy. Forget it, Maggie's being stubborn." Gus pulled his fiancée away despite her protests. "Everyone's gonna think it's the ugliest thing on the planet."

"Whatev," Maggie called out. "I don't care what you or anyone thinks!"

No wonder Barbara Davison was worried. I loved the Grinch, and thought the float had an eclectic, wacky charm. Wendy Clark must have agreed, along with several friends, because they joined Maggie's infectious enthusiasm and pointed out particular details.

"That pig rocks!"

"Hilarious, Mags," someone else called out.

I walked back to the Silver Bear Shop's float. I focused my brain on finding more staff to hire in order to produce the Beary Potter Keepsake wizard bear along with our regular orders, plus manage holiday tours for school, church, and senior groups. My sister and I had reserved a sales table at the Bear-zaar, too. All that, while my new flame,

23

Jay Kirby, taught woodcarving up north. I hadn't seen him since Thanksgiving. We called often, but that didn't relieve the ache of missing him.

I stopped short after bumping hard into someone in a puffy down coat and thick scarf. "Sorry, I wasn't paying attention. My mind's wandering, I guess."

"No, no, Sasha. Don't be. I shouldn't have been standing in the way." Leah Richardson continued to apologize, although it really had been my fault. Her brown hair, over-large nose, and huge blue eyes reminded me of a scared mouse, but a brassy laugh made up for that. "I doubt if your mom knew how much work taking over the parade job would be. I've helped Amy Evans for the past two years, and I doubt she'll do it next year."

"So you're taking over for her?"

"Bite your tongue!" We both laughed and walked the last few feet to the Silver Bears in Toyland float. Leah mimicked tipping a glass. "I'm celebrating after tonight."

"Not with the Bear-zaar coming up this Saturday," Cal Bloom said heartily. "I asked Dave to handle concessions, and he said you'd help. Didn't he tell you?"

"No. He came down sick, and we're hoping it's not the flu."

24

"It's only Wednesday. He's bound to recover by the weekend."

Leah's dismay was evident. "We'll see."

"The pastor's wife couldn't get anyone else to cover the kitchen, so I volunteered you two. No one else wants to work at a hot stove with all that sauerkraut and grilled sausage. Last year I almost passed out from the heat. That's why I talked Dave into it."

I noted Leah's sour look after the mayor turned back to speak with Mom and Barbara. "Oh, brother. Christmas comes early for you." I moved a hidden bear to a more prominent spot, and Leah plucked another to a better position on the float.

"Yeah. We can't catch a break." She lowered her voice. "Dave's family resents him for being such a rebel, not working at the orchard. And Cal always sticks us with thankless jobs. He'll expect us both to be there Saturday. It won't matter if Dave is half-dead."

I felt bad for her, watching her scurry away. It was true nobody wanted to work under an old overhead fan in the church basement's cramped kitchen. Poor Leah — and poor Dave, if he was sick. He'd probably end up working no matter how bad he felt. Whenever the mayor snapped his fingers, the Richardsons always answered the call. I hoped Dave would stay in bed, though, rather than spread his germs to everyone at the Bear-zaar.

The pastor's wife couldn't find anyone to take Holly Parker's place as Santa Claus's main elf at the event, either, but she'd talked Sherry Martinez into portraying Mrs. Claus. My dad wasn't looking forward to that. Sherry always looked as if she'd bit into a sour pickle. But as the church's Women's Circle leader, she seemed the best choice to play the role.

"Too bad you missed the last council meeting, Judith," the mayor was saying. "We sure had fireworks a week ago. You wouldn't believe —"

I tuned his booming voice out while he relayed the back-and-forth arguments over budget adjustments, the last millage vote that barely passed, and the discussion of opening Theodore Lane at Main Street for better traffic flow.

"I'm all for it," Barbara Davison said, "and I'm sure the other residents on the street feel the same. With the tea room in the former bed and breakfast, and the teddy bear shop, it's hard some days to get out of my driveway. I wasn't able to pick up my grandsons from school the other day, can you believe it?"

Mom straightened a strand of lights on our float and then stood back to survey the result. "We really need the street opened, especially now that Flambé built a new restaurant, and my daughter's using their old building for her graphics studio. You've got to convince the council to take action, Cal. Soon."

"I know, ladies, I'm fully aware. We'll get it passed next meeting. I wish Tony Crocker would give up protesting the election results." The mayor waved a hand. "Can I help it if I won in a landslide? I'm not the only one who wonders what's eating him."

"It's not like he had a chance of winning anyway," Barbara said. "He didn't promote himself. That poor girl Holly Parker got more votes than he did, and that's not counting the absentee votes. I could see if someone well known, like Tom Richardson, had been running for mayor in the election. But few people know Tony Crocker."

"And he's never bothered to attend any council meetings," Mom added. "And he never volunteers to help at village events, either, from what I heard."

"I don't even know why he wanted to be a candidate. Do you, Cal?"

"Can't say as I do, although I have heard he thought the job paid a lot more than four thousand dollars a year. Which I never accepted," the mayor said with pride. "I take a dollar and give back the rest. Sure, the dental plan is a nice perk of the job. That more than pays me for my time. But people around here have been saying Crocker's a poor sport —"

"You're the one spreading that gossip around," someone barked from behind the mayor's bulky figure. Tony Crocker, in fact, thin for a man around six foot two, with a John Deere cap on his gray hair, who always wore flannel shirts, jeans, and sturdy, mud-caked work boots. "Go on, admit it! It's not enough that you won the election. You strut around like a puffed-up bantam showing off to a flock of hens. I'm gonna demand a recount."

"Do you realize how much that would cost the village?" Mom asked, hands on her hips.

"I don't care. People were rooked into voting for this clown again. We need new blood in town, and it's too bad voters didn't realize that. No, they fell back on what's familiar and boring. Same old, same old."

Barbara Davison pushed forward. "You had your chance and lost the election, fair and square. Go home to your farm and stop pouting like a child."

"Pouting, eh? I want to see the ballots for

myself. How would anyone know if the whole thing wasn't rigged from the start!"

"We can arrange that, if you insist," Mom said coolly, "but you'll have to pay for it. The village shouldn't be expected to foot that bill."

Tony Crocker snorted. "Think you're high and mighty, you and Alex Silverman. Ever since you moved here —"

"My great grandfather was born in Silver Hollow," I interrupted.

"Nobody asked you!"

"How dare you speak to my daughter that way?" My mother stabbed him in the chest with her index finger. "The Silvermans have been around as long as the Richardsons. But that doesn't matter. The residents didn't vote for you. End of story."

"Cal Bloom is your puppet. Not for long, though. Not for long."

Crocker stalked off down the line of floats, grumbling aloud.

CHAPTER 2

"What was that supposed to mean?" Mom glanced around at us all. "Did that sound like a threat to you, Cal?"

"He's blowing smoke, as usual," the mayor said. "Don't worry about him. Poor sport, like they're all saying. And I didn't start that, no matter what Crocker thinks. You ladies get on with your work. Time to get into my mascot costume. It's a real bear to put on."

Barbara and my mother laughed at his deliberate pun, but I forced a smile. "If you need any help, Mayor Bloom, we could find someone."

"No, no, Sasha. I can manage."

Cal Bloom lumbered off, smiling and stopping to chat with other villagers who wanted to congratulate him on his re-election. I turned back to Mom, who was once more trying to calm Barbara Davison about the Magpie's Nest float. Her quick defense had surprised me. I had to wonder why, but she pushed a white bear in my arms.

"Put that somewhere on the float. I'm sorry, Barbara, but the shop owners pay a fee to participate in the parade. The money goes into the village's events fund. We really don't have any say about how they design their floats."

"If only Maggie would listen to me," Barbara said mournfully. "Maybe she would if you suggest a few ideas about rearranging things."

I stuffed the white bear in between Batman and Spiderman figures in the toy box, fixed the looped rows of white lights along the float's platform, and then walked around to the other side. A clown had fallen onto the cotton batting. I retrieved it and stuck it back in the box.

"Go get yourself a hot cider, Barbara," Mom said. "You're shivering, poor thing."

She rewound the scarf around her neck. "It's supposed to snow, and that cold wind isn't helping matters. I hope they don't run out of hot chocolate like last year."

I waved a mittened hand. "Fresh Grounds, Ham Heaven, and the Sunshine Café all plan on offering coffee, tea, and hot chocolate. Quinn's Pub will be open until mid-

31

night, too."

"So I've heard. Most families will be home by then." Mom stepped back to survey our Silver Bears in Toyland float. "I guess it will have to do, Sasha. Go and find your dad, please, because he'll have to drive this monstrosity. Your uncle wants to stay late at the factory."

"Here, I'll call him —"

"Forget it. I tried," she said with a sigh. "I don't know why Alex bothers to have a cell phone if he leaves it home all the time. He must be in Christmas Alley."

"Okay, I'll go look for him. I don't know why he doesn't trust me to drive the float if he's so averse to it," I said with a laugh. "But I'm still sixteen in his eyes with a lowly learner's permit. He'll never forget how I nicked the fence post."

"Just wait till you have kids." Her voice sounded wistful. "You'll see how fast the time flies, and how hard it is to accept your children as adults. One of my girls has got to give me grandchildren. I'm not getting any younger, you know."

I groaned in silence. Barbara and my mother walked toward the front of the line of parade floats. Guilt descended on me like a net. Mom had mellowed toward me, given her reaction after I survived a second brush with death, so I felt the pressure about having kids. Maddie wasn't ready to settle down, however. We'd all seen very little of my sister since she opened her new graphics studio in the former Flambé restaurant.

With its ground-to-ceiling windows, freshly painted shingle exterior, and gorgeous polished wood floors, her new venture looked a showplace. Maddie had named it Silver Moon. She had a full schedule of work all month and far into the new year. But for one person, the building proved overlarge. My sister only used the front, formerly the dining room area; the back half, including the office, the kitchen, and storage rooms, had been stripped bare. Maddie had no idea what to do with the rest of the building. Maybe rent it, at some point.

I checked the float's lights, making sure no bulbs had burned out, and then glanced at my wristwatch. Five o'clock. The parade would start at seven. Plenty of time to refuel with some hot chocolate and maybe a gingerbread muffin from Fresh Grounds. I headed down Roosevelt Street, admiring residents' hard work to decorate their homes. Every lamppost in the village sported an evergreen wreath. Strands of white lights wound around each pole plus every shop roofline, window, porch railing, and post downtown.

"Excuse me, have you seen my dad anywhere in the village?" I asked Tess and Arthur Wentworth, the tea room owners, who were out walking their pair of corgis.

"No, dear, we haven't," Tess said. "But I wish we'd built a float for the village parade. It looks to be right wicked."

"The parade is a lot of fun."

"Next year, love," Arthur said to his wife. "I'll get Ian to help when he comes over on holiday. Our son owns a pub in Wiltshire. Have you ever been to England?"

"No, but I'm planning to go one day," I said. "Enjoy the parade."

I walked past Bloom's Funeral Home on Archibald. Cal Bloom had long ago restored and expanded a two-story Greek Revival residence into his business, added wings on either side, and surrounded the snow-covered lawn with a white picket fence. Gold Christmas trees flanked the side entrance's large portico, glittering with tiny white lights. More lights outlined a huge picture window facing the street. Inside, a horse-drawn Victorian white hearse sat on display, minus the animals. Most people thought it looked quaint and picturesque.

Mark Fox's vet clinic was down the next

block, so I headed that way. Until I caught sight of someone waving frantically. "Oh, no! I can't deal with Flynn right now —"

When I dashed across the street, the funeral home's van careened around the corner from the side street and shot past me in a blur, cutting off any escape. My ex-husband rushed to meet me, followed by his lanky girlfriend Cheryl Cummings.

"Are you okay? Wow, that was close. Maniac driver!"

He shrugged his camel wool pea coat, his blond hair slicked into spikes like a teen-ager's, sounding annoyed. Cheryl, a weather forecaster for a regional television station, looked festive in a forest green coat, red plaid wool scarf, and laced-up, high-heeled booties. Not the best choice for walking, but she seemed accustomed to it.

"You must have seen my ex around town, right, Cheryl?" Flynn hurried through a quick introduction. "Any idea where I can find Judith?"

"She's checking out the floats, over by the Quick Mix Factory. I didn't expect to see you at the parade," I said. "Heard you've been busy with a big case."

"Yeah, but the parade committee chose me to be Grand Marshal."

"Isn't it exciting," Cheryl said, shivering a

little. Her bright smile was as gorgeous as on television. I couldn't help liking her, despite her flawless complexion, that silky blue-black hair falling over her shoulders, and deep brown eyes. "I'm riding with him, too."

"That's sweet of you." I meant it, too. "And I'm thrilled to meet a real television celebrity. I've seen you plenty of times."

"You were once married to one, remember." Flynn grinned at my skeptical look. "What? I'm famous now in those Flynn Wins commercials. Did you think your mom had to twist the committee's arm to name me?"

"Who else would have suggested you?"

"Oh, come on. I'm one of the hotshot Legal Eagles, too. Besides, with the mayor in costume as the Santa Bear mascot, they needed someone with a higher profile." Flynn sounded smug, not unusual given his ego. "Watch out, Sasha!"

He pulled me out of the way again, this time from a cluster of joggers who'd turned the corner from Kermit Street and raced past. Many wore red and white sweats, some had full Santa Claus suits — beards and hats included. One wore a furry bear mask. I'd forgotten all about the 5K Santa Run. The high school's marching band suddenly started playing, its raucous drum line hammering out a steady beat, the music audible from the football field directly behind the assembly of floats in the Quick Mix Factory's parking lot.

I cocked my head when the band switched from the festive "Deck the Halls" song to a different tune. "*Star Wars*? Really?"

Flynn laughed. "You don't like Darth Vader's theme for Christmas?"

"Not quite what I expected to hear," I said wryly.

"It does sound out of place," Cheryl said. "They're practicing, though, right? Maybe that's not a song they'll play during the parade."

"Oh, I think they will." Flynn took Cheryl's arm. "So what's new, Sasha?"

I couldn't help feeling awkward, however, making conversation with my ex and his new significant other. I scrambled to think of something. "I saw that commercial for Gleaners, where you're collecting food. That's a great cause all year round."

"Charity work is always a win-win, for them and for the Legal Eagles. Everyone in the area, and even the whole state, has heard of me and my winning record."

I quickly changed the subject, not in the mood to hear his boasts. "Have you stopped by Christmas Alley yet? They have live reindeer for kids to pet, and a tent for visiting Santa Claus. You two ought to go see it."

"We'd better find Judith first, or she'll worry." He snapped his fingers, as if remembering something. "By the way, we're engaged —"

"Flynn! You said to keep it a secret," Cheryl interrupted, eyebrows raised.

"Hey, Sasha won't spread any gossip. Right?"

I nodded. "Sure. I mean, I won't. Congratulations."

"See my ring?" She'd already pulled off her thick mitten and flashed her left hand. One huge chocolate diamond was surrounded by smaller white sparkling ones and mounted on a thick gold band. "Isn't it pretty?"

"Gorgeous. Congrats again," I said weakly.

"Let's go, hon. Judith might wonder if we'll ever show up."

Flynn rushed Cheryl away. I raised my eyes to the cloud-thickened sky, wanting to kick him. My engagement ring had been puny, less than a third of a carat, although I hadn't minded at the time. He'd been starting out as a lawyer, but apparently their dual celebrity status merited far more bling. That rock plus the surrounding gems had to be three carats total. Not that any ring guaranteed marital bliss. Despite our divorce seven years ago, Flynn continued to rankle me.

But if Cheryl Cummings could get him out of my hair, I'd be grateful.

I buried a wave of sadness. Jay wouldn't be back in Silver Hollow until Christmas Eve. Neither of us could afford time off, either. I was swamped with the Silver Bear Shop & Factory's holiday rush; I couldn't ask Maddie to cover for me, not with her new business. I missed Jay's cheerful smile, sense of humor, and quiet presence. The snowy weather lately hadn't helped. We'd have to wait until Christmas.

With a sigh, I trudged toward Fresh Grounds again. A muffin and a cookie might help. The dress I planned to wear to Uncle Ross and Aunt Eve's second wedding was tighter than a sausage casing, however. The willowy image of Cheryl Cummings came into mind as well. Maybe I'd better skip a sweet treat. This time.

I quickly searched for Dad. He wasn't anywhere to be found near Christmas Alley with its vendor tents. Where had he gotten to now? I peeked into the busy Fresh Grounds, but he wasn't talking to Gil Thompson. A friendly Labrador wagged his tail at me. I scratched behind his ears, amazed that the dog would wait for his owner, his leash lying on the ground, without running off. Rosie would be halfway to the Village Green, if not the park. Inside, Garrett and Mary Kate worked behind the counter, frantically pulling shots and filling orders. I waited in line, less patient than the other customers, until Garrett took my order.

"Hey, Sasha. The usual?"

"No, I'll take hot tea. Herbal, orange spice. No muffin."

"I'm shocked. Shocked!"

I laughed along with his playful outburst and waggled my eyebrows. "Me too. Especially since those scones are calling my name. La, la, la, can't hear them!"

"Don't tell me you're on a diet, Sasha," Mary Kate called out.

"No, but I had two of your muffins this morning. I really have to fit into the dress I'm wearing to my uncle's wedding. See you later."

I paid up and headed outside, then crossed the street to the church in hopes of finding Sherry Martinez or the pastor's wife. Maddie and I had volunteered to help at the Christmas Bear-zaar on Saturday, held in the church's attached Fellowship Hall.

Vendors would be selling handcrafted items like candy, soap, floral centerpieces, jewelry, quilts, clothing, and other gifts suited for the holidays. A village-wide Teddy Bear Cookie Bake-Off contest was also a big part of the event. We'd advertised that the winner would provide cookies for our staff party and earn three hundred dollars as a bonus. That would more than pay for the ingredients.

But no lights showed in the church office.

"Rats," I muttered under my breath. My sister sprinted across the street to join me in front of the church steps. "Hey, Mads."

"I haven't seen any of the flyers I designed about the cookie contest and Bear-zaar around Silver Hollow. Have they printed them yet?" Maddie's cheeks were flushed, and she panted hard. "They better have. I took time out to do the committee a favor."

"I have no idea," I said truthfully. "Did you come from the studio? Any sign of Dad between here and Theodore Lane?"

"Nope. So what about the flyers?"

"Really, I don't know. I came over this way to ask about the Bear-zaar, but no one's here. Mom will be on the warpath, because Dad's supposed to drive the float in the parade. And he doesn't have his cell on

41

him," I added, since she'd pulled out her phone.

"Okay, I'll send him your way if I see him. You going back to the float?"

"I guess I'll drive it if Dad doesn't show up in time."

Maddie nodded and scurried off, her open parka flapping around her petite form. She didn't need sugar to fuel her energy. Caffeine was her kick while I craved carbs. Someone had to taste test those cookies for the bake-off contest.

Yum. Oh, wait. That dress.

"Maybe I'll find something that fits better before Christmas."

Why kid myself when cookies were impossible to resist during the holidays? I couldn't say no. Maybe by being so busy, planning for our open house and staff party the same week, plus the wedding, I'd forget to eat. A whirlwind of a month, the busiest since I'd started managing the Silver Bear Shop. But I had yet to skip a meal. Maybe I'd get lucky and come down with the flu. Ugh. Maybe not.

I walked back along Kermit Street to the Quick Mix Factory's parking lot, where the high school band milled around in small groups. I waded through the chatting and laughing teens in their navy wool uniforms trimmed with silver, several holding their plumed hats in one gloved hand and their instruments in the other. April Rodgers, the band's director, whistled shrilly to get the band's attention and give last minute instructions.

Mark Fox, the local vet, kept firm control of a pack of gorgeous huskies and Alaskan malamutes with the help of his cousin Jodie, despite the noise and whirl of activity. The animals stood atop a float that advertised Fox's Veterinary Hospital combined with the local pet shelter, Wags and Whiskers, which Jodie managed with Phil Richardson. Another family rebel who'd chosen something different than working at the family farm and orchard.

The fire department's truck, strung with white lights and evergreen boughs, slowly pulled into line after them, followed by the Bloom's Funeral Home's Winter Wonderland, and the Village Bank's carousel. The Quick Mix Factory's float stood on one side, a huge trailer with a theme of Mrs. Claus's Kitchen, complete with the company bookkeeper in full costume. Maggie's float with its hodgepodge items followed it.

Our Silver Bears in Toyland float was squeezed between the Gingerbread House float and Richardson Farm's flatbed, which held the entire Peanuts gang surrounding Snoopy's wildly decorated doghouse. They must have rented the resin characters, who stood with upturned faces, mouths open to sing, while several Christmas carols blared.

"Sasha! Over here."

Mom waved from the shiny red convertible that sat in the middle of all the floats. Banners with GRAND MARSHAL had been fastened on either side of the vehicle. Flynn stood beside her, grinning wide, a steaming coffee cup in hand. Cheryl shivered beside him, her mittened hands cradling a hot chocolate. She sipped with a grateful sigh.

"Did you find your father?" Mom asked.

"No," I said. "Sorry."

"He'll turn up. But I'm more worried about Cal Bloom. He's supposed to be here by now, dressed in his costume. We've got to find him."

"I bet he's behind the factory," my ex-husband said, "fortifying himself."

"What do you mean — oh, his flask of brandy?" Cheryl laughed. "Yeah, he does like to keep warm in this type of weather."

All news to me, since I'd never noticed the mayor with a flask. Mom didn't deny it, though. The cold wind brought a whiff of tiny, needle-like snowflakes into the air, and the temperature had certainly dropped in the last hour.

Flynn took Cheryl's elbow when Mom led the way toward the Quick Mix Factory. Its twin towers had painted murals of their boxed products, and the squat addition held miles of conveyor belts that sent the various items to be shipped. I always used their muffin or bread mixes when in a rush, adding fresh fruit to the batter. My efforts never tasted as good as Mary Kate's made-from-scratch treats. Buying hers was worth the extra money.

My stomach rumbled, thinking of her scones, fried donuts, and the latest holiday muffins she'd created. Raspberry cream cheese, date nut, blackberry lemon, maple pecan, and chocolate chip cappuccino — my latest favorite. I swallowed hard. Veggies, think green. Cabbage soup. Carrots with dip. Carrot muffins would be far better, though. Slathered with cream cheese frosting, too. I tugged my earlobe. Celery, celery. With peanut butter . . .

Every time we stopped to chat with parade volunteers, my stomach grumbled again. And that bitter wind groped through every layer of clothing I wore. I sipped the hot tea I'd had the good sense to grab at Fresh Grounds. Mm. That helped. Especially since the icy snowflakes kept hitting my face. My breath plumed in front of me, too, and I shivered while we stood. Once we started walking again, that helped.

I followed Flynn, Cheryl Cummings, and Mom, who chatted about her efforts to co-ordinate the floats and the various decorated trees in the Village Green, and then explained how she'd talked the mayor into being Santa Bear in the parade.

"I wasn't sure anyone else would want to do it, that costume is so hot. Even on a frigid day. Tom Richardson was the original Santa Bear for the last eight years, but begged off last year. And now he's been suffering with a bad case of bronchitis."

"Tom Junior?" Flynn asked.

"No, his dad," Mom said. "Poor man, almost eighty-six, but he's never been sick a day in his life. Now he's in the hospital, and I feel so bad for him."

"The whole clan is worried," Cheryl said. "I know they'd rather care for him at home, but from what I heard it's turned into pneumonia."

"Anyway, who else could fill out that polar bear costume better than Cal Bloom?" She laughed. "No need for extra padding."

Flynn and Cheryl joined in the chuckles at the mayor's expense. I sipped the last of my hot tea. Did they have any idea how hard it was to keep extra pounds from creeping up whenever the scale loomed? I'd struggled for years, so addicted to sugar. The endless advertising on road billboards, TV, radio, social media, plus the candy train for every holiday, from February to December, didn't help. Exercise had never been my favorite thing, although I forced myself to walk Rosie. The reality of fighting weight gain was a pain.

We passed the last float and walked the entire length of the factory until we neared the playground of the local elementary school on Quentin Street. The band started warming up again, playing the same melodies, so I checked my watch.

"Only half an hour until the parade begins, Mom."

"That must be Cal, sitting over there on the bench." She gestured ahead of us.

"And there's his flask, like I predicted." Flynn sounded smug.

Mom hurried across the empty ground toward the wooden seat. I followed, keeping the factory on one side to avoid the wind, as softer snowflakes drifted down. Not fast enough to blur my view of the mayor slumped to one side, as if asleep. The sleeves of his red Santa suit looked wet, probably from the falling snow. His face was hidden somewhere in the huge bear head, which had one beady eye missing. The mayor's hands hung slack, and his white furry paw-shaped gloves were also soaked. Weird.

My mother shook Bloom's shoulder. "We've got to get you to the parade, Cal." She sounded annoyed now. "Calvin Bloom. Wake up!"

Cheryl backed up until she bumped hard into me. "Oh! Sorry."

"No problem."

"I guess the mayor's had a bit too much brandy."

But my instincts told me something more than alcohol was at play here. Mom pulled off the bear's head to reveal the mayor's grayish skin. That was one clue, and that he didn't budge. Bloom didn't even shiver, which anyone would be doing this late at night. And there were no intermittent clouds from his breath. The wind suddenly snatched my empty cup from my hand and tossed it end over end down the street, scaring me.

Flynn darted forward. "Judith, wait! Don't touch him again."

Snowflakes glistening in her auburn hair, Mom shoved the mayor so hard that he rolled off the bench. We all heard the loud thump when Bloom landed on the damp cement. Even Cheryl gasped aloud. I surged forward in concern.

"Oh, my heavens," my mother said. "Is he dead drunk?"

Flynn knelt and pressed two fingers against Bloom's neck. "The first, actually."

"What do you mean?"

"I mean he can't feel any pain at all." Flynn glanced at us all and then rose to his feet. "Sorry, Judith, but the mayor's dead."

CHAPTER 3

Mom stood aghast, a gloved hand covering her open mouth, eyes widening. "That's not possible —"

"Dead as a doornail, I'm afraid." Flynn rose to his feet and brushed snow from his coat and hair. "No heartbeat. No pulse on his wrist, either. Bloom's a goner."

"I don't believe it!"

Cheryl and I exchanged shocked glances. This had to be a strange nightmare. Breathing deep, I was shaken to the core. How could this be happening? Cal Bloom was always full of life and talked so loud that his booming voice hurt my ears. And now he was lying cold and dead. We'd seen him only an hour or so before, complaining about things, and then greeting people with overt friendliness and charm.

The snow had thankfully ended. Cheryl and I both scrabbled for our cell phones. I dialed 911. A habit, especially after finding two other dead bodies in the last few months, so I reported our location and situation before I hung up. Cheryl was still talking, hunched over, speaking in a half whisper. My mother pulled out her own phone and punched in a sequence of numbers. She must have called Maddie, Aunt Eve, or even Uncle Ross given how she kept hanging up and redialing. At last she succeeded reaching someone.

"Gil Thompson, listen to me. Track down Alex for me, and get him over to the factory parking lot. I'll explain later!" Mom sounded beyond frantic. "I know you're busy. I don't care if there's a huge line — yes, it's an emergency! Send Garrett out then, anyone. Thank you. Yes, whatever it takes. As many people as possible, until you find my husband. And send him to the Quick Mix parking lot."

She hung up, but I waved a hand. "Mom, I couldn't find Dad —"

"I'll find him," offered Flynn, who'd circled the bench a few times.

"We've got to stay here until the police arrive." She knelt by Cal's prone figure. "For the children's sake, the parade must go on. That means your dad will have to be Santa Bear. Come on, Sasha, help me get this costume off him. Why are these paws so damp and stiff?"

Mom tugged off a glove and then gasped. I stared at the mayor's reddened, blistered fingers. Flynn stripped the Velcro apart that fastened the coat over Cal Bloom's chest. The mayor wore only a white ribbed tank shirt beneath, and thin enough that we could all see the charred skin of his chest. Cheryl backed away, although she held out her phone a few times. Was she taking photos? Mom marched over to her, clearly angry.

"I know you're part of a TV crew, but please stop. The police will not appreciate any unauthorized photos ending up on social media. Nor would the family."

"Oh. Yeah, I suppose you're right," she said wanly. "Flynn, I'm freezing. I'd rather wait inside the Grand Marshal's car."

"Uh, sure." He pointed to the mayor's chest. "His hands must have gotten all wet. And if he touched a live wire, it could have given him a shock and caused a heart attack. Didn't he have a bad heart, Judith?"

"Yes. So you're saying he was electrocuted?"

"All of these floats have generators to power the lights." Flynn waved a hand around. "People have been coming and going all day. But I wonder why nobody noticed Bloom over here, or heard him cry out when it happened. That's really weird."

Mom took a deep breath, although her voice shook. "It had to be an accident."

"That's for the police to determine." He rose to his feet. "But greed is a pretty big motive for murder. I've heard and read about plenty of cases where the family offs Grandpa or their parents to get an early inheritance."

"That's ridiculous —"

"Flynn's right," Cheryl cut in. "It doesn't matter what we think. The police will handle this whenever they get here. You two can stay and answer their questions."

"Yeah, and I don't want the cops to get the wrong idea like last time." He stuck his hands into his pockets. "Come on, babe. Let's go."

"You two can't leave," I said flatly. "They'll need a statement from each of you."

"Tell them to call us later."

"Oh, go on, then." Mom sounded hysterical and turned to me. "Now I know how you and Maddie must have felt, finding Will Taylor. And then you found that other poor girl, Sasha! Oh, thank goodness your father's here. At last."

I breathed a sigh of relief when Dad's SUV turned onto Quentin Street. He climbed out and then strode our way. "What the devil is going on?" Dad stared down at Cal Bloom's body while Mom explained how we'd found him. "You called 9-1-1, I hope."

"Of course we did. Now, help me get this costume off poor Cal. You'll have to wear it, Alex, and take his place. Hurry, there's almost no time to spare."

"Judith, we can't touch the body."

"But someone has to play Santa Bear in the parade!"

"Stop. This is a police situation." Dad scrambled for his phone in his pockets, sheepish until I handed mine over. "Thanks, honey. I know, I know. I keep forgetting it at home. I'm calling Ross right now, Judith. He can drive our float instead of me in the parade. Don't fuss. Everything will work out. I'll play Santa Claus instead. The kids won't mind."

"But Dave Richardson is wearing that costume at Christmas Alley," Mom wailed.

"Not today. He went home sick, so I filled in for him. I hope he's not getting that same bronchitis that put his father in the hospital." Dad checked his watch, holding my cell to his ear. "Good thing I stashed the Santa suit in the car instead of leaving it back at the tent. Ross? Yeah, I'm afraid there's been a change of plans. You'll have to drive the float. Get all those packets of gummy bears and toss them out for the kids lining the street —"

"Alex, no! Those are supposed to be for our Holiday Open House." Mom frowned when he hushed her. "All right, but don't complain when we have to buy more."

I patted her shoulder. "We'll manage."

She grasped my hands and dragged me aside. "He made a fuss over what we had to pay for the wizard robe fabric," Mom said, "but never mind that now. I'm so sorry, honey. You have to understand I only wanted you to be happy."

"Huh?"

"Flynn just told me he's going to marry Cheryl," she rushed on, "and all this time, when he talked about wanting to settle down again, I thought he meant with you. That he wanted to patch things up — but I was so wrong. Can you forgive me?"

"Uh, sure." I blinked. "It's okay, Mom. Really."

Mom leaned closer to me, almost whispering. "I hoped you would give him a second chance, that's all. Because your dad did that for me. Oh! We'll have to talk later."

Two squad cars screeched to a halt at the curb. Officers Hillerman and Sykes climbed out of their respective vehicles. Mom rushed over to meet Bill Hillerman at the sidewalk. Digger Sykes sashayed over to join me near the bench, though. I was still reeling from my mother's revelation, and wondering what she'd meant about a second chance.

"What happened here?" He pointed a finger at the mayor, half-hidden in the Santa Bear costume. "Don't tell me you found another dead body."

"I found Mayor Bloom, young man, not Sasha. Along with Flynn Hanson and Cheryl Cummings." At Mom's sharp voice, Digger backed off in surprise. She waved a hand toward the mayor. "Poor Cal must have been electrocuted, although we can't figure out how."

"Wow!"

"Move aside, Officer Sykes. All right, Mrs. Silverman, give me a minute." Bill Hillerman produced a notebook and pencil. Dad walked over and handed my phone over. "Who wants to start telling me the whole story?"

"I wasn't here when they found the mayor," Dad said. "And I've got to get into a Santa Claus suit right now. I'm taking Cal's place on the Santa float. Not much else we can do. It's almost half past seven, and the parade's finally getting underway."

The band's rousing rendition of "Santa Claus Is Coming to Town" blasted out, along with the crowd's excited cheers and rumbling of truck engines pulling the floats. Bill Hillerman quickly jotted down a few notes and then waved Dad off. My father grabbed the Santa Claus suit from his car, pulled on the coat, and then buckled the black belt around his middle. He bolted toward the last float, hat in hand, waving madly.

"Bet you'll find the next body," Digger said in a loud whisper.

"There better not be a next time."

"Ha. Unless your mom's taking over —"

"Knock it off, Sykes," Hillerman interrupted. "I'm sorry, Mrs. Silverman. Go back over that last part. I couldn't hear the details."

"I said it must have been between four and five o'clock when Cal went to get into the Santa Bear costume. So when he didn't show up, we started looking for him."

"What time was that?"

"What time is it right now?"

He checked his watch. "Twenty-two past seven."

"Half an hour ago, I think, or around there." Mom suddenly gasped. "Oh, I have to tell Alison! Before someone calls her, or she hears it on the news —"

"Chief Russell will break the news to her, ma'am."

"I'll go with him. Sasha, take this mike and lead the tree lighting ceremony with your dad. The kids will be so disappointed not to see Santa Bear, so we can't cancel that!"

Her breath caught in her throat and tears rolled down her cheeks. I took the wireless microphone, slid an arm around her waist, and hugged her. "It's okay, Mom. I'll manage, and you can go with the chief. Digger will drive you to the station."

I wanted to kick him when he made a face. "Don't you look so sour, Douglas James Sykes," Mom said. "Your mother's going to hear about your disrespect."

"I'm sorry, Mrs. Silverman." Digger swallowed hard. "I'll take you to the chief."

"I'll call the county sheriff's office," Hillerman said. "We're gonna need their forensic techs to process the scene."

"Why? We don't need them if it's an accident."

"I'm not taking any chances, Sykes. I'll wait until they arrive."

Scowling, Digger took Mom's elbow and escorted her to his police car. I slid behind the wheel of the SUV, knowing word of Cal

Bloom's death would spread fast throughout the village. Especially if Cheryl Cummings had informed her news team via that whispered phone call. I wouldn't be surprised if a television crew showed up as well, but Hillerman would have to keep them at bay.

"Come on, start!" I pumped the gas pedal once and then turned the key again, glad the engine finally roared to life. "Needs an oil change. Great."

I'd have to remind Dad later. Another puff of black smoke rose from the rattling tailpipe, clearly visible in the rearview mirror. Might need a new muffler, too. Nothing else mattered except finding out how Cal Bloom had been electrocuted. My instincts told me it couldn't be an unfortunate accident. We'd found him too far from the floats with their powerful generators. If the mayor had somehow gotten his hands wet, he'd never have fooled around with any electrical equipment on purpose.

But who would target the mayor for murder? Bloom was fairly savvy, too. Wouldn't he get wind of trouble before a killer could take advantage of him? Unless it was someone he trusted. Someone close, someone he'd never suspect. Like his wife or daughter, if what Flynn said was true? But that seemed crazy.

I managed to find a spot behind the bank, pure luck on my part. I caught up to the slow-moving parade at the turn from Kermit Street. Half of the floats had already passed by. My uncle had to be driving the truck that pulled our Silver Bears in Toyland float. Maddie walked behind it with a red metal pail, tossing our small gummy bear packets to kids. They scrambled forward in a mad rush to grab them up from the ground.

"Jon, be careful. Your little brother almost got hit by the car!" One parent pulled both boys back to the curb.

"Maddie! Hey, Mads," I yelled, jumping and waving both arms. Fortunately, my sister heard me over the noise and raced to meet me in front of the Gingerbread House float. "Have you heard about Cal Bloom?"

"Yup. Dad told Uncle Ross who told Gil Thompson, who already heard the news from Mom. And you know what that means," she said with a laugh. "It's bound to be spreading all over the village by now. Hard to believe the mayor's dead."

She clearly regretted not whispering that in my ear, given the crush of people that swarmed us. Older residents, mostly, although one young woman grabbed my coat sleeve.

"Cal Bloom? The mayor is dead?"

"What happened?"

"Was it a heart attack?"

"What if he was murdered," an older man sniggered, but everyone else objected with groans and disapproval.

"Could be murder. I heard his body was found by the Quick Mix Factory." Eric Dyer, who had just opened a local micro-brewery and winery, stepped forward. He was tall and lanky, with golden blond hair all gelled up that reminded me of Flynn. Except Dyer sounded a lot less full of himself. "And he was wearing that furry white polar bear costume."

"It's true the mayor was scheduled to appear in the parade tonight as the mascot," I said, "but the police are investigating what happened."

Everyone gasped and started babbling at once. One woman shook her head.

"That's sacrilege! Like killing the Easter Bunny or the Tooth Fairy."

Eric grinned. "Yeah. So who killed Santa Bear?"

CHAPTER 4

Before I could reply, someone else piped up. "Yeah, and why?"

"Another murder in Silver Hollow, too!"

I held up a hand. "Hold on, everyone. The police don't know the facts yet, and the mayor's death may have been an accident. Let's not jump the gun."

"He was shot?"

"I didn't say that! I have no idea how he died." I winced at my frantic tone and took a calming breath. "The police will figure it out once an autopsy is done."

"But it could be murder," someone said. "Silver Hollow's getting to be a real Cabot's Cove like in that *Murder, She Wrote* TV show. Am I right?"

A few of the others laughed nervously. I didn't get a chance to refute that since the crowd split up and headed in multiple directions. Eric and a silver-haired man whispered together and then left. Maddie blew out a deep breath.

"That didn't go over very well. News here spreads like lightning hitting in a dry forest. Cabot's Cove? Really, how could anyone think this is another murder."

"Because it doesn't make sense, given where we found him." I kept my voice low while explaining how Mom and Flynn had stumbled on the mayor's body, and then discovered burns on his hands and chest. "I mean, if he'd been electrocuted near the generators, he would have yelled or called for help. Someone had to notice, don't you think? Instead it looked as if someone dumped him on that bench, already dead. At least that's my opinion."

"Wow. That is really weird. He's a pretty hefty guy, too. Was." Maddie tossed the last gummy bear packet. "Whoever did it had to be strong enough to carry or drag him."

"I need to get in the Christmas spirit and forget all about murder. Or whatever this turns out to be. Mom went with Chief Ross to tell Mrs. Bloom, since she's her friend. That means I'm stuck covering for her at the tree lighting."

My heart wasn't in it, though, despite watching the various floats with their sparkling lights roll along the dark streets. The major floats looked fabulous, but most of the minor ones also had panache, like the large and elegant poinsettia tree on a small truck bed from Mary's Flower Shop, and the sweet rocking horse from the Pozniak sisters' antique shop. An adorable cat looked ready to pounce on two mice playing hide-and-seek around The Cat's Cradle float with its stack of books. Maddie had designed it for Matt and Elle Cooper's bookstore.

A group of kilted Scotsmen piped like mad behind a troop of Boy Scouts shaking strings of jingle bells. Several World War Two vets rode in heated cars, their convertible tops down so they could wave. The bagpipers who marched behind them played "Amazing Grace" and a rousing rendition of "God Rest You Merry Gentlemen."

The crowd gasped when flames spouted from the fake figgy pudding mold, sponsored by the restaurant Flambé, which startled several of the church's hand bell choir members. Luckily the discordant jangling was soon tamped down by the choir's director. The funeral home's Winter Wonderland marvels passed by, followed by Vivian Grant's Pretty in Pink bakery float — with pink flamingoes, a lighted palm tree, and a plastic Santa wearing only shorts, sandals, and sunglasses under a beach umbrella. Ham Heaven's float with flying pigs reminded me of Maggie Davison's. She must have talked Tyler and Mary Walsh into letting her borrow one.

"Cookies are coming soon! Order yours now," a darling group of Girl Scouts called out, and waved forms at the crowd. Several people dashed forward to sign up.

"Already taking orders?" I groaned. "I need to lose ten pounds. If not fifteen."

"Not gonna cave for Thin Mints?" Maddie teased.

I'd barely resisted the siren song last year. "I'll order a few boxes later this month from Cara. She joined a Brownie troop back when school began."

"Oh, man. That means Dad will buy at least a dozen boxes. Maybe we can stash them in the freezer. Out of sight, out of mind."

"That won't stop me. They taste even better frozen."

"Hey, there's Dad. And looking pretty spiffy." My sister hooked a thumb at the sleigh that followed the high school band. "Santa! It's Santa Claus!"

Alex Silverman waved to all the kids who jumped up and down in excitement, booming out a few "ho ho ho's" whenever he could, and asking if they'd been good. Shouts of "yes" and "no" rang out, with parents' laughter as well. Maddie and I hurried to beat Santa's motorized sleigh before it reached the Village Green. I stood beside the largest evergreen, surrounded by a virtual thicket of smaller trees brought there from Richardson's Farms, either mounted in metal stands or planted in buckets. My knees shook. I tested the microphone, switched it on, and winced at a jarring echo of sound. At last my dad arrived, surrounded by a huge crowd.

"Welcome, everyone!" I cleared my throat and started again. "Welcome to the annual Silver Hollow Christmas Tree Lighting, our most popular event of the year. We'll all count down with Santa until he pushes the magic light button. Are you ready, Santa?"

Dad climbed down from his precarious perch in the sleigh. His knees must have stiffened after sitting so long on such a chilly evening, and he hobbled over to join me. My phone reported the temperature at thirty-five, but not cold enough for the snow to stick. Winter in Michigan could be so unpredictable. Below zero one day, and a balmy forty degrees the next. Or within a span of hours, which always surprised visitors to the Mitten State.

"Ready!" Dad ignored someone's shout about Cal Bloom's heart attack. "Let's get this village ablaze with lights! Start the countdown. Ten! Nine! Eight —"

The crowd joined in and drowned out other onlookers who gathered around in a huddle to exchange information. Once the chant reached zero, although some people shouted "blast off" instead, we all stared at the dark forest of trees. Nothing happened. Groans rose in the air. I blew out a frustrated breath. Dad jiggled the switch once more.

Suddenly the entire block glowed bright from thousands of flickering lights. Everyone oohed and aahed, while I sighed in relief. Dad started singing in his clear baritone.

"We wish you a Merry Christmas, we wish you a Merry Christmas . . ."

Once more the crowd joined in, clapping and happy, although I noted the group that still chatted together. Trina and Arthur Wentworth stood in the middle, clearly eager to hear details; oddly enough, Devonna Walsh, Ben Blake, and Wendy Clark rushed over to listen, along with Dave Fox of the *Silver Hollow Herald*. That didn't surprise me. Fox was always on the lookout for news, and he'd no doubt get a special edition out by Saturday. But I hadn't expected Wendy or Ben to join the vulture-like band of gossipmongers.

"Chattering like a murder of crows." Uncle Ross had joined us. "Disgusting."

Maddie shrugged. "I suppose," I said. "But it's no different than the other times."

"Yeah, look over there."

We all turned to where my uncle pointed. Several television news crews clustered around a different crowd, which included Digger Sykes. That surprised me. If Chief Russell heard that he'd given details without authorization, he'd be toast.

"Is that Cheryl Cummings?" Maddie asked.

"Yes. She and Flynn found the mayor along with Mom," I said, "and I want to avoid being under the gun. Let's go."

"I don't know why people are so curious."

"If they'd been raked over the coals by the cops as a prime suspect, they'd lose interest. And fast." My uncle's breath steamed in the air. "Reality hits hard when it happens to you, not some other sap. At least the parade was a big success."

"Yeah. Mom should be happy." Maddie yawned wide. "I'm beat. I had to work all day on a project that's due Saturday, cram in the stuff for the Bear-zaar, and some of the wizard bear promo. I need some sleep."

"Wait a minute, and I'll walk back with

you." I turned to my uncle and handed him Dad's car keys. "Do you have any gummy bear packets left?"

"Nope. Alex said to use 'em all, that we'd order more."

"Then we better order something else for the open house prizes."

"We could hire the people who don't win the bake-off contest to make cookies for the event," Maddie said. "Then they won't feel left out."

I nodded halfheartedly. Given the circumstances of the mayor's death — and I hoped it was an accident — plus the upcoming Bear-zaar, our usual holiday rush, and decorating the shop and house, I couldn't add one more thing to worry about. Thankfully, the parade and tree lighting seemed to be a success. People were happy, for the most part. Dad continued to greet little kids among the crowd, so Maddie and I threaded our way toward home.

We ducked behind a crowd when Cheryl Cummings pointed in our direction, although one of her colleagues ran over to question me about Cal Bloom. I pleaded innocence. No way would I spread rumors of murder. No matter what my suspicions. And they'd have to wait until Chief Russell decided to hold a press conference.

I caught sight of Digger Sykes again and cringed. "Get me out of here."

"There's Abby and Amanda Pozniak." Maddie pulled me toward them. "Hey, we loved your float with the rocking horse. So adorable."

"We tried to tie a Silver Bear on it, but no dice," Amanda said. "Couldn't find the duct tape, and nothing else worked."

"You up for an early breakfast before the Bear-zaar?" Abby asked. "Sister power!"

"Sure thing." I tugged at Maddie's sleeve. "Come on."

"Hold on, Sasha." Digger Sykes swaggered over, still in his official uniform. "I'm going off duty, but I have to say like daughter, like mother."

I glared at him. "Don't even start —"

"You have a gift for stumbling over corpses," he interrupted with a wide grin. "Did you hear, Mads? Our unofficial Jessica Fletcher passed the torch to your mom."

"What corpse?" Amanda glanced at Abby, who looked surprised as well.

"Mayor Bloom keeled over near the Quick Mix Factory. Heart attack." Digger snickered. "Flynn Hanson found a flask of brandy near him, too. Guess the mayor indulged a bit, since it's so danged cold. Not the first time he overdid it in that department."

70

"I heard he had a DUI once," Abby said.
"More than once."

"Really." I was grateful the topic of conversation had switched from me and my mother to the mayor's personal problems. "I wonder why we never heard much about that."

"I knew," Maddie said, "because Mom told me. But that was long ago, Digger, and you shouldn't spread old gossip. Cal Bloom attended AA and swore off the stuff."

"Then why did he carry that flask with him?"

"How do you know it had alcohol?" I asked. "Could have been tea or coffee in it."

He turned to my sister. "Right. Like that photo the mayor carried."

"Photo? What kind of photo?"

Maddie shrugged, apparently clueless, and Digger changed the subject. "Hope you don't start taking after Sasha and your mom, Mads. We don't need more dead bodies dropping around here. Especially with Christmas coming in a few weeks."

I stared after him when he headed toward the courthouse. "What photo was he talking about? I don't remember Cal Bloom carrying one."

"Forget it, Sash. You know how Digger spouts off garbage."

"I think it's terrible that a local cop would

71

diss the mayor," Amanda said. "Poor Mr. Bloom deserves a little more respect from a city employee."

"Digger hoped for a promotion, so he's sore that the county is always called in to solve these murders."

"Oh, ho," Amanda said. "That's because Sasha solved them before the cops did!"

"No, I only helped. And I'd rather not get involved at all."

I meant that, too. Hopefully the mayor had succumbed to a heart attack. Seeing the news crew on Silver Hollow's street wasn't pleasant, and coverage would spread around the region for days if not weeks. That wouldn't be good for anyone.

Even if bad publicity might be good for business, I preferred peace and quiet.

CHAPTER 5

Yawning wide, I twisted open the blinds in the upstairs rotunda loft on Friday morning. Yesterday had been a blur. Customers trooped into the Silver Bear Shop for new teddies and their accessories, plus any updates about Cal Bloom's death — which I refused to discuss. Today would be the same, no doubt. In the dim sunlight, a dusting of snow shimmered on the sloping roof. From here, I had the best view of our new sign.

Jay Kirby had been careful asking for dimensions before starting the project, and finished it early before he left for his workshop up north. He'd even directed the installation. I adored the carved teddy bear, painted a metallic silver, that glistened in the sun and popped halfway out of the flat surface; huge navy-painted block letters spelled out the shop's name and curved around the bear's face. Maddie loved it, too, along with my parents and Aunt Eve.

Uncle Ross wasn't so thrilled.

"Looks like a frou-frou bear," he'd grumbled at the unveiling.

I had to remind him that our shop sold children's toys, primarily marketing to kids and teddy bear collectors. Our inventory of accessories included frou-frou pink or purple dresses and other clothes with sparkles and sequins, plus sports-like jeans, plaid shirts, hats, backpacks, and sneakers. Both little girls and boys loved dressing up their teddies.

Dustcloth in hand, I descended the circular stairs to wipe each acrylic box of our Parade of Bears, which held teddies holding tiny country flags. Others contained Boyds, Steiff, Lloyd, or GUND branded bears. I climbed back upstairs to snatch a long-handled duster and managed to dispel a few cobwebs in the ceiling corners. Our cleaning crew usually tidied the shop around midnight, or in the early morning hours before we opened, but yesterday Aunt Eve fielded a frantic call about a staff emergency. Apparently, the flu was hitting hard.

Some of our own staff had come down with a stomach virus recently but had recovered. Hilda Schulte and Flora Zimmerman had both called in sick yesterday, and I hoped they didn't end up in the hospital like Tom Richardson. He still battled pneumonia. Bad enough Cal Bloom had died two days ago at the parade. And that reminded me of how we'd found him dressed in the Santa Bear costume, with his awful blackened skin.

Had it been murder, or a simple accident?

I shunted that question away and straightened the wall photo featuring my grandfather, T. R. Silverman, that hung near our large five-foot bear. "Hey, Gramps. I'd better get Mr. Silver new stuffing before our open house. One more thing to add to the to-do list!"

Sighing, I vacuumed the room that displayed our "profession" bears, each dressed in uniforms ranging from military to police and firemen, to hospital workers, and everything imaginable. The machine's whir soothed my frazzled nerves and sent me daydreaming about my last chat with Jay. We'd been so busy lately, but instead of commiserating, we shared memories of the past. High school events we'd attended without being aware of each other, friends we'd hung with, and plans for the future in terms of college and romance.

Jay had a much different experience, born and raised in the area. We often visited my grandparents in Silver Hollow during all the holidays. But it wasn't the same since Grandpa T. R. died before my parents moved back in the middle of my freshman year of high school. I spent the winter and spring in a deep funk. I badly missed my Ann Arbor friends and the urban atmosphere, and resented the transition.

Maddie had adjusted well, since she easily made friends. I was lucky that Elle and Mary Kate had taken me under their wings during that stressful time, and became my best friends. But I wished we'd returned sooner. Grandpa T. R. was a dear, and I so enjoyed listening to his stories and adages. One of his mottos for Christmas was "presence" being more important than presents, and I still missed his beaming smile.

I'd joyfully returned to Ann Arbor to attend college and earn my master's degree . . . met and then married a wonderful man — or so I thought — with hopes of starting a family. But things quickly fell apart.

"And here I am, back in Silver Hollow," I said aloud. "Not that I regret divorcing Flynn. And I hope Grandpa T. R. would be proud of this shop, too. Dad worked so hard to establish it, and I'll keep it going as long as I can manage the job."

Many school friends had moved to different areas of Michigan or out of state to find work, so I was grateful. A few lived in their parents' basements, in fact, working two or three part-time jobs. Things had to improve for the economy soon.

Quickly, I moved on to tidy up the playroom. We designed it to occupy kids while parents shopped, one of the best ideas I'd had since taking over as manager. Especially during the busier holiday season. Which meant I had to dash upstairs morning and afternoon to tidy the room. Kids often left a mess when suddenly called away by their parents. Oh, well, I didn't mind. I'd mind lower sales, so the trade-off was worth it.

A Red Hat Society tour was scheduled for one o'clock, plus I had a Bear-zaar meeting at the church, and needed to set up the bake-off contest table. Maddie would arrange the Magic of Christmas Beary Potter Keepsake display tomorrow before the event opened. This week was turning out to be a real bear, indeed. That reminded me of Cal Bloom's last words, which didn't help improve my mood.

I stuffed the duster in a closet along with the vacuum and returned to my bedroom suite. Before coffee and breakfast, I had to coax Rosie outside.

"Come on," I sighed when she burrowed deeper into the nest of covers on my bed. "What a lazy bum! You're only four, younger than me in dog years. Worse than me in the morning."

"Hey, Sasha. Hurry up, I've got to get to the studio," my sister yelled from the bottom of the stairs. "Move it!"

Rosie whimpered when I shoved the blanket aside and gathered her up in my arms. "Oof. You're almost twenty pounds, and that means too many treats," I muttered. "I'm coming!"

Setting my sweet dog on the floor, I brushed my hair out and twisted it into a ponytail. Checked my silver cable-knit sweater, added some lip gloss and bronzer, then headed for the door. I turned to see Rosie stretched out on the floor.

"Girl! You are not helping. Santa Paws might not leave you anything in your stocking if you keep this up." She still wouldn't budge, so I had to carry her all the way to the back door. "Out you go, and no complaining."

Rosie loped across the porch, claws clicking down the steps, and sniffed the frozen grass. I shivered in the chilly air and returned inside, refilled my coffee and snapped on the lid, choked down a hard-boiled egg sprinkled with salt and pepper, fed Rosie, and changed her water dish. Onyx had stretched out on the sunny window seat, so I scratched behind her silky ears.

"I guess Maddie already took care of your litter box and food dish. See you both later. Be good, and no fighting over the view."

Rosie curled up near the heater vent with a sigh. I collected the fliers for the Bearzaar and bake-off contest. Aunt Eve waved to me when I passed through the office.

"Morning, Sasha! Take a gander at this," she sang and pulled the lid off a large circular box. "I ordered a new hat for today's tour. What do you think?"

I waited for her to slip on the red wool cloche with its sassy swirl of purple feathers, and watched her tuck a few stray blond curls under the brim. "You look elegant, as always," I said and meant it. "You'll be the best dressed Red Hat Society lady today."

"Why, thank you, but Shea Miller will outshine me. She usually does."

My aunt, who had divorced Uncle Ross years ago and planned to remarry him over the holidays, had a certain flair for '50s-style fashion. Today was no exception. Eve Silverman wore a slim wool hound's-tooth skirt with a few pleats on one side; her jacket, nipped at the waist, had a single row of buttons, and a mouton-fur collar dyed red to match her hat. She wore black flats, too, instead of her usual spike heels.

"This hat is vintage nineteen twenties," Aunt Eve explained. "Are you sure it looks all right? The girls might think it doesn't go with the suit."

"I think it's fine, and I love the pattern of your suit. I'm so grateful you're bringing the group in today. Did we order extra red hats and feather boas for the teddy bears? The last Red Hat group cleaned us out."

"I made sure we got a double order."

"Good. It's almost ten, I'd better unlock the door."

"Oh, I ordered little angel bears for the Holiday Open House." Once my aunt set her hat back in its box, she walked me to the shop's front counter. "Mr. Bloom's death at the parade was terrible. It might put a damper on the whole season."

"I'm hoping that's not the case." I flipped the window sign from CLOSED to OPEN. No customers waited on the porch, which I'd expected due to the cold December weather. "I haven't heard the latest gossip, though."

"I figured you'd tell me." Aunt Eve

80

glanced behind her and then froze. "Uh-oh."

"What is it?" I peered over her shoulder and then wilted, seeing my mother storming through the shop. "Looks like she's on the warpath —"

My aunt stepped in front of me with a broad smile. "Judith, how good to see you so early this morning! What brings you in today?"

Mom's face looked flushed and her usually immaculate auburn hair was windblown. "It's criminal! They dragged Alison Bloom to the police station last night, without giving her a chance to get dressed. She had to throw a coat over her pajamas."

I'd forgotten to ask before now. "How did Mrs. Bloom take the news Wednesday?"

"She's been crying her eyes out ever since I told her what happened, Sasha. The poor woman! Her husband is dead, but do the police care? They have no compassion."

"Why are they questioning her?" Aunt Eve looked puzzled. "He had a heart attack."

"Yes. Brought on by touching a live wire, or so they believe," Mom said. "It's true that Alison has been so focused on her mother, she hasn't paid much attention to Cal lately. She feels so bad. But it can't pos-

81

sibly be murder. I mean, really. That's ridiculous."

"But the police always suspect the wife or husband —"

"No matter what anyone believes, she's innocent! Alison would never hurt anyone. I've known her for years, longer than you, Eve. Goodness, we went to the same college. She owned her own boutique in Plymouth, and married Cal after his divorce."

"Maybe they only wanted her to confirm whatever they've learned about the mayor's interactions with people, or his medications," I said. "She may not be a suspect."

"At eleven o'clock at night, they show up at her door?" Mom shook her head. "Why else would they do that if they didn't suspect her. Your father called in Mark Branson to represent her, since Flynn's so busy. They could have asked Alison to come in the morning to answer questions, but no. They insisted right then. Kristen, too. It's all that Digger Sykes's fault."

Aunt Eve looked skeptical. "Oh? What did he do?"

"He's got some bee up his backside. Alison told me that Cal didn't support Digger for a promotion with Chief Russell. So now he's telling everyone that the mayor was a drunk, since we found that flask near the body. I could kick myself for not checking it —"

Mom continued her rant while my aunt and I exchanged worried glances. She always had a strong loyalty for her friends. It was no surprise that she supported Alison and Kristen Bloom, but her outrage seemed overdone. Then again, Mom never did things halfway.

All or nothing, that was her standard MO.

"And one more thing." Mom turned to me and stabbed a finger toward my face. "You've been successful in the past clearing up these things. This time it won't be hard to figure out, so be ready."

"Ready for what?" Clearly, I hadn't had enough coffee yet, although I noticed customers walking to the shop's door. "Can we talk about this another time?"

"No. Come with me, let Eve handle things for a few minutes." She dragged me back to the office, ignoring my reluctance. "I want you to prove that Alison is innocent. Keep close tabs on the police. Ask questions around the village, find out whatever you can about Cal and anyone else who may have had a beef with him."

"But —"

"Talk to that detective, the one from the county, who's helping Chief Russell."

"Okay, but first explain what you said the other day." I closed the office door behind me to prevent eavesdropping. "When you apologized about Flynn, and how Dad gave you a second chance. What did all that mean?"

"Oh." Mom tucked a stray auburn lock behind her ear with a guilty look. "Well, that was a long time ago. Your dad was so busy working. You kids were in school, and involved with Girl Scouts and friends. Dad encouraged me to work part-time at an art gallery in Plymouth. I — I met someone, and things just spiraled from there."

"You had an affair?"

At my shocked tone, she quickly waved a hand. "No, no! Nothing happened. Beyond meeting this artist for lunch or dinner, that kind of thing. He wanted more, of course, like any man would. At least I think he did. I refused. I liked our conversations. We could talk about anything, and he acted like a gentleman for the most part. But Alex found out."

Mom sounded bitter. I was more surprised that my mother had been tempted to stray. She did crave attention, though, much like Flynn. Maybe not at the same level, but my mother had a deep need to feel appreciated beyond mother-and-wife duties. I supposed most women probably did, or so I'd read. Who was I to judge? And what did I really know about my parents' marriage? Not much, clearly. They both had suffered stress over the years. I also knew Dad would have forgiven her, even if she had taken it too far.

He loved her that much.

My mother was certainly attractive, back then and now, curvaceous yet trim, makeup and hair stylish, keeping up with the latest fashions for her age. Intelligent, and fun as well, Mom had always drawn people to share enthusiasm for whatever project she spearheaded.

"Is that why Dad quit the prosecutor's office? And moved here?"

"Not at first. He promised to spend less time at the office, but that never worked out. We both realized it would be better for us to make a change, before it was too late. So we left Ann Arbor. It got me away from Plymouth, although I missed the gallery. I loved that job." She gave my hand a squeeze. "I'm sorry if it disrupted your life. I know it wasn't easy for you, changing to a small town high school. And I helped Dad at first, along with Aunt Eve, setting up the shop and factory, but it wasn't what I really wanted to do with my free time."

I squeezed back. "That's why you wanted to move to Florida. Right?"

"I hoped to find a gallery there, yes, to work in, but your dad never could adjust. He's not a golfer, and he hates to fish. We rarely saw you girls. Alex missed his friends here," Mom said, "and so did I. I even missed the weather and the forests. Palm trees are lovely, but not the same as the oaks, the elms, and birches. The lakes, the lighthouses, Mackinac Island. We agreed that spending a month or two renting a condo would be better than living year-round in Florida."

"You'll miss the tropical flowers, though."

She sighed. "I do love flowers and wish I'd become a floral designer. I'm too old now, and still searching for a better fit when it comes to spending my free time. I want to make a big difference in people's lives, and the community."

I had a sudden inspiration. "Mom, what about serving on the village council? You could even run for mayor. You pulled off handling the parade at the last minute, and I bet you'd get more work done with the council than anyone else. Even Mayor Bloom."

"I'm not so sure," Mom said, "although, I did get results when people balked at paying their fees for the parade floats. But most people want your dad to run for mayor."

"You're younger and healthier."

"Alex doesn't need that kind of stress, you're right." She heaved a deep sigh. "What does matter is proving Alison Bloom's innocence. See what you can find out, okay?"

"I will, but I can't promise much. Oh, and don't forget to pick up Rosie —"

"Your dad said he would. I'm going to visit Alison and boost her spirits."

Aunt Eve knocked on the door behind me, so I opened it. "You two okay?"

"Yeah." I watched Mom head out the door to the parking lot. "We're good."

"Customers, Sasha. Get your mojo on."

I nodded, wishing I could ask Detective Mason about the mayor's autopsy results. He and Chief Russell often warned me that amateurs needed to leave investigating to the police. I knew it was dangerous, and really didn't want to risk my neck a third time, but I had no choice. I had to help Mom's friend. My gut instinct told me it was no accident. Whether or not Alison Bloom had been involved, I'd try my best to find out.

"Welcome to the Silver Bear Shop," I said, pasting a smile on my face when I greeted the family browsing the shelves. I recognized the mother, Amy Monroe, whose husband owned the local movie theater. "What can I help you find today?"

"I want a Santa Bear," the younger girl said, clapping her hands.

Amy laughed. "Lily had her heart set on seeing Santa Bear in the parade. So what really happened? We were surprised that Santa Claus was there instead."

"An unexpected incident came up," I said carefully. The older girl stood admiring our Beary Potter wizard bears in black robes. "We'd be happy to order one for you."

"Emily, would you like that?" When she nodded, Amy turned to me. "Done."

"Fill out this form and we'll make sure you get it before Christmas."

Once she pushed the completed form over the counter, Amy leaned toward me with a hand shielding her mouth. She whispered low, "Is it true that Cal Bloom was murdered?"

"Only a rumor." I held out a hand to Lily. "I'm sorry you didn't get to see Santa Bear, but let's see what we can find here for you."

I spent almost an hour with the Monroe family, showing them all the various bears and special Christmas outfits — from Santa suits to red and green plaid or satin dresses, plus their accessories. More customers arrived, which made for a hectic morning. Thank goodness for our lunch hour. I was grateful when Renee Truman, a college student I'd hired for the season, arrived to cover for me in the shop. I rushed to feed Rosie and take her outside, dropped her off at the groomer's, and then zipped back to the factory. Dodging a flurry of snowflakes, too.

After I stamped my feet on the mat inside the door, I hung my parka with the others in the coatroom. Once I visited the restroom and smoothed my sweater with its applique teddy, I was glad I hadn't worn one of my "ugly" Christmas sweaters. Most of the Red Hat Society ladies would be dressed to kill. Urp. To the nines.

Aunt Eve stood among the group of women, who crowded together waiting for me to guide the tour. They all wore various red hats with purple ribbons or flowers, red or purple vests or sweaters. A few had gone hog wild in their attire wearing red or purple elaborate feather boas, enormous hats, sequined clothing or shoes, handbags, plus all kinds of pins and other bling-y jewelry. They oohed and aahed when my aunt twirled in her suit and red cloche hat.

"How do you pull off that vintage style,

Eve?" one woman said.

"I'm handy with a needle, Vera," my aunt replied with a wink. "Plus, I visit vintage clothing stores every chance I get. Ross says I can't resist a good bargain."

"I'd love to go with you. Is this one of the nieces you always brag about? What a darling sweater with that teddy bear on it."

My cheeks burned in embarrassment. I had no idea Aunt Eve had boasted about me and Maddie, but I thanked her and then greeted the rest of the ladies. Shea Miller had paired her deep purple sweater with a red poinsettia-festooned hat. Vera Adams's jacket sparkled with red sequins in a fancy Christmas ornament pattern. A huge red bow fascinator perched on her blond hair. And her infectious laugh set the whole group off to join in the merriment.

"I skipped Home Economics," Vera said with a wink. "Eve worked as a seamstress at a wedding shop long ago. That's why she can turn a dowdy outfit into a showpiece."

I smiled. "I didn't know that."

"Oh, hemming gowns or taking in seams. That wasn't much," my aunt said. "And it's not hard to rework an old piece of clothing."

Shea laughed. "You told me that skirt was falling apart!"

"It was a bit moth-eaten, and I could only use part of the fabric. I saved the pleats and tailored it down. The jacket was perfect, though. How's my new cloche?"

"Lovely. I hope there's plenty of red hats for our bears," Vera added.

"We ordered extra for today, but you can purchase them after the tour." I beckoned the ladies forward. "If you'll follow the bear paws, we can start."

"Is it true someone was murdered here at the factory?" another woman asked, her eyes wide. She wore a red pillbox in a heart shape, trimmed with glittering white rhinestones. "That he was choked to death with stuffing?"

"The police solved that case in September. Shall we begin?"

"I heard there was a second murder in the village," a third woman said.

Vera spoke up. "Don't forget the mayor, who died right before the parade."

"Ladies, please! That's only gossip," Aunt Eve said. "The police haven't determined what happened yet. I know we love to talk, but settle down and listen while Sasha explains how we produce our teddy bears. The whole process is really fascinating, and if you don't pay attention, you'll miss the steps."

"I have to say that three murders in Silver Hollow are three too many." Shea sniffed. "Who's next, that's what I'd like to know."

"Oh, stop." Aunt Eve pointed at me. "Go on, Sasha."

"All right, ladies, we'll start here at the cutting machine." I raised my voice when one woman signaled that she couldn't hear. "This is where we stack the layers of fabric —"

They listened for the most part while we continued through the factory. I told them how each bear was lovingly sewn together inside out and then stuffed, before the final hand-sewn details of eyes, nose, mouth, and logo tags were added before being stored or shipped. They watched our staff workers closely and asked questions, but many of the ladies whispered together in between stations. I also heard Cal Bloom's name several times.

Clearly the Red Hat Society ladies were far more interested in Silver Hollow's growing reputation for homicide.

CHAPTER 6

I switched the sign in the shop window to CLOSED and locked the door. The week had been nonstop action — preparing our float for the parade, the tree-lighting ceremony, dealing with the holiday rush of customers, producing the Keepsake wizard bears, shipping them out to shops around the country and overseas, along with fulfilling our own local orders and the last-minute details for our Bear-zaar table. I was also due at the church in fifteen minutes.

And I had tickets to a string quartet concert. Laura Carpenter and I planned to relax, listen to excerpts from Tchaikovsky's *The Nutcracker*, Vivaldi's Christmas concerto and *The Four Seasons*, plus a medley of carols. I'd been looking forward to it all week.

In the office, I found Aunt Eve filing receipts. "Wow," I said. "That tour was a huge success, and we're nearly out of our largest size bags. Better order more."

"I already did. I'm pooped." She'd long ago abandoned her red hat and now kicked off her flats. "These puppies need a massage."

I eyed her wiggling toes. "Don't expect me to volunteer."

"I'm hoping Ross will do the honors." My aunt winked. "He's been wanting to see a movie for a while now, but we've been so busy."

"Which one?"

"Whatever's out there. Later this month he wants to catch —"

A hard rapping on the side door interrupted our conversation. I waved Aunt Eve to stay seated at her desk and found Detective Mason outside, bundled in a heavy coat, his cell phone plastered against one ear. Poor Rosie would be so disappointed to miss his visit. She loved the detective and fawned over him every time. Mason held up a finger at me while he listened intently, turning halfway around for a measure of privacy.

"When does he plan to get here? Great. I'm late getting back to Ypsilanti — I know, okay. Keep me posted. Thanks." After pocketing the phone, he pushed his wire-rimmed glasses farther onto the bridge of his nose. "Good evening, Ms. Silverman. I've got a few questions about the parade Wednesday night. Is your mother also available?"

"No, sorry. I think she's visiting Alison Bloom."

"I talked to them both earlier. I had a few more questions about the mayor, though, how you two found the body, that kind of thing."

The detective glanced at Aunt Eve, who waved a hand. "I wasn't there Wednesday night. I helped the staff who were working overtime at the factory."

"Yeah, Judith Silverman told me. But thanks."

While he pulled out his notebook and pencil, I crossed my arms over my chest. "Mom and my ex-husband found Mr. Bloom on that bench, actually. I was a ways behind them."

"She didn't mention Flynn Hanson being there."

"How about Cheryl Cummings, the weather forecaster? She was with us, too." I grabbed my coat. "I'm supposed to be at the church in a few minutes for a Bear-zaar meeting. Can we chat on the way? It's a few blocks."

Mason checked his watch. "I'd rather stay

here if you don't mind. Won't take more than five minutes, tops. Chief Russell asked the county to handle this investigation, given the mayor's position and importance. A good idea, although we're swamped with other cases. So explain what you saw Wednesday night."

Frustrated that I might be late, I led him to the table by the door. This chat, no matter how quick, was bound to affect me getting to the concert on time. Mason scribbled fast while I told him how I'd followed my mother to the bench, how she shook the mayor's shoulder, which then caused him to roll off onto the ground. And how we'd taken off his gloves and peeked inside the costume to discover the blackened skin on his fingers and chest.

"Mrs. Silverman didn't mention that," Mason said wryly. "And Hanson dodged my questions when I dropped by his office. He acts like an ex-con. You'd think a lawyer would be accustomed to dealing with the police."

"Flynn can be squirrely, that's true. But I think he was bothered by being a suspect in Will Taylor's murder."

"So who's this weather forecaster?"

"His fiancée? Oops, that's supposed to be a secret. Maybe you've seen her on television? Cheryl Cummings, the weather forecaster for FOX4."

Mason scribbled for several minutes. "I'll track her down. Sounds like she'd make a good witness, at least better than Hanson. Did you see anyone else in the area? Any sign of a car driving away? No? Too bad."

"My guess is the killer moved the body."

"You don't think it was an accident, like your mom?"

"Well, I suppose Cal Bloom could have been electrocuted by the generators. But then, how did he end up on that bench, so far away?"

Mason ignored my question. "Any idea if Mayor Bloom stopped to talk to anyone after you saw him last? And when was that, if you recall the time?" He kept his eyes on the notebook while he talked, but glanced at me when I hesitated too long. "You did talk to him, before he got into his costume. Right?"

"Yes, but I don't remember what time. I was busy prepping for the parade."

"Okay. Any idea where he went?" Mason checked his notes again. "He was the parade mascot, right? Wearing a big furry head, white suit, gloves."

At his skeptical tone, I couldn't help feeling defensive. "The kids are always excited to see Santa Bear. Most Christmas parades have Santa Claus, but ours is unique."

"Okay. So where did he go to change into the costume?"

"Probably at home. The funeral home, that is. The family lives upstairs." I checked my watch, worried about how long this was taking. "It must have been four-ish. The mayor always stopped to talk to people on the way, but I didn't pay attention after he left."

"Hmm."

"Like I said, I was focused on our float. How was I supposed to know someone would murder him? But I'm planning to find out who."

Mason raised an eyebrow at me, clearly amused. "Oh? Remember the cat."

Confused, I crossed my arms over my chest. "The cat?"

"Yeah, and how curiosity killed it."

"You know he was electrocuted. He couldn't have walked over to that bench, all happy and calm, and then keeled over dead."

He snapped his notebook shut and glanced at the ceiling. I could tell he'd given an involuntary sigh, as if praying for patience. "We won't know for sure what killed Mayor Bloom until the full autopsy report."

"But it was murder."

"Sasha."

"I know, I know. It's a dangerous business."

"You of all people should know that by now. You nearly ended up as a corpse the last few times you decided to sleuth."

"I didn't decide —"

"Whatever. No need to go over all that again."

I breathed deep, hoping my own impatience didn't show. "I'd like to know what was in the flask we found with the body. Brandy, or coffee? Mayor Bloom had a DUI on record, from what I heard, and once attended AA."

"The lab will check that out."

"But who would want to kill the mayor? I mean, everyone liked him."

"The police will find out. Not your job, remember?" Mason grinned. "It's possible he touched a live wire by accident, and then asked someone to drive him to the hospital. Maybe whoever did dropped him off on that bench after he died, instead of calling for assistance. Some people don't want to be accused of wrongdoing."

I snorted in disbelief. "I can't believe anyone would be that heartless. If I'd volunteered to drive him, I would have gone straight to the hospital. Or called the police. That would be the only responsible thing to do."

"Not everyone has the same values you do. Your ex-husband called anonymously from his office back in October, remember, hours after finding that body in the parking lot. In this case, we're hoping Mrs. Bloom and her daughter will give some pertinent information."

"So that's why the police dragged her in for questioning late at night?"

"I'm not actually assigned to this case, so I don't know." He saw my skepticism and shrugged. "I'm only here to start the ball rolling. But Mrs. Bloom said she was at the Silver Birches Retirement Home Wednesday. We'll have someone check the sign-in sheets."

"Don't bother," I said. "Most people walk in and out all the time. Even if they sign the sheet, they leave and return whenever they want with no one the wiser. I've done it myself, in fact. Hardly anyone pays attention until closing time. Then they make sure all the visitors are gone for the day."

"So security is pretty lax overall?"

This time I shrugged. "It's a small town. People come and go, visiting their relatives whenever they get a chance. Or whenever they need something."

"Alison Bloom said she's there every day."

"Her mother has Parkinson's, and I think dementia as well. Mom said Mrs. Bloom helps feed Mrs. Jackson at every meal. One of my friends works on staff as a nurse. She says the staff is always swamped, and they appreciate any help."

My friends, both nurses, had chosen differently. Laura Carpenter worked at a hospital, while Rachel Furness had chosen elder care. Some of her patients refused to take their meds, or waited for home-cooked food from family instead of eating the dining room's offerings. My grandmother expected her favorite Ham Heaven sandwiches, so Dad dropped them by once or twice a week. I explained all that to Mason.

"I doubt if my father ever signs in at the desk."

"Okay, thanks." Mason headed for the door. "By the way, Detective Hunter's on the case. If he ever shows up. But remember, Sasha, stick to selling teddy bears."

The detective tucked his notebook away and headed outside to his SUV. I followed, since I'd have to drive to church, set up the cookie table, and then race to make the concert. Shivering, I slid behind my car's wheel and revved the engine. The temperature must have dropped below freezing. Mason turned onto Kermit. I wondered about the twinge of either regret or sarcasm in his tone when he'd mentioned the other detective. So who was Hunter?

"Sounds like Mason doesn't like him."

I parked across from the church. Digger Sykes wouldn't be thrilled about a new county detective working the case. But no doubt Chief Russell didn't want to risk any mistakes during the investigation. Back in October, I barely prevented Digger from touching a murder weapon without gloves. I hurried into the church, down the hall to the pastor's office where lamp light glowed, and then yanked open the door.

"Sorry I'm late. Ready to —"

I stopped short, shocked to see a stranger sitting behind the pastor's large walnut desk. The committee members sat or stood in the corner. Marianna Lovett sat on a folding chair, and drummed her fingers on her large purse; even her blond messy bun looked messier than usual, and she kept blinking. She sported a cute navy Christmas sweater with a huge snowman in a red hat and scarf, juggling snowballs, plus navy slacks and sensible shoes.

Marianna had an efficiency that amazed most people. She was always on top of things at the church, planning events and keeping the food pantry stocked, and seemed unfazed by any unexpected changes. But tonight, she looked perplexed.

"Have a seat, Ms. Silverman." The man's voice was low and commanding. With dark hair slicked to one side, and icy blue eyes that bored into mine, he pointed to the one empty chair. Straight brows gave him a stark expression that added to his watchful manner.

"Who are you? And where's Pastor Lovett?" I directed the second question to Marianna, who shook her head. Everyone else looked uncomfortable.

"Out of the office. I am Detective Hunter, from Dexter County Homicide."

"I just spoke with Detective Mason about the investigation. You just missed him. He had to return to Ypsilanti —"

"Good." He sounded pleased by that. "Now you can tell me what you told him."

"I'm supposed to set up for tomorrow's Bear-zaar. Everyone else is, too."

His mouth thinned, as if my daring to question him was a sin. His tone sharpened, too. "It'll have to wait. Mayor Bloom's death is more important, of course. So I hear you're the local amateur sleuth. Mason warned me about you."

Baffled by his hostility, I took a seat and studied Hunter while he consulted his notebook. His stark black suit coat, with sunglasses tucked into his white shirt pocket, matched the severity of his personality. He didn't wear a necktie, either.

"So. Looks like I'm in luck, interviewing a number of villagers in one spot. Who was at the parade on Wednesday, and spoke with the mayor?"

No one raised their hand except me. "I did, but I already told Detective Mason everything I saw and heard."

"Now you can tell me what you told him." Hunter's smile held no warmth.

"Of course I want to cooperate with the investigation, but this isn't a good time." I glanced around the room, aware of their discomfort. "No one else has any information. Let's arrange to meet tomorrow."

Hunter leaned over the desk, shoved aside Pastor Lovett's Bible and papers — probably Sunday's sermon notes — and narrowed his eyes. "I'm not in the habit of waiting."

"But you don't mind wasting everyone's time."

"You're in no position to dictate terms to me, Ms. Silverman."

"Am I a suspect in Mayor Bloom's

death?" I asked.

"I never said that."

"Then call Detective Mason for the information." I rose and turned to Marianna. "Let's go. You have to check on vendors, and I've got that cookie table to set up."

She quickly jumped to her feet. "Yes, please!"

Hunter rose from the desk chair, sputtering protests, but I ignored him. Marianna had already scurried out, and I preceded the other committee ladies. Many attended church here and knew my mother. I suspected many would report this incident to the gossip network at the first opportunity. Wendy Clark followed at the rear, trying hard to repress her laughter.

I didn't glance back at Hunter. The nerve of the guy, making ridiculous demands like that. The door banged shut behind us. Let him stew. I'd wasted enough time, and I wasn't going to miss the concert tonight. All he had to do was call Mason.

"Boy, oh boy! Did you tell him off." Wendy chuckled while we rushed to the basement. "I almost told him that I saw the mayor. Only on Wednesday morning, when he came into Fresh Grounds for coffee."

"Did he have his brandy flask with him?"

"I dunno. Bloom looked fine, joked about

the weather as usual, and how hot that Santa Bear costume would be. He was strolling around the floats later on, but I was so busy, I never talked to him. So what's going on? I mean, was it murder like everyone's been saying?"

"I have no idea," I said honestly, "but they won't know for certain until the autopsy."

"Ben was so shocked to hear about Cal Bloom's death. He drove his pharmacy float, the first one in the parade with all the presents and a big Christmas tree."

"I missed seeing that one."

"He had to redo the wrapped presents, too. Some wiseacre kids tore them apart Tuesday night." Wendy stopped outside the hall's double doors. "Maybe they thought Ben hid drugs in them. Like, how stupid is that? He had to get all new empty boxes and wrap them."

I yanked one door open and stopped cold. "Wow. Look at all this!"

Amazed at the transformation, I admired the red and green tinsel looped across the ceiling, held up by hooks, along with golden bells, red and white candy canes, and sequined ornaments. Slim evergreens dazzled with white or multicolored lights. The aisles between vendor tables were far narrower than I'd expected, but artists didn't seem bothered by it. They hurried to set out their creations in their booths. One woman wore a sweatshirt with green buttons all over it, in the shape of a tree, with a big red bow beneath her neck, and she hung other painted or appliqued blouses and sweatshirts on a portable rack beside her table.

"Everything is great," the vendor told Marianna. "The rental price, the lighting, the food court. I'm hoping we get a big crowd in tomorrow."

"I'm sure we will. We advertised all over the place."

Wendy nudged me. "Your sister's flyers sort of fell through the cracks," she whispered. "That was a big mistake. But a few village shops tacked them up today."

"Better late than never, I suppose." Maddie wouldn't be pleased. She'd worked extra hard getting those designed and printed on time. At her own expense.

While the committee trooped through the hall, checking things out, I set up the Teddy Bear Cookie Bake-Off contest table. We'd paid extra to host it at the Bear-zaar, which Marianna appreciated for the church fund, and expected a good turnout of entries. Aunt Eve had fielded more than two dozen calls for information, about how many cookies to bring, what types were allowed, including gluten-free, whether children could bake them, and if the cookies had to be iced and decorated. Even whether they had to be shaped like teddy bears.

Maddie and I had even taken out an ad in the *Silver Hollow Herald* to explain the contest and its rules. As long as the cookies were edible, we would accept any kind. The grand prize was large enough to attract plenty of entries. Or so we hoped.

Once I finished, I raced to my car and broke the speed limit to make it to the concert on time. Laura hugged me and laughed at my shaking hands.

"We've less than five minutes, come on!"

"You're still in your scrubs."

"I didn't get a chance to change — shh!"

We slipped into our seats since the violinists and cello player had already begun warming up. Every time my stomach growled, we giggled. I'd forgotten to grab something to eat on the way. We thoroughly enjoyed the musicians' skill, the haunting melodies, and catching up with our busy lives during intermission. After the concert, we promised to have tea at the Queen Bess before New Year's. On my way home, I grabbed a fast food burger and wolfed it down.

My thoughts returned to the taut exchange with Detective Hunter. He'd acted cold and smarmy, to say the least. No wonder Mason seemed ambivalent about him. Clearly, they didn't communicate, since Hunter hadn't been aware that Mason came to "start the ball rolling." That probably stuck in his craw. I also resented Hunter's quick summary of me as an interfering busybody. Come to think of it, he made it sound like Mason had told him that.

If so, I'd really be steamed.

CHAPTER 7

I had to drag myself out of bed the next morning. After a hot shower, I donned jeans and a sweater with OH SNAP! in large letters and broken gingerbread cookies appliqued on the front. An homage to our bake-off contest. Winners would be chosen next week, but we hadn't decided on rules for judging. What if we couldn't agree?

"Hey, Sash! Are you coming or not?" Maddie's shrill voice floated upstairs from the kitchen. "We'll be late! It's almost five forty-five."

I groaned and dragged Rosie off the bed. "Come on, girl. I know it's an ungodly hour, but it can't be helped. Let's get you outside."

She resisted, however, so I slid her toward the bed's end and carried her down to the kitchen. Again. "You better not make this a habit, Rosie."

Maddie had two travel mugs of coffee

ready. "That concert last night did you in, huh?"

"Talking to Jay so late is the real reason." I yawned so hard, my jaw hurt. "The concert was wonderful, and Laura's as busy as I am. It was great seeing her."

When I strapped on Rosie's plaid doggie coat around her neck and middle, we both laughed at her sad expression. Rosie hated mornings more than I did. And winter. Once Maddie opened the back door, I set Rosie on the slick porch. A glimmer of weak sunlight slanted through the trees' bare branches, and darker clouds hung in the west. The cold bit through my sweater and made my teeth chatter.

"Go on, girl. You can catch up on your beauty sleep after this." I stamped my numb feet while Rosie reluctantly picked her way over the snow. "And don't complain about cold paws. I bought you boots but you refuse to wear them."

"Aunt Eve said she'll feed Rosie and Onyx around eight thirty," Maddie said, "so let's go. Amanda and Abby are waiting at the Sunshine Café."

Since the cat was already curled on the window seat, Rosie crept into her crate with a chew toy and her ragged bear for company. I grabbed my purse, parka, fur-lined gloves,

111

and jammed a knit hat on my wet hair. Bleary-eyed, I stumbled to the car over the rutted snow in the darkness. Maddie's back seat held boxes crammed to the ceiling, and the trunk was full as well. She parked in the bank's lot and dragged me across the street to the former hardware store, which had been converted to the café. Empty flower boxes lined the huge picture window. Yawning, I crunched over the rock salt scattered near the front door.

Inside, customers filled half the booths and tables. Vintage photos of Silver Hollow, one showing Model T's with a horse and buggy on Main Street, cheered me. This town had such an interesting history. Indirect lighting washed the bright yellow walls and low ceiling, warming the place until real sunshine streamed through the front window. I breathed in the delicious smells of fresh coffee and bacon. Mmm.

"Morning! Sit anywhere," Lenore Russell said, bustling behind the counter.

I blinked. Uncle Ross, Gil Thompson, and my dad sat in a row before her with full coffee mugs, earlier than usual, exchanging the latest village happenings. Lenore set three huge dinner plates before them with stacked pancakes plus eggs, bacon, toast, or her flaky buttermilk biscuits. If anyone asked about police business, the chief's wife remained mum. I didn't blame her.

Maddie led the way to the booth where the Pozniak sisters waited. "Hey. Wake up, Sasha!" Amanda snapped her fingers with a laugh. "Coffee, stat!"

"Yes, please," I mumbled, and poured half the cream into an empty mug with a hefty spoonful of sugar. Lenore topped it with coffee and set a full cup at my sister's elbow.

"Bring us the specials, all around." Maddie poked me. "Drink up. It's gonna be a long day, and you'll need an IV if you keep yawning like that."

"I'll be fine." I gulped half of the coffee and felt better. Maybe that was wishful thinking. Maybe I should have skipped talking to Jay, but I'd wanted to update him on events here. "Has anyone else heard about Cal Bloom's DUI record? I didn't know he had one."

"That's old news." Abby hooked a thumb in Gil Thompson's direction. "He and Cal Bloom both attended AA, plus did community service. They've been sober ever since."

"But we found a brandy flask near the mayor's body."

I'd lowered my voice to keep anyone from eavesdropping, although the other customers' chatter in the café, the sizzling grill close by, and the scraping of chairs on the wooden floor, masked most of our conversation.

"I'm surprised at that. He kept saying he was over booze," Amanda said. "And even though Cal Bloom stuck his foot in his mouth countless times, everyone forgave him. That's why he kept getting re-elected."

Abby nodded. "That was awful, Sasha, finding him dead."

Janet Johnson must have overheard that when she brought over our breakfast plates. "So it's true you found Cal Bloom at the parade. Did he die of a heart attack?"

"The police haven't determined for certain what happened." I crunched a piece of burned bacon and shook salt and pepper over my scrambled eggs. "Yum, and the hash browns are nice and crispy, too."

"Not overdone, I hope."

"Nope. Perfect for me."

Janet tucked a strand of long dark hair behind an ear and leaned closer to the booth. "You ought to know Cal Bloom was drinking again," she whispered. "He was in here maybe a month ago, telling Gil Thompson that his wife threatened to divorce him if he didn't get sober."

"Really?" Surprised, I noted how Mad-

114

die's friends also looked shocked by that news. "You heard him say that?"

"Yup, and so did Lenore. Enjoy your breakfast, and let me know if you need anything else. Hot sauce? Sure thing, right over here."

Janet grabbed the small bottle off another table and plopped it down in front of Abby. We ate in silence for a few minutes, ingesting that information along with our food, before Maddie finally spoke with her coffee mug in hand.

"So the mayor slid backward, but everyone knew he wasn't a saint. I'm surprised Mom didn't mention that Mrs. Bloom wanted a divorce."

"Either she didn't tell her, or Mrs. Bloom wasn't serious about filing," I mused. "But I'll ask Mom next chance I get. If I remember."

"If you don't, I will." My sister pushed her plate away. "Come on, Sash, it's twenty to seven. We still have work to do at the Bear-zaar."

Reluctantly, I followed her out with my unfinished toast wrapped in a napkin. Maddie groaned when some strawberry jam dripped on the car seat, but I swiped it clean and finished eating. Not before she turned onto Kermit, fish-tailing on the slippery pavement until regaining control. Maddie braked hard in the church parking lot and nearly sideswiped a truck. Luckily no one was present to witness.

"Whoa, there," I said. "Remember what Grandpa T. R. always said."

"Yeah, yeah, 'we'll get there when we get there.' We made it just fine. Uh-oh. Looks like Uncle Ross is mad about something. Wonder what's up."

His obvious annoyance wasn't new. And his swanky pale blue vintage Olds took up two spaces in the lot, so no one could park too close, bump it, or scratch the paint. What was up? We hurried over to join him.

"We can't leave our cars here. One of you better follow me back to our parking lot," he grumbled. "They want this one and the streets around for customer parking."

Maddie handed me the keys. "We have to unload first, though."

"They should have paved this lot three times bigger."

"Except they couldn't, because of the small cemetery behind the church," I told Uncle Ross. "Pastor Lovett sent paperwork in for a historical marker, but they haven't heard back yet. The mayor wanted to move the ten graves to the county cemetery in Ann Arbor."

"Cal Bloom meddled in too many things beyond his mayoral duties."

"Like what?" I asked.

"His spat with the police union over the latest contract negotiations, for one thing, and he disagreed with the Silver Hollow Beautification Committee. They want to put a picket fence all around the Village Green to keep people off the grass."

"Oh, I hope not! Rosie loves walking there."

"That's the biggest problem. Too many dog owners don't pick up after their pets. Mayor Bloom was on your side, though. Who knows what the committee will do now."

"A lot of people had disagreements with him," Maddie said, "but let's get our work done and then you two can gossip."

Uncle Ross huffed. "Who's gossiping? Not me."

I grinned and carried a big stack of boxes down the steps to the Fellowship Hall. We had samples of our specialty six-inch wizard bear for taking orders, but the other bears we brought to sell all wore Christmas outfits — red and white pajamas, fancy dresses, Santa suits, and the like. We also had a dozen bags of our tiniest and cheapest bears in a rainbow of colors. Uncle Ross had assembled the booth yesterday, and it glowed with lights and tinsel garland.

" 'Fa La La Llama,' how adorable!" Marianna Lovett pointed to the lettering on my sister's navy sweatshirt, which included a white llama and a striped scarf. "And your sweater is perfect for the cookie competition, Sasha."

"The Teddy Bear Cookie Bake-off contest," Maddie corrected. "I asked Isabel French to register the entries for us."

I liked Isabel, who co-owned the Silver Scoop Ice Cream Shoppe along with Kristen Bloom. I often stopped by for a scoop of mint chocolate chip during the summer. She was so friendly and nice, while Kristen remained aloof. Oh well.

"Hey, when are we gonna decide about decorations, food, and entertainment for the open house? Plus the staff party."

"That's up to you and Aunt Eve," Maddie said. "I'm busy with my own shop."

"Oh, come on. You're better at those details."

"Sash, I don't have time with all the projects I'm doing. You're lucky I agreed to help today back in the summer. Otherwise, I'd be at Silver Moon all day."

"Gee, thanks." I was half-kidding, but my sister's crankiness got on my nerves. Maddie didn't look happy with me, either. "Never mind, I'll manage with Aunt Eve's help. Wanna bet we'll be swamped today like last year? It was a madhouse."

"Come on, let's find out if anyone's registered for the cookie contest yet."

Maddie led the way to the wide table near the church kitchen, where Isabel French sipped from a Fresh Grounds coffee cup. She wore a gray sweatshirt with battery-powered lights tangled around a sheep, and the words FLEECE NAVIDAD printed in white.

"Morning! I love the gingerbread teddies you painted on the cookie banner, Maddie," she chirped. Isabel tugged the white table-cloth back into place. "The red and white bunting is so festive, too. I've gotten a dozen entries already."

"Really? Can I see them?" I asked, but Maddie emphatically shook her head.

"Don't you dare show her a single cookie. I don't trust Sasha within an inch of any-thing resembling one. Especially Christmas cookies."

"I'm no better, really." Isabel patted her plump stomach with a smile. "But I promise not to touch or even sniff. I've lost twenty pounds in three months on Weight Watch-ers. And I'm exercising a few days a week."

"Good for you," I said. "But I can't wait until the Silver Scoop opens again."

"I hate to tell you, but Kristen is pressuring me to buy out her share of the business." Isabel looked morose. "She wants to open a yoga studio instead."

"Wow. I had no idea."

"Okay, you two, back to the cookie contest. The cutoff for entries is thirty," Maddie told Isabel, "although you might not get that many. I'll check back later today."

While they discussed the contest rules, I crossed the aisle to the Fresh Grounds table where Mary Kate arranged her goodies. "Almost ready?"

"Yep. Want this broken maple pecan scone? I can't sell it."

"Say no more." I scarfed that down in two bites, moaning with the delicious flavors and tender flaky pastry. "Look at those gorgeous snowflake cookies."

Wendy Clark joined us with a huge smile. "Aw, thanks! I used silver sugar pearls instead of dragees, which really shouldn't be eaten. We have Christmas trees with edible dots, though. They're supposed to look like ornaments, but I like the poinsettias best."

I admired the rest as well, bright yellow stars, Santa faces with scrolled beards, and reindeer with cherries for noses and piped icing harnesses. I hoped Mary Kate had a few leftover cookies at the Bear-zaar's end, so I could buy extras.

For my secret emergency stash.

CHAPTER 8

By the time I returned to the Silver Bear Shop display, my sister had almost finished setting up. Maddie fussed over where to place the various Christmas bears and stashed the wizard bears on a shelf behind the table.

"Remember, we're only taking orders."

"Yep. Are we guaranteeing delivery before Christmas?" I asked.

"We'd better, or no one will want one." Maddie readjusted the lights, switched them on and off a few times, draped more on either side of the crimson cloth-covered table, and at last pronounced it finished. "But I think we need more tinsel."

"I'm gonna check out the other booths before the Bear-zaar opens."

I rushed off before she could send me home for that tinsel or other decorations. I thought the booth looked fine. Dressed as Santa, Dad straightened his "throne" in a corner next to a stack of colorful wrapped presents and a droopy Christmas tree with faulty lights.

"Can you unplug that strand for me, Sasha?"

"Why not toss another set of lights on instead?" I'd spotted a new box under our table and managed to spirit it away while Maddie was distracted. Then I unwound the strand from the plastic holder. "Easier than trying to replace bulbs."

"Thanks." Dad connected the lights to a working set and then filled in some of the bare spaces. "Dave Richardson's still sick, so I'm filling in for him in the kitchen."

"But —"

"Mrs. Claus can sit here, if any kids want to give Santa their list."

I suspected that Dad didn't mind missing Sherry Martinez's company, who was never a bundle of joy. "I hope you're not gonna wear that suit, or you'll cook from the heat at the grill."

He stripped off the white beard and mustache. "You're right."

Dad headed off to change, so I wandered around the aisles to see the other vendor displays. The church's Bear-zaar was always popular, with people coming from miles around Southeast Michigan to peruse the hand-crafted items.

One young man set out exquisite pottery on shelves, some as translucent as china. A middle-aged woman's booth displayed lovely knitted and crocheted items. Her daughter had filled the next booth with elaborate hand-sewn doll clothing. And an elderly man with gnarled fingers, wearing a red baseball cap and a shirt with OLD GEE-ZER spelled out on it, sat behind a table displaying realistic carved birds and animals. Some were highly polished to show off the natural wood grain, while other colorful Santa Claus figurines, teddy bears, angels, and snowmen were cleverly painted.

The tantalizing scent of simmering spices drew me to the booth across the aisle, where a slow-cooker held hot apple cider. "These packets have fresh-grated cinnamon and sticks of cloves." The bearded man pointed to small tins. "I also have holiday spiced teas."

"It smells divine."

I bought five packets of the cider mix and moved on to see a woman dripping with gold and silver chains and sporting rings on every finger. She stood behind a glass counter filled with gorgeous jewelry, some vintage, all unique.

"How much is that silver teddy bear?" I

asked, pointing to the pins on display.

"He's darling, isn't he? His arms and legs swing back and forth." She retrieved the pin and flicked a finger to show the tiny bear's movements. "Only twenty-five dollars."

"Sold." I paid for the bear and then pinned him to my name tag. "I manage the Silver Bear Shop and Factory, so he's perfect."

"Indeed! I love your shop. Are those wizard bears new?"

"Yes, our Beary Potter wizard won the Teddy Bear Keepsake contest for the Child's Play Toy Box Co.," I said. "Their main branch is in Cincinnati. We have an exclusive contract to produce them for the company."

"If I did order a bear, would it arrive in time for Christmas?"

"The cutoff date is December fifteenth, so you're good."

"Wonderful," she said. "I'll get two bears for my niece and nephew who are big Harry Potter fans. I'm booked every weekend this month, and traveling in between, so I won't have much time for Christmas shopping. I'm always looking for unique things."

"Me too." I dug out a card from the dozen I carried in my pocket. "Stop by anytime today at our booth, over by the entrance, and you can fill out an order form."

"I will. Thanks so much!" The jeweler leaned forward to whisper. "I heard a rumor that the village mayor was murdered on Wednesday. Is that true?"

"The police are still investigating."

I slipped away before she could press the issue. The last thing I wanted to do was discuss Cal Bloom's death, and preferred to focus on the festive atmosphere. In the next aisle, Cissy Davison caught me by the arm. Her sweater was festooned with sequined red and white candy canes and her blond hair glistened with rhinestone-studded pins.

"I've got to talk to you, Sasha. It's important."

She half-dragged me toward the farthest corner of the Fellowship Hall, close to the kitchen with its wide serving window. A line of people waited for coffee. Leah Richardson wiped tears with a sleeve while she arranged donuts on a platter. Oddly enough, she wore a turtleneck sweater, which had to be stifling in the hot kitchen.

"Leah, what's wrong?" I asked.

She sniffed. "Nothing."

"Is there something I can do to help?"

"No, it's okay. I'm okay."

"You don't look okay," I said flatly. "Tell me what's wrong."

"I feel so bad. My kids told me how all

126

the little ones at the parade were so disappointed when Santa Bear wasn't in the parade. And Dave is so sick, he couldn't be Santa Claus, either. Everything's such a mess."

"Things will get better."

"I'm so worried." Leah filled cups from one coffee urn, tears rolling down her cheeks. "Now that the mayor's dead, what will Mrs. Bloom do with the funeral home?"

"Get a grip, Leah." Cissy waved a hand in dismissal. "It's the only one for miles around, so I highly doubt Alison Bloom would close it."

"I hope you're right, but what if she decides not to sell after all? And I'm swamped here in the kitchen. My girls have a school fundraising project today. I'll never be able to handle this crowd by myself!"

"I'm here to help." My dad squeezed through the narrow doorway into the hot kitchen, his shirt sleeves rolled up, and began measuring coffee grounds into two other stainless steel coffee urn trays. "I'm glad Dave's home recovering. He needs to stay in bed."

Leah blew her nose and then washed her hands, although she swiped her face with a sleeve. "Yeah, he's running a fever and has a terrible headache. Thanks, Mr. Silverman."

She snapped lids on the coffee cups, apologizing for the delay over and over to waiting vendors who swarmed the table and grabbed donuts as well. Cissy Davison pushed me into an alcove far away from the kitchen.

"Really, Sasha, you've got to help me. Have you seen Maggie's dump of a shop? It's filled to the rafters with trash. She's ruined what I worked so hard to establish, and that parade float was a joke. Our family's the laughingstock of the village."

"I doubt that," I said. "You're blowing it way out of proportion."

"You haven't heard the gossip! Stuff is piled so high, the fire department issued her a warning." Cissy snorted. "Unbelievable, really. Can't you talk to her?"

"Me? Why —"

"Maggie won't listen to Mom, me, or Gus," she interrupted, "no matter what we say. Mayor Bloom asked her to put half of her stuff in storage to make it easier for people to walk in the shop. Now he's dead. Mom and I thought you could talk to her, and maybe explain how the village has a reputation to uphold. For quality."

"I think her shop is really cool. I had no

problem walking around."

"Oh, for heaven's sake," Cissy said impatiently. "I'll ask Maddie, then. She's an artist. She would understand at least about that awful float."

Cissy stalked toward my sister, who'd somehow found more tinsel garlands to hang over our booth. I knew Maddie wouldn't agree with her. She supported all artists, whatever their odd quirks, but Cissy and Barbara Davison probably didn't realize that. I checked my cell phone. Five minutes before the doors opened. I stashed the cider packets under our table, straightened the chairs, and suppressed a grin while Cissy explained about her flighty cousin.

"You've got to be kidding," Maddie said. "I went to school with her, and I'd never insult the Magpie's Nest. It's a perfect haven for vintage collectors. We both love her shop."

"Clearly you have no taste whatsoever." Cissy tramped off, fists clenched, high heels clicking on the tile floor. Maddie snickered.

"What a trip and a half. Digger showed me a racy photo of her a week or so ago, half-naked. Cissy's the last person to talk about taste."

"You're kidding! How did he get that kind of a photo?"

"He never said directly, but probably Cal Bloom." My sister lowered her voice. "Digger would get in real trouble if Cissy knew."

"What if her fiancé found out? Ugh."

I imagined Gus Antonini would be livid. Why would Mayor Bloom have shared a photo like that with anyone? And how did he get it in the first place? Too creepy. Maddie quickly changed the subject.

"Last-minute check, Sasha. Is the iPad charged? Did you run through a transaction to make sure we have internet access? Never mind, I can do it."

"Hurry up, because the stampede has begun."

A huge crowd streamed through the double doors, the majority women, although a few men with children in tow headed for the kitchen to buy coffee, cider, and donuts. Maddie and I handled a steady influx of customers over the next few hours. We sold bears so fast, I had to call the shop to replenish our supply within the first hour. Tim Richardson and Deon Walsh arrived with several large boxes, followed by Aunt Eve with extra logo bags. Her dangling Christmas tree earrings swung back and forth when she surveyed our depleted shelves.

"I hope we brought enough bears. Here's

more order forms, too."

"Good. People are going gaga over the Beary Potter Keepsake wizard bear." I handed her the forms we'd already filled out and then stacked fresh ones on the table. "I only hope we can get them all done in time for Christmas."

Maddie quickly slit the tape on a box and handed me various bears to set on the shelves behind our table. "Did you bring any of our smallest size, Aunt Eve?"

"I'll send Deon and Tim back for them. I had to leave Joan in charge of the shop. Oh, Sasha! Where did you get that darling little silver bear pin?"

"Over at the jewelry booth." I waved past the busy kitchen with its line snaking around the basement. "Good luck finding a way over to it, though."

"I'll check it out while I'm here."

Aunt Eve merged into the crowd, looking smart in a black cloche hat with a sprig of holly on the brim, red slacks, a black wool pea coat, and sensible boots instead of heels. I knew she'd love the vintage pins and necklaces. My mother suddenly appeared and overtook her. I hadn't noticed when she'd arrived, but turned back to the onrush of new customers.

"Good thing we restocked," Maddie said

when the crowd finally thinned. "Santa will be leaving a lot of them under Christmas trees this year. The tea room hosted half a dozen baby showers since they opened."

"They're doing well."

"Too bad Tess and Arthur didn't have a float in the parade. I wish you'd gone with me to that shower for Cheri Furness. Remember she married your friend Rachel's brother. They want to wait until the birth to find out if it's a boy or girl. She loved our largest silver bear inside a bassinette. It looked more like a big basket, and so adorable with pink ribbons."

"Aww. Sweet."

I sighed, wishing my future wasn't so bleak when it came to a family. Jay and I were committed in our relationship, but we hadn't discussed marriage. Or children. We both loved our families and traditions, and shared so many interests — books, movies, games, friends, and more. Ever since Thanksgiving weekend, when we'd stolen a few days together, our busy schedules prevented more than a ten- or fifteen-minute phone chat late at night. Jay didn't expect to come home until Christmas Eve, if then. The weather this year didn't help, either.

"Is it snowing again?" Maddie pointed to

wet puddles on the tile floor from the crowd's boots. "I'll get some paper towels before someone slips and falls."

She rushed off toward the bathroom. Grateful for a lull in customers, I tidied up our table and the cash box. Mom hurried over, one hand on her hip.

"This is terrible! I don't know what to do."

I hoped she wasn't referring to Alison and Kristen Bloom, or the investigation into Cal Bloom's death. "What's terrible?"

"Your uncle! He wants to get married by Judge Starr at the courthouse and skip any kind of reception or family dinner. How can we celebrate their second wedding? I wanted to have it during the staff party. That would be perfect —"

"Mom, I know they don't want a big fuss."

"But what better way to observe such a special occasion, with everyone there? We could have a wedding cake, and poinsettias on all the tables. Maybe silver bells, too."

"It's their decision, Mom." Maddie had returned from wiping the wet floor. "Maybe they don't want anyone feeling obligated to give them a wedding gift."

"Oh, pooh on that. Nobody would mind in the least."

I groaned to myself. Mom often ran roughshod over other people's feelings or desires when she immersed herself in planning something. The day Eve showed off her engagement ring, Mom had started gushing over plans — and we both knew she was capable of taking over everything. Dad was usually able to talk sense into her, but apparently he'd failed making any headway. And while my aunt no doubt appreciated help, she had her own ideas.

While Maddie handled a new order for the wizard bear, I packaged up a red and white Christmas sweater for a large teddy and swiped the customer's credit card on our iPad. Once she signed, I had her fill in the email address on the line for a receipt.

"Thank you! All this new technology is so convenient. And my grandson will love this sweater for his bear."

"I hope he enjoys it, and thank you." Once she walked away, I nudged my sister. "Uh-oh. Big trouble."

"What?"

"Someone's not a happy camper, that's what."

Lois Nichols stood before the Fresh Grounds booth, glowering at Mary Kate, hands on her hips. Lois had formerly worked in the factory and had given Uncle Ross a hard time about work conditions, pay, and benefits. Now Wendy Clark argued right back at her, shaking a fist. Mary Kate's soothing words didn't get either of them to stop. Lois's face turned purple.

Maddie raised an eyebrow. "She looked that way after we fired her."

"You stole my cookie recipe!" Her screech stopped people in their tracks, but Lois didn't seem to notice. "Why don't you come clean and admit it?"

"I didn't steal your recipe." Mary Kate sounded calm. "Mine is traditional shortbread from Scotland. You bragged the other day that yours is from Pinterest."

"So? Maybe the recipe is different, but you stole the name. Sugar Plum Teddies sounds exactly like my Sugar Plum Teddy Bears. And you expect to win the contest because you're best friends with Sasha Silverman!"

I hurried over, leaving Maddie to cover our booth before the situation got out of hand. "My friendships will not be a factor in judging the contest, Lois."

"So you say! I'll sue you if you win, Mary Kate. Wait and see."

"You can't sue anyone, Lois," she replied with a small smile. "You signed the entry form to accept the judge's decision."

"That's true." My mother had joined us. "No lawyer would take your case on those grounds alone, Mrs. Nichols."

Lois waved a hand. "I'll sue the Silverman family business, too, if I can prove any hint of favoritism in judging."

"The entries won't have the baker's name on them," Mary Kate said.

"Like that matters. Some of those entries aren't even bear-shaped cookies! What kind of teddy bear bake-off contest is this supposed to be, anyway?"

"The cookies can be any type," I said, "according to the contest rules."

"The fix is in. Everyone in the village knows it."

CHAPTER 9

"That's ridiculous." My mother sounded firm.

"Some of those entries aren't even baked cookies," Lois retorted, remaining calm.

"We hired a pastry chef and two other people to judge," Mom said. "They have no ties to our family or friends in Silver Hollow. They'll choose five entries today in the final round, and those five will be judged for the final winner."

"We hired — Oh, we did." I nodded, hoping Lois wouldn't catch my slip. Maddie and Mom hadn't told me of this plan, and it meant I'd miss out on taste-testing. Dang. "That's as fair as possible."

Lois continued to scowl. "I'll only be satisfied if my Sugar Plum Teddy Bears make the final round." She stalked toward the exit.

"Oh, brother." I breathed a deep sigh of relief. "I have a bad feeling this isn't over, not by a long shot."

Mary Kate agreed. "We won't mind if we're not in the finals. My Christmas Scookies are selling like crazy. We can't bake them fast enough."

"Wow, what's a Scookie?"

"Sort of a hybrid cookie, cakelike, shaped like a scone. I use flour, sugar, buttermilk, eggs, both baking soda and baking powder, plus raspberries. I'm sure Lois only wants to win the bake-off contest as a way of getting revenge against you and Maddie for firing her."

Wendy Clark nodded. "I heard her saying exactly that. And how she wasn't given a second chance. Everyone at the Quick Mix Factory thinks she's nuts, though. And I've heard horror stories of what she used to pull while she sewed teddy bears."

"Like what?" When Wendy clapped a hand over her mouth, I laughed. "Come on, spill. Who told you all that, and what kind of stuff did Lois do?"

"Joan Kendall and I meet for dinner at the pub once in a while. Boy, does she have great stories. Like Lois messing up a sewing machine so she could go home early —"

"On purpose?" I winced, recalling how often that had happened. Not only did it cost us a bundle in repairs, we even had to buy several new machines.

"Yeah, and she often skipped a few steps in sewing bears. Joan had to trash one teddy bear completely. Half the seams hadn't been sewn properly, and it looked lumpy."

"Why didn't she tell my brother-in-law, the supervisor?" Mom demanded. "Ross would have put a stop to that, for certain."

"She threatened Joan to keep quiet," Wendy said. "Lois even cowed Flora Zimmerman, and she doesn't scare easy. Harriet Amato couldn't take Lois's threats, so she quit."

That surprised me. "I always wondered if she had another reason besides Will Taylor's murder. Especially since we walled off the stuffing machine. It satisfied everyone else."

"She wanted to retire anyway. Plus Harriet's daughter had trouble finding babysitters whenever school closed, or her kids were sick."

"I can't believe Lois bullied so many people at the factory."

"Sasha, you always think the best of people." Mary Kate smiled. "That's why you're so shocked when you find out their secrets. I'm wondering if Lois will do something drastic if her cookie isn't chosen for the contest. Like sabotaging the winner."

Mom rubbed her arms as if a sudden chill

hit her. "Eve told me she served time in some prison. Is that true?"

"Yes, for assault. She never mentioned her conviction on her employment application, either. Since that's required according to our policy handbook, we had no choice but to fire her. Lois must have figured we'd never find out."

I watched Wendy box up a customer's order and then tie it with a red-and-green-striped ribbon while we chatted. A line had formed, and Mary Kate deftly wrote up receipts and cashed them out. I tapped a finger against my chin.

"I was hoping to see your contest cookie," I said, hinting broadly.

Mary Kate giggled. "You're out of luck, Sasha. Our entry is safe with Isabel French. Now get back to your booth. Maddie's swamped."

Wendy pulled me aside and whispered low. "You can tell our Sugar Plum Teddies by my style of decoration. Lace collars and cuffs on a blue suit."

"Like *Little Lord Fauntleroy*? How cute! I can't wait to see them." I hurried back to help my sister, while Mom headed toward the kitchen. "Guess she's checking on Dad. I bet she won't volunteer to take over for Leah, who really ought to go home and take care of Dave if he's so sick. Maybe I ought to help Dad —"

"Oh no, you don't," Maddie said. "Make sure these wizard bear order forms are filled out in full. We need email addresses, shipping addresses, and see if any orders were duplicated by mistake. I was in such a rush. Hope I didn't mess up any of them."

Once I finished that task, I bagged up a customer's bear in tissue and set it within our logo bag along with a pink ballerina outfit and a tiny teddy bear nutcracker. "Your granddaughter will love these," I said to the older woman.

"We're taking her to see *The Nutcracker* ballet, so this is perfect."

I handled four other orders before Aunt Eve insisted she would cover the booth so that Maddie and I could take a twenty-minute break. This whole week felt like I'd been running a 10K marathon. My sister walked slow, shoulders slumped, when we headed to fetch more coffee and a sandwich. Usually she had so much energy.

"I'm surprised Leah Richardson hasn't gone home. Wendy said the whole clan is at the hospital. Her father-in-law isn't expected to survive."

"That's a shame, really."

My phone chirped, signaling a message. I

read Jay's text with delight and set a time to call that night. He'd finally gotten through a tough week, planned to work on a commission for a few hours, and then relax while talking to me. Four new inches of snow had fallen up north on top of a base of about half a foot. Local roads were rutted and icy, too. I hoped salt trucks and plows had gone out to clear the streets in Silver Hollow.

Maddie smiled knowingly. "If you left now, you could make it in four or five hours, give or take. Even though you don't like winter driving."

"Yeah, but I'd have to be back tomorrow afternoon." I sighed. "Plus it's gonna snow more tonight. We'll just talk on the phone."

I wished I could drive up north for a visit with Jay, but knew I'd never make it. A gallon of coffee wouldn't get me safely there. We returned to the booth, where I helped one customer choose a bear for a friend's child. Despite being tempted to see Jay and his most recent work, I couldn't leave early. Dad had taught us to stick with a commitment, even if it meant missing out on something else. I missed Jay's smile, though, his easygoing nature and infectious laugh.

"Guess we're both stuck at home tonight," my sister said. "I wanted to finish that project for the microbrewery, but I'm too beat."

"What's this plan about hiring a pastry chef to judge the cookie contest?"

"I had a feeling we ought to, since everyone knows everyone around here. We don't want to alienate people or hear complaints of cheating. There he is, too."

"Who? The chef?"

Maddie pointed out a hefty guy with a beard, in ratty jeans, a leather jacket, and a flat cap, who strolled through the hall. Two women followed behind him, chatting together, looking fashionable in wool coats and scarves, and carrying trendy tote bags — one a Kate Spade, the other a Coach. Unless they were knockoffs. Maddie nudged me again when the threesome stopped at the jewelry booth.

"Christophe Benoit of Flambé told me about this guy, who's French. Georges Martin is his name, and he teaches an advanced pastry class at a culinary school in Ann Arbor. He's always judging contests. Even international ones."

"Who are the women with him?"

"I think they're his best students, from what he told me on the phone. I asked Mom to cover for me here while the judging takes place, but maybe she forgot."

"Go on, you can watch them. I'll be fine. Things are winding down anyway."

Maddie hugged me. "Thanks, Sash! I'm dying to see which five they choose."

"Give me the full rundown when you get back, then."

She rushed off. Luckily I wasn't swamped with customers buying bears or accessories, and only took a few orders for the wizard bear. Sherry Martinez ambled by at four, in a white wig, round glasses, and a calico dress; the white cap she wore on her head as Mrs. Claus matched her apron. She looked glum. Her husband, who owned the La Mesa Mexican restaurant on Main Street, was the polar opposite. Always smiling, super friendly, and generous to the community when he sent food to the local cops and firefighters. He often volunteered at fundraisers, too.

So did Sherry, but she never looked like she enjoyed it.

"A few vendors have already started closing down." She frowned in disapproval and patted her wig. "They're supposed to stay until five o'clock. I suppose they're worried about driving home, since we've gotten at least three inches of snow this afternoon. The roads are getting worse by the hour."

"Wow. Hope no one gets in an accident

out there."

"It wasn't too bad between ten and two o'clock, but then it started snowing harder. Make sure to clean up your area before you go. Trash thrown away, chairs folded. The take-down crew will put them away along with the tables."

Sherry moved on. Her news decided the question about me driving anywhere but home. Disappointed, I straightened what was left of our products and counted the minutes until the Bear-zaar closed at last. Then I began to pack what was left of our inventory. Maddie danced her way toward the booth, ecstatic.

"You should see the five cookies the judges chose! They're wonderful."

"Is Mary Kate in the running?"

"What did hers look like?"

"Shortbread teddy bear, blue outfit, with a lace collar, and cuffs. Wendy decorated it."

"Oh, yeah, all the judges raved about the icing skills. I didn't think Lois's Sugar Plum Teddy Bear looked that great, but the students thought the tiny sugar plum noses were adorable. And Chef Martin said it had good flavor." Maddie whooped over the huge stack of order forms for the wizard bear. "Wow! Look at all these. I hope we can make it before the deadline. That only doubles the pressure to deliver on time for Christmas."

"We'll make it," I said. "I've got four new people trained to sort pattern pieces and sew. That will help with production. And two of Tim Richardson's friends will help with shipping orders every day after school. Don't worry.

"So what are the other three cookies? I'm dying to know who's up against Lois and Mary Kate in the bake-off contest."

"A Cranberry Walnut Snowball, a Ginger Caramel Buttercream Macaron, and Date Nut Jingle Bells," Maddie said. "A miniature gingerbread house almost got in the final round, but when one of the judges picked it up to examine, the roof cracked apart. The little house perched on the edge of a mug, with a tiny teddy bear in the window. Too bad. I really loved it."

"So, Mary Kate's Sugar Plum Teddies —"

"She renamed it the *Little Lord Fauntleroy* Bear," Maddie said. "Wendy said you came up with that idea, so now Lois can't complain about the name competing with her Sugar Plum Teddy Bear. I don't know who entered the other cookies, but they're all delicious."

We stacked boxes on a cart and then

rolled it to the stairs. Uncle Ross and several factory staff members helped us to carry everything to the company truck. Dusk had deepened into night when our staff headed home. Mom had ordered pizza from Amato's, so we sat or stood around the kitchen island to eat.

"Tom Richardson passed away at the hospital this afternoon," Dad announced. "Despite his fever, Dave dragged himself to his father's bedside in time."

"The entire clan's headed to the funeral home, from what Tim told me." Uncle Ross bit into another slice of pizza. "My guess is the family will choose Tuesday or Wednesday of next week for services. Don't know if that will clash with Cal Bloom's, though."

"I don't think so," Mom said, "although Dave and Leah have their hands full helping Alison and Kristen plan the details."

My uncle wiped his mouth. "That detective hasn't been around much. The hefty guy, Mason. Instead there's some dude in a fancy suit asking questions around the village. Even came to the factory today, nosing around."

"Detective Hunter is assigned to the case. He came around when the judges were tasting the cookie contest entries." Maddie blew out a breath, clearly annoyed. "He kept bugging me when I couldn't give him my full attention. I didn't like his attitude."

The clock struck seven, so I sneaked upstairs. I'd taken Rosie outside when we first returned and now she padded after me. Poor thing, she'd been alone most of the day — and must be desperate for attention. Until I noticed shredded tissue on the carpet. She crept into a corner of the bedroom, half-hidden behind the tufted armchair.

"Oh, no, Rosie. What did you get into?"

I stared at the strips of paper on the bathroom's tile floor and the empty cardboard tube. "I knew I should have taken you to doggie day care last night instead of leaving you alone with Nyx. You found another way to amuse yourself."

Once I cleaned the mess, I changed into flannel pajama bottoms and an old sweatshirt, brushed out my hair, and braided it. Then I curled up on the window seat with a book and an afghan. Rosie jumped onto my lap after a half hour, so we watched the light snowfall together. She rolled over so I could rub her belly. Jay was scheduled to call at eight o'clock, but the long minutes ticked by. I left a message on his cell at eight thirty.

That wasn't like Jay to promise and then forget. I'd hoped to catch him up on everything that had happened, in depth, since the mayor's murder. He had a logical bent. Too often, I relied on my gut instinct, which was sometimes just plain wrong.

Rats.

My mood worsened with each passing minute. The soft lamplight didn't soothe me, and I wasn't in the mood to turn on the TV or plow into the stack of magazines piled on the end table. Not even *Tea Time,* one of my favorites, with its eye candy of teacups and lovely treats. Not that I'd ever have the time to bake. Sometimes I gave Mary Kate an issue if she wanted to try out a new scone recipe among its pages.

Even the *Teddy Bear Times* didn't keep my interest, which showcased the most recent holiday-themed bears for collectors. Dad had gotten me into the habit long ago, checking out doll and teddy bear show announcements. Instead I fetched my iPad and checked the Child's Play Toy Box Co.'s website. At last they had posted an explanation of the Teddy Bear Keepsake contest. That meant the Silver Bear Shop's feature would appear in the next print issue, since I'd sent in a photo and answered interview questions.

Setting my iPad aside, I plucked up the PS4 video controller. Jay had introduced me to *Overwatch,* which proved addictive. I'd been too busy to devote time in learning the characters and their skill kits, or exploring the maps, and preferred casual play rather than competitive. Jay had no time to play at all. His sister, Lauren, had hooked him into the game first. She'd broken up with her boyfriend and dedicated a lot of time to playing.

I felt bad for her and sympathized with her coping mechanism, but hoped she wouldn't get too sidetracked. Younger than Jay by nearly ten years, she had a sweet vulnerability. With her upcoming EMT exams, however, Lauren couldn't afford to fail.

I flopped across the bed. Rosie abandoned the window seat and curled up on the warm heater duct near the floor.

"I bet Jay got distracted by his project. His deadline's Christmas, after all —" Startled by a knock on the bedroom door, I rolled onto my side. "Who is it?"

"You decent?" Maddie poked her head inside. "Mom and Aunt Eve need your opinion about the wedding. Come on downstairs."

"An opinion on what?"

I couldn't help sounding grumpy. Rosie raced out the door, so I grabbed my phone in case Jay did call and followed them downstairs. My parents sat at the table, but Aunt Eve and Uncle Ross were getting into their coats.

"— would be perfect. The food's already taken care of, Eve, and I promise to keep it as casual as possible," Mom was saying. "You didn't want a classic wedding, so no champagne, no fancy dress. I'll take care of everything."

"You think you're going to wear us down, right?" Aunt Eve waved a gloved hand near her red-cheeked face. "Oh, these hot flashes! We'll more talk tomorrow, okay?"

Dad rose to his feet. "We're leaving, too. Come on, Judith. Let's go."

I shivered from a blast of cold air when Uncle Ross opened the door. My sister blocked any retreat, however. Dad brought Mom's coat and then followed my aunt and uncle outside. Yipping wildly, Rosie darted past them all into the snowy yard.

I nudged Maddie. "Everyone's leaving. Why did you drag me down here?"

"You'll see."

When Jay walked through the door, my jaw dropped. Rosie jumped against his damp jeans and wagged her tail. She waited while he rubbed clumps of snow off her paws and belly. With his slicked-back wet hair, apple cheeks, and bright smile, he looked adorable.

"No, it's not a dream." Maddie pinched my arm. "Have a great time catching up. See you in the morning at breakfast. A late one, I hope."

Jay pulled off his boots and padded toward me for a big, thankful bear hug. The kitchen seemed empty with only the two of us and Rosie, who circled us and barked until I hushed her. After a few wonderful kisses, I leaned away from him.

"What are you doing here?"

He laughed. "Surprising you. Are you? Surprised, that is."

"Yes, but what about the snow? It's still coming down."

"Yeah, your dad asked me about that, too. I'm lucky I didn't end up in a ditch like a few smaller cars. A heavy truck sure helps in this weather." Jay kissed me soundly again, sending a thrill down to my toes. "Took a few extra hours, since I had to drive slower."

"I thought you were working on your new commission. That was rotten of you to text me instead of calling!" I kissed him lightly. "But it is a wonderful surprise."

"I stopped at a Starbucks in Mount Pleasant to text you. It was so noisy, and I didn't want you to overhear anything with a phone call."

"Driving must have been terrible. Have I got a lot to tell you."

I hugged Jay tight, overjoyed that he was here, tracing the stubble of his beard from his jaw to his ear, and noting how his light brown hair fell over his flannel shirt collar. He nuzzled my neck while I told him about the Bear-zaar. Breathing in his scent of musk and sweat, I had a hard time focusing. Rosie whined, so I let her outside one last time.

The falling snow looked so peaceful against the dark sky, filling in the holes where people had tramped from the house down the drive to the parking lot. We laughed to watch Rosie frolic in the snow, racing in circles, her tracks resembling a rabbit, and stopping to sniff every so often. Once she returned, I toweled her dry and mopped the kitchen floor's puddles.

"So you must know more about Cal Bloom's death, right? You never did explain the whole story about the parade." Jay leaned over to rub Onyx, who purred against his hand and curled her lithe body around his ankles. "Tell me what happened."

"I think he was electrocuted. We found him near the Quick Mix Factory, nowhere near the floats and generators for the parade. He couldn't have gotten a shock without a power source." I draped the dog's wet towel on the baker's rack and locked the deadbolt. "So murder's a strong possibility."

Jay groaned. "No way, Sasha. You aren't joking?"

"I wish I were. The police won't know for certain until the autopsy report is finished. If Detective Hunter ever bothers to tell us anything, that is."

"Who?"

"A different county detective is investigating. Nothing like Mason, who's a decent guy. Sharp, too, and on track most of the time. Hunter's full of arrogance."

I left a few treats on the cat tower, plus filled a Kong toy with peanut butter, before we headed upstairs. I took my time and explained everything — the floats in the parade, how my mother found Cal Bloom, and that Flynn and his latest girlfriend had accompanied us. When Rosie jumped on the big bed, I shooed her off.

"Oh no, you have to sleep in your own bed tonight, over there." I set the Kong treat down on the thick cushion and turned back to Jay. "The whole thing's a mess about the mayor, but who would want to kill him? It takes a lot for someone to do that. Tony Crocker was so sore about losing the election, but would he have offed him? And then there's Cissy Davison. She might have been mad if she found out Cal Bloom had a half-naked photo."

"I hope you mean of her, not the mayor." Jay winked.

I playfully tossed a pillow his way. "And now Mom wants me to prove Alison Bloom is innocent. If she's a suspect —"

"How about we skip talking over the whole murder business," he murmured against my ear and pulled me close. "I'm still pretty chilled from that long drive."

"I can help you with that."

I grabbed the afghan blanket off the window seat and held it out. I laughed hard at his sour expression and then ended up in a tug of war over it. Jay let me win, but snatched a pillow from the floor and swung it; I danced aside before it landed on my backside. Giggling, I tripped over Rosie and fell backward on the bed.

Jay stretched out beside me, one arm keeping me in place. "I'd rather you warm me up in a different way." He trailed a few kisses on my neck and mouth. "Unless you're too tired?"

I kissed him. "Maybe you can convince me to stay awake."

CHAPTER 10

Jay and I lazed around the next morning, chatting during a late breakfast of thick waffles and an egg casserole. Maddie had made it all before she left for the graphics studio. The kitchen was a huge mess, but Jay helped clean up; after that, we curled up together in front of the cozy fireplace, sharing the warmth, memories of previous winters, stories of our families, friends, and holiday fun. At last I nudged him in the ribs.

"So what do you think about the mayor's death? I think someone killed him."

"Wow. You really won't let that go." He smoothed a stray blond strand of my hair away from my eyes. "I'm not sure what to say. I barely remember what happened on Thanksgiving, except for that pumpkin pie. You apologized fifty times for the burned crust."

"Thank goodness whipped cream hides mistakes."

"Very true." Jay planted a kiss on my ear. "I've seen Bloom around the village my whole life. Everyone thought he was a real character. Always played Santa Claus at the K of C hall on Baker Road every Christmas, before the city council voted for the parade and tree lighting. Your dad came up with the Santa Bear mascot idea, you know."

"Really?" I smiled. "All I remember is how Dad tried to talk Uncle Ross into wearing the costume. That went over like a lead balloon."

"Your uncle doesn't like kids?"

"From a distance. I don't think it bothered him he never had any."

"Too bad. Hope you want a few."

I snuggled against him, smiling. "You bet. When Cal Bloom volunteered, he didn't need any padding with the bear costume. Everyone thought he was perfect. The mayor loves — did love — the spotlight, as you know. Now we'll have to come up with a different mascot."

"I don't see why. Everyone will forget what happened by next year."

"I doubt it. Murder seems to be increasing around here."

Jay rubbed my shoulders. "Relax, Sasha. Forget it and focus on everything between now and the New Year. Once I'm done with

158

this woodcarving class, I'll open my studio near the village. Maybe you can help me find the perfect spot. I'd rather not freeze in my parents' barn over the winter."

"Hmm. I'll have to think about that. The city council is supposed to open Theodore Lane at Main Street, but they may postpone the vote due to Cal Bloom's death. Depends on who the mayoral pro tem is, I guess. I never paid attention to local politics. Or national, either."

"Did you vote in the last election?"

"Forgot. Totally."

He laughed and kissed my temple. "I'll remind you next time."

A comfortable silence reigned. I savored the last few minutes before Jay had to leave. Reluctantly, I posed a question. "Do you know Kristen Bloom at all? Cal's daughter. Your older brother, Paul, graduated with her, I think."

"Yeah. Want me to ask him if she's capable of patricide?"

"Stop teasing."

"Sorry. Your dad said it might have been an accident, though."

"Remember, no power source was anywhere near where we found him. But I'd like to cross both Alison and Kristen off the suspect list."

"Okay, I'll call." Jay retrieved his phone from the end table and punched in a series of numbers. "Hey, bro. Got a few minutes?"

While they talked, if you could call a series of grunts, short words, uh-huhs, and mumbles as conversation, I made a thick sandwich of turkey, leftover bacon, tomato, and lettuce on rye for him to eat on the long drive back to Grayling. I also filled a thermos of fresh coffee and added a handful of cookies I'd bought yesterday from Mary Kate's Bear-zaar booth. That would tide him over. Jay would only need to stop for gas.

He slid his arms around my waist while I stood at the kitchen island, nuzzling the bare skin of my neck. "Thanks for breakfast, and now lunch. You're too good to me."

I turned to accept a deep kiss. "So what did Paul say?"

"Kristen blew him off when he asked her out once, so he never bothered her again. Paul doesn't know squat about anything that happens in Silver Hollow. He keeps his head down. Not much to tell me about our family, either. I hear more than he does."

"That's because you're close with Lauren. How's she doing? Assuming you've talked to her recently. She told me about breaking up, and how terrible that was."

"Yeah, she's bummed. Swamped with —"

Rosie jumped up from her spot near the fireplace, barking like mad. I heard a hard rap on the back door. Wishing I'd exchanged my fleece robe for clothes, I jumped to my feet. Who would drop by on a snowy Sunday at noon? My parents had a key, along with Ross and Eve. They knew Jay was here, and like Maddie, wanted to give us privacy. Then again, maybe it was Detective Mason coming with news of the investigation.

Flynn stood on the back porch in his wool coat, hands in his pockets, his blond hair frosted with snowflakes. I yanked the door open. "What are you doing here?"

My ex-husband pushed past me with a smirk. When Jay rose from the sofa, Flynn jerked a thumb his way. "Aha. Having a little booty call?"

"None of — What do you want?"

"Hey, no problem, Kirby," he said and shook Jay's hand. "I figured you might be curious about something I found out, Sasha."

"Oh?" Jay scratched his stubbly jaw. "What's that, Hanson?"

"That other detective who's investigating Bloom's death came by to question me."

"Detective Hunter?" I asked, noting the gleam in Flynn's eye.

161

"Yeah, on Friday. Guy looked familiar, but I couldn't place him. Until last night. I'd been meeting with a client for dinner about a few weeks ago at the Gandy Dancer, over in Ann Arbor. That's where I saw him. Guess they didn't figure that you can't keep a secret for long, even outside of Silver Hollow."

"That's true. So you went to that expensive restaurant near the train station?" I slid an arm around Jay's waist. "What a nice tax write-off."

"Hey, I gotta keep up my image. Remember that Flynn Wins. So if you ever need a lawyer, Kirby, call my office."

"The Legal Eagles? From what Mike Blake said, you've pretty much erased your partners out of the spotlight. Bet you'll rename it Hanson's Law Firm soon."

"So what if I do?"

I hushed them both. "Back to Detective Hunter, guys. He's gotta eat, so what's the big deal about seeing him at a restaurant?"

My ex grinned. "You might ask who was with him that night."

Despite his annoying smugness, I took the bait. "Okay. Who?"

"Kristen Bloom."

"So? Maybe they're friends —"

"More than friends," Flynn interrupted.

"Holding hands, and kissing between sips of champagne. Then he handed her a velvet box. That's when I paid more attention, because the necklace had a huge diamond. Sparkled so much, no one could miss it, or how she squealed like a prize pig. Hunter seemed pleased, too."

"You're sure it was him?"

"As sure as you're standing here."

"Wouldn't that be a conflict of interest, investigating his girlfriend's father's death, and possible murder?"

"Like, yeah. Big time." Flynn slapped his leather gloves against the palm of one hand. "So I told Blake and Branson, since Mark is representing Mrs. Bloom. He needed to know. You might want to mention it to Detective Mason the next time he comes around. And he will. The cops' success rate in Silver Hollow depends on your help, remember."

I ignored that. "What else do you know about Kristen?"

"Money problems, at least rumors of it. So long. I got work to do."

"Hey, have you heard about a racy photo of Cissy Davison?"

That stopped him in his tracks. I repeated my question, since he'd already descended the porch steps. The wind tore the door out of my grasp and nearly slammed it shut. Flynn cocked his head and grinned, almost wickedly, his eyes gleaming.

"What about it?"

"How would Cal Bloom have gotten that photo, or a copy?"

"No idea. If he'd stolen it, or tried to publish it, that would be a statutory violation." Flynn glanced around, as if we were being spied upon, and then leaned forward. "All she could do was ask me to send him a letter demanding its return. It's her private property, after all. But Bloom denied having it."

"Wow."

"I'd guess that Gus Antonini showed it around to his friends, and probably had more than one copy. I learned my lesson about incriminating photos." He tapped a finger against his cheek. "Let me tell you, Mrs. Bloom wasn't happy to see that letter."

"So what if —"

"Gotta run, I'm late." He rushed toward his car in the parking lot.

I shut the door and turned to Jay, who'd walked up behind me. "That is seriously creepy about the photo. The mayor always seemed so family oriented."

"Who knew he was such a dirty old man

in secret," he said, chuckling. "I'd better head out, Sasha, before it gets dark."

"Already?"

I kissed him hard, hoping to stave off his departure. It worked for another half hour. Once Jay left, though, I cuddled with Rosie before the gas fireplace. Detective Mason probably didn't know about that photo, or that his colleague was dating Kristen Bloom. Mason seemed a stickler for protocol and standards, while Hunter had an attitude problem. How could he keep an open mind about suspects? Especially if Mrs. Bloom was first on the list.

Only time would tell.

The snow stopped by three o'clock, so I decided to take a long hot shower. Once I dried my hair, I donned jeans, a heavy sweater, boots, coat, gloves, and hat. When I grabbed Rosie's leash, she raced around me with eagerness.

"Good girl. Time for a nice brisk walk after a lazy day."

The hired snowplow had cleared our driveway, parking lot, and Theodore Lane to the curve. I fastened Rosie's Velcro boots on her four paws, and doubled over with laughter at how she high-stepped in an awkward gait until she grew accustomed to the weird feeling again. Rosie disliked snow more than the boots, however. We skirted the few drifts that covered the sidewalk and walked along the street instead. I saw few cars out this late in the day.

Warm sunshine cheered me, but more clouds scudded across the sky. Hopefully Jay would make it back safe and sound. He'd promised to text once he arrived at his friend's cabin. I'd have rented an apartment for that long, but he liked roughing it. I crossed Kermit and headed to Fresh Grounds. A little pick-me-up sounded good, with a cookie. Maybe two. Hang the tight-fitting dress. The more I heard about the wedding, the more confident I felt that Aunt Eve wanted a casual event. All eyes would be on the bride, anyway.

I tied Rosie's leash to the lamp post outside the coffee shop. "I'll be right back, sweetie, with a treat for you. I promise."

Inside, I waved to Wendy Clark. "Congrats on getting into the final round in the bake-off contest. The *Little Lord Fauntleroy* bear's adorable!"

"Thanks. Mary Kate's not all that thrilled with the name change, but I figured we'd better steer clear of any trouble with Lois Nichols."

"I totally get that."

Wendy had wiped crumbs off the counter

with a damp cloth. "Enough about her. What can I make for you this afternoon, miss?"

I had to laugh at her teasing tone. "A chai latte, skim milk, and don't skip the whip. Plus, hmm." I eyed the Christmas cookies in the case and pointed to a huge tree with red cinnamon imperials. "I'll take one of those. And two doggie treats for Rosie, of course."

"Two for her, one for you? It's usually the other way around." Wendy snickered while she bagged up my purchase and then handed over my tea. "Enjoy."

I headed outside into the cold once more, fed Rosie her treats, and munched my cookie. Wendy's stories about Lois Nichols bothered me. How could Maddie and I have missed such obvious character flaws when we hired her? Lois had worked in our family business for over a year. I'd heard a few inklings of trouble with other workers, but we hadn't dug deep enough to discover the problem. That had been a big mistake. We hadn't anticipated Will Taylor's sly attempt to control production back in late summer, either.

Maddie and I planned our cookie contest to include locals, whether or not they had real baking experience. We wanted village residents to feel a part of our holiday celebrations. I truly hoped Lois wouldn't undermine the bake-off contest.

That would sour everything.

The coffee shop's door swung wide, knocking my elbow, but I managed to hang on to my chai tea. The short dark-haired woman looked vaguely familiar when she apologized.

"You're Sasha Silverman, right? I'm Alison Bloom."

"Oh! Hello —"

"Surprised I'm not in jail?"

"No," I sputtered. "I didn't expect to meet you here. On the street, I mean."

She laughed, a pleasant sound that made me sympathize with her plight. Alison Bloom wore carefully applied makeup that made her look forty instead of closer to sixty; her eyes had a puffiness from a crying jag, however, that couldn't be hidden. Her spiked hairstyle, with barely noticeable strands of gray, also lent an appearance of youth. And her black jeans, camel coat, plaid scarf, plus chunky gold jewelry gave her a classic look. Genuine snakeskin boots with three-inch heels lent a bit of pizazz.

"Judith said you helped prove Ross Silverman's innocence. I hope you can do the same for me." Alison sighed. "I'm only guilty of neglecting my husband since my mother went into the Silver Birches. Cal and I have been through a lot together, but I never expected this."

"I'm so sorry for your loss. And for Kristen, too."

"My stepdaughter? Yes, she's quite upset about her dad."

"Stepdaughter?" I blinked. "I thought —"

"Most people assume that," Alison interrupted, "but Cal's first wife divorced him when Kristen was seven or eight. I tried hard to be a mother to her. We had a difficult time adjusting over the years. Thank you, though. We appreciate everyone's support." She eyed my dog. "What a sweet puppy."

"She's full grown, actually."

"Do you have time to spare for a longer chat?"

"I can't take Rosie into Fresh Grounds, but how about the bookstore?"

Alison glanced at The Cat's Cradle bookstore. "Sure."

After I gulped most of my tea, I tossed the cup in the trash and led the way to the shop. Elle was on the phone with a customer. I waved Alison toward the back and then mouthed "we need privacy" so my friend wouldn't interrupt us.

169

"I know Mom expects me to prove your innocence," I began, "but your alibi should take care of that. I mean, you do have one. Right?"

"Yes. I was with my mother at the Silver Birches on Wednesday."

"At night, too, before and during the parade?"

Alison gazed at the ceiling and bit her lip. "Let's see, I didn't leave until very late. But Kristen came to visit with — oh, um. A friend."

"You mean Detective Hunter."

Her eyes widened. "You know about him?"

"I heard they're dating, yes. Secrets don't stay secret for long in a small town."

"Yes, I'm beginning to realize that. Kristen went home, oh, around four o'clock or so. I'm not sure. With Detective Hunter."

"Do the police know they're dating?"

"I have no idea. But I'm grateful to the Legal Eagles for keeping them at bay. You must have heard they took me in for questioning. In the middle of the night."

"Is it true you were planning to divorce the mayor?" I asked, watching for her reaction. Alison looked annoyed but quickly hid that. "Over his drinking problem."

"I threatened, of course, but I didn't file the papers."

"What about the matter of an intimate photograph?"

"You know, I'd better get back to check on my mother," she said quickly. "But thanks, Sasha, for whatever you can do to help."

I didn't get a chance to reply, since Alison Bloom rushed past me out of the shop. Clearly, she didn't want to answer further questions about her marriage. So Kristen was her stepdaughter. How had I missed that? I didn't remember Mom mentioning it. Or about the Blooms being on the brink of divorce. Both interesting facts.

"What gives, Sash?" Elle hung up the phone and joined me near the front window.

"How about a Guilty Pleasures Gossip Club chat?" I laughed when she rubbed her hands in glee. "Ask Mary Kate and let me know when."

Rosie tugged at her leash, so I headed outside and across Main Street. A few other people walked around the village in the sunshine. Maggie Davison emerged from her shop, although the screen door thwacked her shoulder. Her curly red hair stood out against her green sweatshirt, and a faint smattering of freckles marked her pale complexion. Maggie wore a hint of pink blush and eyeliner to emphasize her gorgeous blue eyes. Gingers had all the luck.

She waved me over. "Hey, Sasha! I saw the wizard bear yesterday at the Bear-zaar. I'd love to sell them here in my shop and online."

"Sorry, but we're under exclusive contract with the Teddy Bear Keepsake contest sponsor." I couldn't help feeling pleased by her interest, though. "We're tied up for a year to produce them, if not longer depending on how many orders. How's business going?"

"Good, so far, even though Cissy thinks I'll tank over winter. I'm so glad I asked Emily Abbott to help me out part-time. She's a real whiz at the computer." The sun disappeared among the thicker clouds, and Maggie shivered in the chill wind. "Come in out of the cold."

She pulled me inside the warm shop, which Rosie appreciated. My dog shook herself and then enjoyed the rubdown Maggie gave her, with plenty of slobbery kisses in return as a reward. I perched on a wooden bench next to a stuffed alligator. Or crocodile, whichever. Half a dozen children's toys and books and a vintage rotary telephone, similar to my mother's princess-style one, sat on the floor in front of a rusted, barely legible Sinclair Gasoline sign. I tried out a vintage Bentwood rocker and then jumped up, but Maggie waved me back to sit and relax.

"Isn't it comfortable? Here, I'll show you my latest paintings." Shyly, she brought me a leather portfolio with several delicate watercolors. "I'd like to send them off to a greeting card company, but I doubt they'll take them. Nowadays, you have to do everything yourself. Print and sell them on Etsy for peanuts. It's almost not worth it."

"Bet you can sell them here, in the shop, if you mat and frame them." I loved the one showing delicate white daisies against a purple background. It wasn't what I expected, given her unconventional personality. "This is gorgeous. Can I buy it?"

"I've got a five-by-seven, already framed. Twenty bucks."

"Great. It'll look perfect in my bedroom. You ought to show these to Maddie. She might be able to use some of the designs."

"Wow, never thought of that. Maybe I will."

We sat in silence for a few minutes. I sensed that Maggie heard about Cissy badgering me and my sister at the Bear-zaar yesterday. I waited her out, figuring she might feel awkward about bringing up the subject. She petted Rosie for a few minutes in silence, her curly hair hiding her face, and then turned to me with reddened cheeks. When her voice faltered, Maggie drew a deep breath and started again.

"I guess you must know how things stand with this shop. Aunt Barb isn't happy. She won't accept how different it is from the Time Turner. Cissy stops in every day, and she's driving me nuts. They both claim I'll have to close soon."

"Why would they think that?"

"I'm not the best with sales, or keeping the books straight. Math was always hard for me." Maggie pushed a lock of hair from her eyes. "Those story problems drove me crazy. Why would two trains be on the same track, heading toward each other? Who cares what time they crash and at what speed? What about the people? Like, call an ambulance!"

I'd joined in her laughter but sobered now. "You can always hire someone to handle the account books and tax filings."

"Yeah, I better do that. But I swear, I wish Cissy would leave me alone. Get married and have babies. Gus is so ready. He wants three sons and at least one daughter."

"That should keep her busy."

"I hope so! But I'm grateful to you and Maddie, sticking up for me yesterday." Maggie ducked her head again, petting Rosie. "It's none of her business what I do here."

I frowned. "I wonder why she's targeting you so much. Word's getting around that the mayor had a half-naked photo of Cissy, although apparently he denied it."

"Yeah, I heard that." She laughed. "Cissy had several photos taken, boudoir ones. As an engagement present for Gus, from what Aunt Barb said."

"How intimate?"

"Nothing worse than what you'd see in a Victoria's Secret catalog. Bikini panties, garter belt, stockings, a push-up bra showing her cleavage. Retouched to conceal any flaws, too. Gus showed them off to his friends. I bet one of his friends pocketed one on the sly."

"And somehow it got into the mayor's hands."

"Probably. Cissy found out when Cal Bloom came to her shop. Caught her alone, and showed it to her. I guess he made a pass, groped her a little. What a jerk."

"Whoa. What did she do?"

"Nothing." Maggie gathered up her loose curls into a ponytail, secured it, and tossed it over one shoulder. "It was a 'he said, she said' kind of thing, so she couldn't prove anything. But Cissy and Gus both have hot tempers."

"Hot enough to electrocute the mayor?"

"Whoa. I never considered that."

"Well, no matter what, the cops need proof."

"Yeah, like what happened with your dog!" Maggie rubbed her eyes. "Poor, sweet baby was almost killed. Horrible."

I leaned over to rub Rosie's silky ears, unable to meet her gaze. "It was touch and go, but Rosie pulled through."

"Anyway, thanks so much for supporting me. You and Maddie both. Aunt Barb's always poking around the flat upstairs to see if I'm keeping it clean. Thank goodness for Emily. She doesn't judge."

"That's too bad. Not Emily judging you. I meant your aunt —" I joined in when she collapsed into a gale of giggles. "If you hear anything else about the mayor, let me know."

"I did overhear something weird. You know how Cal Bloom always put on a front, like he was the happiest guy in the village. But at the parade, he sounded downright nasty. I couldn't help thinking how awful he sounded. To his wife, no less."

That intrigued me. "What time was that?"

"I have no idea. They were arguing, really bad, but every married couple argues.

Right? Nobody's perfect. Only Cal Bloom was furious. All red in the face, almost purple. Complaining how his wife is always at the Silver Birches."

"She does spend a lot of time there."

"I didn't pay that much attention to them, not at first. But Mrs. Bloom started crying, and that's when Mayor Bloom got right in her face. Yelled that he wasn't gonna 'spend another red cent on that old battle-ax' and they could both go live in the town dump for all he cared. Like, wow. That was freaky, let me tell you."

Startled by that information, I forced a smile. "Yeah, that is pretty disturbing. I'd better head out. Thanks again, Maggie."

I led Rosie to the street. The news about Cal Bloom intrigued me. I'd have to ask Mom what she knew or heard about the issue with Alison's mother. Plus any financial problems the family had. Clearly, things had grown more serious than anyone realized.

It also meant that Alison Bloom had good reason to kill her husband.

CHAPTER 11

Monday morning, I doctored my coffee and sat at the kitchen table to eat leftover brunch eggs. I'd posted a sign that the shop would be closed today due to Saturday's event, and also spread the word online. Business in the shop was always slow early in the week, although the factory would be running nonstop. Aunt Eve also appreciated a day off. She had plenty to do for the wedding, plus Christmas shopping.

Maddie appeared in the kitchen doorway, her large drawing case in hand, purse swinging by its strap, and cursed when her keys crashed on the floor. I snatched them up and waved her over to join me at the table.

"Got a minute, Mads? I warmed up a plate for you."

"Not hungry. Plus I'm late."

"Oh, come on. Take a load off, relax for one day." I poured her a mug. "You prefer mud, but I like a little coffee with my sugar."

Maddie dropped into the chair. "You're getting positively domestic."

"Ha. Fat chance of that." I started eating the fluffy eggs, bits of bacon and veggies, and cheese. "Breakfast is the most important meal of the day, you know."

She sipped her black coffee with a weary sigh. "Sleep is better. And I haven't gotten more than four hours at a time. There's so much to do."

I stabbed my fork into a soggy waffle. "Mads, if you ever need to talk things out, about anything, just ask."

"Like what?"

"Well, like the stuff back in October."

"I broke up with Kip. It wasn't going to work out anyway."

"But —"

Maddie cut me off. "Don't worry about me, I'll be fine. You ought to think about what kind of future you'll have with Jay."

"I already know. He's going to set up a studio in the village."

"I'm not sure that's wise. Silver Hollow's too out of the way from the big money, I mean. People who come to the Bear-zaar for Christmas novelties are not gonna buy pricey carvings. Or sculptures, or paintings like at the Ann Arbor Art Fair."

"There are plenty of galleries in small

towns up north, far from the 'big money' like you said," I argued, "and he's getting commissions."

"Hmph." Maddie sipped coffee with a thoughtful gaze out the window. "Jay's talented. I'm not saying he wouldn't make it as a woodcarver, but what if interest in his work fades or the market dries up completely? Then what, if you two are serious about getting married? I know it's none of my business, Sasha, but don't settle. Not after what happened with Flynn."

"You're a bundle of cheer this morning." My joke fell flat, since she rose to her feet with an irritated sigh. "Hey, I didn't mean anything by that."

"I know." Maddie snatched up her portfolio. "The Silver Bear Shop is doing well now, but competition in the toy market is fierce. Uncle Ross, Dad, everyone realizes it."

"We're getting a lot of exposure due to the Teddy Bear Keepsake contest."

"That won't last. Two other companies who won in the past ten years went belly up. What will you do if Dad decides to sell out like they did?"

I stared at her in disbelief. "Why would he?"

"Forget it. I'd better go."

My sister had crammed a wool hat over her short hair and grabbed her coat while talking, and now rushed out the door. I was tempted to race after her and demand if Dad had hinted to her about selling the business, but she was halfway down Theodore Lane. I'd seen her stressed-out before, but this was different. Now I was sick with worry. Maybe Maddie needed counseling for depression. We'd both suffered trauma after what happened at the Oktobear Fest, but I'd shared my feelings in depth with Jay. I hadn't thought of including my sister, however.

Maybe I should have.

Even if Maddie claimed she didn't need help, I knew something was wrong. I'd have to warn my parents without alarming them, though. If Mom smothered her baby, pressuring her to spill her worries, my sister would blame me. Maddie hated unwanted attention.

I dialed my cell phone. Mom answered, her tone clipped. "What's up? I'm with Dad for his cardiologist appointment."

No wonder I heard so much background noise. "Want me to call you later on?"

"No, I can only play Candy Crush on this phone so many times."

Suppressing a laugh, I broached the subject of Maddie's possible depression. "Have you or Dad noticed how down she sounds lately?"

"Not really. She acted perfectly fine on Saturday."

"Because of all the work we had —"

"She's so busy, but she'll snap out of a funk before too long. Madeline doesn't brood over stuff for too long, thank goodness."

Mom sounded flippant, which worried me further. She was right about one thing. Mads didn't dwell on negativity for long. Maybe I was making too big a deal out of her earlier bad mood. Everyone had them once in a while. I hesitated bringing up what I'd heard about Cal Bloom and his wife's mother, but Mom was the best source to confirm that.

She dismissed Maggie's claim, however. "Ridiculous. Cal never had any problems with Mrs. Jackson. He did complain that Alison spends too much time with her, that's true, since the staff is capable. But I never heard him say a mean word about anyone."

"Maybe he never said it when you were around."

"Maggie's a little wacko, Sasha, so take what she says with a grain of salt. Barbara told me she couldn't take the pressure of her last job, and might not last too long running her business. Richard is floating Maggie until spring, since he promised his brother. But no one in the family believes the Magpie's Nest will make it."

"Really. That's too bad." I liked the shop's quirky nature. "But why would Maggie tell me something that wasn't true?"

"She might be begging for attention. Look at that awful parade float she put together at the last minute. People certainly criticized it. All the other floats looked wonderful, classy, and smart. Hers was a royal mess."

"It wasn't that bad —"

"Oh, believe me, people were laughing and pointing, making fun of it. Why else would Barbara and Cissy be so upset? And I don't blame them. For next year, I'm going to recommend that the parade committee approve any new design two months before the event."

I rolled my eyes heavenward. "But Maggie's was the only new float this year. She'll know she's being singled out."

"Uh-oh, the nurse just called us."

Mom hung up. I suspected that by using "us", she meant she'd tell the cardiologist how Dad wasn't eating properly or getting enough sleep, and that he needed more tests. I slid my phone into my pocket, sensing in my gut that Maggie had heard Cal Bloom correctly. I couldn't convince my mother, though. She'd ignore what she didn't want to believe about her friends.

After starting the dishwasher, I wiped the kitchen table. The cleaning crew was due any minute for their weekly rundown of the place, and I'd left specific instructions on getting the shop ready for the season. That meant extra work — moving the accessory racks and polishing all the wood, plus taking down and rehanging the Christmas decor. I didn't want to hang around and give them the idea of supervising, either, and grabbed my coat, scarf, and gloves.

I relished the chance to gather more information. At ten o'clock, I'd meet with Elle and Mary Kate at The Cat's Cradle bookstore. They were looking forward to a break from their usual schedules, too. We all wanted to discuss the mayor's death and the Bloom family.

Rosie and Onyx had been fed and seemed content, sharing the sunny window seat, so I snatched up my car keys. Outside, the cold hit me like a hammer and squeezed the breath from my burning lungs, but the bright sunshine warmed my heart. The wind had already swept most of the accumulated snow into drifts closer to the shrubs and houses. The weather forecast predicted fair skies for this week. I was thankful for that.

I was lucky to squeeze into a parking spot across from Fresh Grounds. Inside the coffee shop, a smattering of people worked on their laptops or chatted at the larger tables. I passed by the window and opened the door to The Cat's Cradle. Elle Cooper had married my cousin a few years before I returned to Silver Hollow. Matt worked at the Quick Mix Factory weekdays and manned the store evenings and on Saturdays.

Elle roused herself from the sunken saucer chair braced on its bamboo frame. "Hey, Sash. You're late, it's ten fifteen."

"But I'm not that late."

"Gave me a chance to catch up on some reading." Elle waved the book in her hand, a cozy mystery featuring a berry basket shop. She beckoned me over to the armchair by the frosted window. "The Bear-zaar brought in a bunch of new customers yesterday. Online sales, too."

"Hey!" Mary Kate stuck her head through the side door that led to Fresh Grounds, her strawberry-blond ponytail swaying. "I'll grab a few lattes. Scone or muffin?"

"Either one."

"Some of both, then."

Elle drew her knees up and tucked her slipper-clad feet under her. "I'm glad I put Celia in that all-day Kindergarten program. She's making loads of friends."

"Such a social butterfly." I pulled over two chairs and sat by the window. "Did she ever get over being lost at the Oktobear Fest?"

"She had a few scary nightmares in November, but nothing recent."

Mary Kate swept into the shop with a tray and set down the offerings. "Mocha for Sasha, but we're low on mint syrup, sorry. Chai for Elle. Hot cocoa for me."

"No caffeine, Mary Kate?" Elle sipped her tea. "Mmm, nice and spicy."

"I have good reason to skip the caffeine." She perched on the third chair with a secretive smile. "I'm gonna need more baby clothes. Newborn ones, without spit all over them. And I'm hoping for blue this time."

"You're preggers? Wow!" Elle struggled to rise from the saucer chair, but soon gave up. "I know you and Garrett wanted another baby."

I hugged Mary Kate, who glowed. "Congrats! When are you due?"

"Next May. We're thrilled." She slid a hand over her belly, which seemed flat to my untrained eye. "I was early before, so this baby could come in late April. If we do have a boy, we absolutely refuse to name him after Uncle Gil. He was so disappointed when we had Julie and expected us to name her Jill."

"Wow." Elle grabbed a cinnamon muffin. "You know what they say about becoming a mom. You lose brain cells every day. That's a nine-month loss. Scary."

"That's not funny," Mary Kate said, although she laughed. "But I sure don't have time for my own problems when Julie comes first."

"All right. The Guilty Pleasures Gossip Club is officially open," I said, "unless you don't want to hear everything about what happened at the parade."

"We do! I missed out on all the fun last Wednesday, stuck in the coffee shop."

"That's your specialty. Sasha's is finding dead bodies." Elle pretended to duck behind her book at my wrathful glare. "Just kidding!"

"I wish Digger Sykes would stop saying that all the time. Besides, my mom found Cal Bloom. Not me."

I explained the whole story once more, how the parade grand marshals, Flynn and Cheryl Cummings, had tagged along to search, and about finding the mayor's blackened skin underneath the Santa Bear costume.

Elle whistled. "Freaky. He must have come into contact with an electric current."

"So either the shock fried him, or he had a heart attack?" Mary Kate asked.

"No idea, and the cops haven't reported the autopsy findings yet. What's odd is that the mayor's gone. He was larger than life, you know?" I sipped my latte. "I guess Alison Bloom has been questioned a bunch of times at the station."

"I haven't heard anything," Mary Kate said sadly. "I'm so busy, and exhausted —"

"You need a break or you'll get sick," Elle interrupted. "Why not hire another barista or two? Julie will need more attention before and after the baby comes. Let Wendy Clark do more baking. She's a whiz at decorating, so I bet she could manage your recipes."

"You're right, but it's so hard to let go."

"And you're better off not knowing the sordid happenings around the village," I said. "Did I tell you Mom wants me to prove that Mrs. Bloom is innocent?"

"I can't believe she'd kill her husband."

"You can't believe anyone would steal from the penny dish, Mary Kate." Elle snorted with laughter. "Happens a lot more than you'd think."

"Let's get back to the Blooms," I said. "Maggie Davison overheard them arguing at the parade. Tell me what you think."

I related what I'd learned from Alison Bloom about Kristen, and added my mother's reaction to Maggie's story. Both of my friends looked puzzled.

"No way would she lie about that," Elle said firmly. "If Maggie heard the mayor threaten to stop paying for Mrs. Jackson's care, he said it. And he must have been serious. So Alison threatened to divorce him, but hadn't gotten around to filing the paperwork? I bet it's more than that. He had a real drinking problem."

"Yeah. And maybe having an intimate photo of Cissy Davison —"

"What?" Elle's screech hurt our ears. "Sorry, but that's so wild!"

Mary Kate also looked shocked when I told them that juicy bit of gossip. "So Cissy and Gus are suspects, too," I said. "Not just Alison and Kristen."

"But how did someone get him to that bench by the Quick Mix Factory? You said he wasn't killed there, right?" Mary Kate asked. "I mean, if he was dead weight, that would take serious muscle. He was a hefty guy."

"Someone had to notice something," Elle

said, "no matter how far away from the parade floats and generators."

"It was pretty dark, though, by that time. So maybe not."

"Okay, go back to when you last saw him. What time was it?"

"I figure he left to go put on his Santa Bear costume between four and five thirty. The parade was set for seven. So it had to be six thirty when we started looking for him."

"He could have stopped by the courthouse or a restaurant before going home to change." Mary Kate tapped a finger on her chin. "Alison Bloom is what, five foot five or six? If that, and Kristen is tinier. I doubt the two of them could have handled it together. Cissy and Gus, yeah. No problem there. That dude's got muscles."

"But Kristen is pretty fit with all that yoga. Plus she lifts weights."

"No matter what, it's always money at the heart of something like this," Mary Kate said. "Although any inheritance would go to Mrs. Bloom before Kristen."

"Not unless the mayor set up a trust fund. He might have designated a big chunk for her directly," I said. "But listen. Flynn dropped by over the weekend. He told me that Kristen is secretly dating the detective assigned to investigate her dad's death."

Elle smirked. "My, my. Isn't that a strange coincidence. What if he helped Alison and Kristen take the mayor's body over to that bench?"

"Are you kidding?" Mary Kate asked. "He's a cop!"

"He could be a dirty cop. And it seems shady, if you ask me. If Chief Russell knew, he wouldn't want Hunter to investigate."

"And when I met him, he acted like a real jerk," I said.

"Sounds like the perfect match for Kristen, then."

"Stop it, Elle. She's not that bad." Mary Kate leaned forward in excitement. "I know someone else who might have had a reason to kill the mayor. Tony Crocker."

"I can think of someone else, too," Elle said, "although you're right. Crocker was pretty miffed that Cal Bloom won re-election in a landslide. His son Jake used to cut and bale the Christmas trees grown on the family farm, but he moved up north. Maybe Crocker wanted to retire and add the mayor's salary as a source of income."

Mary Kate sighed. "It's not much money, though, according to Uncle Gil. He's acting as Mayor Pro Tem until the council can set up a new election. But I'm glad. Gets him out of the shop for a bit, and Garrett needs the break from being bossed around."

I turned to Elle. "Didn't you say you thought of someone else who'd murder Cal Bloom? Like who? Or is it whom, if you want to be grammatical."

"Lois Nichols and her husband." She grinned at my surprise. "Matt told me Lois is a real pain in the you-know-what to work with at the Quick Mix. She complains nonstop during her shifts. Lois goes on and on about how Harry asked the mayor to help him battle HR over his health benefits. I bet Cal Bloom never promised him anything."

"But would they kill him over such a minor thing?"

"Who knows? Lois strong-armed her way into the finals of your cookie contest," Elle said. "How crazy, threatening to sue Mary Kate over a silly recipe. And your family, too."

"The judges chose her cookie, to be fair. But that reminds me. Isabel French told me at the Bear-zaar that Kristen wanted to sell her share of the Silver Scoop. Now I'm wondering why." I finished off my second muffin, chock-full of blueberries, and wiped my mouth with a napkin. "Mmm, so good. It looked so lonely on the plate, I had to put it out of its misery."

"Poor muffin." Mary Kate gathered up the empty cups. "It's odd that Kristen and Isabel decided to be business partners. They seem like polar opposites."

"They are." Elle rushed off to answer the phone.

"Isabel wasn't happy when Kristen closed for the winter. Last year they stayed open, remember?" Mary Kate shrugged. "They did okay, since the weather wasn't all that cold. I'm not surprised Kristen wants to sell out if her heart isn't in it. But I'm not sure a yoga studio would have a better chance to thrive."

"I know. Everyone loves ice cream, but yoga? We'll see," I added. "You need to take care of yourself, Mary Kate. Remember how you ended up on bed rest last time, two months before Julie was born."

"How could I forget? All right, keep me posted on whatever you find out. I'd better get back, or Garrett will murder me."

Elle hung up the phone. "Fat chance of that, he'd do anything for you. Cara's teacher said I could bring birthday cupcakes over this afternoon. Oh, the joys of motherhood."

"That sounds like fun. I hoped Cara liked her present."

"Oh, she loves Mary Poppins, and the boxed set was a great idea." She groaned, though. "The cupcakes can't have peanuts. Can't be homemade, either. I had to buy thirty packets of juice, too. At least I don't have to deal with the sugar high in the classroom."

I gathered up my purse and coat. While Elle sounded flippant, I knew she didn't mean it. And I'd trade places with her in a heartbeat. That would be so fun to see the kids' excitement. Instead, I had to satisfy my mother and root out more information about the Bloom family. So Kristen wanted to try her hand at a yoga studio. Isabel French had mentioned that at the Bear-zaar, although I hadn't really paid much attention.

Shivering in the cold wind, I drove off to visit Isabel French.

CHAPTER 12

I drove past the courthouse and the Village Green and turned on Oyster Bay Street. A row of Victorian homes stood far apart and back from the narrow road, their ironwork fences draped with lights or evergreen and red velvet ribbons. The vista reminded me of old-fashioned Christmas cards my grandparents sent. Only one house seemed out of place, a Sears Roebuck kit house built in the early 1930s, with half timber and stucco, red and brown bricks, plus an overhanging gabled front porch.

Isabel lived here with her mother. Since her husband's dementia had worsened, Mrs. French reluctantly placed him in the Silver Birches Retirement Home. I wondered if Isabel found a temporary job already, and what her future would be when the Silver Scoop closed for good.

After knocking several times on the wooden door, I gave up. Dang. I'd wanted to see the interior. I favored the Craftsman style and hoped to own one someday. Although I enjoyed living above my parents' Silver Bear Shop since returning to manage the family business, I couldn't see myself raising a family there. I'd want far more privacy.

After divorcing Flynn, I realized I didn't want another empty marriage. I wanted an equal partner, a man who shared the same values of faith and family. So much had changed since Will Taylor's death, which hammered home the reality of life and its unpredictability, along with unfulfilled dreams. An odd restlessness had taken hold of me, along with my yearnings for a husband and kids of my own. After divorcing Flynn, I'd also never expected to meet someone living right in Silver Hollow, who'd gone to the same high school. I was thrilled to discover that Jay brought me such happiness.

I drove back to the village's heart and stopped at Blake's Pharmacy to buy two boxes of Godiva chocolate. Ben had finished filling a prescription and hailed me.

"Hey, Sasha. Wendy wants to know if you'd like to meet at the pub tonight."

"Sure. Anything special going on?"

"She has a question for you. Didn't tell

me about what, though."

"Okay, see you later."

Next, I drove to the retirement home's parking lot off River Street. The long, one-story building had been a former elementary school, its windows framed in black. Two wings marched down either side of the front entrance. Leafless oaks, elms, pines, and various shrubs surrounded the Silver Birches, without a birch tree in sight. I chuckled at that. Strands of Christmas lights stretched along the roof, but failed to lend a festive spirit.

The lobby, however, made up for it. A riot of Christmas ornamentation filled the space, including a huge lighted tree swathed in shiny silver and gold tinsel, plus glass balls of every color. Several garish wreaths adorned the walls, and red poinsettias filled the tables along with a nativity display, Santa figures of various sizes, and plastic snowmen.

No one guarded the large desk. The pen by the register book had run out of ink, too, so I groped for a pen in my leather purse. At last, I scribbled my name on a fresh line — not that anyone would check. I flipped through the pages over the last week. Only a few names were logged, most nonresidents with addresses outside of the village. Frequent visitors didn't bother, like I'd mentioned to Detective Mason.

A staff nurse happened to walk by. "May I help you?"

"I'm here to see Mr. French."

"Yes, the family's in the dining room. Poor Henry takes a long time to eat." She pointed down a hallway with a strong scent of Listerine and bleach. "Take that to the end."

"Thank you."

I ambled down the hall, eyeing the framed tepid landscapes and floral watercolors that hung on the walls. Each room had two names with photos of the residents in their younger years; most showed women in their wedding gowns or formal church attire. I had a panicked moment. Would my parents end up here? I dismissed that thought outright. Dad and Mom, in their early to mid-sixties, had plenty of time yet to live independently.

Then again, nothing was guaranteed.

Guilt filled me. My parents deserved to enjoy grandkids soon. Time hung heavy, and the ticking clock echoed in my brain every night before I tried to sleep. That insistent sound plagued me each time I passed the Silver Birches. I'd often avoided visiting my grandmother, too, despite my mother's urging. That added another layer to my remorse. I swallowed hard and inched along until a wide room opened before me.

Overhead piped-in music played familiar Christmas medleys sung by Dean Martin, Tony Bennett, and the Ray Conniff Singers. All tunes my parents and grandparents loved to hear over the holidays, but no longer played on the radio. Residents sat four to a table, most sitting in wheelchairs, while staff distributed trays with stainless steel–covered plates. An early lunch, since it wasn't half past eleven. I spotted Isabel with her parents at a back table and threaded my way around the curious residents.

"Sasha, what brings you here?" She waved me toward an empty chair. Isabel wore faded jeans and a sweatshirt, more casual than her mother's tailored navy pantsuit. "I haven't seen your grandmother today, but several residents are down with the flu."

I shrugged off my coat. "Hello, Mr. French. Mrs. French. I brought something for you both." I slid the smaller box of chocolates over the table's surface. "Merry Christmas."

"How nice, thank you." Suzanne French turned to her husband. "You remember Sasha Silverman, don't you, Henry? You have a silver teddy bear in your room."

He gave me a blank stare. Isabel looked

sad, her eyes misty. "Dad's not having a good day," she said in a low voice. "I was telling Mom about the Bear-zaar and those adorable cookies in the bake-off contest. I can't wait to find out who wins."

"It sounds wonderful." Mrs. French studied me for a moment. "I also understand you found the mayor at the parade after he suffered a heart attack."

"Uh, yes," I said.

"I'm not surprised, given how overweight he was. Not like poor Tom Richardson. That man was never sick a day in his life. He managed the orchard and farms that his grandfather started, did you know? It's a centennial farm, designated by the state."

"My dad told me that."

"Good thing his oldest son took over so he could retire. Tom Junior expanded beyond cider and donuts in the fall. He added school tours, the corn maze, the pumpkin painting for little kids, and the haunted houses."

"They had zombies this year, too," Isabel said. "They had to turn away several dozen kids from Silver Hollow High who wanted to dress up in costumes."

Suzanne sniffed. "All that zombie stuff on television and in books. Disgusting. Your father would never approve, and I don't, either."

"Oh, Mom, don't be so old-fashioned. It was all in good fun."

"It's too bad Mr. Richardson passed away." I steered the conversation back to a more neutral topic. "He had a long, full life, though."

"Very true." Mrs. French patted Henry's arm and then encouraged him to eat with a soft word before turning back to me. "I wonder how Dave and Leah Richardson will manage, now that Cal Bloom has passed."

"He was loyal to the mayor," Isabel said, "so I bet they'll take over the business now. They've managed it for a long time. Right, Mom?"

Suzanne French nodded. "I remember when Victor Blake sold the place to Cal Bloom back in the mid-seventies. And from what I understood, the mayor planned to sell it to Dave Richardson. Who knows if Alison will honor that now."

"Undertaking seems so weird. Cremation is better."

"Oh, Isabel. Kids today are too modern. Anyway, Alison Bloom is always here taking care of her mother. I'm not sure the mayor approved of that, but I'm hardly one to blame her." She smoothed her husband's hair. "Henry gives the staff less trouble whenever I'm with him. I don't worry so much, either."

"It must be stressful, caring for an aging parent or spouse." I glanced around the dining room. "Is Mrs. Bloom here today with her mother?"

"I suppose, but Mrs. Jackson is in the advanced nursing care wing."

That answered my curiosity. This area served the residents like Grandma Silverman and Henry French, who walked or made their way to the dining room in wheelchairs, and needed less assistance. The cost per month for advanced nursing care had to be enormous. No wonder Cal Bloom objected to paying. Before I could ask if she'd seen Alison last Wednesday, Mrs. French changed the subject.

"I was quite surprised the other day," she began, "when a police detective came to the house. Asking Isabel about the mayor —"

"Mom, don't worry," she cut in, but I heard a tinge of fear in Isabel's voice. "Detective Hunter questioned a lot of people besides me around the village."

"About the parade Wednesday night?" I asked.

"Yeah, only I never saw the mayor there." Isabel wrung her hands. "I did see Detective Hunter, so I texted Kristen. I think she told him what I said, about how obnoxious he was. I bet Hunter resented it, because he came out two days ago and grilled me like a sausage."

"Sounds like something he'd do."

"I called Kristen again, but she yelled at me. Mom even heard her, she was screaming like a witch. Kristen defended Hunter and called me a big fat liar."

I sensed Isabel was close to tears. "That's harsh."

Mrs. French looked angry, too. "I'm not happy with how she treated you. Do you want me to speak to Mrs. Bloom?"

"No, Mom. Don't get involved, please."

"Kristen would defend Hunter," I said, "since they're dating."

"You know they're dating?" Isabel groaned. "She accused me of spreading gossip about her around Silver Hollow, but I didn't! Now Kristen won't talk to me. At. All."

"It wasn't you —" I stopped, mortified. Flynn had seen Kristen and Hunter together at an Ann Arbor restaurant, and then I'd mentioned it to Mary Kate and Elle. Even Alison Bloom knew that I knew. Uh-oh. "I mean, their dating wasn't that big of a secret. Right?"

"I don't care, to tell you the truth. She

ought to know people find out every little thing that happens around here. I think Kristen's more mad that I can't afford to buy her out of the Silver Scoop. I explained why in a voice mail and told her to call me back, and then texted her, but she never replied. She's mad, all right. Who knows if she'll ever talk to me again."

"You said Kristen wants to open a yoga studio. Right?"

"Yeah, only she needs a boatload of cash to pay off a loan. Kristen wanted renovations at the Silver Scoop, and she wouldn't listen to me that we couldn't afford it. I told her she'd have to find another way of paying. I wasn't putting in any money. But Kristen resented that."

"I thought the Blooms were pretty flush with cash."

"Yeah, they own the building. I think Kristen expected her dad to cough up the dough for the drive-through, but he balked at the last minute."

"Plus Cal Bloom didn't like cars lining up on that little alley beside the funeral home," Mrs. French said. "In the summer, of course, but people blocked access to the parking lot where his visitors park. No wonder he wanted her to give up the Silver Scoop."

Isabel nodded. "Except Kristen refused. At least back then, only maybe she's changed her mind. But no one can easily manage two successful businesses at one time."

No wonder Leah was so worried at the Bear-zaar. "Did Kristen ever tell her dad about the yoga studio?"

"They had a huge fight about it. Now that he's dead, she'll inherit a bunch of money and pay off her loan. First she'd better pay me my share after selling the Silver Scoop before doing anything. Then I can pay Mom what I borrowed to help start the ice cream shop."

"Isabel, I told you not to worry," Mrs. French said. "Find a better job first."

"But Dad's care here is so expensive, and you need the money."

I snapped my fingers. "If you're looking for a new job, we need extra help at the factory filling orders for our wizard bear. You'd fit in perfectly with our staff."

"Really? You'd hire me?" Isabel's eyes brightened, but her hopeful tone faded. "I don't have any experience, though. In sewing."

"Flora Zimmerman will train you. We need someone to help with shipping right away, so see Aunt Eve in the office tomorrow morning. She can start the paperwork."

"I will, and thanks! That sounds great."

"I hope Detective Hunter steers clear of you, Isabel," Mrs. French said. "Promise me you'll tell Chief Russell if he shows up again with questions."

"Okay, okay."

"Well, I'd better go." I rose to my feet, reclaimed my coat, and the paper bag from the pharmacy. Henry French had been eyeing me sideways with suspicion, and I didn't want to cause trouble. "Have a wonderful holiday season, and thanks."

Isabel walked with me back to the hall. "I can't thank you enough for the job offer. Mom's been pretty worried."

"Really, you'd be helping us out." I suddenly remembered something she'd said earlier. "You overheard Hunter being obnoxious, but when was this?"

"At the parade. He was talking to Tony Crocker, who ran against Mr. Bloom in the election. Hunter cornered him near the mayor's float, and threatened him."

"In what way?"

"He warned Crocker about not bothering with an election recount. Hunter said he heard him saying all kinds of things, how Cal Bloom didn't deserve to win, and that the mayor cheated people right and left."

Isabel shrugged. "It sounded pretty crazy to me."

I shrugged into my coat. "Thanks, Isabel. If you hear anything else —"

"Sasha, is that you?"

My grandmother's shrill voice startled me. I turned to see her wheeling down the hall, thin arms akimbo. Her white hair looked unkempt, and her cardigan sweater was buttoned all wrong. Isabel smiled and retreated to the dining room.

"How are you today, Grandma? I was coming to see you in a few minutes."

"Did your mother send you to spy on me?"

"Of course not. I brought you an early Christmas present."

"Trying to make me fat?" She eyed me up and down, as if some of the candy had already attached itself to my thighs. "Thank you. Godiva is my favorite."

"I know. Let me help you with your sweater."

"Not here, child. Back in my room — no, no. I can get myself moving. I've got to keep my strength, or they'll have me sitting all day in bed."

She muttered an apology when she bumped into another patient's wheelchair. Stifling another smile, I followed Grandma to her private room. The photo posted outside the door showed Grandpa T. R. holding her hand on their wedding day. They'd celebrated fifty-one years of marriage, so Grandma turned bitter after his death. The whole family missed him. He was always a joy and so happy. Everyone had adored Grandpa T. R.

"There you go." I'd re-buttoned her cardigan and searched for the comb in her bedside table. "Let me fix your hair, okay?"

"Thank you, Sasha. Here, use these." Grandma handed over several bobby pins with trembling fingers. "Are you sure Judith didn't send you?"

"No. I came to see Isabel French, who's visiting her father."

"Yes, that poor man." She waved a hand at the television set in the corner. "I heard the news on television and read the *Silver Hollow Herald* about the mayor. Is it true he died at the parade from a heart attack? I wouldn't be surprised. And his poor wife, running back and forth to help with her mother. Mrs. Jackson's not long for this world, either."

"Is she that bad?"

"She can barely eat without help. I saw Mrs. Bloom feeding her mother, you know, last Wednesday. But then she left suddenly, right in the middle of dinner. The staff had already taken Mrs. Jackson back to her room by the time she returned. We had a group of carolers in, and hot chocolate with those tiny butter cookies while we listened."

My ears had perked up at this news. "Are you sure it was last Wednesday, Grandma? The day of the parade."

"Of course. I'm not senile like Mr. French. Yet."

That was interesting. Why would Alison claim to be here until after the parade ended? If she had left — that meant she'd lied. Deliberately. Where had she gone? To the funeral home, to murder her husband?

Grandma tapped my knee. "I'm glad you came to see me, Sasha."

"I am, too." I kissed her forehead and then thumbed the remote until I found a *Matlock* rerun. I knew she loved Andy Griffith's charming portrayal of a Southern lawyer who always won his case. "This is one of your favorite shows."

"Perfect." She flashed a wan smile. "I suppose it reminds me of your dad, and how Alex had so much success in the courtroom."

I sat with Grandma until she nodded off, within the hour. Then I set the box of Godiva chocolates with its puffy gold ribbon next to her elbow on the bed and headed out. Maybe Tony Crocker and Dave Richardson would answer a few questions.

Whether or not, it wouldn't hurt to ask.

CHAPTER 13

I parked on the side street off Archibald. The shortcut to the Silver Scoop's drive-through window led to the parking lot, which served both the funeral home and the Pretty in Pink bakery. Tire marks had left deep ruts in the snow. Cal Bloom's white van was parked in its usual spot at the end, but the funeral home's black hearse remained out of sight. Probably behind the building, close to a double door in back.

The sun's warmth felt wonderful on my face. I crunched my way across frozen snow, marked with footprints tracking back and forth to the picket fence gate. Something winked in the light on the ground, so I picked it up. A marble? I stuck it in my coat pocket. Onyx loved to roll all kind of toys across the kitchen floor. The funeral home's entrance door was unlocked. Most people didn't lock their homes in the village, in fact. I marched inside.

The lack of Christmas decorations surprised me at first. Then I realized that decorated trees and lights might deepen the sadness and grief of families who had lost loved ones during the holiday season.

But the foyer had abundant greenery. A tall parlor palm tree and two huge dieffenbachias stood beside the wide stairway that led to the second-floor residence. A basket of trailing ivy sat on a side table, flanked by twin plush armchairs. Inside a carved walnut étagère, frames held antique family photos showing people in clothing styles of the 1800s and early 1900s. Had Cal Bloom bought them for mere decoration, or were they of his relatives?

I avoided the roped-off parlor that held the Victorian hearse. Soft music played overhead, Beethoven's *Moonlight Sonata* if memory served me right. I'd practiced it a million times for a piano recital in sixth grade and winced, recalling my nervous mistakes. Lessons had been my mother's idea. She'd never had the chance to learn, and was determined to give Maddie and me that opportunity. I enjoyed piano but hated practice. My sister excelled, of course.

Maddie also played oboe in Symphony Band. But lately she'd been listening to Chopin's more depressing pieces. Hmm.

Another sign of her recent moodiness.

I peeked into the office, since the door stood open. Dave Richardson wasn't behind the walnut desk. Maybe he was still sick and Leah was busy downstairs preparing the deceased for visitation. The information for both Cal Bloom and Tom Richardson Senior filled a sign near the front entrance. Tom would be laid out tomorrow, with services on Wednesday morning. The mayor's family had planned visitation on Thursday evening and a Friday funeral. Silver Hollow residents would spend the entire week in mourning.

That meant we'd be crunched for time to churn out wizard bears and prepare for our Holiday Open House the following Tuesday. If only it were already Christmas. I wished everything, including my uncle and aunt's wedding, would be over.

I felt like Ebenezer Scrooge.

Forcing myself to banish my stress, I checked the hall for Dave or Leah and then returned to the office. A row of silver and brass cremation urns sat on a shelf behind the desk. Another shelf held our quality teddy bears with black silk ribbons around their necks, encased in plastic. I'd arranged the contract several years ago to provide for the Bloom's Funeral Home's consolation package for deceased children. Given their dusty covers, I was glad they lingered here. The next room, much smaller, held filing cabinets and a desk with ledgers.

Perhaps I should have called ahead of my visit. Too late now.

I wandered into the first parlor. Carved, ornate furniture and rows of padded chairs stretched toward a drapery-covered wall. A low, wide stand must have served to hold the casket. I stared at numerous cheap black teddy bears perched on sofas, chairs, or end tables. I picked up one and saw the label BEARS FROM THE HEART, our rival toymaker. How could Cal Bloom buy these, when my parents were his best friends? They looked brand new.

To me, teddy bears represented childhood joy and happiness. I knew many people bought them to memorialize a lost loved one, but I preferred seeing a boy or girl hug their stuffed toys for comfort. It made my job at the Silver Bear Shop so meaningful. All the extra hours planning events, tours, the long holiday hours, even working at the factory to meet deadlines, was worth it. Sure, our bears might be more expensive, but their quality couldn't be beat.

So why did Cal Bloom buy half a dozen from our rival? That puzzled me.

"Hello, Sasha. Did you need help?"

I jumped out of my skin at the voice behind me. One hand over my pounding chest, I turned to see Leah Richardson. Eyes wide, wearing a turtleneck sweater, blazer, and black trousers, she pushed a strand of her dark hair behind an ear. I clutched a chair's high back.

"Sorry, I didn't hear you come in."

"It's this thick carpet in the parlors," Leah said with a grin. "Dave's always sneaking up on me. I've screamed, oh — I don't know how many times. It's kind of funny."

"Yeah, the carpet is soft. Like walking on a sandy beach."

"Cal Bloom had it redone in the spring. Dave thought Berber would be more durable, but Cal wouldn't hear of it. Nothing but the best quality and the deepest pile. I suggested tile floors and Persian area rugs, but nope. He didn't want that. We have to get the carpet cleaned at least three times a year, too."

Nothing but the best quality. Hmph. I glanced at those cheap bears and then squeezed her forearm in sympathy. "I'm sorry about Mr. Richardson."

"Yes, thank you. We figured my father-in-law might not recover, and he had all the plans set in place for his funeral and burial for years. But Dave said Cal Bloom didn't have anything prepared, which is odd. Owning this place, I mean, and urging pre-planning so much."

"Did you hear that he was electrocuted?"

"Yeah, and that it triggered a heart attack."

"The police are still investigating, of course."

"Dave was so sick, and with his dad dying . . . Well, we haven't kept up with the latest news around the village." Leah gave an awkward shrug. "Too much going on at one time."

I took the chance to ask a few questions, even if I didn't get far. "I heard Kristen Bloom is selling the Silver Scoop so she can open a yoga studio."

"Really? I didn't know that."

She sounded relieved, so I continued. "You must be expecting Alison Bloom to sell this place to you and Dave."

Leah fiddled with the registry book on the stand by the parlor door, straightening it and testing the pen for ink on the back of her hand. She pulled at her turtleneck, too, although that only drew my attention. I glimpsed a dark bruise on the skin just above her collarbone. How had she gotten that? And in such an odd spot. She finally met my gaze.

"We hope so. We've worked long and hard for Cal, for fifteen years."

"I heard he wanted Kristen to take over the business."

"Yeah, that wasn't gonna happen." Resentment flooded her words. "Not many people know this, Sasha, but Cal was a hard, hard man. To work for, to deal with — it was his way or the highway, you know? He came across as all jolly and nice in person, but he was never easy to please. No matter what we did."

I nodded, unwilling to interrupt. Leah plunged on.

"He started the paperwork to sell us this place months ago, but then suddenly balked. We've been living in limbo ever since."

"That must be hard."

"Worse! Dave never thought of leaving Silver Hollow, not with his family so near. He could have bought a funeral home in another town, or worked for one of those chains in Ann Arbor or Ypsilanti. Cal knew that, too. He took advantage of Dave's good nature. Used him, like he used other people in Silver Hollow."

I wondered what my mother would say to that. "In what way? I heard something about how the mayor cheated people."

"He did. Dave covered for him," she added. "He paid suppliers out of our bank account when Cal delayed, on purpose. Like he figured they'd stop bugging him and tear up the invoices, but word got around to other companies. It made things more difficult. A few suppliers refused to do business with us anymore, in fact."

"But why would he do that?"

"He didn't think anyone would find out, that's why. Cal believed he was too important for his reputation to be tarnished."

"But it was bound to affect his business," I said.

Leah's bitterness rang true. "Oh, I admired him when he first asked Dave to manage this place. But once he was elected mayor, Cal loved the attention. Running the council meetings, pretending to be a role model, talking to people everywhere. But if anything went wrong here, he blamed me and Dave. And people sometimes complain even if things go right. Cal Bloom never wanted to hear that, though. Only the compliments."

I wasn't surprised, given what I'd heard that the mayor shifted blame to others instead of accepting responsibility. "That's nuts."

"Remember that stink over how Cal

wouldn't pay that poor girl? The one who was killed before the Oktobear Fest," Leah added. "She worked on his re-election campaign."

"He wasn't happy with Gina Lawson's promotional spin."

"But she finished the work. Cal told her whatever she came up with would be fine, and then, he hated it! That wasn't her fault." Leah smoothed a lace doily on an end table, hesitating before she met my gaze. "And now Alison Bloom might sell this place to ⸺"

"Sasha!" Dave Richardson hurried into the parlor. "How good to see you."

"Hi, Dave," I said, my heart sinking. Leah looked stricken at being caught gossiping. "You must have recovered from the flu, then."

"Yes, I'm over it."

Tall and thin, Dave resembled his dad with gray hair and bright blue eyes. The late Tom Richardson had raised six children with his second wife, Cleo, who was twenty years his junior. They lived in homes on the same road as the huge family farmhouse built in the late 1800s, except for Dave and Leah. Tom Junior managed the farm and orchards with his brother John, with most of their kids and grandkids to help.

Dave had chosen to work for Cal Bloom instead. I'd always wondered what brought on that rebellion, and noted a spark of anger in his tone when he spoke to his wife.

"Leah, go back downstairs and finish up for Dad's visitation tomorrow. Do all the last-minute checks. Go on!"

She threw me a desperate look and then scurried toward the back. Leah pressed a button, stepped inside the elevator, and then vanished when the double doors closed. How odd that Dave dismissed her in such a sharp tone, as if she were a wayward child.

Curious of her skittish behavior, I yearned to follow her to the basement. Dave gripped my arm, however, and led me out of the parlor. He only loosened his hold in the foyer and drew me toward his office. I shook him off, however.

"I can't stay, but I'm sorry for your family's loss. You have my sympathies."

"Thank you. Dad lived a full life and is no longer suffering. His bronchitis developed into full-blown pneumonia. He couldn't shake it."

"Leah was so upset on Saturday at the Bear-zaar. I was worried about her, and that's why I came today. To make sure she was all right."

"Her nerves have gotten bad. Dad's death

came at a bad time, when we're so focused on helping Mrs. Bloom and her daughter get through this difficult ordeal. Cal Bloom is — was — our boss, after all. We've been loyal to his family for years."

"Did you know the mayor's death may not have been an accident after all?"

Dave looked guarded. "What makes you say that?"

"Rumors I heard. Mr. and Mrs. Bloom were on the brink of divorce. Kristen also had financial problems. Murder requires a motive, after all."

"Murder?" He barked a laugh. "You can't honestly believe Alison Bloom would kill her husband. That's ludicrous. And Kristen would be the last person to lift a hand against her father. She adored him, and he doted on her. His only child, remember."

I bristled. "Perhaps, but it seems odd that her detective boyfriend is assisting with the investigation. Some people might think that's a conflict of interest."

"I wouldn't know. But let me assure you, the last thing Alison or Kristen would do is murder anyone. And certainly not Cal Bloom."

"What about Tony Crocker? He's pretty sore over losing the re-election."

Dave scoffed at that as well. "Tony's a

windbag and off his rocker about so many things. He showed up at the last council meeting and accused several people of fixing the election."

I changed the subject. "Is it true you covered delayed vendor payments for the funeral home? I heard Cal Bloom sat on supply invoices for months."

"Who told you that?" When I didn't reply, Dave blew out a long breath. "Yes, I did. Cal was too busy, and I wasn't going to let him down — so I took care of it. He treated me like the son he never had. I trusted him to repay me. Cal had that huge bill every month for his mother-in-law at the Silver Birches. I'm sure you know how expensive it is, since your grandmother lives there."

"I don't, really, but my dad —"

"Listen, Sasha. I'd advise you to stop spreading rumors around town. Cal Bloom met with an unfortunate accident. End of story."

Despite Dave's aggravated tone, I stuck to my theory. "But he wasn't found near any electrical outlet. Someone must have taken him to that bench, after the mayor was dead."

"Then let the police figure out what happened. If they can."

That last comment stung me. I tossed out

that last hint from Leah. "What a shame Mrs. Bloom might not sell this place to you after all." He narrowed his eyes, but I plunged on. "After all, Cal taught you everything. And how inconvenient, getting sick last Wednesday."

"These things happen."

"Cal Bloom also expected you to work at the Bear-zaar Saturday. Leah was stuck doing everything in the kitchen, although my dad helped her."

"I was so sick, I barely got to see my father before he died." Dave cocked his head. "I've heard how clever you are, Sasha, tracking down murderers. Maybe the police find it helpful, but go home and forget about it. Cal Bloom wasn't murdered."

With that, he steered me out the door. Miffed by his admonishing words, I marched down the walkway to my car. For some reason, his stubborn insistence about an accident rang false. Leah had acted fearful, too. That bruise on her neck — how did she get that? Had she suspected her husband of being involved, questioned him coming down sick before the parade? It did seem beyond coincidence. Or perhaps she'd witnessed something.

I was clueless about identifying domestic abuse, or helping a woman in that situation.

Even where to go for assistance. Maybe I should find out more information.

But Dave didn't strike me as violent. I'd been wrong in the past, but this seemed too strange. I knew anyone could do anything when pushed to the breaking point. Was it possible that Dave faked his illness? That he hadn't gone home, and met Cal Bloom instead. Maybe near one of the generators beside the floats, when Dave pressured him about his promise to sell the funeral home . . . If Cal told him he'd found another buyer, someone who could afford to pay more than what Dave could afford, it might have been the last straw.

He'd get what he wanted by making the murder look like an accident. It sounded like Dave expected the police to accept that ruling. No matter who was guilty, no matter how much evidence was found to form a theory, any detective had to have one vital element.

Proof.

CHAPTER 14

Back at home, I unlocked the door and laughed when Rosie raced over to greet me. Her leash's end dangled from her muzzle. "Poor thing! I get the hint, but it's cold."

Onyx was curled in the hollow of her new microbead pillow, soaking in the late afternoon sunshine. Clouds to the west promised a hint of overnight snow. First, I checked the cleaning crew's progress in case they hadn't finished, but spotted the invoice on the kitchen counter. Then I toured the shop. The floors gleamed, all the Christmas decorations had been put back into place, and the crew accomplished every task. I logged into PayPal and then forwarded the paid invoice email to Aunt Eve so she could print and file it in the morning.

I shrugged into my coat and fastened Rosie's on before adding her harness and leash. "Hope this place stays clean for the open house. Come on, girl."

She led the way outside. I needed to think over everything I'd learned today and sort out the possible suspects and motives. Who had last seen Cal Bloom, and where? Despite Dave Richardson's forceful words, the mayor's death seemed too pat. Whoever killed him hadn't thought of taking him so far away from a source of electricity. It didn't seem natural. And it smacked of an arrangement, in my opinion.

The mayor was also nowhere near any homes, only the closed and locked Quick Mix Factory. I doubted if Lois Nichols had a key. Although the elementary school was close, no cars had been parked in that lot — which meant teachers and students had all gone home, too. No witnesses, unless one of the custodians had been around, but I doubted that. Had anyone seen a car? Someone arranging the mayor's body on that remote bench?

Rosie sniffed a strip of grass beside the picket fence on Theodore Lane. The Davison's house, a near perfect match to ours, had been swathed with real evergreen boughs, red velvet ribbons, and swags of pinecones. Nothing artificial for Barbara Davison. Her husband wouldn't have cared, but she embodied Martha Stewart's homemade and handmade style. Mom tried to convince me to match Barbara's elegant style for the Silver Bear Shop's exterior, but I wouldn't budge. She'd have to compete with her friend in other ways.

I glanced back at the Silver Bear Shop. The oversized snow globe on the lawn, with its teddy bear in a rocker and falling flakes, looked so sweet — and Santa and his sleigh perched on the roof with more bears spilling out of his sack. Both emphasized our brand as a fun place for children. Once darkness fell, bright lights would outline every window, door, railing, and the eaves. And inside the shop, more lights decorated the Christmas trees, wreaths, and garlands. Our customers adored it all. That counted far more in my book.

Thanks to Maddie's clever marketing, too, online sales were booming.

Rosie barked at a squirrel who dashed across the lane and tugged me along in a frantic chase. My scarf half-strangled me, so I unwound it and left it hanging loose. My breath steamed in the air when I stepped over the rusty cement pylons that blocked traffic. If only the village council would vote to open Theodore Lane. And soon. It would help the Queen Bess Tea Room, our shop, and my sister's business. Maybe they'd vote to pave the empty lot, too, but keep most of the trees intact. I'd have to mention that possibility to Gil Thompson.

I headed away from the village and skirted Silver Lake's shore. A large array of pine and fir Christmas trees stood in a lot near a truck hitched to a small camper. Tony Crocker, wearing an orange hunter's jacket, heavy pants and boots, and thick leather gloves, took a customer's cash and then hefted a baled tree onto the waiting car's roof. He looked strong for his age and tall build, lashing the tree tight with rope. Crocker hailed me in a loud voice.

"Hey, aren't you one of the Silverman girls? The one who found the mayor?"

I walked his way, although I kept my dog from crossing the rutted, dirty snow. "My mother found the body, actually."

"Didn't figure Cal Bloom would go belly-up like that. Heart attack?"

"The police aren't certain yet," I said, "but they're asking questions —"

"Yeah, yeah. I know." Crocker spat on the ground. "That fancy detective accused me of offing Bloom. And he'd threatened me at the parade about asking for a recount. Jerk."

"You also said something about Cal Bloom not being a puppet for much longer. Don't you think some people might have taken that wrong?"

"What the — I wasn't talking about him ending up dead!"

When Crocker waved another car into the lot, I stepped back to avoid a splash of mud. "You accused people of fixing the election, after all. From there, it's only a few short steps to get revenge on your political rival."

"Listen, missy. If I wanted Bloom dead, I'd have shot him with my hunting rifle and then waited for the cops to arrest me," he snarled. "Go walk your scrawny dog somewhere else. I've got a business to run."

Rosie growled, apparently unhappy at being called scrawny, but I pulled her down Main Street toward the village. "He's the one who wanted to talk to me," I muttered under my breath. "And his trees looked scrawnier than Rosie."

I grumbled over that unfortunate meeting until we reached the porch steps. I hadn't noticed walking back to the shop, being so angry. Rosie refused to linger outside, despite the squirrel that raced up a tree. She jumped onto the window seat, however, and barked like mad with her paws against the glass. Onyx hissed her displeasure.

"Oh, stop. There's plenty of room for you both, Nyxie."

The cat swatted Rosie anyway but then curled around, rump to my dog's nose. Rosie sniffed, the usual disgusted behavior, and then stretched out once I unfastened her leash. Guess she didn't mind wearing her coat and harness, so I left her alone. The cat's tail whipped back and forth, hitting Rosie a few times. I sighed and left them to their shenanigans. No voice mail messages blinked on my cell phone, which I'd left on the counter by mistake, but Ben had texted to meet at Quinn's pub. Seven o'clock, so I had a few hours to kill.

I pulled out a chair at the kitchen table. Should I check the latest news, or email?

Neither. Channeling my super-organized sister, I powered up my laptop and created a document. Added three columns. Titled them with "Suspects," "Whereabouts," and "Motive." Then I plugged information in the rows below the headings.

"Alison Bloom, at Silver Birches until Grandma saw her leave at some point before the parade started. Maggie Davison overheard her and Cal arguing over money to pay for her mother's care. She didn't know what time that happened, either."

I stopped talking to myself, feeling silly. Whatever the case, Alison had a strong motive, given the possible divorce. Alison might have thought the court would side with her husband, given his popularity. Plus being widowed would save lawyer fees.

I typed in Kristen Bloom and Phil Hunter's names next, although I wondered if Alison had also lied about them. Had they gone to the funeral home, or was she pointing suspicion her stepdaughter's way? Alison admitted to their difficult relationship. Most motives boiled down to money, and with her dad's death, Kristen inherited a lot of dough. Enough to pay off her loan and fulfill her dream of a yoga studio.

Next, I added the names Cissy Davison and Gus Antonini. They both had a beef with Cal Bloom over that intimate photo and a possible groping incident, according to Maggie. But maybe the mayor got rid of the photo after Cissy sent that letter via Flynn's legal firm, demanding its return. It could be a motive for revenge. The mayor had shown it around to certain people in Silver Hollow, after all. Embarrassing, to say the least.

"I saw Tony Crocker at the parade, too." I added his name to the Suspects column with satisfaction. "He claims he'd have shot the mayor and confessed, but that sounds like bragging. He resented losing the election, given his demand for a recount."

I chewed a fingernail, and then typed Dave Richardson's name next. I added "home" under Whereabouts with a question mark. I only had his word for it, but Leah would certainly cover for him. Most victims of abuse did, according to my quick research on domestic violence. She might also be too loyal to admit that Dave faked his illness. What if he'd confronted Cal Bloom, killed him, dragged the body to the bench, and then continued his pretense of being sick at home? Missing the Bear-zaar lent credence to his story.

How could I confirm that?

"Maybe I can get Leah alone again without Dave interfering."

I added Lois and Harry Nichols next as suspects. I hadn't seen them at the parade, and couldn't imagine the two of them dragging Cal Bloom's body, given Harry's cancer. But Lois might have asked someone else to help her. If she'd expected the mayor to help negotiate health care benefits with the Quick Mix Factory, heaven help Cal Bloom. With her violent past and jail time, Lois was capable of anything.

Sighing, I saved the document. Then I headed to Pinterest, a website with glorious photos of colorful flowers and gardens, cozy books and nooks, teddy bears, gorgeous teacups and teapots, or historical pictures. I found it relaxing to browse through and click the links. It also eased the overwhelming stress from our frantic production of the Beary Potter Keepsake wizard bear, the bake-off contest, the open house, and our staff party.

Thank goodness I shopped year-round for family gifts, which saved me come December. And online ordering was also a lifesaver for last-minute items. But I loved visiting bookstores to relax and find last-minute gift items. Nothing else could beat that.

Guilt plagued me, though. I should put a few hours in at the factory, but the thought ratcheted my stress level back up a few notches. I wasn't competent at sewing. The stuffing machine scared the daylights out of me. I couldn't get the image of finding Will Taylor's dead body in front of it. Even the thought of boxing up finished bears gave me a headache. I'd go tomorrow. Unless Renee Truman couldn't cover for me.

"Hi, Sasha!" Mom breezed in through the back door, followed by my father, who carried bags of groceries. "Playing on the computer again?"

"Working, actually." I'd switched to checking out holiday teddy bears for sale a few minutes before their arrival, but closed my laptop. "Dad, did you know Teddy Hartman's Bears From the Heart company is going out of business? I read an online article in a New Hampshire newspaper. What a shocker."

"Really?" He dumped the bags on the kitchen island and breezed over to plant a kiss on my forehead. "Closing down, or just selling out?"

"Sold out to that larger teddy bear company in Vermont. Didn't say why, though."

"Given the competition lately —"

"Are we ever going to sell the Silver Bear Shop and Factory?" I sounded anxious, and my tone stopped both my parents in their tracks. They looked surprised. "Just curious."

"You'd have to make that decision," Dad said. "You and Maddie both, since it's your company, along with your uncle. Our fingers are not in the proverbial pie."

"Oh." That answer surprised me in turn.

"Why aren't you at the factory, Sasha, helping to sew the wizard bears?" Mom stashed milk, eggs, butter, cheese, and meat in the refrigerator. "Ross told me the staff is getting behind, and will need overtime hours."

"Sasha deserves a break," Dad said, "so why don't you help at the factory, Judith?"

"Me? I worked my tail off getting the parade off the ground. That wasn't a walk in the park, you know. The phone calls alone were staggering. And all those meetings." Mom washed her hands at the sink. "Now I understand why Amy Evans worried about leaving all of a sudden. She felt bad, but family comes first."

"Did you talk to Maddie yet? About feeling stressed."

"Yes." She washed celery, tomatoes, and carrots in the sink and fetched a knife from the block. "That's why I wanted to cook a few meals for you two. Your refrigerator is empty, and you're both exhausted. I told Mads to scale things back, but she won't."

"She has more clients than she expected at first."

"A one-person company." Dad grunted. "She wants to do it all herself, too."

"Maddie can handle it," Mom said. "By the way, I'm making Brunswick Stew in the Dutch oven for later, plus Swedish meatballs for dinner. I hope you don't have plans, Sasha."

"Actually, I'm meeting friends at the pub —"

"You'd rather have a greasy burger?"

"You didn't let me finish." I waved my cell phone. "I'd rather have dinner here and then meet them. I'll text Ben and Wendy that I might be a little late."

"Good."

Now that Mom was satisfied, I followed Dad to the adjoining room. He sank into a leather armchair near the fireplace with the *Silver Hollow Herald.* "I need to ask you a few questions about Dave Richardson. Remember he got sick the day of the parade."

"That's what he told me in Christmas Alley."

I sat cross-legged on a floor pillow near the bookshelf. "How sick was he, really? Like, with the flu or a bad cold? Did he look pale, or nauseated?"

Dad lowered the newspaper, one eyebrow raised. "No idea. He told me he was going home, so I took his place. The line of kids to see Santa stretched for almost a block."

"Do you think it's possible — oof!" Rosie had jumped on me and licked my face, begging for attention. "I can't help wondering if he was faking. I mean, Cal Bloom promised to sell him the funeral home a while ago but then balked. Maybe the mayor found a different buyer, and when he told Dave, he lost his temper."

Dad looked startled. "You think Dave killed Cal Bloom? That's not possible."

"Why?"

"Dave Richardson is more loyal than

anyone I've ever known. Cal Bloom treated him like a son, and taught him the business from the ground up."

"But what if Dave lost his temper? I mean, Mr. Bloom wanted Kristen to take over the business, so maybe —"

"Sasha, listen to me." He'd folded the newspaper and set it aside. "Dave Richardson wouldn't harm a fly. And Alison or Kristen aren't cold-blooded killers, either."

"That's right," Mom called out from the kitchen. "They're heartbroken over Cal's death. Besides, a little family squabble over paying off loans, or inheritance money is common. Look what happened after Grandpa T. R. —"

"It's not the same, Judith," Dad said sharply. "Let the police do their job, Sasha. They're bound to find the truth of what happened."

"But . . ." I paused, wondering how to word this. "Isn't it frowned upon if a detective gets involved with either a suspect or the victim's family? Couldn't they get in trouble?"

He narrowed his eyes. "You're talking about this new detective, correct? I've heard a rumor that Hunter's been spending a lot of time with Cal's daughter. And I saw them together at Ham Heaven on the day of the parade. It's up to Chief Russell, though. He should make the call about taking Hunter off the case and avoid any future problems."

"Hello, everyone," Aunt Eve called out from the kitchen. "Ross said he'll be late. They have half a dozen wizard bears to finish tonight."

"See, Sasha? I was right about the staff needing your help," Mom said. "I'm glad you're here, Eve. I could use some help finishing dinner. The noodles are boiling, and the colander is in the bottom cabinet. Meatballs are almost done. Roasted vegetables, too."

I rose to my feet, intending to set the table, but Dad waved a hand. "Wait, let them chat. Your mom is dying to wring some answers out of Eve about the wedding."

"Okay, no problem."

I heard them chattering away while they worked about what Aunt Eve might wear, either a simple suit or something fancier, whether the wedding should take place before or after the staff party, and if they wanted to invite other friends. My mother wouldn't rest until everything was settled. She was a natural-born organizer.

I turned to Dad. "So. Back to Cal Bloom's death."

"As for your previous question, yes. Detective Hunter ought to take himself off the case, but it is optional."

"What time did you see them at Ham Heaven?"

"Before I took over for Dave in Christmas Alley, I think. Don't hold me to that." Dad winked. "I can pass along a word of caution to the police chief, if you prefer, about Hunter dating Kristen. That way Tom Russell can handle it."

"Sure." Relieved, I plunged on with more questions. "Have you heard that Cal Bloom had an erotic photo of Cissy Davison?"

Dad shook his head. "Cal did have a reputation as a womanizer, though, and some found him too friendly. Hugging them, that kind of thing, but don't tell your mother. Judith would deny it. She claims he acted like an angel from heaven."

"Yeah, no kidding. What did she mean about Grandpa T. R.?"

"Oh, a little spat between brothers. That's all."

"You and Uncle Ross?" I asked, astonished. "You argued over inheritance money?"

"Let's just say that family squabbles are common."

"Hey, Sasha. I meant to tell you some-

239

thing." Aunt Eve stood in the doorway, wooden spoon in hand, and an apron over her plaid pants and cashmere sweater. "Remember those tiny gingerbread house cookies?"

"The one perched on a mug?"

"Oh, you should have seen them, Judith, they were so cute." My aunt sighed. "Too bad one broke during the judging, but they may have had help. I ran into the pastor's wife today. Mrs. Lovett saw Lois Nichols handling those cookies. She asked why, of course, but Lois said she hadn't touched them. Wouldn't you call that suspicious?"

I frowned. "So you're saying Lois tampered with them? Oh, man. I'll text Maddie and see what we should do."

"I would confront Lois, that's for sure," Mom said hotly, "especially since she threatened to sue us if her cookie didn't make the finals."

"I watched the judging with Maddie," Aunt Eve said. "The gingerbread house ended up tied with Lois's entry. When the chef noticed a crack, he picked it up and then it broke. So since Lois lied about touching them, I'd say she did it on purpose. Whose entry was it?"

I'd already sent my sister a text and waited for a reply before answering. When my cell pinged with a text, I read it with a sinking heart. No wonder Lois tampered with them and then lied to cover up her actions.

"Flora Zimmerman baked the gingerbread houses. Maddie said Flora insisted they were perfect when she registered. I believe her. She's far too honest."

I didn't add that Flora drove Uncle Ross crazy with her scrupulous honesty, reporting any problems with factory equipment or supplies. She'd also tattled on Lois's laziness. Apparently Lois found a way to get revenge on Flora by cheating in the bake-off contest.

"Maddie also said she'd call Mrs. Lovett on the way home."

I knew she planned to announce the contest winner any day. Thankfully, we had a reliable witness. The pastor's wife had no reason to make up a story like that, since Lois Nichols didn't attend church and probably had never met Marianna Lovett before the Bear-zaar. I had a feeling that disqualifying Lois would bring trouble, though.

We'd have to risk it.

241

CHAPTER 15

Once Maddie arrived, we ate and chatted about the upcoming open house, the staff party, and Uncle Ross and Aunt Eve's wedding. Mom droned on and on about adding more wedding-theme decorations until Aunt Eve stopped her cold.

"Judith, we don't want any fuss. Please —"

"Leave everything to me."

"That's what I'm afraid of," Uncle Ross grumbled.

"Hoo boy." I turned to Maddie and changed the subject to Lois's cookie tampering. "Did you talk to Marianna Lovett?"

"Couldn't reach her, so I'll try again tomorrow."

"So what are we going to tell the judges?"

"Lois threatened to sue us," Mom said. "Toss her entry."

Maddie looked troubled. "It's a serious problem."

"That woman always gave me a headache at the factory," Uncle Ross said. "Complained about the hours, the working conditions, the pay, and the benefits. Did Harry Nichols actually have cancer? Emphysema, yes, from smoking for years."

"Lois showed me the doctor's treatment orders," Maddie said. "I'm worried that she'll follow through with a lawsuit. She has major anger issues."

Dad disagreed. "I doubt she'd sue given the court costs involved if she loses. You have a reliable witness. That alone should make her tuck tail and run."

"Speaking of running, I'm late." I rose from the table and grabbed my coat, purse, and boots. "Night, all. And thanks for the advice."

Maddie jumped to her feet. "Wait for me. I need a break tonight, too."

We rushed outside into the cold. Luckily the wind had died down. My sister trudged beside me in silence, head down and hands in her coat pockets. I decided to gauge how far the gossip about Kristen and Detective Hunter had gone around the village. If Digger Sykes found out, he'd be sure to tell Mads, and everyone else living within a hundred miles. I broached the subject and explained what I'd learned so far.

"Yeah, I heard the news from Digger. I'm surprised the local police allowed Hunter to investigate the case."

"Flynn thinks it might be a sticky issue. So does Dad."

No live band music poured out of the pub when we entered, and I was grateful for that. We both needed tranquility, although this place might not be the best spot to find it with all the noise from guys playing pool in a side room, and others laughing at the bar. Brian Quinn waved behind the line of people and motioned to the back where Wendy and Ben sat in a booth. We hung our coats on a rack and joined them.

"Hey, Mads. Didn't expect you to tag along," Wendy said.

"Wine should improve my mood."

"Sounds like your business is getting off the ground fast." Ben signaled the waitress so we could order. "That's a good thing."

"I guess." Maddie turned to Wendy. "Someone witnessed Lois Nichols tampering with a cookie at the Bear-zaar last Saturday. Did you notice anything? You were at Mary Kate's Fresh Grounds booth, right across from the contest table."

"Hmm. Lois did hang around after she turned in her Sugar Plum Teddy Bears." Wendy set down her beer bottle with a thunk. "I didn't see her doing anything, but I wouldn't put it past her. Which cookie did she target? One of our *Little Lord Fauntleroy* Bears lost an ear, so lucky thing we brought extras."

"I wonder if Lois broke if off, on purpose," Maddie said.

I shrugged. "All we can prove is that she handled Flora Zimmerman's gingerbread house cookies, and likely caused it to break. That ruined any chance of getting into the final round."

"Lois probably figured that cookie would beat hers," Wendy said. "The little house with the tiny teddy bear in the window, right? That was a nice touch, and unique. Have you asked Isabel French whether she saw anything?"

"Not yet, but we will soon." I changed the subject. "Did either of you hear rumors or know about Cal Bloom's DUI record?"

Wendy shook her head. "Nope."

"That's because you weren't raised here, like I was," Ben said to her. "It's not common knowledge around town, but I saw him during my presentation at the local AA meeting. They asked me to speak after I earned my pharmacy degree."

"A presentation about alcohol abuse?" I asked.

"Any kind of substance abuse. People start with booze to dull the pain in their lives, or to reach a level of euphoria. The body craves more to achieve the same intensity. Or they go with pot first, and that can lead to harder drugs like cocaine or heroin," Ben added. "Not that Cal Bloom ever got to that point. Gil Thompson attended, too."

Maddie shifted beside me, clearly uncomfortable. "Kip O'Neill was an alcoholic."

I stared at her in amazement, wishing she'd shared that insight with me before now, and recalling the time I'd joined the two of them for dinner at the hotel with Jay. Kip wanted to celebrate, ordered the most expensive champagne, and was angry when Maddie objected. I'd been mortified by my sister's embarrassment, and felt uneasy witnessing their spat. Even Jay never realized the extent of Kip's problems.

Wendy nodded in sympathy. "It's easy to fall into that kind of trap. The mayor carried a flask at the parade, but he joked it was only tea. I took a sip when he passed it around. From the way it burned my throat, it had to be brandy."

"A lot of people knew about that flask," Maddie said. "Flynn did, and Digger. So is it true his wife wanted to divorce him?"

"I doubt she'd have gone through with

it," Ben said. "Although Mrs. Bloom increased her husband's life insurance policy. But you didn't hear it from me."

"You're serious? Mom wants me to prove her innocence, you know. Who told you that?" I was disappointed when he shook his head.

"Oh, come on, Ben," Maddie coaxed. "How did you find that out?"

"Sorry. I was told in confidence."

"But for how much?"

"Over a million bucks. Hearsay, though."

"Okay, okay. But that means Alison Bloom expected to collect a big windfall after her husband's death," I said, still reeling. "That kind of money would pay for her mom to stay at the Silver Birches for years, if she lived that long."

"And whoever killed the mayor had to have help," Maddie said. "He was no lightweight, especially dressed in the Santa Bear suit with the big head."

Her cell phone rang, playing the "Peanuts" theme music, so she slid out of the booth and took the call near the restroom door. I watched her for a minute and turned back to Ben and Wendy, who finished her burger and licked her greasy fingers.

"Just remember, innocent until proven guilty," Ben said with a frown.

"Of course," I said. "So what do you know about Dave and Leah Richardson? Cal Bloom planned to sell them his business, but apparently that didn't happen."

"The mayor figured he'd sell since things were going so badly before the election. His popularity took a hit when Gina Lawson filed a lawsuit over that botched campaign. Things were really messed up, but then Bloom won. Shocked him right out of a funk, he told me that. I guess Cal decided not to sell after all."

"I heard Dave Richardson was furious," Wendy said.

"I overheard them arguing," Ben said with a shrug, "but Dave's a rock. I've never seen him lose his temper. He always puts the family first. The Richardsons are careful about their name and reputation in Silver Hollow."

I was tempted to bring up the bruise I'd seen on Leah's neck, but changed the subject. "So Wendy. You had a question for me? That's what Ben said at the drugstore."

"I'm dying to know about the bake-off contest results," she admitted. "Even if the *Little Lord Fauntleroy* Bear loses, we want a heads-up. Okay, I do. Mary Kate's too wrapped up in being pregnant. She even said I could do all the baking. That surprised me."

"We'll announce it tomorrow." Maddie returned to the booth and slid back onto the wooden seat. "But first we'll inform Lois Nichols that she's been disqualified. I'm not sure how that will go over, but whatever."

"Badly. She's bound to rant and rave that you made it all up."

"Dad always says, 'Never back down from a bully,' but good thing we have a witness," I said. "Wish us luck."

I tossed a few bills on the table for our drinks, grabbed my coat, and followed my sister outside to Main Street. She kicked a clump of dirty snow, silent again while we crossed the street and wandered down deserted Theodore Lane. The Davisons' house had lights on in the front, along with the Tyler's cottage. One security light glowed in the doorway of the graphics studio. Maddie rattled the locked doorknob with satisfaction.

"Good. I was worried someone might break in."

"Like Lois?"

"It's more likely she'd do something after I call her. Marianna Lovett called, and verified that she saw the whole thing. Lois handled more than one gingerbread house, and refused to admit it. She even accused Marianna of lying. Imagine that."

"Oh, brother. Don't bother to tell Lois anything," I said in disgust, "and let the judge choose a winner from the other four entries. I don't care if that's fair or not."

"Wow, Sash. That's not like you."

"Blame it on all this month's stress. We're swamped, and there's two funerals to attend this week. Maybe Lois won't even protest."

Before we reached the Silver Bear Shop's parking lot, an SUV drove in our direction. The headlights flashed in my eyes, temporarily blinding me, before it stopped. I recognized Detective Mason's bulky figure when he climbed out, looking official in a shabby unbuttoned trench coat and rumpled suit. He reminded me of TV's Columbo; in fact, minus the fat cigar. Mason looked so different in a suit than his usual casual attire.

"Court appearance today, Detective?" I asked.

"Yeah. Seen Detective Hunter or Officer Sykes?"

"Nope."

"Thought one of them might have updated you on the autopsy report." Mason hooked a thumb in the direction of the village. "In a nutshell, the mayor did suffer a minor heart attack. But a skull contusion finished him off."

Whoa. That was a shocker. "Someone hit him over the head?"

"It's not official yet." Mason pulled leather gloves from his pocket. "But corpses don't bleed, so that means he was alive, given the blood matted in his hair. The killer wanted to make sure he was good and dead."

"So it was murder after all," I said slowly.

"The ME's pathologist ruled it as pending. It may take a while to review reports and get all the lab results back. And gather more information, of course. As always."

"Did he give any opinion on whether the body was moved?"

"Nope. But you can't really tell for the first six hours or so, before lividity sets in." He shrugged. "Still a homicide, so we'll stay on the job. We need multiple sources of information to make anything stick in court."

"So 'we' includes Detective Hunter? He doesn't seem to be making much progress, and spends most of his time around here with his girlfriend."

"Girlfriend? Here in Silver Hollow?"

"Yeah," Maddie said, her tone sour. "Kristen Bloom."

"Wait a minute." Mason poked his glasses farther up on the bridge of his nose. "The dead mayor's daughter? You sure they're in a relationship?"

"Someone saw Hunter giving her a diamond necklace. And they were together the day of the parade, having a meal at Ham Heaven." I shrugged. "I didn't see them myself, so you'd have to verify that."

"Oh, I plan to," he said, looking pained. "You can bet on it."

"By the way, I did hear something interesting. Alison Bloom raised the life insurance policy benefits on her husband. Over a million dollars."

"No joke?" Mason had retrieved his notebook and scribbled fast. "I'd better jump on this business with Hunter right away. Could blow any chance of a fair trial."

"By the way, did you tell him how I've helped investigate cases?"

"Never told him anything."

Maddie shook her head, mouthing, "Digger." My anger seethed. That weasel.

"Anything else, Sasha?" Mason asked. "Okay, but text me if either of you come across anything else important."

He returned to his SUV, while I followed Maddie inside. Multiple sources. Hmm. Maybe I could find out if one of the staff at the Silver Birches had seen Alison leaving the day of the parade, when she'd claimed otherwise. Brother. This investigation business could be tricky.

In my mind, the only absolute was murder.

Chapter 16

"It's all set," Maddie announced on Tuesday morning. "We have a winner."

Bleary-eyed, I poured myself a second cup of coffee. "Okay, who? Or should I say which cookie came out on top? Did you get a chance to call Isabel?"

"Yes, but she was too busy to notice anything. Everyone entering crowded around her with their boxes and trays, blocking her view." My sister shrugged. "I couldn't get a hold of the chef, Georges Martin. I let Mom, Dad, and Aunt Eve do a final taste test, but they thought all four entries were wonderful. So I let Dad choose the winner."

"Wow, better not tell anyone that."

"He's as fair as I could get at the last minute. Mom and Aunt Eve thought Mary Kate's was the prettiest, but that doesn't count. I wanted it judged on taste."

"Bet they were all good." I snapped the

lid on my travel mug. "I've got to open the shop in five minutes, so please tell me who won."

"Mary Kate's teddy bear came in second place. Dad detected a touch of peppermint in the dough, or the icing. I'm not sure which, and you know he doesn't like it."

"Okay, so who came in first place?"

I knew I sounded testy, but Maddie could really pull my chain. Especially early in the morning — if you called nine forty-five early, that is. She flashed that mischievous smile and handed me a small box tied with a red ribbon.

"Here you go."

"What's this?"

"The winning cookie. I should say the leftovers. Ah, ah, ah, you might get powdered sugar on that black sweatshirt. Wouldn't look good with that silver teddy bear graphic."

"The Cranberry Walnut Snowball won? So who baked them?"

"Amanda Pozniak."

"Really? Wow, will she have time to make enough? I mean, she and Abby must be swamped with holiday customers at the antiques shop."

"Amanda's on break from her part-time job at Great Strides Therapeutic Riding.

255

She's a certified instructor, and loves helping kids and adults with disabilities," Maddie added. "She told me she'd have plenty of time to bake them for the staff party."

"So what about the others? I hope they'll make cookies for our open house. We can pay them, too. Only not as much as the prize winner."

"You know Mary Kate and Wendy will, and Hilda Schulte already offered to make her Date Nut Jingle Bells. I'll ask Flora, too."

"Great, that's a big relief. I'm helping in the factory later today, if you need me."

At her nod, I headed to the shop. Although my fingers itched to open the box and gobble a snowball cookie, I restrained myself. Several customers waited on the porch. I set my coffee mug and the box under the counter, then unlocked the door.

Tuesday morning flew by, although we didn't have a deluge of customers. At twelve thirty, I traded places with Renee Truman and raced to the factory. Not to work on a sewing machine, thank goodness, but in shipping with Deon Walsh. Tim Richardson was with his family for his grandfather's visitation. I shared the Cranberry Walnut Snowballs with Deon before we started and pronounced them buttery, sweet perfection.

We'd gotten seriously behind boxing up orders for the wizard bear, to the shops selling them, to customers who ordered via email, telephone, and at the Bear-zaar.

Deon worked fast, and I had a hard time keeping the pace of adding packing materials around the plastic-wrapped bears, taping the boxes shut, labeling, and stacking them for pickup by either FedEx or UPS. I also bandaged a finger with a nasty paper cut. It wasn't deep enough to bleed much, but red stains wouldn't have looked good on the cardboard box or labels.

The afternoon zipped by as well. I checked my watch, suddenly aware that darkness had fallen outside. "Deon. Deon!" I waved a hand in his direction, so he pulled off his headphones with an easy smile. "It's half past six. The visitation's tonight at the funeral home."

"I'm going, too. Are you working with me tomorrow?"

"You're stuck with me the rest of the week until Tim's back. But we hired Isabel French. She's starting in a few days, so that will help. We'll probably have to put in a lot of overtime to make sure everything gets out before Christmas."

"No problem, boss. Don't mind the extra pay, to be honest."

"Okay then."

I headed to check the magazine rack by the door. Staff had taken most of the *Teddy Bear Times* copies I'd placed there, which had our article about winning the Child's Play Toy Box Co.'s Magic of Christmas contest. I'd have to order more. Matt and Elle were also selling them in their bookstore. Apparently villagers had been buying multiple copies as keepsakes, to go along with their Beary Potter wizard bears.

"Sasha, come on," Maddie called from the doorway. "Dad took his car into the shop, and mine needs brake work. We'll all have to pile into your car."

"Can I change first?"

"No time, sorry."

"Let me wash up, then, at least."

I trudged to the restroom, grumpy that they couldn't give me fifteen minutes to look more presentable than my dust-smudged pants and teddy bear shirt. I could have used a makeup retouch, too, given my reflection in the mirror. After washing my hands and swiping a damp paper towel over my clothes, I grabbed my coat and purse. Dad and Maddie waited by the car, but Mom was nowhere in sight. Uncle Ross and Aunt Eve were also missing.

"Mom's inside changing," Maddie said.

"We'll give you five minutes if you want a new outfit. Hurry up!"

I dashed inside and ran upstairs. Rosie nearly tripped me in her excitement, tail wagging. "Sorry, baby, you can't tag along tonight. I hope they let you outside, though."

Knowing my mother would take her time, I washed my face and quickly reapplied my makeup. After I twisted my hair up, I chose a maroon top, long black skirt, and boots, and then knotted a thick scarf over my gray wool coat. By the time I rushed down the steps and joined Dad and Maddie, my mom had yet to appear. Rosie followed me outside. I stayed on the porch and hoped she wouldn't linger in the cold.

"Come on, Rosie. That's my girl."

Once I sent her inside, I rushed back to the car. "— hounding her," Mom was saying. "It's a shame, Alex. How can they treat her so unfairly?"

"Because Alison Bloom's a suspect in her husband's death."

"But she's innocent!"

He sighed. "The police have to ask questions, many times, in case the story changes. They'll ask Kristen and other family members. Including Cal's first wife —"

"Who is she, by the way?" I interrupted.

"Does she live around here?"

"No." Mom sniffed in disdain. "Joyce lives in California. She left and took Kristen out there when she was four or five. And sent her back to attend high school when Joyce found another man, although she didn't marry him."

"Cal told me she preferred alimony to remarriage." Dad started the car.

"At least she won't get any more," Mom said. "That's ended now. Joyce lived in a commune for years, so no wonder Kristen is into yoga and meditation."

I sat back and pondered this new information. I didn't know Kristen lived in California during early childhood, and returned to find Alison as her stepmother. Perhaps she didn't want to conform to rules after living in such a free, communal environment.

Dad stopped the car behind the hotel on Archibald Street, which brought me out of my thoughts. "I should have dropped you all off, but at least I found a parking spot."

"But Alex, it's so cold."

"I've circled the block twice, Judith. I can't park illegally —"

"Look at that car, over there, in front of the fire hydrant." Maddie grinned. "Digger probably wrote up that ticket. He loves making the guilty pay."

"You'll have to find another spot," Mom said. "Go back and drop us off, please. I'm wearing heels, not boots."

Maddie was already out of the car, however, so I followed her. We trudged past the courthouse toward the funeral home. Cars lined the road, and no doubt filled every parking lot in the village. It looked as if everyone in Silver Hollow, and maybe every other community for miles around, decided to pay their respects to Tom Richardson. By the time we squeezed through the crowd in the foyer, the chatter of people was deafening.

The Richardson clan numbered over two dozen. That didn't include Tom Senior's first wife and two daughters, who moved to Lansing. Mom had updated us in the car about Paula marrying a state-level politician, retired now, plus everyone else in the extended family. Her memory would be a huge bonus if Mom ran for mayor. Dad would have more freedom to explore his own interests if she did. Retirement suited him.

The family's matriarch, Cleo Richardson, greeted visitors in the main parlor. Floral arrangements, baskets, large potted plants, and several framed memorial plaques filled the back wall on either side of her husband's casket. A crowd stood around three easels with collages of family photos. Muted organ music played overhead.

I recognized one of our largest silver bears in the middle of a heart-shaped, huge red poinsettia wreath placed on a wire stand. Eight small white bears were woven in between the red flowers. I felt a touch of pride seeing the card that read THE SILVERMAN FAMILY. Mom had mentioned ordering the floral tribute earlier today, and how the eight bears symbolized all of Tom's children by both wives. Mary Monroe had outdone herself with the display.

Once I signed the registry with Maddie, we watched Dave and Leah Richardson roll out extra wheeled coat racks into the foyer. Tom Richardson Junior; his brother John; their wives, Ann and Nickie; plus their sister Diana, all gathered around Cleo. Phil and Claire Richardson, the two youngest kids, both single, chatted with a group of friends. I had no idea if Mr. Richardson's first wife and children were present.

Richard and Barbara Davison stood talking with Mom, so I pushed my way through the crowd to join them. "It's adorable with all those bears," Barbara said and nodded to me. "You've met our son, Sasha. Rob is married to Diana, and they have two boys."

He extended a hand, so I shook it with a wan smile. In my opinion, Silver Hollow had too many intermarriages. I supposed other small towns had the same problem. I also sensed tense competition between my mother and Barbara Davison, who gushed about her grandsons' private school, their sports activities and prowess, their height and slim builds. I noticed Mom chewing her lip, pea green with jealousy.

No wonder she wanted grandkids so badly, but I refused to pop out babies to please her. In my own time, when I was ready, thank you very much.

Maddie nudged me and nodded to a close-knit group on the farthest side of the parlor. They all glanced around, uneasy, and only spoke to each other in whispers. No one bothered to greet them, and the woman in their midst looked forlorn.

"That must be Tom Senior's ex-wife, Paula, and her two daughters," my sister whispered. "Mom told me that Diana Davison took Paula's job at the Quick Mix."

"What doesn't Mom know."

"No kidding. I bet they feel like outcasts here."

Maddie was right about that. One little girl with two pigtails fidgeted and hung onto her grandmother's hand. I felt sorry for the poor child, who looked confused among strangers. The noise and crush of people were giving me the jitters, too. And I lived here.

Suddenly I caught sight of Lois Nichols, her eyes narrowed, her mouth pursed in a grim line. And she was heading my way.

Oh, joy.

CHAPTER 17

I squirmed my way through the crush of visitors to avoid her, but ran straight into Cissy Davison. She gasped in pain. Gus Antonini helped her balance while she hopped on one foot. "Are you all right, honey?"

"I'm so sorry," I said. "Totally my fault."

"Where's the fire?" Her voice dripped sarcasm. "I probably shouldn't have worn these heels tonight, but they're one of my favorite pairs."

I glanced down at her strappy, navy suede shoes that paired well with her matching skirt and muted cashmere sweater. Cissy sank into an empty chair. I quickly grabbed the nearest one before someone else could sit beside her. Gus stood vigil, hands behind his back, as rigid as a bodyguard. His black suit, black shirt, and silver tie added to that stereotypical image.

Avoiding Lois Nichols was worth the price of listening to Cissy's complaints. Eventu-

265

ally she got around to her cousin's tawdry Christmas decorations, as expected, along with Maggie's lack of business sense.

"I managed the Time Turner without any problems, even after I started planning our wedding. It's going to be on Valentine's Day, did I tell you?" Cissy flipped her blond hair from one eye. "Did Maddie mention I asked you both to be in the wedding party? We're having an even dozen, satin red gowns, and white roses. It'll be gorgeous."

"No, she didn't tell me." I groaned inwardly, knowing we'd be only fillers to round out that number. "Thanks for thinking of us, but —"

"We can discuss everything later. I can't tell you how many vendors have signed up, for the chocolate fountain, musicians for the ceremony and the reception, of course. Oh, and the photographer, but the hall we put a deposit on is trying to change our date! Can you believe it. Why would we agree? It's the best day to have a wedding."

Cissy rolled her eyes. I waited her out, hoping for the chance to bring up the disputed photo. I was dying to know whether Cal Bloom had groped her, since Maggie never explained. Some things made the rounds of the village gossip mill, while others were quashed on purpose. No doubt due to Barbara Davison's diligence.

Unless it never happened.

Cissy's ramblings cut into my thoughts. "— how they'll be taking those cement blocks away. So my parents are selling. My brother is against it, of course, and Debbie, too."

I blinked, wishing I'd paid more attention. "They're selling their house? You mean after the city council votes to open Theodore Lane and connect it to Main Street."

She nodded. "That's not the only reason. They usually spend a few months in Florida for the winter, but they're moving because of all the murders here."

"People are murdered in Florida, too."

"I suppose, but they want a gated community. Safer, you know."

Repressing a laugh, I didn't reply. Any criminal could find a way in, gated or not, locked or not, to a community, a house, a safe. But Cissy wouldn't appreciate hearing that.

Gus winked. "I think they ought to renovate their house into apartment units. Keep a finger in the pie, real estate-wise. They own that block downtown with the Magpie's Nest and the Bird Cage, plus the Walsh's cottage."

"And the florist and hair salon," Cissy added.

"Really? I didn't know that," I said.

"Yeah. Let's mingle, Gus. My foot's better."

"Hang on a minute." I'd scrambled awkwardly from my chair and cleared my throat. "So, I heard something about a photo of you that Cal Bloom had —"

"That louse! You saw it?" She seemed relieved at my denial. "I wasn't half-naked at all, like some people said. It was quite tasteful."

"Forget it, honey. It's all water under the bridge," Gus said, although I caught a flash of guilt in his dark eyes. Cissy flounced off toward her parents. "She's kind of sensitive about that photo, Sasha. It was meant for my viewing pleasure only."

"But you showed it around to your friends."

"Aw, come on." He gave a sharp laugh. "She's hot! Can I help being proud of my babe? But I didn't appreciate that jerk stealing it. What kind of privacy is there nowadays. Who knows what happened to it."

"Did Mr. Bloom make a pass at her? When he visited her at the Time Turner."

"I don't know, but I wouldn't spread that around." Gus sounded terse. "He's dead.

Leave it at that, in terms of the photo or anything else."

"Given his murder —"

"Who said it was murder? That detective, Hunter, stopped to talk to us last Sunday. He said Bloom had a heart attack," Gus said. "Now you're telling me someone killed him?"

"The investigation is still ongoing. I'm sure Chief Russell will hold a press conference when he has more information to share."

"Thanks. Maybe I'll ask him."

"You were at the parade last Wednesday, right?"

He blinked. "Yeah, but not for long. We left about five or six o'clock, around there. We had a dinner reservation at the Regency. Why?"

"People might think you both had reason to take revenge. But like you said, it's all water under the bridge."

"Yeah. Right."

Clearly aggravated, Gus stalked off and whispered in Cissy's ear. Her cheeks flushed red, but she didn't glance at me. The two of them cut into line, spoke with Cleo Richardson, and then surged toward the exit. Uh-huh. The Regency Hotel was less than a block from Bloom's Funeral Home. The timing was right. Motive and opportunity also played a role. And I wondered what connections Gus Antonini might have, if he asked for help.

An interesting development, indeed.

"Sasha Silverman!"

I wished now I'd made my escape along with Cissy and Gus. Instead, I turned to face Lois Nichols, who resembled a witch more than ever, in a ratty coat over a plain black dress. Silver threaded her dark hair, and her sour tone washed over me.

"I heard who won the bake-off contest."

"Yes, Amanda Pozniak with her Cranberry Walnut Snowballs."

"Maddie's best friend, ha! No different than if Mary Kate won."

"The judges' decision is final, I'm afraid."

"I expected to lose. Now I can hire a lawyer —"

"I wouldn't, if I were you," I said coolly. "Someone witnessed you tampering with Flora Zimmerman's gingerbread house cookie."

"That's a lie."

"You and Flora had problems at the factory. You didn't want her to beat you, so you made sure she wouldn't make it into the final round. Admit it."

"I don't have to do squat. You're not the

boss of me anymore! All you Silvermans were born with a silver spoon in your mouth."

"You're wrong about that. My parents worked hard to earn what they have now, and they didn't give me a free ride to college. My sister and I worked for everything we have, and to achieve our goals in life."

Lois sneered. "What rot. Harry and I sold our house and we're leaving this stupid town. Nothing but trouble here, that's all we've ever gotten. I'm glad Cal Bloom's dead. Old codger promised to help Harry, but did he? No. He only helped his close friends." She snatched up a black teddy bear. "Might as well get something free from your shop."

"Um —"

Lois pushed her way toward the front door and disappeared. I shrugged. She was welcome to steal a cheap Bears From the Heart toy from the funeral home. Good riddance to her and her bad attitude. I doubted if anyone would be sorry to see the Nicholses leave.

I made my way to join Mom, who'd finally gotten the chance to speak with Cleo, Tom Junior, and John Richardson. Thankfully, they didn't expect me to add to the conversation. But Maddie wormed her way through the crowd and gripped my elbow, drawing me away toward the group's edge, where Dad talked to Gil Thompson. She hissed under her breath.

"What was that all about? With Lois?"

"Tell you later."

Dave Richardson appeared at my elbow, startling me, and reached out to shake hands with my father. I edged sideways around Maddie, uneasy about visiting the funeral home only yesterday, although it seemed like a year ago. Especially after such a busy day. My feet ached in my damp boots. I wanted to go home and sleep until the weekend.

If only.

"— at eleven," Dave was saying. "I hope you'll be there."

"Of course," Dad said. "Silver Hollow has suffered a big loss. We'll miss your dad. The Richardsons have always been a big part of the community."

"Pastor Lovett and his wife have arranged everything. The service, the luncheon, the burial out at the cemetery," Dave said. "Mom's so grateful. She'll be lonely, but we'll keep a close eye on her. Thanks for coming. We'll see you and your family to-morrow."

I glanced at Maddie, who didn't look

pleased at the idea. I knew she'd wanted to work at the graphics studio tomorrow. We planned to close the Silver Bear Shop & Factory, since staff members wanted to attend Tom Richardson's service and lunch. And the mayor's was on Friday, which meant we'd lose more precious time. It couldn't be helped.

Dave and Leah weren't the only ones burdened by two funerals.

Hot from the crush of bodies, I walked into the hallway. Waited in line at the drinking fountain, and decided to hit the restroom. A line snaked out the door, so I gave up that idea. A few acquaintances from outside the village came over to greet me.

Maddie soon dragged me off again. "What did Lois Nichols say?"

I checked into a side room where Jodie Watson, Phil Richardson, and the rest of the Wags and Whiskers pet rescue volunteers gathered. Instead we headed down the hall, past the busy lounge with its curtained glass doors, and found an alcove with an antique phone stand. Double doors led outside behind the funeral home.

I picked up the receiver, but didn't hear a dial tone. "For looks, I guess."

"Will you please tell me what Lois said?" Maddie folded her arms over her chest.

"She was furious about losing. That much I knew, but what else?"

"Your friend took first place. Guess that was as bad as if Mary Kate got it."

"Amanda is your friend, too!"

"I know that. Lois would have complained no matter who won." I leaned closer. "She did tell me something interesting."

"Oh? What did she say, tell me."

"I'd love another box of cookies. Snowballs, or shortbread —"

"Okay, okay already. So spill."

"Wow, you're too easy. I don't need a bribe." I laughed at her narrowed-eye glare. "Lois and Harry sold their house and plan to leave Silver Hollow."

She tossed her head. "For your information, they rented that house. You can't believe anything Lois says. But I know how to verify it."

I trailed after her down the hall. Maddie joined Mom and Aunt Eve, who chatted with Barbara Davison in the front parlor. All three women, wearing traditional black suits, teetered on high heels. The netting of their small hats half hid their eyes.

"— already arranged with Mary and Norma to deliver all the poinsettias," Mom said, "and they'll arrange them on different levels, like a Christmas tree."

"It sounds lovely," Barbara said. "So no church ceremony, I take it."

Aunt Eve shook her head. "Ross and I didn't want a big fuss. Judith arranged everything for the party, so all we have to do is show up."

"But I hired a photographer and arranged for a wedding cake," Mom added. "I also found the perfect shoes to go with Eve's dress."

"Vintage, I assume?"

"The most darling pair of kitten heels, with red velvet bows."

"Excuse me, Mrs. Davison?" Maddie apologized for interrupting, but Barbara waved that away. "I only have a quick question. Didn't you rent the little Cape Cod house on Kermit Street to the Nichols? The middle one."

"Yes, and our property manager mentioned how they broke their lease," she said. "We have a lot of cleanup to do before it can be rented again. The Nicholses will lose their security deposit, but that won't cover all the costs. Who knows if we'll be able to rent it this late in the year, or even in January."

"I know someone who's interested." I stepped around Maddie. "Jay Kirby is looking for a studio to do his carving. Not in the house. He'll live there and work in the garage. It's not a shed, right? It's a full-size garage?"

"Oh, yes. I'll keep him in mind, then. And thank you."

"Ross told me Lois Nichols quit her job at the Quick Mix Factory," Aunt Eve said, her voice low. "He heard they planned to fire her anyway. Nothing could be proven, but a co-worker accidentally left her purse in the restroom. She'd cashed her paycheck at lunchtime, and when she realized her mistake and rushed back, the purse was there. But not the money."

"How terrible," I said.

"Lois had been washing her hands when the woman first left. By the time she called security, Lois had already gone home. Said she had a bad headache."

"Maybe the police could check if she deposited the same amount in her bank."

"I doubt it. Cash is easier to hide." Maddie sounded disgusted. "I bet she left before they could accuse her of stealing the money. And never went back. Now she's leaving."

They all nodded sagely. I suspected Lois would make off with more than a cheap teddy bear, but no one could prove it. I glanced around. The crowd hadn't lessened much. Or the noise, either, muffling the hallway's grandfather clock when it struck nine.

"There's Kristen and Alison Bloom." Maddie gripped my elbow tight. "I wondered if they'd show up tonight."

Ow. I rubbed my arm once I escaped her clutch. I also lost track of Alison and Kristen in the crowd, and shivered when a chilly gust of wind blew through the foyer. Dave Richardson struggled to shut the door after the departing visitors.

"Sasha?"

I turned to see Leah Richardson. Pale, her eyes red and puffy, she twisted a handkerchief between her fingers. Her dark hair fell into soft curls over her shoulders, and once more her neck was hidden with a high-necked blouse under a dark blazer.

"I know this has all been a lot of work for you," I said.

"Yeah. Things will get better once this week is over. Thank goodness Dave recovered fast. I'd never have been able to handle all this without him. He knows exactly what to say, and how to comfort grief-stricken families."

I didn't know what to reply. I was nervous, since I suspected her husband of faking his illness. Leah glanced around, as if checking to see if Dave was near. Why would he keep such close tabs on her if there wasn't domestic abuse? And she always looked fearful. I'd researched the subject on Google and found a list of red flags. Controlling behavior was near the top.

When Paula Richardson strolled by with her family, Leah leaned close to my ear. "She reminds me of Joyce, Cal Bloom's first wife, who moved out to California. At least Dave's dad didn't fool around like the mayor did with Alison."

"You mean —"

"Yeah. When Joyce found out, she divorced him and got full custody. Took Kristen with her, so he had to fly out to LA to see his own kid. Alison shouldn't be surprised that Cal cheated on her. Some people never change." Leah's bitterness had returned. "And Alison's as cheap as Cal. Can you believe she told Dave we owe her a thousand bucks?"

I raised an eyebrow. "I thought the mayor owed you money."

"Yeah, but she claims Dave signed for stuff when Cal never — Uh-oh."

Leah clammed up at the sight of her husband and then rushed to join him in the front parlor. Dave glared over his wife's shoulder at me. Ignoring him, I wandered among the smaller groups still sharing memories with the Richardson clan. Poor Leah. I remembered being afraid of Flynn's moods, although he'd never abused me in the physical sense. A mental slap in the face was just as painful, however.

"If it isn't Silver Hollow's chief snoop."

Kristen Bloom raised an eyebrow, as if expecting a reaction from me. Her three-inch heels lifted her to my eye level, so I couldn't miss the fierce anger that blazed in her eyes. I had no chance of dodging her, either. I swallowed my pride and smiled.

"Sticks and stones, huh?"

"I heard you were spreading rumors about me. I've got one thing to say to you —"

"I hope it's four words actually, like 'Sorry, I was wrong,' " I said. "I wasn't gossiping about you. Isabel French didn't, either. You owe her an apology, too."

"Mom said you knew about me and Phil, don't try to deny it." She had deflated a little, but Kristen's sarcastic tone remained strong. "And you're asking all kinds of questions and stirring up nasty stories about my dad."

"I'm trying to find out the truth."

"Dad was fabulous, and everyone here knew it! Why else would they have voted for him again in a landslide? Tony Crocker might be unhappy, but he hasn't accomplished anything compared to what my father's done for Silver Hollow."

"I know that."

"Do you really?" Kristen cocked her head, one hand on her hip. "He made sure all the lamp posts in town remained Victorian in style, but with modern fittings. He improved council meetings, worked hard with all the commissions to improve the village in so many ways. And he made sure business owners coordinated their Christmas and other holiday decorations, instead of letting them be tacky and cheap."

I wondered if that was a dig at Maggie Davison, but I let that go. "My parents were good friends with your dad —"

"Then you ought to know better. Quit being such a troublemaker, Sasha."

Kristen marched toward the Richardson clan surrounding Cleo. I ground my teeth in frustration. How unfair, calling me out in public, but she was grieving. I retreated to join my family, knowing the day would come when I lost my dad. I'd probably feel as heartbroken as Kristen. I hoped I never lashed out at other people, though. Deserving or not.

How odd that she hadn't berated me for gossip about her stepmother. Alison had the strongest motive for murder. Three reasons to be rid of her husband.

Adultery, alcohol addiction, and that big insurance policy payoff.

CHAPTER 18

The next few days were a blur. My exhaustion tripled, and mainlining coffee during the day didn't help much. Sleep eluded me at night, too. I barely remembered Tom Richardson's funeral service, lunch, and burial on Wednesday, except for the bitter cold. Thursday seemed the same, another mad race to sell, produce, and ship out wizard bears. Even Aunt Eve complained that the Child's Play Toy Box Co. had sent multiple email reminders of the deadline.

"Like we don't know," I grumbled and taped another box shut.

Cal Bloom's evening visitation turned out to be another noisy crush of people at the funeral home. Triple the number of floral arrangements, baskets, and plants in every parlor and alcove, but minus the warm atmosphere. Everyone whispered and tiptoed through the parlors. They'd been prepared for Tom Richardson's death, given his long illness, but the shock of the mayor's death left everyone uneasy.

Suspected murder had that effect.

Alison Bloom looked every inch the grieving widow in a modest black suit and flats. She maintained a calm mask that only slipped when my mother hugged her tight. Alison sagged visibly as if close to collapse.

"It's been so awful, Judith. You understand what I'm going through."

"We're here for you," Mom said, her voice soothing, and she reached for Kristen's hand. "How are you holding up, sweetie?"

"I'm fine."

Kristen pulled away, her tone cold. I suspected she didn't appreciate her step-mother getting all the attention, for one thing, and her own friends hadn't yet arrived. That might be to blame. No one could miss the glittery diamond pendant that hung over her lacy-sleeved black mini-dress, too. Alison wore simple pearls in comparison. Neither shed any tears while they greeted people, which seemed awkward to me.

I'd be inconsolable — like I was at Grandpa T. R.'s services. Maddie as well, and we chose to hang his photo near Mr. Silver in the shop and display his tools. We'd never forget his humor, love, and steady influence in our lives.

I joined my sister to murmur a prayer at the mayor's casket, but quickly moved on. I'd lost respect for Cal Bloom due to his condescending attitude toward women. And after learning he wasn't all jolliness and fun, my admiration fizzled.

But no one deserved to be murdered.

On Friday morning, Silver Hollow residents gathered at the church for the funeral. A line of cars stretched along Kermit Street all the way around the curve that ended at Archibald. Leah and Dave Richardson greeted mourners in the church narthex; Pastor Lovett stood beside Alison and Kristen. The rest of the Bloom family consisted of his niece, Zoe Fisher, and her widowed mother, plus Alison's brother, Tim Jackson — the entire Bloom family. I saw no sign of Phil Hunter. The haughty detective had not put in an appearance at the visitation last night, either.

I bypassed the sanctuary and slipped into the restroom. I'd slapped on makeup without paying attention, so I fixed that and brushed out my blond locks as well. Pinned them up a few times, and finally gave up, choosing a simple braid in surrender. I smoothed my burgundy skirt and sweater, wishing I'd had time for a second mug of coffee.

"Out into the fray —"

"Excuse me?" Vivian Grant, the owner of the Pretty in Pink bakery, had emerged from a restroom stall. "Did you say something to me?"

I blinked. "Oh! Um, no. I was talking to myself. Sorry."

She only nodded. Strands of frizzy dark hair swirled around her face, and she yanked her dress down on one side. Vivian slung her hot pink purse over one shoulder and departed without another word. I waited a few minutes for the heat in my cheeks to recede. How embarrassing. And then outside the restroom, I bumped into an older gray-haired man, who looked rail thin in a suit that hung on him. I blinked. Tony Crocker? I hadn't recognized him.

Thankfully he ignored me and shook hands with a tall, muscular man who had silver hair, pale blue eyes, and a ruddy complexion. "Keith Dyer, right? You and your son opened that microbrewery, out past my Christmas tree farm."

"That's right. Eric's business permits came through before the mayor's death, so we're grateful for that, given the soft opening we planned for this month."

"Good thing. Gil Thompson's Mayor Pro Tem, and he's slower than a Galapagos turtle getting anything done. Doesn't like outsiders complaining. No different than Cal Bloom."

"That's not what I heard," Dyer said, but Crocker shrugged.

"All the village council members have their hands in each other's pockets. Especially Alex Silverman, his brother, Ross, and Thompson. Don't say I didn't warn you."

Crocker stalked off and took a seat in the sanctuary's last pew. I introduced myself to Mr. Dyer, hoping to set the record straight. "That's not true, what Mr. Crocker said."

"I figured that." He lowered his voice and smiled. "Given my son's business, I know the taste of sour grapes."

I stifled a laugh. Keith Dyer slipped past me and chose a pew halfway up the aisle. The pastor's office door was slightly ajar, and I heard Alison Bloom chiding Kristen about some detail in the service. When their voices raised in argument, I rushed into the sanctuary. No way would I be caught listening outside and accused of spreading more gossip.

My parents, Maddie, Uncle Ross, and Aunt Eve all sat together, so I walked around the side to slide into the pew closest to the window. Five minutes later, Kristen marched toward the front row and joined Zoe and her mother. Alison sat with her brother in the opposite front pew. Clearly their feud had festered deeper now to be on public display. I noted several people with raised eyebrows and heard a few whispers.

Pastor Lovett started the service with a prayer, led the hymns, and then offered the microphone to those who'd been invited to give eulogies. After Gil Thompson, my father, and Tim Jackson finished, Vivian Grant stood and began addressing the crowd, her voice inaudible. Pastor Lovett hurried to her side and held the microphone, so she started over. I guessed the family hadn't expected her to speak.

"I want to remind everyone here that Cal Bloom, despite his few faults, championed small businesses in this village. He supported us whenever asked, and at unexpected times, too. I'm sorry I didn't tell him in person. But I thank him from the bottom of my heart."

When she sat down, I whispered in Maddie's ear. "What was that about?"

"He loaned her money. Remember that huge food fight she had with Carolyn Taylor, when she found out Will had been carrying on with Vivian? But Alison made sure she paid back every penny, with interest."

"Mee-ow!"

"No kidding." Maddie snickered. "Who knows, but maybe Cal fooled around with Vivian before he married Alison. Or after."

"Or both."

Mom hushed our whispers, since the pastor had started reading the poem on the memorial card's back side. " '— for some the journey's quicker, for some the journey's slow . . .' "

How apropos. Someone had hastened his journey to the other side, all right.

Once the service ended, the family slowly left the sanctuary. Alison remained dry-eyed, but Kristen wept openly and leaned against Zoe Fisher. Her friends Nickie Richardson, Cissy, and Debbie Davison crowded behind her, too. While the rest of the mourners filed out of the pews, I scanned their familiar faces. No signs of evident guilt, of course. If only it were that simple. Otherwise, the cops would attend every murder victim's funeral.

I followed my sister out to the narthex. Alison Bloom squeezed my mother's hands and exchanged air kisses, and accepted Dad's murmured condolences. Maddie skipped the line of people waiting to speak with the family and dragged me outside.

"Did you see Vivian Grant, sucking up to Kristen just now? What's going on?"

"I have no idea. You didn't give me a chance to overhear anything."

"Oh, something's up. Alison and Kristen look ready to tear each other's throats out." Maddie gestured toward the church. "They didn't sit together, and they're leaving in separate cars. A house divided, huh? Cal Bloom must be turning over in his grave."

"He's not there yet," I said wryly, "but you're right, he will. They're lining up cars to head to the cemetery now."

"Yeah, but I'm skipping the rest to finish some work." My sister headed toward Theodore Lane. "Update me if any more bombs drop in the war."

I sighed, wishing I could follow, but my parents beckoned. We drove to the burial service which proved to be a simple reading and prayers at the mausoleum. Pastor Lovett then invited mourners back to lunch in the church's Fellowship Hall.

"You're not getting out of this," Dad said when I tried begging off. "Maddie doesn't have anyone else in her business, so that's a good excuse."

"And Alison wants to know if you've made any progress on proving her innocence," Mom said. "Thank goodness the police aren't harassing her further."

Reluctantly, I rode in the back seat of my parents' car. My thoughts returned to what I'd seen and heard at the parade over a week ago. When had Cal Bloom left to change into his Santa Bear costume? I know he'd met people, but who? Someone with a good reason to confront him. Was it Lois Nichols? Tony Crocker? And when had he spoken to Alison? Had she enlisted help from Kristen and Detective Hunter to move the body?

Maybe their public spat was a cover for their collusion.

Unless Cissy Davison and Gus Antonini abandoned their plans for dinner at the Regency Hotel. Had they waylaid the mayor and taken their revenge? Or was it Dave Richardson, whose expectations to buy Bloom's Funeral Home had been put on hold again?

Then again, Alison Bloom was desperate to keep her mother at the Silver Birches.

"Sasha? Wake up," Mom said when Dad parked the car on Kermit. "I'm so hungry, it's almost two o'clock. And you won't hear me complain if it's the same chicken, ham, and green beans like at all the church pot-lucks."

I followed my parents downstairs but hung back, wishing Elle and Mary Kate had come. I'd seen them briefly at the visitation last night, but I was on my own today. Mom chatted with Dad, Tim Jackson, and Gil Thompson. Kristen stood at the far end of the hall with her friends, plus Mary Monroe. Zoe Fisher tapped me on the arm with a bright smile.

"Hey, Sasha, where's Maddie?"

"Working."

"Ah. I hoped to talk to her about the graphics studio. She asked me to help her out."

"Yeah, she's having a hard time keeping up with stuff."

"I'll head over there once this is over and figure out what she needs."

Her dark eyes sparkled with eagerness. Zoe wore her sleek dark hair in a pageboy, minus the purple or teal shades Maddie favored. Her black jumpsuit, silver belt, and outrageous jewelry had a similar flamboyance to my sister's style, though. They'd be a perfect team.

"Well, well. If it isn't Jessica Fletcher. Any new bodies drop lately?"

I turned to see Digger Sykes waiting in the buffet line, clearly off-duty given his tight and well-worn sport coat. He held a fistful of memorial cards printed with Cal Bloom's photo. The mayor's beaming smile jarred again with his secretive past.

"One of these days you'll find a corpse," I said, "and it won't be a joke."

Digger grinned. "Lighten up, Sasha."

"You're a cop, so act professional like Chief Russell. Or Detective Mason."

"Ha. Haven't seen him around."

I suddenly remembered what Mom had mentioned. "Is it true you weren't happy about the mayor not supporting your promotion?"

"I didn't expect him to do anything. And Bloom called me lazy after the last two murder investigations, thanks to you."

Boy, would I lose a popularity contest. Tony Crocker, Kristen Bloom, Lois Nichols, and now Digger Sykes had all expressed their displeasure with me lately. I tried to push past, but he grasped my arm and leaned close to whisper.

"There's a new rumor about your ex-husband."

"Now what?" Digger must have heard about Flynn's engagement to Cheryl Cummings, but I wasn't about to confirm that. "I haven't seen Flynn for days."

"Hanson's in big trouble. Again. That flashy lawyer in Detroit filed another lawsuit against him."

I shrugged. "Probably as bogus as the first

one, since the judge tossed it out of court. You mean Vince Sheffield? What's his beef now?"

"Apparently, he's claiming Flynn made 'unwelcome advances' against one of his clients. Met her at a restaurant, grabbed her during their meeting. Sheffield's out for blood." Digger sounded gleeful. "Hanson walks around like he's God's gift to women and the entire planet. What goes around always comes back to bite you where it hurts."

"You're a fine one to talk. Remember you're in Chief Russell's doghouse, and don't try to blame me for that. You knew better."

"Yeah, yeah. Whatever."

He swaggered off toward my dad and Gil Thompson. I didn't care what Digger Sykes thought. Or anyone else, for that matter, since Flynn's hotshot style and over-the-top friendliness with clients could very well be taken wrong. But that kind of lawsuit, even if it was thrown out of court, could affect the other Legal Eagles. Branson and Blake had worked hard to establish their practice. I hoped Flynn wouldn't bring it crashing down with a reckless mistake.

Speak of the devil. I'd glanced around the large hall and spied Flynn with Mike Blake.

Cheryl Cummings cooed over Lisa Blake's new baby in a car carrier. For a woman who'd given birth recently, Lisa looked great. And in pink to match her infant's outfit and blankets. Clearly, she was ecstatic having a daughter. Her sons had to be in school or the local daycare.

I turned away, filled a plate, and chose to sit with Tyler and Mary Walsh. While we ate, they shared a brief, funny memory of Cal Bloom. "He came in for our pecan pie two or three summers ago," Mary said. "He was so disappointed that we'd run out that day."

"Cal said he'd try the lemon instead, remember?" Tyler laughed.

"He expected a chiffon pie," Mary said. "You should have seen that man! Said my lemon icebox was so tart, he kissed his tonsils."

"You'd put in less sugar than usual, honey, by mistake."

"I felt so bad about it, I promised him a pecan pie at Christmas. He got the biggest kick when I delivered it to him, all wrapped like a present!"

Her husband nodded. "Didn't share it with nobody, either."

"And Kristen never forgave him!"

We all laughed together this time. I nearly

dropped my fork when Flynn leaned over my shoulder to greet the Walshes. Then he hissed in my ear.

"Got a minute, Sasha?"

Displeased by the interruption, I rose to follow him to the coffee urns. Everyone had finished lunch and lingered now over dessert, chatting in low voices. Why did people think they could confide in me to solve their problems?

I wasn't a miracle worker.

"Let me ask you something first," I said. "What's this lawsuit against you?"

"Total fabrication."

"That's not what I heard."

Flynn snorted. "Vince Sheffield's been after me for months. He's sick. Sick and jealous, trying to discredit me because my television commercials are so popular. They're making him look like a loser. I can't help that."

"This lawsuit sounds serious, though, and you can't blow it off. Did you actually meet his client at a restaurant?"

"It was a setup." He glanced around, although I could barely hear his whisper. "That woman has a history of luring guys and recording them on her phone. I doubt if the case gets to the investigation stage, and then discovery could take six months to a year. Vince Sheffield is well-known for frivolous litigation. The judge threw out his last lawsuit against me. That's bound to happen again."

I didn't reply. Swagger had always been part of his game, but Flynn hadn't learned to be more careful. I noted a few white strands mingling in his spiked blond hair. Maybe I was wrong. Maybe he'd learned a hard lesson this time.

But Pastor Lovett interrupted us. "Well, Mr. Hanson! I hear congratulations are in order. Have you chosen a wedding date and venue yet?"

"I'm sure it's too early for that." Marianna had also joined us and beamed. "We watch Ms. Cummings every morning on FOX4 for her weather forecast."

Flynn flashed a shocked look in my direction. I mouthed, "Not me" and slipped away, figuring that Dave Fox had somehow found out. Or maybe Cheryl Cummings told a friend and somehow the news spread. Flynn reported seeing Kristen and Phil Hunter together in Ann Arbor, so what did he expect? He must have forgotten his own words, that secrets couldn't be kept for long even outside the village.

Besides, Digger was right. What goes around comes back around, and not always in a good way. Call it karma, or payback. Best to avoid that altogether in the long run.

Since Pastor Lovett kept Flynn talking, and I'd seen Uncle Ross escape with our factory staff earlier, I grabbed my coat from the hallway rack. Outside the cold wind froze me to the bone. Before I reached the corner of Theodore Lane, Maddie honked her car horn and pulled to the curb. I climbed inside.

"Going to the post office," she said, "so keep me company. Did you hear that Zoe agreed to work for me the rest of December? That will really help."

"She's so talented."

"And then, Digger told me before the church service that Flynn's engaged to Cheryl Cummings. Did you know?"

So that was how news had gotten around. "Yes, Flynn told me at the parade, but swore me to secrecy. Sorry about that."

"Mom said she knew, too." Maddie pumped a fist toward the sky and then turned onto Baker Road. "Hallelujah. He'll finally leave you alone!"

"Don't bet on that. And what if he gets cold feet, like with Gina Lawson?"

"Oh, I don't think so the way Cheryl's flashing that diamond. That rock's bigger than Mom's and Barbara Davison's combined. Everyone's settling down except me."

"You'll get married before I will," I said wryly. "Wait and see."

"At least the parade and tree lighting was a success —"

"The mayor was murdered."

Maddie waved that away. "You sold a ton at the Bear-zaar, and the Beary Potter wizard bear production's on track. All that's left is the Holiday Open House."

"Don't forget the staff party and wedding."

"Hang on a minute." My sister parked in front of the small building, ran in, and then returned with a plastic crate holding multiple small packages. "They called and said I'd better pick up all this stuff. Wouldn't fit in my box, and I have to switch to a bigger one. I'll take care of that next year. I'm too busy to exchange keys and fill out paperwork."

"You should have your mail delivered to the factory."

"And risk getting stuff mixed up? No way. Plus, I can take the cost off my taxes." Maddie drove back toward Silver Hollow, explaining the various specialty items she'd ordered. "I didn't expect to run out of printer ink so fast, even though I do so much online."

"We're always ordering that, plus boxes, tape, foam noodles. You name it."

At last we left busier traffic and entered the outskirts of Silver Hollow. "Okay," Maddie said. "Remember you were gonna update me about the war."

"The war. What war?"

"Kristen and Alison. And the whole bit with Vivian Grant, too."

"I have no idea what she's up to, although she was talking to Kristen at the funeral lunch. Alison stayed far away from both of them. I've got to get back to shipping teddy bears, though, and forget all this craziness."

"Stop acting like a Grinch. Be a Holiday Cheermeister instead."

"As long as I don't have to sit in the Chair of Cheer." I stuck out my tongue. "Or taste all kinds of Who Pudding. But you owe me Christmas cookies."

"I stashed a box on the shelf where we keep the Bubble Wrap. You, Deon, and Isabel French can treat yourself while you're slaving. Compliments of Silver Moon, by the way, but save a few for Tim Richardson. I know he's busy helping his parents."

"No rest for the weary, I swear."

"We're all working overtime." Maddie turned onto Theodore Lane. "Christmas comes, ready or not, remember. That's what

Mom always says."

"True enough." I spotted a low-slung sporty red Camaro in our parking lot. "Whose car is that? Anyone you know?"

"Nope."

I squinted in the dim afternoon light and saw Detective Hunter emerge from behind the wheel. He stood waiting, his expression unreadable, one hand on the car's slick roof, watching me climb out of Maddie's car. I waited for my sister to park, though, half-turned away. Together we walked toward the shop. Hunter's deep voice sent a chill through me.

"Ms. Silverman. A word with you, if you don't mind."

I did mind, but replied, "Sure."

I wasn't about to allow him the chance to accuse me of hindering the police investigation. Or not cooperating. Besides, I hadn't gotten far with either Kristen or Alison and might learn something new from Hunter.

If I was lucky.

CHAPTER 19

"I've got to take this stuff to the graphics studio, so I'll see you later."

Maddie winked. A subtle message to tell her everything the first chance I got, and she hurried off with her packages. I sensed she knew the last thing I wanted was to waste precious time with Detective Hunter. He pulled leather gloves from his coat pockets and tugged them on. His ears looked bright red. The wind stung my cheeks and lips, and I shivered.

"It's colder than I thought out here." He eyed the gray clouds overhead.

I'd gotten the hint. "Might as well come inside for a cup of coffee."

"Thanks."

The detective quickly followed me to the back porch, but hung back when I explained about Rosie's uneasiness with strangers. If my sweet dog accepted him, he could be trusted. Rosie had bonded with Mason, but

I wasn't so sure about Hunter.

"Hey, sweet girl. It's okay —"

I'd grabbed her leash and harness, buckled it on, and sighed in relief. Rosie barked, of course, and I was grateful he stayed on the walkway when I led her past to the yard. Once she was finished, however, Rosie sniffed his pant leg and walked past him back into the house. He didn't reach a hand down to pet her, however. Hunter seemed disinterested, standing in the kitchen door-way, hands in his pockets, and eyeing the Christmas decorations. My sweet teddy bear dog looked adorable. Who wouldn't fall instantly in love with her curly hair, those bright black button eyes, and wagging tail?

He was startled when Onyx jumped down from the cat tower's top ledge. She curled her sleek, lithe black body around his legs. Then he crouched, gloves off, and slid a hand over her silky fur, head, and ears.

"What's her name?" Hunter smiled at her purring rumble. A cat lover, apparently. "What a gorgeous animal."

"Onyx is that, and more."

Disappointed, Rosie grabbed her squeaky snowman between her jaws and bounded up to claim the abandoned window seat. Squeaking it over and over, as if she was insulted. Onyx continued to soak up the love Hunter lavished on her, circling him, rubbing her head against his hand whenever he stopped. And when he rose to his feet, she meowed. Insistent. The detective squatted again to pet her.

"That's her way of telling you she's the queen, and you're her subject," I said, "but she'll get tired of it. Eventually. Or bite you."

"Uh-huh."

Hunter rose and straddled a pub chair at the kitchen island. I'd made coffee earlier today in the programmable maker, but dumped the leftover brew and fetched the can of grounds from the refrigerator. He reached down to stroke the cat again.

"Toss something in the Keurig for me. Less trouble."

"Any particular brand or caffeine strength?"

Once he'd chosen, I plucked a pod from the metal carousel, added filtered water to the machine, and placed a medium-sized mug beneath. I slid the sugar bowl closer after I brought his mug. Surprisingly, Hunter added two spoonfuls. He seemed so hard-nosed and gruff, as if he chewed nails for fun. How odd that I'd learned more about him from a cat's affection and a coffee-making ritual. I'd chosen Lady Grey tea and then perched on a chair opposite.

Onyx leaped to the pub seat beside him for better reach.

"Can't get enough, huh. Typical female."

I gritted my teeth. "Are you here to update me on the mayor's death, Detective?"

"I'm no longer on the case."

Hot tea burned my mouth. I'd gulped too much in surprise, and snatched a napkin from the tree-shaped holder. Yowza. I hoped he didn't suspect me of influencing Chief Russell in booting him, when my dad had probably called.

"Been reassigned," Hunter added, "to the Ypsilanti case Mason's working. I'm surprised he isn't here yet. Should be coming any minute."

"Oh. I see."

I fetched the can of grounds again, filled the pot with water, and started the coffee brewing. By the time the pot filled, Rosie had hopped down and barked with excitement at the back door. She raced in circles when Detective Mason knocked. I'd already filled the creamer and set it on the island, and waved the detective inside. The minute he held up a finger, Rosie's rump hit the floor and she whined, low. Mason praised her obedience.

He glanced at Phil Hunter, who was petting the cat on his lap now. Mason draped his jacket on the pub chair at the end of the island and sat. Rosie curled up at his feet. The two policemen couldn't be more different. Mason reminded me of a teddy bear, stocky and round, with light brown hair and glasses. Hunter had a lean, hungry air with an angular body, wary blue eyes, and sleek dark hair. He looked catlike, come to think of it.

"Jamie."

"Phil."

I poured fresh coffee, eyebrows raised at their terse first-name greeting. But Mason's tone had more than an underlying hostility, with a sharp nip to it. Maybe I needed to wave a white napkin for a truce. They ignored each other and sipped from their mugs.

"Guess I shouldn't have been surprised, getting yanked from the case," Hunter finally said. "You behind it?"

"Yeah, what of it? If you had an ounce of integrity, you'd never have taken —"

"I'm already over it."

"Huh. You said that about the Heritage Park case."

"How was I supposed to know you'd already interviewed those gang members?" He glared at Mason. "Like they gave me any worthwhile information anyway. Turns out they were involved in both murders, remember."

"I sent you the file. You could've read it first."

Another long silence reigned. I gulped my cooler tea and crushed my insatiable curiosity. Cramming it back into a Pandora-like box was impossible. If only I could cast a spell like Hogwarts's Professor McGonagall and transform myself into Onyx, or one of our wizard bears. The two detectives would battle it out minus the velvet gloves without me around, given their past history of clashing over cases. Clearly, they frayed each other's nerves. I kept an eye on the clock. Counted out one minute, two, and then a third.

Wow. The tension prickled the hair on my neck, making me shiver. I was dying to know who'd break the silence first. Hunter stared out the window, while Mason twisted his mug around, eyes downcast.

"Never got reports about the Bloom case," he finally said. "I checked every day."

"I sent 'em. Email." Hunter shrugged. "Never got a reply."

"Are you accusing me of —"

"Whoa." I held up a hand to interrupt. "Maybe one of you had the wrong email address," I suggested. "Transposing one letter is pretty common."

Hunter glared at me, but Mason wrote something and pushed the notebook over toward his colleague. "Whatever. So I'll re-send 'em."

"And then," I said to Mason, "you hit reply with 'thanks' or some other response."

"Yeah, gotcha. The big question is, are you gonna mess up my federal case while I clean up after you on this one?"

Hunter turned beet red and set Onyx on the floor as if preparing to pounce on the other detective. "I didn't mess up anything."

"Bunk! I had to redo all the —"

I whistled sharply. "Do I have to use the kitchen sprayer, the way you two are acting like junkyard dogs? Or send you outside so you can finish fighting."

Mason leaned back against the stool and took a deep breath. The last thing I needed was acting as referee between two cops. I wasn't in the mood for a chess match, either. I was terrible at strategy. No matter how disgruntled, they'd both beat me hands down. I also had no idea why they'd chosen the Silver Bear Shop as neutral ground for such a tense meeting.

"That's better," I said, glancing at them both. "Get to the facts."

"Okay." Mason flipped to a new page of

his notebook. "Chief Russell is convinced Cal Bloom's death was accidental."

"I agree with him, except his daughter insists it was murder." Hunter shrugged. "Kristen hadn't spoken to her dad in a while, so it could be guilt. She's pretty upset."

"I think it's murder as well," I said, deciding not to be a mere spectator, "but there's too many people with motives. I don't know if they all have alibis."

Mason tapped his pencil on the table. "Run down the list of suspects and motives."

"Tony Crocker, who resented losing the election."

"So what." Hunter's scoffing tone made his opinion clear on that score. "He had no chance of winning whatsoever. He'd be insane to kill Bloom over that, even though that dead girl, Holly what's-her-name, got more votes than Crocker did."

"That 'girl'? She was my age," I said tightly.

"Okay. Woman."

Now I wished I hadn't invited him inside. Hunter definitely pushed my buttons with his bad attitude, but I continued when Mason nodded in encouragement.

"There's Cissy Davison and her fiancé,

308

Gus Antonini."

Hunter raised an eyebrow. "Who?"

I ignored him. "Cal Bloom somehow got hold of an intimate photo —"

"Oh, the curvy blonde. She owned some fancy boutique on Main Street."

"What kind of photo? Nude?" Mason looked skeptical when I explained.

"I wouldn't be surprised if Bloom did suggest trading that photo for sex," Hunter said, "but she can claim anything. He's dead and can't deny it. Convenient."

"You don't think that's a substantial motive for murder?" I asked.

"Hey, consenting adults."

"But Cissy didn't consent! And how did the mayor get that photo in the first place? He may have denied having it, but Digger saw him with it."

"I'd like to know what happened to it, too," Mason added. "You must have questioned Ms. Davison, Phil. What about Officer Sykes?"

Hunter plucked a few cat hairs from his wool suit jacket and pants. I didn't offer him the lint roller. When you encourage a cat, you deal with the consequences. The detective slouched in the chair, hands curled around his empty mug, as if deciding how to reply.

"Yeah, I asked Sykes. He didn't know how Bloom got it, or where it is now. I pressured him. You know the idiot nearly contaminated the last murder scene, right? So I asked if he found it inside the mayor's polar bear suit. Copped it instead of letting the forensic techs process it. He got all hyped-up, and denied it half a dozen times."

"He must be telling the truth." I thought back to that night, and related how Flynn had unfastened the costume. "There weren't any pockets in that suit, or photos."

"It's probably gone for good, so tell Cissy baby not to worry."

Mason glared at Hunter and turned to me. "Who else?"

"Alison Bloom, the widow, had motive and opportunity."

"Kristen would love to accuse her stepmother of murder, but she's got an alibi." Hunter folded his arms over his chest. "Let's be honest. This was just a stupid accident. I met the mayor a couple of times. Typical blowhard. The guy loved to hear himself talk and impress people. Friendly on the surface, but a real jerk once you got to know him in person."

"Many people around here would not agree," I said.

"Okay, I get that your parents are tight

310

with him and his wife. But Cal Bloom wasn't one to admit a mistake."

"That doesn't mean —"

"I think he shocked himself at the parade," he continued, ignoring me. "Got a jolt and then staggered off. Didn't tell anyone he was having a heart attack. Maybe Cal fell, hit his head. Managed to make it as far as that bench. And then died. The end."

Hunter looked at me as if I'd agree with him. I didn't. I also thought he liked the sound of his own voice, just like Cal Bloom. We stared at each other for a long while, waiting. Mason finally broke the silence.

"Not buying into that theory, Sasha?"

"It's a theory like any other, but with a big flaw."

Mason grinned. "Why is that?"

I chose my words with care. "A lot of people hung around the generators where they tested the floats' light strings. If the mayor got a shock there, someone would have noticed. And they wouldn't have let him wander off, either."

"Hmph." Hunter eyed me with derision. "Maybe. Maybe not."

"When I talked to Alison Bloom on Monday, she told me you and Kristen had been visiting the Silver Birches the day of the parade," I said. "That you both left around

311

four o'clock or thereabouts. So did you go to the funeral home after that?"

"No. Kristen wanted something to eat before watching the parade."

"Which restaurant, then?"

"Ham Heaven."

"That checks out, my dad saw you."

"Gee, thanks." Hunter rolled his eyes upward. "What else?"

"Did Kristen tell you she fought with her dad, about the business? Cal Bloom wanted her to take over the funeral home business. Like how I manage this shop."

That last bit was a guess on my part, but easy to conjecture given Cal's close friendship with my parents. Hunter stared into his empty mug. Maybe wondering how much to disclose what he knew about his girlfriend and her family.

"Yeah, okay, but Kristen hated the idea. It was a petty feud. She had her own plans, and his bad behavior around the village embarrassed her," he added. "Cal Bloom was a scumbag, but he was still her dad."

"Scumbag?" Mason glanced up from his notebook. "Sounds harsh."

"The mayor was a drunk, a womanizer. Nobody here realized half of what he got away with," Hunter said. "He cheated on his first wife and didn't change that bad habit with the second one. Plus sweet Alison wasn't around much. If you want my opinion, Cal got tired of her playing saint and martyr at that retirement home. So he looked elsewhere."

"Then who was he involved with?" I asked. "The woman might have a motive to kill him if Mr. Bloom decided to end the affair."

Hunter shrugged. "I got nothing on that. Never asked, never heard."

"So why would Alison Bloom use her mother as an alibi," I said, "when someone at the Silver Birches saw her leave? And she didn't return until after the parade."

He straightened up, shoulders back, eyebrows knitted together. "No way. I asked all the staff there, and no one saw her leaving."

Mason finally spoke up. "Then maybe you asked the wrong people."

I smiled. "Alison was at the parade, because someone overheard her arguing with her husband. And not much later he was found dead."

"So who saw them together?" Hunter asked.

"You're off the case, remember?"

I set aside my cold tea, yearning for a cookie. Or three. I deserved it after sitting through this prickly encounter, with Hunter acting like a jerk and Mason clearly enjoying our exchange, by his sly smiles.

"That's more legwork for Jamie, then, once you tell him who to hunt down." Hunter cracked his knuckles. "If you do."

"Sasha's gotten more results than you did over the past ten days," Mason said, "while you wasted time with your girlfriend."

The other detective muttered a curse, or at least that's what it sounded like to me. "This whole case is a waste of time."

"Nobody asked your opinion. Kristen wants justice for her dad," I said, "and every murder victim deserves that."

"Sure, sure. And we solve every case, just like on TV. Right, Jamie?"

Hunter's sarcasm burned me. I was thankful when he rose to his feet, though, signaling the end of this exchange. I collected the empty mugs, set them in the sink, wiped down the coffee machine, and then straightened the row of wooden nutcrackers in their holiday colors on the counter. Mason leaned down to rub Rosie's belly and then slid off the tall chair onto one knee. He didn't bother to acknowledge Hunter, who sauntered to the door.

"One last thing," the lanky detective said, hand on the knob. "When Kristen's mom dumped her back on Cal Bloom, Alison resented that. Sure, they had a bad relationship, but now her dad's dead, she has to share the inheritance. Money soothes a lot of wounds."

"Does Kristen actually suspect her stepmother of murder, though?"

Hunter exchanged a cautious glance with Mason. "She hasn't come out and said it, but Kristen told me that Alison didn't give a fig about Cal being mayor, and she hated him owning the funeral home. And her dad mentioned something about a possible divorce."

"So now you're on board," I said with satisfaction. "That witness who overheard Cal and Alison Bloom arguing said he threatened to stop paying the bills for her mother. It costs a lot to keep her at the Silver Birches. That alone is a solid motive."

"What the hell." Hunter waved a hand at Mason. "Give her a detective shield. But can you blame the mayor? A cold wife, who milked his bank account for all it was worth. All right, Jamie. You still have a lot of ground to cover, but maybe your little Christmas elf here will make it easier for you."

The door slammed after him. I turned to Mason, glad he'd be handling the case now. "Do you think Hunter will mess up your federal case?"

"Can't worry about that now." He shrugged into his leather jacket. "Chief Russell wants to solve this case quick, and I agree with you. Everything points to murder, where the mayor was found, and that blow to the head. Keep in touch. And even though Phil Hunter thinks you're a big help, I think you've done enough."

"Hey. Can I help it if people always confide in me?"

"Just remember —"

"Yeah, stick to selling teddy bears." I smiled. "Right."

CHAPTER 20

Maddie, Aunt Eve, and I all pitched in over the weekend, both Saturday and Sunday, at the factory. I refused to skip church, though, and raced back to work in the shipping department. We had to push hard to finish the Teddy Bear Keepsake orders for Child's Play Toy Box Co., or there'd be the devil to pay. Uncle Ross reminded us that Michigan's state laws didn't require breaks for workers. I insisted that everyone stretch their legs after four hours, refill water bottles, and use the restroom.

Meals were also mandatory, and snacks. Pizza from Amato's, tacos and burritos from La Mesa, plus Mary Kate's delicious half scone, half cookies topped with jam, to accompany coffee or tea. Uncle Ross grumbled about the cost. I ignored him. It definitely kept our staff motivated to pull an overnighter that continued into Monday. We fueled ourselves with coffee, bagels with cream cheese or peanut butter, hard-boiled eggs, and a huge bowl of fruit that Mom put together for breakfast before getting back to the grind.

My mother joined me to pack wizard bears, too, since Maddie had gone to meet Zoe at the graphics studio. I counted myself lucky that Renee Truman was free to cover the shop for me. But when Aunt Eve brought news of a predicted blizzard, we sent the staff home.

"I hope we don't get any more orders for the wizard bear," Mom said.

"It's long past the deadline," I said, taping a big bandage over my thumb. A cardboard box was capable of nastier cuts than paper. "We only have another three dozen bears to finish, and we'll be all caught up."

Aunt Eve sighed. "Ross isn't sure we'll make the deadline. I'm going home. I only want soup and some crusty bread. Sorry, Judith, and I know you made lasagna."

"More for us!"

I was joking, but Mom's Italian meals truly were amazing. Dad had refused to eat only one dish she created long ago. "Heavenly Hash" had been declared inedible, and my sister and I rejoiced. We'd dubbed it "Hell Hash" and tossed it in the garbage. Shamefaced, Mom ordered fish and chips instead from Casey's Tavern. After that, she stuck to favorites. And Mom was a whiz at making linguini, spaghetti pie, shrimp scampi, and the like.

Isabel French looked exhausted. I'd sent her to quality control earlier since she had a sharp eye for details. She also proved a deft hand at fastening Beary Potter's special wizard robe at the neck, and tacking on the wand to prevent it being pulled loose during shipment. That was a lifesaver. She punched her time card with pride and thanked me again.

"This is fun! So much better than serving ice cream."

"I'm gonna miss your Silver Scoop creations, though." Yawning wide, I glanced out the window and shook my head. "It's already snowing."

"Great." She sighed. "See you tomorrow, if it's not too horrible."

"I'll have to work in the shop, since Renee Truman can't make it."

"I could do that! I love interacting with people, and helping kids choose a new teddy bear or some outfits. But only if you need me to switch."

"I might take you up on that. Right now, we have to get those wizard bears done."

"Sure."

Isabel headed out to her car. I ambled over to the house, dead tired, yearning for a nap. The spicy tomato scent and the sound of bubbling cheese on top of Mom's lasagna in the oven boosted my flagging energy. Mmm. I fastened Rosie's coat, harness, and leash. I'd better walk the dog now before the snow piled up on the walk.

"Alexandra Victoria Silverman!" Mom waved a wooden spoon at me, but I quickly ducked back outside again. "I've got a bone to pick with you —"

"What's up now?" I watched snowflakes drift around Rosie while she sniffed the frozen, dead grass. "Guess I'll have to face the music, Rosie. But let's get you moving."

Dad parked the car and waved, heading inside with a bag from Jackson's Market. Rosie and I walked fast to Kermit Street and back. A short stroll, but the snow had already covered our foot and paw prints by the time we returned.

Inside, I found Dad slashing a long bread loaf lengthwise. He buttered both halves and added the garlic Mom had chopped. Since they were busy, I rushed upstairs to change into my warmest flannel pajama pants and a cozy sweatshirt. Then I dragged myself back to the kitchen. I should have joined Aunt Eve for soup and avoided

320

Mom. Too late now.

"So what gives?" I asked in my most innocent tone.

She pointed the chef's knife at me. "You're supposed to prove Alison's innocence, not guilt! For heaven's sake, Sasha. You told everyone about Kristen dating Detective Hunter, and then got him tossed off the case."

"Wasn't me."

"You can blame me for that, Judith." Dad kissed her cheek and slid the pan under the broiler. "Alison ought to thank me for it, too."

"She's not thankful at all, since that other detective dragged her back to the police station for another interview! That makes three times already. They keep asking the same questions, too, over and over."

I gathered up plates and flatware and started setting the table. "If you must know, Flynn told me he saw Phil Hunter with Kristen in Ann Arbor. At a restaurant."

That stopped Mom cold. "He's sure it was Kristen?"

"Yes, and Hunter gave her that diamond necklace," I added. "The one she wore to the funeral. You must have noticed it."

"Hard to miss, really. Who else knew they were dating?"

"Digger Sykes told me, if you're talking about Kristen Bloom." Maddie had breezed inside, bringing a whiff of cold air and swirling snowflakes with her. "That means everyone in the whole county knows."

"I'm glad Chief Russell asked Mason to take the case," I said. "Hunter should have refused to investigate in the first place."

Dad popped a bit of bread crust into his mouth. "Any sharp defense attorney would have used that relationship to help his client. Hunter's too close to remain objective."

Mom drew the lasagna pan out and then retrieved the garlic bread from the second oven. "I'd like to know why that hefty detective —"

"His name's Mason," I interrupted.

"Why is he hounding Alison? She was with her mother, the whole day of the parade. And she didn't leave until late that night."

I glanced at Dad, wondering how they'd both react. "Actually, someone saw Mrs. Bloom leaving the Silver Birches. Mason has yet to confirm it, though."

Mom waved a hand. "Alison would never lie."

"Ask her if she increased the benefits of her husband's life insurance policy."

Both my parents stared at me in shock, as if I'd reported that the Leaning Tower of

Pisa in Italy had toppled to the ground. Maddie tiptoed around them to fetch glasses, uncorked the wine, and poured. I grabbed the salad bowl and set it on the table. While my parents muttered together, Mom kept shaking her head.

"I won't believe it," she said. "No. I won't."

"I've half a mind to go ask her," Dad said, "but it won't matter. Alison's business is hers, not ours. If the police find evidence, they'll arrest her."

"Alex, she wouldn't have killed Cal."

Mom's pleadings continued when we started dinner. My sister and I picked at our large portions, pulling the cheese into long strings like we used to do as children, but I didn't touch my wine. Even the garlic bread wasn't appetizing. A lump had formed in my stomach. I felt bad for my mother, who must feel betrayed. What if Elle or Mary Kate had lied to me and killed their husbands? I'd feel horrible.

It couldn't have been an accident. The killer had bashed Cal Bloom's skull, making sure he was dead.

"— told me Vivian Grant planned to expand her bakery."

My ears pricked up at that. "Pretty in Pink? It's right next to the Silver Scoop on

Kermit Street, before the curve."

"I know," Mom said. "The last time I talked to Alison, the night before the funeral, she was furious. Cal had paid off Kristen's loan the day before the parade. And he signed over the deed for that property to his daughter. Now she's selling the Silver Scoop."

"And sitting pretty now," I said slowly. "She can open her yoga studio without Isabel French or any other business partner."

"A yoga studio! Of all the crazy ideas."

"Is that Alison's opinion?"

Mom refused to meet my gaze. "Maybe, although I agree. That kind of thing might be popular in Ann Arbor, but here? Besides, the Silver Scoop has been around forever. Why let Vivian Grant take it over?"

"Maybe I should buy it," Dad said, although I suspected he was joking.

"Kristen always dreamed of opening a yoga studio. Why shouldn't she?" Maddie set aside her empty glass. "Nobody has the right to criticize that."

"Hear, hear," I said.

My mother swiped my glass, her cheeks as dark as the burgundy wine, and gulped half the contents. Dad cleared his throat and changed the subject.

"So, Judith. How are the wedding plans

going for —"

"Don't patronize me, Alex Silverman. You just said you should buy it!" Mom launched into a heated defense of Alison Bloom once more. "Maybe that was bad timing about the life insurance policy. I bet Cal wanted to make sure there'd be plenty for Kristen and Alison in case something happened to him. He was prediabetic, after all, and refused to change his diet. Plus everyone knew he had a weak heart."

"The timing does seem unfortunate," Dad said mildly.

"No matter what, Mom," I said, "it's impossible to prove that Mrs. Bloom is innocent. She left the Silver Birches, argued with him before we found him, and didn't say where she was all that time. It wasn't an accident, either."

"Maybe she ran to Jackson's Market for something. Her mother always needs adult diapers. You could ask —"

"That's Detective Mason's job," Dad interrupted. "Let him do his job. And leave Alison alone for a while. She needs time to grieve."

"But she's not. Alone, I mean," Maddie said. "Digger saw her Saturday night at Quinn's Pub, with some guy. I think he's helping Eric Dyer with his microbrewery.

Might be his dad."

"Keith Dyer? Wow." I explained meeting him at the funeral home. "Nice guy."

"I doubt if he's anything more than an acquaintance," Mom said at last.

"That's not what Digger said."

"I'm calling Alison." She rushed off, while we sat in shocked silence.

Dad finally spoke. "I talked to Keith. He retired last year from one of the big three auto companies. Chrysler, I think. Told me how difficult ice wine is to make, waiting for the right moment. The grapes on the vine have to be partially frozen, and then they harvest them by hand. Working fast, night or day, or else they're ruined."

"I thought that place brewed only beer."

"Apparently not. The grapes begin to freeze but the sugar inside doesn't. If they miss the timing, they have to toss the whole crop."

"Wow." I was interested to taste ice wine now, and turned to my sister. "Have you met Eric and his dad yet?"

Maddie shrugged. "Yeah. Didn't really impress me."

"Keith, or Eric?"

Dad was teasing her, but my sister scowled.

"When did you talk to Eric?" I asked.

"He hired me to do a flyer for their holiday event between Christmas and New Year's. A tasting of all his most popular brews. Some caterer from Ann Arbor is making the food. Crème brûlée, pecan pie, and all kinds of stuff. You'd think Eric would hire a few local bakers."

"Why didn't you tell him that?"

She sniffed in disdain. "Said he doesn't know what Silver Hollow can offer. Like that's any excuse. Lame."

"It took a while for us to be accepted, remember," I said. "Some people will never come around, either. Like Jack Cullen."

"I heard he's in the hospital now. Flu, I think." Dad sounded sad. "And he's not expected to make it. First Cal, then Tom Richardson, and now Cullen."

"Threes, they always come in threes," Maddie said. "Weird."

"That's a silly superstition," Mom said, returning to her seat. "I didn't get Alison on the phone, so I left her a voice mail."

I had a feeling she wouldn't get a return call. It sounded strange to me that Alison Bloom would be spending time with Keith Dyer so soon after her husband's funeral. In a pub, of all places. Talk about inviting gossip. Mom tore chunks of garlic bread and then shredded them onto her plate, lost in thought. Dad and Maddie returned to discussing ice wine's unique flavors, although neither of them had tasted it yet.

My thoughts wandered back to Vivian Grant. Now I knew the real story — she wanted that building. In order to expand Pretty in Pink, taking over the Silver Scoop would be a cheaper alternative than building a new addition or moving to another location.

Given what Phil Hunter said, plus Kristen's grief and difficulties with Alison, I no longer believed she'd taken part in her dad's murder. But could Alison have lifted her husband's dead weight? Had she enlisted Keith Dyer's help? He seemed so friendly, but who could tell what a person was really like after one encounter? Given her husband's affairs, Alison may have gotten involved with a lover as payback or promised Dyer a cut of the insurance money.

I'd have to tip off Mason about that new development.

I still hadn't cleared Cissy and Gus, though. That intimate photo was still floating out there. Somewhere. Tony Crocker also remained on my list, however unlikely. With Mason investigating, things might start heating up.

That might make the killer uncomfortable and lead to a mistake.

CHAPTER 21

I glanced at the clock. Nearly one, but I didn't care. I couldn't sleep after eating Mom's spicy lasagna anyway. Jay had called two hours ago, as we weren't caught up on events since his brief visit after the Bearzaar. It felt like a month ago.

"The visitation was so awkward. Nobody mentioned what happened at the parade."

"Bet they talked about it nonstop beforehand," Jay said with a chuckle. "Everyone was all talked out by the funeral."

"Ha. Anyway, remember how Flynn told us about Kristen dating Phil Hunter? Chief Russell booted him off the case, and Mason took over. He's been buzzing around the village every day since. But he hasn't come by to tell me anything."

"I hope he doesn't. Stay out of it, Sasha. I'd feel terrible not being there in case you run up against major trouble like last time. Don't take any risks."

"I wish you were here, right beside me."

"Miss you, too. It won't be long before Christmas Eve. Hey, got any ideas for a present? I'd hate to give you something you don't want."

"Anything. Books, earrings. Mostly you, back home."

"Soon as I finish up, I'm there. This workshop hasn't turned out like I expected. They run things with a ton of red tape and hassle. I'd rather take students on my own terms. But I'm gonna need a studio to get that going."

Jay breathed a long sigh. I pictured him snuggled in a down sleeping bag. His friend's run-down hunting cabin had to be cold without heat. He cooked in the fireplace, and used a rigged shower and portable toilet. Way too extreme for me. I preferred to camp at the "Hamp." Heated hotel, thick and comfortable mattress, clean bathroom with a hot shower, soap, fluffy towels, plus a coffee maker, hair dryer, and maid service. He thought I was joking, at first.

Some things were worth the money, and absolute necessities in my life.

We'd agreed that he could go camping and hiking to his heart's content, whenever he wanted. If Jay wanted me to tag along,

I'd make a reservation. He could sleep in a tent and fend off real bears. The only bears I wanted to meet were in my shop.

"So Mrs. Davison has a Cape Cod on Kermit Street for rent?" he asked. "Are you sure it doesn't have a measly shed out in the yard?"

"A garage with a space heater. Harry Nichols used it for taxidermy before his cancer. At least that's what Digger Sykes said. His brother Larry helped out, too, skinning the critters before Harry had to undergo chemo treatments."

"Now I remember. Paul took his prize fish to Nichols, who did a decent job."

"I'll ask Mrs. Davison again." I nestled deeper into the pile of pillows behind me on the bed. Rosie snuggled close. "The open house is tomorrow, remember. Actually, today. We've got a lot to do this morning, making room for tables, the games, and everything else. I'd better get some sleep."

"Hard to believe it's halfway through December," Jay said. "I'll be home a week from tomorrow. We'll celebrate big time."

"I can't wait."

We exchanged our usual sweet nothings before promising to talk again by the weekend. No chance until then, for sure, given everything we had on our plates. I gave Rosie an extra hug and then tried to sleep. After a restless night, with maybe four hours under my belt, I groped my way into the shower and dried my hair.

"Six thirty. We did this already for the Bear-zaar," I grumbled. "How do some people get up so early with a smile on their face?"

Maddie's singing in the shower answered my question. Ugh. My nerves didn't help, plus I'd had a bad dream where I dropped all the cookies and dumped a whole bowl of punch.

"Lucky we're not serving that." I headed to the closet. "But the cookies!"

My dog snored on the bed while I dressed in a special outfit for our open house. The gorgeous burgundy Mikado silk midi skirt had pleats at the waist but flared at the bottom, and looked sleek with a cashmere sweater. I chose flats for comfort, added my silver teddy bear pin and sparkly earrings, and twisted my hair up into a messy bun. I shoved a few rhinestone pins to tame the loose strands near my face, then swiped a layer of gloss over my red lipstick.

"Come on, Rosie. Time to get you outside before breakfast. No whining, either."

Maddie was already in the kitchen, in black velvet leggings and a fire-engine red top studded with flashing lights. She laughed at my surprise. "I can turn them off and on. See? Battery operated, the wires are all hidden inside. Isn't it sweet?"

"Your feet will be sore," I said, pointing to her four-inch red satin heels with ribbon bows at her ankles. "How do you expect to walk around in those things all day?"

"Let me worry about that." Maddie twirled, cocking her head. "Like my haircut?"

"What's — oh! I see the difference now. It's all red underneath."

"Lynn did it, at Luxe Salon. It's called an undercut pixie and she talked me into adding the reverse ombre effect, dying red in the back and leaving my normal hair color alone. Perfect for the holidays." My sister poured our coffee into large travel holders. "Doctor your own. I don't know how much sugar you want."

"How's Zoe Fisher working out at Silver Moon?"

"She knows a lot about computer software, that's a big plus. She produces newsletters for companies on the side, so I'm hoping we get new contracts. Next year, of course. We're swamped right now."

I waved a hand at our coffee. "No muffins? Not even a bagel. Yeesh."

"Tighten your belt. Work first."

Rosie returned from outside. Thankfully, the weather forecast predicted a warmer day than usual. The snowstorm had ended up as a dud. What little remained would melt by noon in the bright sunshine. But the wind this early in the morning had a bite and sent a shiver through me. Rosie refused to eat anything. Instead, she trotted to her crate where her teddy bear waited and tugged the soft fleece blanket over herself with her teeth.

I laughed, wishing I'd gotten a video. Instead I snapped a photo.

"That's something you can use for our Facebook page or newsletter."

"Good. Remember to take as many pictures of kids with their bears. Everyone loves to see selfies, and customers who can't make it will love seeing what happened. Mary Kate and Hilda dropped off their cookies. Flora's bringing her own, she wants to set them up. Carry that stack and I'll open the doors for you."

"If you weren't wearing those silly heels, you could help," I said. The boxes, while not heavy, blocked my view. I hoped my nightmare wouldn't come true.

Maddie led the way down the hall, opening doors for me, until we reached the office. Once I set my burden on Aunt Eve's desk, Mary Kate carried in a tray. Elle popped up from behind in a red and green elf outfit with pointy ears and a cap over her dark hair.

"Ta-da! We wanted to surprise you, Sasha." She pointed to one ear. "I borrowed these from the hobbit costume I wore on Halloween."

"Cute! And I thought I smelled bacon." I stared at the scrambled eggs, hash browns, a jug of orange juice, fruit, and a platter of donuts and cinnamon buns. "We all need aprons."

"Bingo. Elle the Elf has come prepared," Mary Kate said. "I only brought the pastries. Maddie ordered everything else from the Sunshine Café. I almost never get a chance to relax in the morning, so Wendy baked all these. And Garrett said to spend the morning here. I'd love to help. I can replenish the cookies or do whatever you need."

"That sounds great. We'll find you a chair so you can stay off your feet."

We chatted and laughed over breakfast. I ate too much, of course. Who could turn down a sticky bun oozing with pecans, and a sugar-coated brioche donut? Aunt Eve arrived, festive in a red skirt and an embroidered sweater with sequined holly leaves and red berries. Dipping her donut into coffee, she took a bite and sighed in satisfaction.

"My goodness! I've never tasted anything so decadent."

I puffed out my cheeks, groaning. I'd be lucky to fit into my sweats for the wedding, but everyone would be looking at the bride anyway. Maybe I could fast for a day or two. Drink green tea, maybe even black coffee. Uh, no.

We all pitched in to move the accessory racks to the conference room. That left plenty of open space for the crowd to walk around and view the Christmas trees, the bears on our shelves, plus fill their plates with treats. Besides the tiny savory pinwheels, meatballs, and other canapés, Mary Kate and Elle arranged a variety of cookies on trays. Date Nut Jingle Bells mixed with plain shortbread and iced sugar cookies from Fresh Grounds. They set out peanut-free and gluten-free assortments as well.

"Keep these near the door, so people can take them home when they leave." Maddie placed the box with cellophane-wrapped, exquisitely iced *Little Lord Fauntleroy* teddy bears. "I'm hoping we won't run out by noon, though."

"We bought two hundred," I said, but wondered if she was right.

Aunt Eve put out cups and lids, napkins, and plates near the coffee urns. "There won't be enough people to eat all these treats," she joked.

"One year it snowed so much, we sent leftovers to the Silver Birches. But today we'll have perfect weather. Forty degrees!"

The Silver Bear Shop hosted this event to entertain and give back to the community. If we didn't sell one bear, I'd still be happy. People always came to eat and drink, peruse all the photos of bears donated to Toys for Tots and other organizations throughout the year, and drop donations, cash, food, or cat litter for Wags and Whiskers, the pet rescue. Maddie had mounted a poster of Rosie with her teddy bear above the large box.

"Is Dad ready?" I asked my sister.

"He will be. I told him to come out between ten thirty and eleven."

"Great. I'll go feed Rosie and Nyx."

That didn't take long, since they both gobbled their kibble without protest. Rosie trotted back inside after a quick potty break while Onyx curled up on the sunny window seat. I checked my hair and makeup and rushed back to the shop.

Flora Zimmerman arrived at nine thirty

with her gingerbread house cookies, carefully packed. "Enjoy, and I hope you get a big crowd," she said.

"I promise not to break them," Mary Kate called out. She looked adorable, her slight baby bump showing beneath a blue and white snowman sweater. "It won't be easy, though, since they balance better on a china mug. Not a paper cup."

"Do the best you can," I told her, and taped the laminated page from the *Teddy Bear Times* magazine onto the wall. It showcased how the Silver Bear Shop & Factory had won the Teddy Bear Keepsake contest. "Maddie, where's the wizard bear photo?"

"Here, and we'd better open up. People are lined up outside."

Customers streamed into the shop, mostly women, holding babies or carrying toddlers, red cheeked but excited. Everyone oohed and aahed while they walked through the rooms or waited for cups of hot chocolate, coffee, tea, and treats.

"Yes, this is our Magic of Christmas Beary Potter Keepsake wizard bear," Maddie said to several women asking questions. "We're no longer taking orders, however, but you can find them through the shops listed in the brochure."

"It's so clever. What a wonderful costume."

"I bet they'll bring a high price on eBay," someone said.

No doubt, but that was beyond our control.

One little boy held his six-inch wizard bear with its black robe, maroon and gold scarf, and wand. Round-rimmed glasses perched on the nose, and we'd included a tiny lightning scar applique sewn onto Beary Potter's furry forehead.

"Sean, have 'Beary' cast a spell on another bear," his mother said.

"Ally kazam! You're a cat."

"A cat bear? Interesting," I said with a laugh.

Mary Kate was swamped at the hot chocolate table, while Elle showed several girls how to dress their bears for the holidays. I snitched a Date Nut Jingle Bell cookie and then replenished the tray, tossed my latex gloves, and refilled the coffee urns.

At exactly eleven o'clock, a voice boomed from the loft. "Beary Christmas, one and all! Have you been good boys and girls? That's paws-itively fantastic!"

Everyone craned their necks to see my dad dressed as Santa Bear at the top of the stairs. Joan Kendall and Pam North had designed and sewn a new costume, making sure it was different than Cal Bloom's polar bear outfit. Dad wanted it to be lighter and more breathable. The end result was a tall brown bear, oddly similar to Paddington Bear except for the head and a longer snout. He wore a red and white Santa coat and hat, glittery black belt, and boots.

Elle the Elf waved to the delighted children. "Who wants to visit Santa Bear? Right this way, no running! Up the stairs, that's it. He's a special friend to Santa Claus, so tell him what you'd like under the tree this year. He can't promise that you'll get every toy on Christmas morning, but he has a special treat for every child." She held up a tiny bear with angel wings.

"Santa Bear! Santa Bear!"

I guided the few mothers carrying babies to the elevator. "Easier than climbing the stairs. And thanks for attending our open house."

"We've never missed one yet." A young woman shifted her toddler to the other hip. "How wonderful to have Santa Bear back in the village, and in a new costume. It can't be the mayor. That was awful, hearing about his heart attack."

I nodded, grateful that the elevator doors opened. The mothers joined the throng waiting their turn with Santa Bear. Dad was in his element, sitting in a padded rocking chair, and Elle was helpful in keeping the line moving.

I headed back downstairs to check on the treats, which had depleted fast. Aunt Eve and Maddie were refilling everything, and Mary Kate had gone to the restroom. Someone wanted a cup of hot chocolate. I managed to perch the tiny gingerbread house without breaking it.

"These cookies are scrummy." Tess Wentworth held up a Date Nut Jingle Bell. "Any idea where I can get them, love? Our last Christmas tea is being held this Sunday."

"I'll write down the information." I jotted Hilda's, Flora's, and Amanda's names and phone numbers after looking them up on my cell. "Mary Kate at Fresh Grounds made the *Little Lord Fauntleroy* Bears, but you probably know that."

"Oh, yes. We ordered a good number in their little plastic sleeves. A marvelous take-home for guests." Tess winked. "Ta, what a lovely event. I'm so glad I toodled over today. Any word when they'll open the street at Main?"

"Sorry, I haven't heard anything."

"Could be the village council has a bit on their minds, what with the mayor's death.

Ah, well. Happy Christmas, Sasha, to you and your family."

"Same to you. Thanks for coming!"

Tess wove her way through the crowd. I managed to dodge a question about the mayor, glad they didn't press the issue. I wanted to enjoy this event without thinking about Alison or Kristen Bloom, or anything else about the investigation.

I took a break to check on Rosie. She wasn't in her crate or on the window seat. Onyx blinked from the top ledge of the cat tower, yawned, and then jumped down to saunter into the laundry room. My dog had to be in there. What had she gotten into now? Rosie raised her head, stretched across a basket of clean towels, and then returned to her nap. Kibble pieces were strewn over the tile floor, too. I scolded her, carried her back to the kitchen and shut the crate door. I'd have to clean up the mess later.

"I hope you know you're in trouble, little girl." She looked so forlorn, I unhooked her crate door. "No more getting into trouble. And I'm putting up the gate so you can't go upstairs."

I returned to the shop, wondering if getting another dog might help keep Rosie company. Or would it double the trouble? I'd have to think on that.

The crowd hadn't thinned much by two o'clock. Mary Kate and I added other treats to the empty cookie trays — chocolate-coated pretzel rods, peppermint bark pieces, and teddy bear gummies. Maddie abandoned her red high heels and donned my teddy bear slippers. Dad took a break from the costume, although the lighter fur fabric and foam base for the head was a big improvement. Despite a tiny battery-powered exhaust fan inside, he felt too warm.

"I'll be back, an hour or less."

By four o'clock, school-age kids had arrived. Parents must have spread the news about our Santa Bear, and even though the older ones had given up believing, they wanted to high-five Dad and get a photo taken. Elle had left to pick up her kids. I'd sent Mary Kate home long ago, when we'd run out of gingerbread houses. All of the angel bears were gone. We'd planned to close at five, but decided to keep going until we ran out of treats or people. Garrett Thompson sent over more boxes of iced sugar cookies. They vanished within an hour.

Mom arrived at six. I'd expected her earlier, though, and wondered where she'd been all this time. Christmas shopping? Not that she promised to pitch in, of course, but we would have appreciated an extra pair of hands. She stared openmouthed at a broken teddy bear cookie in its wrapper lying on the floor, along with chocolate candy crushed underfoot, and a scattered mess of coffee, tea, and hot chocolate cups.

"Looks like a tornado went through this place."

I collected the abandoned cups and broken cookie. "Third time I've done this."

Aunt Eve brought a fresh plastic bag. "I'll help clean up the mess."

"So it's over now?" Mom asked.

"Ten minutes." I glanced at the stragglers leaving out the front door, and then called up to the loft. "Hey, Dad. Check to make sure no kids are hiding up there!"

She eyed me in disbelief. "Really, Sasha?"

"Last year we found a three-year-old eating cookies under the loft table. He made a tent with an afghan, so yeah, it happens. And some parents are forgetful. Or don't you remember leaving Maddie and me behind one day at the mall?"

"You were nine, and old enough to not panic." Mom looked sheepish. "That was a horrible day. I'm glad you had enough sense to flag down one of the security guards."

"They took us to the management office,

except you didn't know that."

"I should have checked there before running around the mall, searching, and then calling the police. Thank God we have cell phones now."

Dad emerged from the elevator, alone. "No kids, and I'm bushed. Takes a lot of energy to listen to so many kids, asking for *Star Wars* lightsabers, Legos of all kinds, the Elsa doll from *Frozen,* Barbies, and Pet Shop toys. What are those? I knew dinosaurs would never go out of fashion, but hoverboards? What happened to tea party sets or Tonka trucks?"

"Boy, are you dating yourself." Maddie chuckled. "Don't forget all the video games for Nintendo and PlayStation. One kid wanted his own motorized car."

"Can't wait to grow up, I guess."

"Elle told me one little girl wanted a job for her dad," I said.

"Heartbreaking, isn't it," Aunt Eve said. "I looked up some numbers of organizations for the mother, plus gave her Marianna Lovett's number. They have a food pantry."

Mom waved her hands. "Hello? I have news, good and bad. But I ordered dinner brought in from Flambé. I figured we'd be tired of pizza, tacos, and lasagna."

"First we have to clean up and move

everything back into place," I said, "because we're still open until Friday. Then we have the staff party to prep for on Saturday."

"Nah, you all look beat." Uncle Ross had arrived, and drew Aunt Eve to her feet. "Leave it for morning, and I'll send over Tim and Deon, plus a few others. They can get the shop ready for business tomorrow."

"But —"

"Sasha, really. You look exhausted." Mom glanced at her wristwatch. "Dinner should be coming any minute. Are any staff still working at the factory, Ross?"

"Nope. I sent 'em home at five today. They deserved it." He sounded gruff but with an underlying tone of pride. "They worked hard on that Santa Bear costume, too. How was it, Alex? I hope you didn't suffocate, since heat rises to the loft. Did you roast?"

"Baste me, I'm done." Dad set the foam head aside. "Actually, it wasn't bad at all. That fan is a real lifesaver."

"Joan Kendall watched a YouTube video on mascot costumes," I said. "That's how she knew about crafting the head and installing the fan."

Dad gingerly removed the hat, belt, and the Santa coat by its Velcro fastenings. Maddie and I each pulled off a boot, while Mom helped him out of the furry body.

"We'll dress you up for St. Patrick's Day with a green hat and bow tie," Maddie said. "And a stars and stripes shirt for the Fourth of July parade."

"Hire someone younger, with more stamina."

Mom herded us out of the shop and down the hall to our living quarters. I ran upstairs to wriggle out of my skirt and change to comfortable sweats. I also reclaimed my slippers from Maddie and held Rosie tight when she began barking.

Christophe Benoit, the restaurant owner, carried in the boxes from Flambé. "My assistant was detained, that is why your order is late. My apologies."

"I heard that Gus Antonini is at the police station," Mom said. "Detective Mason took him and Cissy Davison in for questioning."

Benoit shrugged. "Yes, Madame. You ordered tenderloin medallions of beef in cream sauce, potato croquettes, salad, chicken portobello linguini with spinach and sun-dried tomatoes, and raspberry cheesecake. Bon appétit."

"Hope things work out for him." Dad shook his hand and tipped the chef.

Once he departed we all sat down, Mom rapped the table. "Finally I can tell you the good news. Alison Bloom is bringing in several of Cal's colleagues, members of the Michigan Funeral Directors Association, to survey the business. She wants to know how much it's worth, for one thing, and if Dave Richardson has kept it up to standards. She hopes that a corporate chain will be interested in buying it."

"That's good news?" Dad looked dismayed. "Dave has his heart set on taking it over, and wants to keep it a family-owned business."

"That's the bad news. Alison has no intention of selling to him. Ever."

CHAPTER 22

Dad laid down his fork. "Did Alison tell you why?"

"No. I tried talking to her, but she wouldn't discuss the matter," Mom said. "Not until Friday, when she has more information."

"Judith, you've got to talk sense into her. Dave's been there for —"

"You don't have to tell me! I know how long he's worked for Cal, how much he did for Cal, how much he learned from Cal, and how Dave kissed his feet. And backside."

"That's unfair and you know it."

I mouthed, "Wow" to Maddie. Aunt Eve caught that and nodded, twirling a finger near her temple. Meaning Alison, not my mother, I hoped. Uncle Ross had his usual sour look.

"Family owned is better than a corporate chain."

"But she wants to get the most she can get out of it," Mom said. "Everything depends on the investigation, you know that. The police believe Alison had motive, and this latest news won't help one bit. Especially since she raised the life insurance benefits. But they have to prove her guilt. Right, Alex?"

"All the paperwork to transfer the business was drawn up by lawyers —"

"But without Cal's signature, it means nothing. Alison swore he changed his mind. Mark Branson is representing her, you know. He's sharp, intelligent, but quiet. Sasha, is he older or younger than his sister Mary Kate?"

"Older. Number three of six kids, and Mary Kate's the youngest."

"I didn't realize she had such a big family." Mom turned back to Dad. "Anyway, Mark is quite different than Flynn, who can be a little full of himself."

"A little?" I choked on a piece of beef. Maddie pounded on my back, which didn't help. Finally, I managed to swallow and gulped some water. "That's an understatement."

"Never mind. I'm glad the open house went so well."

My sister changed the subject. "Speaking

of cookies —"

She rambled on about how everyone had loved the gingerbread houses and iced teddy bears. I'd been surprised at how moist the Date Nut Jingle Bells tasted, more cake-like, chockfull of fruit and delicious.

"What about the snowballs that won the contest? They were melt-in-the-mouth fantastic," Aunt Eve said. "And so pretty with the cranberries and nuts inside."

"Amanda is making eighteen dozen for the staff party," Maddie said.

"That should be plenty. So we don't need a wedding cake —"

"Already ordered it." Mom wiped her mouth with a napkin. "You never told me what flavor you wanted, so I chose cherry nut. The design is a surprise. And we're buying you a new living room set for your condo, as a wedding gift from all of us."

"What?" Aunt Eve's mouth dropped open. "No, Judith. Our furniture is perfectly fine. The cake, yes, but —"

"I'm not listening." She blocked her ears. "You can choose vintage style if you want, since it's all the rage now, but you're getting new stuff. If you don't pick out the items, I'll choose for you. We want it delivered by Christmas."

Dad laughed. "You know Judith. Better

smile and say, 'Thank you,' because you'll lose the battle in the end."

That was also an understatement. Mom always meant well, though, unlike Flynn. He wasn't generous to a fault like my mother, either. Except for the huge diamond he'd bestowed on Cheryl Cummings. I snuffed out that twinge of jealousy. Flynn was out of my life, a blessing, and I ought to be grateful. Maybe Maddie was right. With a new wife, he'd be too busy to come nosing around and bothering me.

Once everyone finished dinner, Maddie and I cleared the table. We'd have two pieces of leftover cheesecake for breakfast. I rinsed the dishes and then loaded the dishwasher while my sister wiped the table. Our usual chores from childhood. Why did we fall back into old habits so easily? Some things never changed. Except for the funeral home, evidenced by Alison Bloom's vehement rejection of Dave Richardson. I couldn't help wondering what was behind that.

Maddie and I trudged upstairs after the others left for home, weary, our pets following. My sister sat cross-legged on my window seat and switched on the tiny battery under her top. The lights flashed merrily in the glass's reflection. Onyx jumped up beside her, curious, eyeing her shirt, while

Maddie stared out the window. I kicked off my slippers and nestled in an armchair. I wanted to crash, but something was on her mind.

"So what did you think about Alison and Dave?" she asked at last. "Maybe they have some bad history. Something has to be wrong, or she'd sell the place to him."

"Yeah, so it seems."

"Oh, come on. Don't tell me you're not curious to find out."

I waggled my index finger. "I never said that."

"Aha." Maddie grinned. "So the sleuth will get busy."

"It depends on what Mom can wrangle out of her first. Alison lied to my face, remember, and I bet she blames me for Mason questioning her again." I yawned. "Anything else? I am so whipped. I didn't get much sleep last night."

"I can tell by the bags under your eyes. Girl, go put some night cream on or you'll look like an old crone," she teased. "Keep me posted, although I'll be busy all week. Text me if you do find out anything. Mom tells you stuff before she does me."

"That's not true —"

"Don't go there, Sash." With a laugh, Maddie headed to her room. Onyx followed, still fascinated by her shirt's flashing lights.

I slid under the covers, hoping to reclaim the hours I'd lost last night. But sleep eluded me again. Tossing and turning gained nothing but a neck ache, so I switched my Kindle on and tried to read. A wonderful historical mystery, with a duo of private inquiry agents much like Holmes and Watson. I immersed myself in Victorian London for a few hours, at least, until my eyes refused to stay open. And slept through my alarm clock.

"Sash, wake up! It's after nine. I'm late for work, too." Maddie shook me again, hard, and then rushed out when I rubbed my eyes. "Coffee's getting cold."

"Nnngh." I needed a hefty swig to fuel my energy. "What day is it?"

"Wednesday," she called out. "Happy Hump Day."

I felt like a hump, or more like a lump of lead. Yesterday was Tuesday, and the open house. Memories flooded back. The noise, the excitement of kids seeing Dad dressed as Santa Bear, and all those wonderful cookies. And cheesecake for breakfast. I headed for the shower, pulled my wet hair into a ponytail and dressed. Turned my shirt right-side-out, and then grubbed through the dresser drawers for matching socks. By the time I got Rosie outside, fed, and grabbed my coffee mug, the clock showed ten fifteen.

"You're late, but thankfully, no customers showed up yet." Aunt Eve smiled when I sank onto a chair with a huge yawn. "I tried calling you. I even texted, although I don't know if I did it right. These newfangled phones are beyond me. Tim, Deon, and Flora Zimmerman came in at seven this morning. Everything's back in place, so that's good. Flora supervised the whole thing, telling them where to put the racks, and making them spot clean the floor."

"Wow. We'll have to give them extra in their Christmas bonus."

"Flora deserves double for making all those gorgeous gingerbread houses. They were the hit of the open house."

"The staff party on Saturday —" I yawned again. "Everything's been ordered, right?"

"Yes, and it starts at two o'clock. I'm praying it won't snow."

"I hope so, too. I'd hate for people to not come, after we ordered all those cookies from Amanda. She's working so hard."

Aunt Eve laughed and then waved at the phone. "People will love them. I've had three calls in the last ten minutes, asking which bakery made the cookies yesterday.

Everyone knew the teddy bears came from Fresh Grounds, though."

She snatched up the receiver when it rang again. Pulling out my cell, I noticed several missed texts. Not from my aunt, but from Maddie, Mary Kate, and Isabel French, who'd left a voice mail as well. I listened and felt bad that her dad had fallen last night. Mrs. French needed her help today, since he'd been taken to the hospital for X-rays.

I texted back, telling her to take as much time as she needed. Family first, that was the Silverman family's mantra. Then I called Mary Kate. "Hey, what's up?"

"Uncle Gil's on the warpath," she whispered. "He's here, ranting about what happened, so I can't talk loud. Did you hear that Alison Bloom refuses to sell out to Dave Richardson? And she wants a big chain to buy the funeral home! Even Garrett's upset. The whole village is talking about how unfair it is."

"I heard. But people can't boycott the funeral home, like Starbucks or Amazon."

That was a poor joke, but Mary Kate giggled anyway. "We'll talk later, okay?"

She hung up. Next, I called Maddie, since she'd called while I was either in the shower or getting dressed. Before I had a chance to share what Mary Kate said, my sister cut me off.

"Mom's probably blowing a gasket. Digger stopped by the minute I unlocked the door and said Mrs. Bloom was taken in for questioning last night, at midnight. I guess Mason wanted to grill her again about stuff," Maddie said. "And you won't believe who saw her leave the Silver Birches on the day of the parade!"

"Grandma Silverman."

She gasped. "You knew, and didn't tell me?"

"First, I wasn't sure if I could trust what she said, and I haven't had a chance to confirm it with anyone else there. We know Grandma's sharp, but other people might not believe it."

"Digger said two other residents saw Mrs. Bloom returning, around eight o'clock. So she must have left for sure at some point."

"Hey, I have to call you later. Customers."

Reluctantly, I hung up. Three strings of jingle bells made a merry sound, but it felt more like hammers tapping on my skull. I gulped coffee while the couple browsed the shop. Not that it helped. Other people arrived to pick up their wizard bears, and a number of visitors expressed their disappointment over missing our open house for one reason or another.

"Put it on your calendar for next year, then. We enjoy hosting it."

"I heard it was wonderful," one woman said, "and who baked the cookies?"

Maybe Mary Kate would end up with more competition than from Vivian Grant's Pretty in Pink bakery. I made a list of the contest bakers' names and phone numbers and gulped a second and third cup of coffee. The day dragged on forever, and missed opportunities defined the hours. Jay left a voice mail, since I'd set my cell phone to vibrate and forgot to reset the ringer. When I called him back, his phone went to voice mail. So did Maddie's.

Frustrating wasn't the word.

At six o'clock, I turned the sign to CLOSED. I'd enjoyed watching a dad shop with his two daughters. They'd insisted on choosing their own teddy bears for Christmas, instead of trusting Santa Claus. One wanted a Santa suit, but the other sister wanted a purple summer dress. I sent Aunt Eve to hunt through our storage rooms upstairs. She brought two dresses, sandals, and a tiny beach umbrella. Delighted, the family bought the lot plus a sled to fit both bears.

I brushed away a tear after they left. I

couldn't wait to share such moments with my own kids. One day.

Thursday proved easier. I'd finally caught up on sleep, and talked to Jay on Friday during my lunch hour walk with Rosie. While she wandered over the Village Green, and I hung onto her extended leash, Jay suggested all kinds of things to do between Christmas Eve and New Year's. He also made me promise to call on Saturday night after our staff party. Bright sunshine warmed my face and boosted my mood.

Even the investigation into Cal Bloom's death had taken a back seat.

"Sasha! Over here," Maggie Davison called out.

She beckoned from her shop doorway on Main Street. I tugged Rosie's leash when she resisted at first but she trotted into the Magpie's Nest in hopes of a treat.

"Sorry, Rosie. I don't have a cookie for you," Maggie said, "unless you want a piece of leftover bacon? Oh, you do? Why am I not surprised."

We both laughed when my dog gobbled the strip in one bite. "What's up?" I asked. "I've got to get back to the shop."

"You haven't heard, then?"

"Heard what?"

"Alison Bloom's in the hospital."

"What? How did she end up in the hospital?"

"Kristen took her in last night. Alison was so dizzy with vertigo, and she couldn't stop throwing up." Maggie made a face. "Yuck."

"Alison Bloom must have caught a bug. I heard plenty of residents at the Silver Birches have come down sick. Jack Cullen's in the hospital." I straightened my shoulders. "Wait. Didn't she have that meeting today, with the funeral directors?"

"Yeah, bad timing. And Mr. Cullen passed last night. Why do so many people die during the holidays?" Maggie sounded wistful. "My mom did. Not that Aunt Barbara ever cared, and she expected me and Dad for Christmas dinner anyway that year. I absolutely refused. Maybe that's why Aunt Barb hates me so much."

"She doesn't hate you."

Maggie tossed her curly hair. "Yes, she does, and so does Cissy. They both want me to give up this shop. I'm thinking it's not what I want, since Uncle Richard talked me into it. I'll sell or give away all this stuff to whoever wants it, and move to Chicago."

I sympathized with her but took my leave. Rosie and I crossed the street to Fresh Grounds, where I picked up my lunchtime bagel. Wendy pulled shots for lines of customers, while Garrett worked the cash register. I didn't get a chance to ask either of them if they'd heard anything new. I headed back outside and dialed my mother's cell phone number. Her voice mail kicked in, too. Dang.

Mom was bound to know everything about Alison. She might be at the hospital right now, in fact. I walked faster toward the shop. Being late twice in one day — horrors.

"The manager might dock my pay," I said to Rosie, but she didn't laugh.

We made it back with one minute to spare, with no waiting customers. When Renee Truman showed up at two, I rushed to the factory's shipping department. Deon and Tim didn't need an extra pair of hands and sent me to Flora Zimmerman. She frowned, and then directed me to help sort fabric pieces once they were collected from the cutting machine.

Not the most glamorous job, but it kept me well away from the sewing machines. Sorting took more brain power than I realized. I had to recheck my work several times and count the pieces, making sure I didn't miss a limb or an ear piece for each individual bear.

"Ms. Silverman?" Tim Richardson waited

until I glanced up from the board in front of me. "Detective Mason's here to see you. Over in shipping."

"Uh, okay. Thanks."

I glanced around, hoping no one had heard Tim, but Joan Kendall and other workers watched with curiosity when I followed him. Mason stood chatting with Uncle Ross. That was a big shock. He'd been the prime suspect in our sales representative's murder earlier this year, and resented being targeted. Apparently, my uncle had gotten over that. They laughed together and then shook hands. Mason turned to me next.

"Mind if we find someplace private?" he asked. "Unless you want to come over to the station. I've got a closet for an office."

"A closet?"

"Literally." He pushed up his glasses. "I like this place better."

"Follow me, then."

I led the way to the stuffing machine, enclosed in its own room. Jay had put up the walls, installed the door, and even added shelves for storing the huge twenty-five-pound bags of polyester fiberfill. I didn't like being here, but there wasn't another option.

"That's a lot of stuffing," Mason said.

"Each sixteen-inch bear takes half a pound, so we go through a lot of these bags every week." I leaned against the edge of the shelves without glancing at the machine. "Have you caught up on Detective Hunter's notes?"

"Still haven't gotten them. Unless they ended up in my Spam folder. If he printed them out, they could be buried with the other case folders on my desk."

"How many others?"

"A dozen or more." He shrugged and took out his notebook and pen. "Some are from a couple years ago. We keep hoping for a fresh lead, a witness who decides to talk. You never know what might turn up. Okay, did you happen to see Tony Crocker at any point during the parade? And what time."

Everything seemed fuzzy, since so much had happened. The days and weeks all jumbled together. Taking a deep breath, I closed my eyes to concentrate. "I did see him, before the mayor went off to get into his costume. They argued about the election. Crocker demanded a recount. Mom wasn't happy about that, since it would have cost the village a lot of money."

"Yeah, he admitted that. He also claimed that Phil Hunter threatened him."

"Isabel French told me she overheard

them. I guess Hunter told Crocker he'd better not make trouble for the Blooms. Or something like that."

Mason looked disgusted by that information. He was silent, jotting it all in his notebook. "Okay, thanks. I'm tying up loose ends, since Hunter didn't follow through on much. Anything else you might want to add? Rumors about the murder, I mean."

"No, but how is Mrs. Bloom? I heard she's in the hospital." I hesitated, and then rushed on. "Maybe this sounds silly, but she was supposed to have a meeting with many of Cal Bloom's colleagues from the Michigan Funeral Directors Association. She wanted to find out how much the business is worth, and find an interested buyer."

"Okay. So?"

"Remember that Dave Richardson wanted to buy it. Expected to buy it, in fact. Cal Bloom had papers drawn up for the sale in the spring."

"I don't see the connection."

"What if —"

"What if it was something she ate for dinner? There's always some kind of food safety alert coming out about E. coli or other types of contamination." Mason thrust his notebook into his coat pocket. "I'll go check out what the doctor thinks, but I'm due back for a meeting on the Ypsilanti case. I can't miss it. I don't trust Hunter to handle things."

"So does Chief Russell agree, that Cal Bloom was murdered?" I asked.

"I never said that."

"But what about the blow to the head?"

"Yeah, well . . ." Mason sighed. "Your chief finds it hard to believe someone would target such a friendly guy. Me, I know anything can happen."

He headed for the exit. I shut the door to the stuffing room, shivering a little, and returned to sorting fabric pieces for our teddy bears. My curiosity gnawed at me while I worked. Even if Chief Russell didn't agree, no one had to convince me.

Murder will out, as Chaucer once wrote.

CHAPTER 23

I spent Friday night preparing for the next day's combination staff party and wedding in the factory. I'd bribed my friends Elle and Wendy into helping, too. Elle brought Mary Kate and insisted she sit to supervise while we worked.

"But I'm past the miscarriage stage —"

"You've been on your feet all day, Mary Kate. Give those puppies a rest," Elle said. "Come on, Sasha. Help me with the wedding decorations."

"Mom's bringing them tomorrow morning, so we need to set up tables and then tape the floor for the Reindeer Race."

We laid down long strips of duct tape in the space that Deon, Tim, Uncle Ross, and my dad had cleared. They'd lined the sewing machines against the windows, so we covered them with white sheets. While Christmas songs played on Elle's phone, "Santa Baby," and "I Want a Hippopotamus for Christmas," we arranged the tables, covered them with green linen cloths, and set up chairs. Amanda Pozniak had delivered her boxes of Cranberry Walnut Snowball cookies earlier that day, so I led my friends on a raid.

After we sampled a few and brushed away any evidence of powdered sugar, I handed them pairs of elastic gloves. "Ready to fill the trays?"

Elle snapped a glove over one hand. "Yes, Dr. Silverman."

"It's not brain surgery!" Mary Kate giggled. "Behave."

Once we arranged the cookies and covered the trays with plastic, they headed home. I let Rosie outside before bedtime and curled up with a blanket, a book, and my dog for some relaxed reading. I woke at one o'clock in the morning, the book tilted sideways, and rubbed my stiff neck. Rosie and I headed upstairs to bed. I rolled over and closed my eyes. Hmm. My mind raced between the investigation, the upcoming wedding, and the wizard bear deadline.

Sitting up, I reached for my cell and checked for any text messages. Nada from Jay. But there was a voice mail notification. Mom had returned my call, which I missed since I'd left the phone near the bed. And she sounded worried during the playback.

"Alison hasn't regained consciousness. The doctors aren't sure what brought this on, but it's not flu. They're doing all kinds of lab tests, blood work and such, but it could have been something she ate that had given her —"

Beep. I winced at that loud and annoying sound, signaling the cutoff time. Mom hadn't called again with more information. Could it be food poisoning? After what happened to Cal Bloom, I wondered if the killer also wanted Alison dead.

Was Kristen that greedy? Things would fall into place for her after the sale of the Silver Scoop. She'd get her yoga studio. But what if that million dollar life insurance policy tempted her? That I couldn't answer. I didn't know her that well, but it seemed so vicious.

I rolled over again, still restless. Our shop was closed for the party today, and I'd be able to sleep in. Our staff wouldn't arrive earlier than one thirty. I forced myself to count sheep. Then counted numbers, from one hundred backward, until I lost track in the forties . . . and woke when Rosie's stomach grumbled near my ear. I shoved her off my pillow.

"Girl, you need a bath!"

Rubbing my eyes, I checked the clock. Half past ten. Whoa. That couldn't be right, given the bedroom's darkness. I sat bolt upright. At a rumble of thunder, Rosie trembled and crept closer, whimpering. I hugged her to my chest.

"It's okay, baby. I'll find out what's going on."

I padded over to the window and stared in awe. Snowflakes swirled, mixed with a misty rain, and lightning flashed in the distance. Once again thunder rolled farther off. Wow. Michigan weather could be unpredictable, but thunder snow was the coolest phenomenon ever. I sank onto the cushion and watched until I was thoroughly chilled. A hot shower warmed me up, though. Once I used my hair dryer, I rushed Rosie downstairs and outside.

She hated rain and snow, but I refused to sympathize. Once she returned, I toweled my dog dry and fed her breakfast. Ate a quick bowl of yogurt and berries, then hurried to don what I'd chosen to wear for today's party.

Maddie had long ago planned an "Ugly Christmas Sweater" theme for the party, but we scrapped that after adding Uncle Ross and Aunt Eve's wedding. When the happy couple decided no one needed to dress up, I'd rejoiced and shoved the too-tight dress back in my closet. Instead, I wore comfortable black jeans and a red sweater with a huge green stocking appliqued on the front. A perfect pocket for the tiny candy canes that I planned to give all the kids attending.

"Hooray, no heels today."

Or Spanx, come to think of it. I brushed my hair and braided two pigtails, then tied them with red velvet ribbons. I checked the mirror for mascara smudges and shoved my feet into red ballet flats. After checking that Onyx was happy, I barricaded the kitchen so that Rosie wouldn't get into trouble. I donned a warm coat, opened an umbrella, and walked slowly to the factory. Uncle Ross had scattered salt over the parking lot and paths, which crunched underfoot. I waved to Maddie who was busy hanging silver bells over the doorway.

"Sleeping Beauty, at last. I took pity on you, since Mom drove over at six this morning to put up the wedding decorations. She wanted a Scottish theme, but I'm glad she didn't overdo it. What do you think?"

Each table had a bouquet of purple heather in a glass vase, with raffia and a lovely plaid ribbon bow. The "tree" of white poinsettias in the corner looked stunning.

My mother had strung more silver bells from the rafters, which tinkled softly from the overhead fans. And each place setting had a pair of Belgian chocolate bears in gold foil. In the center, a table for two had been covered in white linen and pinned with an ivy garland. Purple heather had been added to an evergreen and holly berry floral arrangement surrounding an unlit cream candle.

"Reserved for the newlyweds? Fabulous. Are Mom and Dad acting as witnesses?"

Maddie nodded. "Last week Aunt Eve dragged Uncle Ross to apply and pay for the marriage license. She had to search for their official divorce papers, too. And Mayor Bloom was supposed to marry them, you know. Aunt Eve asked Pastor Lovett instead."

"I bet Uncle Ross wasn't happy about that."

"He wanted Judge Starr, but the courthouse isn't open on Saturdays."

I snickered. "So he will be married in church, after all. We ought to crash it."

"Uncle Ross always said he'd be struck by lightning if he walked through the doors. Maybe the weather today is cooperating."

After another rumble of thunder, we cracked up and then clapped a hand over our mouths when Joan Kendall arrived early. Deon also carried in his DJ equipment and set up in the corner opposite the poinsettia tree. He'd promised to play all the Christmas favorites, old and new.

"So what else needs to be done?" I asked Maddie.

"Nothing until the caterers arrive."

Harriet Amato, who'd retired in late summer, breezed in with her family along with Pam North, Renee Truman, and Tim Richardson.

"Is Jay coming today?" Pam asked me.

"He's near Grayling, teaching a woodcarving class."

"Oh, that's right." She looked crestfallen for a minute. "I'll have to call and remind him about my New Year's Eve party. He said he'd drop by at some point."

Pam wandered off to join the other staff. I wondered why she sounded so pleased. Jay insisted their relationship had ended long ago. I swallowed hard, recalling the New Year's Eve when I discovered the truth about Flynn's cheating. Finding him and a friend in our bed had been devastating. It had taken years for me to trust anyone again.

I turned my attention to Harriet and her husband, trying hard to keep their grandkids from touching everything. Harriet's bluish-silver curls hadn't changed, and she still wore the chain with a pair of magnifying glasses around her neck.

"Welcome to the party!" I greeted each of the kids with a tiny candy cane. "I see you brought gumdrops. Is that for the Head Start program?"

"Nana says the kids will make candy trains," one boy said. "How come we can't make a train? I wanna make a train today."

"We'll make one at home. No touching, I said!" Harriet pulled him away before he could grab one of the largest candy bars from a bag. She held up a large tote with a knitted afghan. "So where do we put the gifts for Ross and Eve? I made this for them."

"It's lovely," I said. So much for specifying "no gifts" on the invites we'd sent. "Your daughter and Mary Monroe did a beautiful job on my family's teddy bear and flower wreaths for both funerals last week."

"She's very talented, my Norma." Harriet scolded the other grandson when he jumped to hit the doorway's silver bells. "Leave them be, or we'll have to go home."

More staff members arrived and dropped off bags of peppermint candies, licorice ropes, pretzels, gum, crackers, and smaller chocolate bars. I sent Tim Richardson to scrounge around the shipping department for a box to store it all. At a table where we planned the "Wrap a Bear" contest, Maddie set out rolls of holiday paper, bows and ribbon, tape, and other decorations. That was always another fun game.

"Hey, Sasha." Mary Kate looked adorable, her strawberry-blond hair curling over her shoulders, and wearing a sweater with Cookie Monster and NO COOKIES FOR SANTA spelled out. "We'll set up the Hot Chocolate Bar over there."

"That game's too easy," Garrett said, shifting little Julie to his other arm.

"No boxes or bags, just the teddy bears which are harder to wrap than you'd think. And whoever does the best job will get a plastic headband with bear ears."

"I'd be all thumbs," Mary Kate said.

"Some people go for the 'worst job' prize instead," I told them. "It's all in good fun. We donate the bears to the police department, and they're given to comfort kids after a car accident, or if a social worker removes them from abusive homes. Another group donates blankets, and that helps when the kids end up in foster care. The power of teddy bears!"

"Julie's blanket and teddy bear give her

comfort." Mary Kate wiped away tears with her thumbs. "Sorry, I cry over everything now."

Isabel French arrived with her mother, although Mrs. French seemed uneasy until my parents arrived. Mom greeted her warmly and chatted about the Silver Birches. Relieved, Isabel rushed over to greet me with contagious enthusiasm.

"I love working here! I can't thank you enough for hiring me."

I smiled. "How's your dad? Did he break anything in that fall?"

"No, thank goodness. But he was pretty upset and bruised."

"This party is designed to kick back and relax, so enjoy yourself. It will help, especially given the craziness with our wizard bear."

"My aunt said she bought one in Chicago. She loves it."

Flora Zimmerman sidled over and squeezed Isabel's arm. "This one's a fast learner, Sasha. The best you've hired in a while."

"Thank you." Isabel blushed.

"I'd recommend two other seasonal workers if you want to hire them full time. Chevonne Lang is a whiz at sewing, she's over there with all those braids. And Karen

Anderson has past experience crafting new patterns for outfits."

"Thanks, I'll talk to my aunt and uncle about them. I wish I could hire Renee Truman, but she's finishing her degree."

"In what?"

"I'm not sure, but I can ask her. She's over by the church pantry table."

Renee looked up from arranging a large donation of canned goods and boxes when we joined her. "My mom sent all this," she said. "Dad lost his job a few years back, and it took him a while to find a new position. We're grateful for the church's help."

I nodded, although my family never experienced such hardship. My college degree had been paid for in full, minus a few scholarships, but I researched for Dad whenever he needed more than his law clerks could handle. So many people lived paycheck to paycheck, juggling loan payments, mortgages or rent, utility, health, and grocery bills, and my woes of a bad marriage and divorce paled in comparison. I resented Lois and Harry Nichols, though, who expected easy money and perks without putting in the work.

"So what kind of degree are you working toward?" Flora asked Renee.

"I started in physical therapy, but now it's

a seven-year doctoral program. I switched to occupational, which is a lot less time and money. But it's hard, taking classes, studying, and working part-time, too."

"We were just talking about that," I said. "If you can, I'd like you to keep working for us. I'm willing to work around a flexible schedule."

She hugged me tight. "It's an answer to prayer. Oh, look!"

Dad carried in the four custom-made plastic reindeer heads, complete with antlers and blinking red noses, from our shop's storage room. And Mom brought the four child-size hobby horses, along with several rolls of duct tape. Maddie had come up with the idea at our first staff party, but the papier-mâché heads proved too fragile. Everyone loved the game, though, and it had quickly become a favorite tradition. I started tearing strips of duct tape.

"I volunteered to videotape the Reindeer Race," Garrett said to me. "Elle and Matt are jealous that we were invited to the party this year."

"After you baked all those teddy bear cookies for the open house? But Matt and Elle are coming with the kids, too, because they can't miss the wedding. Plus, cake!"

"That's a bonus, especially since Mary

Kate baked it."

We all pitched in to prepare for the game. Part of the fun was straddling the hobby horse sticks with their taped-on, awkward reindeer heads, despite being lightweight, and much too short for adults. Maddie also attached "reins" of sturdy rope beneath the heads. The rest of the staff who arrived gave a rousing cheer for the games, which drowned out the "Grandma Got Run Over by a Reindeer" song that Deon played over his speakers.

"I'll beat you today," Tim said, but Deon shook his head.

"No way, bro. Not gonna happen."

Dad walked over and showed off his YETI TO PARTY sweatshirt, with the blue and white furry and toothless Abominable Snowman from the *Rudolph the Red-Nosed Reindeer* television special. Mom's red OH DEER sweater with appliqued antlers looked cute on her, and she wore dangling reindeer earrings.

"Did you both wear those outfits to the wedding?"

"Of course not." Mom laughed, eyeing the polished wood floor. "I don't think I'll risk my neck playing the reindeer game. It's bound to be slippery in stocking feet."

"That's the fun part," Dad said, "seeing

who breaks a leg."

"Not fun, actually. Someone always sprains an arm or ankle."

My cousin Matt and Elle arrived with Cara and Celia, who proudly carried two huge bags of candy and placed them on the Head Start table. When I tickled their necks, they both wriggled in excitement.

"Looks like you two robbed a candy store. Did you? I bet you did."

"No, we didn't!" They both giggled in delight.

"Oh, look at Aunt Maddie. I want a dress like that," Celia said.

My sister twirled around for the girls. "I made this from a Christmas tree skirt. See the snowman, and a penguin, and Santa Claus in his sleigh."

"With all his reindeer," Cara said, wide-eyed. "And it says, 'Merry Christmas,' too."

I hugged her. "You're a fantastic reader. Good job."

Celia clapped her hands. "I want tights, Mommy, and a skirt like Aunt Maddie's. Can you make me one?"

"Oh, sure. I'm so handy with a needle," Elle joked. "At least I can buy the tights."

"Maybe Mrs. Claus will sew her one." Maddie winked. "I'll ask."

She wore red tennis shoes with flashing

lights on the soles instead of precarious high heels. Her gold headband had half a dozen small glittery ornaments glued on top. Maddie pulled it from her head and smoothed her short pixie cut back into place.

"This thing hurts. I made it last night, but it would fit someone else better."

"Let's see." I tried it on and winced. "Ow. Nope, my head is way too big, so it must be perfect for a little girl."

Maddie handed it to Cara, who proudly slipped it on her head. "I'll make one for you, Celia, before Christmas. That's a promise."

Disappointed, she tugged on Cara's arm. "Can we take turns wearing it?"

"No, pumpkin." Matt swung Celia up to perch on his shoulder. "Aunt Maddie promised to make you one, but your flashing shoes are prettier than hers."

I smiled at his red sweatshirt with BITE ME and a one-legged gingerbread man. Elle's green shirt had a red satin box-shaped present with a gold lamé bow. Both girls looked sweet, too, in sweaters adorned with Santa and his reindeer. I handed them each a candy cane from my stocking. Elle agreed that they could to eat them and then handed me a card.

"For the newlyweds. Or is that 'oldyweds?'

381

Maybe we should call them 're-weds,' huh? They're not here yet, I take it."

"Sounds like them now."

A trumpet fanfare blared over the speakers. Everyone applauded when Uncle Ross and Aunt Eve walked into the factory, arm in arm. Tim stuck two fingers in his mouth and whistled shrilly until the newlyweds stopped at their special table.

"Oh, Ross, this is beautiful!"

"Looks like Judith outdid herself, as usual. What happened to casual?"

"You two don't look that casual," I teased.

Aunt Eve's classic pearls, red velvet dress, and matching heels with tiny bows reminded me of a vintage Barbie doll. Uncle Ross didn't resemble boyfriend Ken in the least. Instead of a tux, he wore a black suit, red plaid vest, plus a deep green tie, and immediately stripped off his jacket. He looked so different without his trademark hat, although he'd trimmed his hair and beard, but the grumpiness remained.

"Why the big to-do? We've been married before."

"Congratulations are still in order," Mom called out, beaming.

The crowd rushed over to offer handshakes, hugs, and cheek kisses. Aunt Eve waved her clutch purse to stave off a hot flash, her face flushed, and laughed when I handed her a sandwich baggie with white rice.

"We decided not to throw it," Maddie added, "even though it's traditional."

"No chance of that, heavens! I'll let you two pop out the babies."

"And when is that going to happen?" Mom asked me and my sister. "I'm ready to spoil some grandkids, you know. Dad and I won't live forever."

"You might hear the pitter-patter of little feet sooner than you think!" My sister hooked a thumb my way. "Don't look at me. Way too busy with the graphics studio."

I snorted. "Like I'm sitting around, eating bonbons."

"Cookies, more like it."

"Stop it, you two," Mom said. "Bickering's not allowed at a wedding."

Relieved, I changed the subject. "Here I thought you'd wear your Scottish kilt, Uncle Ross. That would make it interesting in the Reindeer Race."

"You mean showing a bit of bare skin, I suppose," he shot back and winked. "When do we eat? I'm starved."

"You're first, so lead the way," Mom said.

The newlyweds filled plates from buffet spread of carved hams, roast beef and turkey, plus potatoes, roasted vegetables, fresh rolls, and butter. As a nod to our family heritage, Mom had added English and Scottish dishes — puffs of Yorkshire pudding, stewed cranberries, tiny mince tarts, trifles, and Scottish cream buns.

"What, no haggis?" Uncle Ross chuckled when Aunt Eve hushed him.

Mary Kate and Garrett ate close to the Hot Chocolate Bar, which proved popular with the kids. Garret kept watch on the coffee and tea urns, and handed out small bottles of water. Isabel French slid into an empty chair at my nearby table.

"Sasha, have you heard any more about Alison Bloom?"

I dabbed at a cranberry stain on the tablecloth. "Mom said she regained consciousness, but that's all I know."

Inching closer, Isabel chose not to whisper due to the noise surrounding us. "Kristen said that Dave Richardson stopped by the funeral home to apologize, on Thursday. Remember Mrs. Bloom had that meeting yesterday with the funeral directors. I guess he wanted to know why she wouldn't sell the business to him."

"Wait. Kristen's talking to you again?"

Isabel nodded, a little sheepish. "Yeah. She needed my input about selling the Silver

Scoop. Lucas Vanderbeek's buying our inventory and proprietary rights to the name."

"So Vivian bought only the building." I pushed aside a half-eaten mince tart and bit into a cream bun. "So who's this Vanderbeek?"

"Lucas moved here this summer from Grand Rapids or Holland. His parents own a dairy farm, somewhere close to Lake Michigan, and they're sending him fresh cream and whatever else he needs to make specialty products."

"He'll need to rent a shop. Somewhere."

"He wants his dairy bar built close to the park."

"That's bound to triple the business in summer," I said. "Smart move. I've never seen him around the village, but we've been swamped lately. What's he like?"

"Nice, polite. Tall, blond, and he speaks a few languages. Lucas used to participate in all the Tulip Festival events in spring, dressing up and dancing in wooden shoes." Isabel smiled with a wistful sigh. I wondered if she had a slight crush on him. "He's awful cute. Anyway, Kristen's opening her yoga studio in that little Cape Cod house on Kermit —"

"What?" I'd yelped so loud, everyone

around turned to look at me. "Uh, sorry," I said and then whispered to Isabel, "the one that Mrs. Davison rented to Harry and Lois Nichols? But she said it wouldn't be ready until February."

"Guess she changed her mind."

I banged a fist on the table in disgust. Despite being a close friend with Mom, Barbara Davison had rejected Maddie's request to rent the Time Turner shop. But Maggie was family and took precedence. That I could understand. But now she hadn't even given Jay Kirby a chance to ask before Kristen Bloom snapped it up. Resentment spilled into anger. Not that she'd promised anything, but still. I repressed a few choice curse words.

Maddie clapped her hands. "Attention, everyone! I'd like to present the winner of our Teddy Bear Cookie Bake-Off contest. Amanda Pozniak, come over here. Looks like most of you tried her fabulous cookies. They're almost gone."

More cheers rang out. Red-faced, Amanda walked over to join my sister. "Um, thanks for awarding my Cranberry Walnut Snowballs first place."

"And here's your three-hundred-dollar grand prize!"

When Maddie handed her the check,

Amanda waved it high. "I'm donating this to Great Strides, the therapeutic horseback riding program."

"Amanda works there part-time, it's a great place," Maddie said.

"What is it?" someone called out.

"It benefits people with disabilities and challenges, like kids with cerebral palsy or vets with PTSD. Volunteers lead the horses around the corral, and side-walkers help the riders keep their seats." Amanda smiled. "Fifteen horses need a lot of feed and fresh hay for their stalls."

Everyone applauded, while Deon and Tim both stomped their feet and whistled. Isabel and I devoured frosted cupcakes from the Pretty in Pink bakery, unable to resist the buttercream swirled on top, and tiny red and green sprinkles. I wished I'd worn sweat pants. Once again, I'd eaten way too much. The games might help, or a long walk with Rosie later. She had to be getting restless, cooped up in the kitchen all this time.

The kids rushed to greet Santa Claus, who arrived with a bag of gifts. "Ho, ho, ho! Merry Christmas, and I hope you've all been good boys and girls."

I'd hired a nonlocal performer for today's party. Dad deserved to enjoy the festivities, and had pulled up a chair to Uncle Ross and Aunt Eve's table. Maddie danced her way over, red tennis shoes flashing their lights.

"Plastic cups and forks don't work. We should have hung mistletoe."

"Huh?" My uncle leaned back, puzzled.

She waved her arms. "Kiss! Kiss!"

"Ross, lean this way." Aunt Eve planted a smooch on him, to the cheers and whistles of our entire staff. "There. Don't expect any more, though!"

"Then it's time to cut the wedding cake," Maddie announced.

Mom led them over to a pub table that held the single-tier wedding cake, covered with white fondant and a tiny house amidst sparkly green trees. Mary Kate had baked it and Wendy added the decoration. I loved the design. The photographer directed the newly remarried couple to feed each other a bite, snapping several shots, before returning to take other photos of the staff. Mom had certainly outdone herself in planning everything.

Isabel peeled off a second cupcake wrapper. "Looks like that Santa Claus scared a few kids. He's a little too enthusiastic."

I thought I'd recognized that crying baby. Mary Kate hushed Julie and carried her back to the Hot Chocolate Bar. "Poor thing."

"Your dad did a better job when I saw him in Christmas Alley. The day of the parade."

"Did you see Dave Richardson that day?"

"You mean before he went home? Yeah." Isabel licked frosting from her fingers. "He didn't look that sick to me."

"Really."

"I mean, he wasn't coughing. He only said he had a headache, but isn't that part of the job? Listening to kids about what they want for Christmas. I ought to volunteer, if they'd let me. I wouldn't get a headache. I love little kids."

I wondered once more whether Dave faked his illness. Dad had accepted his excuse and took over as Santa Claus. Maybe Leah would know whether her husband was really sick or not. But would she tell me the truth?

The Reindeer Races had begun, so I focused on watching groups of four straddle the awkward, unbalanced hobby stick "reindeers." They lined up inside the long strips of shiny duct tape that marked the slippery floor. Uncle Ross and Aunt Eve took turns being the judge, although it wasn't even close in some races. Two of Evelyn Dolan's older grandsons raced against Pam and

Joan, which resulted in a tie. I slid and fell in the next race, tangling legs with Garrett and Deon, so Tim Richardson did win after all.

"I'm such a klutz! Sorry, guys."

"Bet you did that on purpose," Deon teased. "It's okay. Next year I'll win."

I flexed my arms and legs, but only my elbow felt sore. Lucky me. Deon helped Garrett to his feet. Mary Kate rushed over to check on her husband, who crossed his eyes and stuck out his tongue.

"No concussion. Wait, who are you again?"

"Your wife, who's gonna clobber you."

"I won a prize!" Tim held up a 100 Grand candy bar with a wide grin.

Maddie and Elle helped Cara and Celia straddle the "reindeers" on their short sticks, while two seasonal workers, Bryce Miller and Dallas Peterson, kept watch over Harriet Amato's grandsons. I covered my ears from the girls' raucous screams and yells from the encouraging crowd. Celia won, only because Maddie plucked her up and half-carried, half-ran to the finish line. Aunt Eve gave miniature candy bars to all four children.

"Again, again," Celia begged.

Elle shook her head. "Let other kids have a turn."

"But I wanna —"

"We'll go home if you can't settle down."

Both girls obeyed. My friend had always followed through whenever she gave them a warning, and I filed that away for future reference. Harriet's grandsons ran wild through the factory despite her frequent threats. What a difference.

I turned back to Isabel. "So how did Kristen talk Mrs. Davison into renting her that house on Kermit Street? Jay Kirby hoped to live there. He wanted to use the garage as a studio for his woodcarving business."

She shrugged. "Once Kristen heard the Nicholses moved out, she volunteered to clean it up if Mrs. Davison would rent it to her. She's gonna live above the yoga studio, and I guess she couldn't get away fast enough from her stepmother."

"So that's why."

"Yep. I guess the Nicholses totally trashed the place. Ripped the chandelier from the dining room, stole the drapes and blinds. All the light fixtures, the wall switch plates, whatever they could carry off. I'm surprised they didn't take the appliances."

"Wow," I said glumly. "Wouldn't be worth going to claims court."

"The Nicholses never did say where they planned to move, either."

Tracking them down would be near impossible. Despite my deep disappointment, and dread in relaying the bad news to Jay that night, I changed the subject back to Alison Bloom, Dave Richardson, and the funeral home.

"Dave brought the Blooms a gift basket for Christmas," Isabel said, "with wine, cheese, crackers, and fruit. I guess he was trying to schmooze a bit. Didn't work, though."

"I'm surprised he bothered to visit."

"I know, right? She really doesn't like him at all. And now Mrs. Bloom is too sick to do anything. What if she dies? Kristen will inherit the works. The business, all of her dad's money, and everything that would have gone to his wife first."

"Plus his life insurance payout."

"Yeah. Kristen doesn't care who buys the funeral home. She'd sell it quick."

How interesting. I wondered if Dave knew that. "Maybe it does seem odd that Alison came down sick after that visit."

"Kristen doesn't drink wine, but her stepmom opened the bottle for dinner that night. Then Alison got an important phone call. That's what Kristen told me. She was so distracted, she forgot to finish her glass."

My gut instinct didn't just ring a bell, it

clanged aloud. "You mean —"

"Who can say for sure? Kristen dumped the rest of the wine down the sink, and stuck the bottle in the fridge."

"And then Alison got sick. Right away, or a few hours later?"

"I'm not sure, but she passed out before the EMT's could get there." Isabel waved a hand. "The cops questioned Kristen, of course, but she only put two and two together after they asked what they'd eaten for dinner. I should say what Mrs. Bloom had, but the only difference was that wine."

"Huh. And Dave Richardson gave it to them."

"You can guess why the cops collected the bottle, then."

I didn't have to guess. I knew without a doubt they'd test it for poison.

Chapter 24

"The staff party last night was wonderful, all around," Mom said, "but I'm glad we didn't clean up afterwards. I was too full from the food and that fantastic cake."

"I should have hired our cleaning crew." I stacked the last chair in the rack with a sigh and pushed the heavy cart toward the door. Dad had left the folded tables leaning against a wall earlier. "The rental company will pick these up tomorrow morning."

Maddie finished sweeping the floor. "Now that we're finally done, I'm taking an afternoon nap. I am bushed."

"Party leftovers for dinner tonight." Mom headed for the door. "I'm going Christmas shopping, although it's bound to be a madhouse. Sunday's no better than Saturday, I suppose. Your dad has some kind of meeting this afternoon, girls. See you later."

I followed my sister home from the factory and greeted Rosie. Once she visited the yard, my dog followed me upstairs to my bedroom suite. After powering up my laptop, I browsed online and ordered a few last-minute items. What joy to avoid parking hassles, crowds, and lines. I saved so much time and effort. And delivery was guaranteed before Christmas. I added a few books to my Amazon Wish List while I browsed.

My cell buzzed with a text. Jay had sent an attachment of a student's finished project. Then he called to share the news of his latest commission. A new seafood restaurant in Ann Arbor had asked for a huge carving of a marlin to mount above the door.

"Congratulations!" I was delighted to hear his voice again, and sensed a touch of underlying pride. "What kind of wood will you use?"

"Mahogany, or kiln-dried pine. Depends on the size they want. I'm pumped. Once I get my studio ready in that garage, I can start."

"About that —" I hated to burst his bubble, but Jay took the news well. "I'm sorry. And I'm sorry I didn't call you last night, but I totally crashed."

"No problem. Maybe I'll ask my brother about that outbuilding at the lumber yard. All I'd need is a space heater."

"Kind of dangerous, with all that wood

lying around."

"Yeah, but Paul will figure it out. So tell me about the staff party."

We shared laughs over the Reindeer Games video that Garrett had uploaded to a private YouTube channel. I texted a video attachment of the "Wrap A Bear" contest while I related the party and wedding details. Despite the niggling doubt I had about Pam, I didn't bring her up. We had so many other things to talk about, and I had plenty to accomplish before Christmas Eve. Maddie and I hadn't had time to put up the tree yet. Baking, decorating, plus working.

And I had yet to find the perfect gift for Jay.

My dad's sharp rap on the door startled me, and I almost dropped the phone on Rosie's head. "Say hi to Kirby from me," he said, "and don't forget Mr. Cullen's funeral visitation. After dinner, like seven o'clock. I'd like us all to go as a family."

"What meeting do you have?" I asked, while Jay patiently waited.

"Dave Richardson wants to see me, so I'm going to Quinn's pub. I never had a chance to talk about his dad. Grandpa T. R. was good friends with Tom Senior, you know."

"Okay, Dad. I'll be ready." I returned to

my conversation with Jay. "Sorry about that. I've got to take Rosie for a long walk. Poor thing deserves it after spending yesterday afternoon cooped up in the house. And this morning, during church."

Jay chuckled. "I bet she's lying in the sunshine right now."

"Bingo. She just rolled over, belly up."

"We'll talk later. Take her out while it's warm."

After ending the call, I slid Rosie off the bed. "Okay, you need some exercise before you turn into a stone dog. Do I have to carry you again?"

Downstairs I slipped her Sherpa-lined coat over her head, set her on the floor, and then fastened her harness. She did perk up, given the sunny weather. I wound a scarf around my neck, hoping to elude the bitter wind, and pulled up my hood. Tugged on fur-lined gloves, and then walked briskly down Theodore Lane with Rosie.

I'd also thought of a brilliant plan.

With Dave Richardson gone, I could drive over for a quick chat with Leah Richardson. She was bound to tell me the truth about her husband. How desperate was he to buy the funeral home? Enough to tamper with that wine bottle? The lab results might not be back for a while, but another possibility had come to my mind. If Dave suspected Alison of killing her husband, and was truly loyal to Cal Bloom, could he have meted out a form of justice?

Dave Richardson is more loyal than anyone I've ever known. My dad had said that with conviction, and I believed him. I only hoped that loyalty hadn't led to murder.

Leah was sweet and a good friend. I worried about Dave mistreating her, and my gut instinct wasn't usually wrong. She acted deathly afraid of him. I had to discover the truth. I only had so much time before Dave returned, though. If he found me with Leah, who knew what he'd end up doing? I ignored that. I couldn't pass up this chance.

Once Rosie had her fill of sniffing the entire Village Green, we hurried home. She shook herself hard and then curled by the fireplace with her teddy bear. I was tempted to join her with a mug of hot chocolate and a book, but I plucked up my car keys and cell phone. Hopefully Dad would keep Dave Richardson occupied for a few hours.

I drove over to Archibald Street. No cars sat on the small side street beside the funeral home, and the van wasn't in its usual spot. Had Leah accompanied Dave to the pub? I should have called first.

Instead, I walked to the picket gate. That

reminded me. I took off a glove and groped in my coat pocket. My fingers closed over the piece of glass I'd found here, on the sidewalk, and it had fallen deep into the pocket's bottom. I held it up and examined it close, letting the sunlight shine on the surface. It wasn't a cat's-eye, like I'd first thought, given the boy who had dropped a whole bag before the parade. No marble could have bounced this far from the curb.

Not to land by the gate.

The glass piece resembled more of a pebble, flatter on one side, white with a large black spot on it. I'd seen something similar, recently. Dad, wearing his Santa Bear costume, with the same kind of big glass eyes. And that brought back the memory of seeing Cal Bloom near the Quick Mix Factory. Slumped to one side, his gloves wet, his red suit damp also. Wearing the furry white polar bear head that hid the mayor's face.

One glass eye had been missing.

"This is it. The eye," I said aloud and glanced at the picket gate. "So Cal Bloom changed into the costume here, but then what? Did he lose this before or after that? Did Dave confront him here, and not at the parade? Or maybe he dragged the mayor to the van, and the eye came loose. Dropped on the ground and he didn't notice."

My dad's words replayed again in my memory. *Dave wouldn't harm a fly . . .*

What about a pesky fly? Maybe Dave had gotten so mad, he'd lost all sense of right and wrong and swatted that fly. Everyone knew that Cal Bloom bullied the Richardsons into doing menial volunteer work. He'd angered plenty of vendors by refusing to pay bills. Worst of all, he'd reneged on his promise to sell the funeral home.

Maybe Dave forced Leah to help him kill their boss, and then dump his body. Especially given the bruise I'd seen on her neck. She might be hiding other such marks, in fact. Victims of domestic violence often made excuses, believing their abuser's lies.

That they deserved being beaten, that they were ugly, or stupid. That they brought all the punches, slaps, and kicks on themselves. I'd never encountered that before and didn't know how to help. But the way Dave watched his wife's every move was proof of his fear.

That Leah would let the truth slip.

Maybe I should let Mason question her. I rejected that. He was sure to be miles away in Ypsilanti. Precious minutes had already passed. I couldn't waste more time. Taking a deep breath, I walked toward the funeral home's entrance. A delivery of flowers sat on the wooden bench outside, so I carried it inside the foyer. A great excuse if I needed one. Leah wasn't in the office or the parlors.

I returned to the office and set the box down on the desk. Was she in the basement? The elevator near the front door could only be summoned with a key. I tried other doors marked "Private," but the knobs were all locked.

In the main parlor, I walked to the side door and smiled in relief. It led to the service elevator, big enough for a full-size coffin. How else would they get the deceased up from the prep room? Leah might be getting Jack Cullen ready for tonight's visitation. I checked my cell phone for the time. Dave was bound to return in less than an hour. I had to move fast.

"Keep him there, Dad, for a second beer."

My voice echoed inside the elevator. I wiped clammy palms on my coat and punched the B button. The floor beneath my feet slowly descended. The room below surprised me in its neatness and sterile whiteness. Walls, cabinets, counters, flooring — everything sparkled from the bright ceiling lights, too. I also didn't smell anything. I'd expected a hint of nasty formaldehyde, the scent an ugly reminder of high school biology. A metal table looked scary. So did the odd machinery above it, and the weird sink with its long attached wand.

"Sasha! What are you doing here?"

I whirled to see Leah in the adjoining room's doorway. She wore a blue gown over jeans and a sweatshirt, plus matching shoe coverings. A face mask dangled around her neck. Red powder smeared one cheek. She wore clear latex gloves, too.

"Stopped in for a chat." I waved a hand. "Is Dave here?"

"No. He's meeting with someone, but I don't know who."

"Good. I hoped to catch you alone."

Smiling, she beckoned me to join her in the next room. I didn't want to remain near that metal table, or muse on what occurred there. Leah sidled over to the plain casket, where a man in a suit and tie lay inside, eyes closed, hands folded. I almost didn't recognize Jack Cullen. He'd always walked around Silver Hollow in ragged clothing, and looked as if he hadn't shaved for days. He was clean shaven now. His gray hair had been slicked to one side, too.

Another doorway beyond led to a large open room with two rows of caskets, some plain pine like Cullen's. Most looked elaborate with carvings on the corners or sides, in various polished woods. I recognized mahogany, oak, and cherry.

"So this is the makeup room?" My face felt hot. I hated how nervous I sounded. "Um, you must have training in cosmetics, then."

"I'm licensed in embalming," Leah corrected me, "but that includes using makeup." She held up an airbrush tool, its slender cord plugged into a nearby compressor, and handled it with loving care. Clearly, she took pride in using it. "This helps make our clients look as natural as possible. Have you ever tried an airbrush?"

"No."

"I love it." She picked up a round jar. "This is called hot chocolate, but it's just a brown shadow powder I use for contouring. Around the nostrils, the chin, the little cleft above the upper lip. And a tiny bit under the cheekbones."

"Not an easy job," I said, gazing around me. "I never would have known."

"It can be tough sometimes." Leah set down the tool and picked up a makeup brush. "Families want to see their loved ones looking peaceful, like they're asleep."

I was impressed by all the items spread out on a side table. Palettes of eye shadows held shades of blues, greens, browns, even gold and pink. Mascara, eyebrow pencils, tubs of finishing powder, bottles of nail polish, various tubes of lipstick and gloss, along with combs, brushes, nail files, and other tools filled a separate box. Leah was truly skilled, given the way Jack Cullen looked better dead than alive.

"You have a real gift, doing this job."

"Thank you." Her cheeks flushed pink. "So does Mr. Cullen look okay? He was a mean son-of-a-gun from what I've heard. Not much family, either. Poor guy. I usually get a photo from the family, but this time I had to guess."

"A hundred times better than when I saw him in the summer," I said honestly. "He was dehydrated, of course, but he recovered."

"Too bad I couldn't do much for Dave's dad. Tom Senior had been sick for so long. But Dave wanted Cal Bloom to look his best. That was important."

When Leah glanced expectantly at me, I nodded. "I only had a quick glimpse, though. The parlor was crowded." The truth was I hadn't wanted to see the mayor's body in the casket. Not after finding his body, but I didn't want to admit that.

"More people came to his visitation than we've had in years. Cal Bloom didn't deserve that much hoopla, though." She frowned. "Poor Alison. I heard she's in the hospital. Did she come down with the flu, too?"

"I'm not sure." I changed the subject, not wanting to get sidetracked with time running short. "Can I ask you how sick Dave was, the day of the parade?"

Leah had been powdering Jack Cullen's neck, focused on the job at hand, and glanced my way after a long pause. "He mentioned how you'd asked him about that."

"I'm curious whether he was. Sick, I mean."

"Don't you believe him?"

"No," I said simply. "It's too much of a coincidence."

"But Dave never lies. Not about anything. He's the most honest guy in Silver Hollow. He never thinks badly of other people. He didn't believe me when I told him about — well." She leaned closer toward Jack Cullen's body. "It doesn't matter. Not anymore."

"About what?"

Her hands shook, and she twisted so fast that powder from the brush flicked into the air. "You wouldn't believe me, either."

"Yes, I would." I checked my cell again.

Dave might be on his way now. I was nervous about getting off the main subject. "Tell me what you told him."

"Dave said what's done is done. And besides, he's dead."

What an odd phrase — *what's done is done.* It sounded ominous. Shivers ran up my arms and chest. "You mean about Cal Bloom?" I asked. Leah hesitated, so I touched her arm. "Maybe you'd feel better talking about it. I know the mayor bullied both of you. I heard him at the parade and the Bear-zaar. Remember?"

"That's not the half of it." Her bitterness had returned, a hundredfold.

"Then tell me."

"I can't." She sounded stubborn. Leah fiddled with Cullen's shirt, collar, tie, and then the cuffs of his sleeves. "Dave deserves to own this place, you know. Alison Bloom should sell it to him, not to some stupid funeral home chain. None of the villagers around here would want to deal with strangers taking care of their loved ones. Dave and I have worked here almost fifteen years. Everyone trusts us."

"I agree —"

"We've worked so hard," Leah continued, as if I hadn't said anything. "We've been respectful of everyone's family members.

Even Mr. Cullen. And he's broke."

"I'm sure people around here will help pay for the funeral," I said. "My uncle paid for his coffee at the café. I know the church pantry sent over groceries, and so did Tim Jackson. Gil Thompson helped out, too."

"Cullen wasn't a nice man."

"But he was a veteran. That's why they wanted to help him." I felt like I was beating a dead horse, and grew desperate for an answer. I didn't have time to discuss Cullen or anyone else except her husband. "When Cal Bloom came to change into the Santa Bear costume, before the parade began, did Dave meet him?"

"Here?" Leah turned to face me. "Why would you think that?"

I held up the piece of glass. "Because I found this by the gate outside. On the sidewalk. One eye was missing from the bear's head that Cal Bloom wore. We found him sitting on that bench by the Quick Mix Factory."

She peered closer. "Looks like a marble to me."

"It's the missing eye. I've been wondering how it got there, too." She shrugged, so I kept talking. "I think your husband killed Cal Bloom. I think Dave asked you to help him cover up the crime. Or did he force you

407

to help?"

Leah stood frozen, half-turned away, drawing in shallow breaths. Slowly exhaling, so I waited. She finally swiped at her face with a sleeve. Was she crying? Uh-oh. I hated to upset her more, but I had no choice. She started shaking like a tree in a stiff breeze, still silent.

"Is that how you got the bruise on your neck, Leah?" I asked. "Dave grabbed you? I saw the mark the last time I was here."

She scrunched her shoulders upward, as if trying to hide the offending mark. "It's not much of a bruise." Using her face mask, Leah held it against the base of her neck. "You don't know. You can't know what it's like. Lying to everyone. Praying no one finds out."

"No, I don't. But I'm willing to help. Whatever you need. Counseling, or even if you want to get away from Dave. From the funeral home."

"Dave says I can't. It wouldn't be right. His family, they're everywhere."

"They'd never want you to keep that kind of secret," I said. "Cleo Richardson would want to help. Nickie and Ann. Diana, too."

"You don't understand!"

I cringed at her wailing tone. "The van almost ran me over that night when I crossed the street. Dave drove it that night. After he put Cal's body in the back. Right?"

Leah turned haunted eyes toward me. "No. I was driving."

CHAPTER 25

I reached out to her, but Leah backed away. "Dave forced you to help, after he killed the mayor. Is that true? Please. Just tell the truth."

"He — he deserved to die. For what he did."

My heart thumped so loud in my ears, I could barely hear her whisper. I took a deep breath. "What did the mayor do?"

"Cal Bloom was sick." Her eyes looked huge. "You don't know what kind of man he really was, Sasha. No one does. Nobody in Silver Hollow knew, except me and Dave."

"Okay. So explain what you mean." I waited, and spoke again while she hesitated. "Did Alison and Kristen have problems with him, too? What did Bloom do?"

When Leah kept shaking her head, I sighed in frustration. She finally spoke, her tone sharp. "No, they don't know anything."

"Okay."

"He kept saying nasty things. Telling dirty jokes. And showed me photos."

I took a wild guess. "He showed you a photo. Of Cissy Davison?"

"Yes. He said she posed for him. That if I did the same thing, he'd reward me."

"Reward you. In what way?"

Leah picked up a pair of scissors and a makeup brush, tossed them down, and then picked up other tools. Threw them into the box, harder and harder. Her growing rage scared me. What had I started? Next she picked up a razor blade and stared at it. I wondered if she'd hurt herself, and how I could stop her if she attempted it. I hoped not.

"He lied about so many other things, to me and Dave. I didn't believe him at first," she whispered, "but why else would he have that picture?"

"Cissy posed for her fiancé, Gus Antonini, not Cal Bloom," I said firmly. "She told me that herself. So yes. He did lie."

She drew a shuddering breath. "And about signing the papers."

"The papers —"

"To sell us the funeral home."

I slowly nodded. "He had them drawn up by a lawyer in the spring, I heard that. But

Cal never signed them."

"He promised!" Leah wept openly now. "Cal swore he would sell. Dave was like a son to him, he deserves to own this business. I didn't have a choice, Sasha!"

"So you posed for him?" Shocked, I touched my own neck in sympathy. "Was Dave so mad, he gave you that bruise?"

Her eyes bulged with fear. "No, not Dave. Cal had no sense of decency. He wasn't easy to please. He was always complaining to Dave, always yelling at me. Then one day he grabbed me by the neck. Right here."

She pulled down her sweater to show the fading bruise on her neck, tinged yellow, with finger-shaped marks. But that didn't jibe with what I knew about the mayor. I'd never heard any rumors of physical violence. Not with his first wife, or with Alison. Cheating, yes. But not abuse. And why would Cal Bloom hurt the wife of the man he treated like a son? I was beginning to doubt her story. Maybe Dave had abused her, and Leah didn't want to admit it.

Except Cal's reputation for womanizing hadn't died with him. I had to ask. Hated to ask, but I wanted the truth. I'd come this far.

"Did you have an affair with the mayor, Leah?"

412

She licked her lips, eyes shifting down to the floor. "Ugh, no."

I sensed Leah was lying. "You showed Dave the bruise, though?"

"He saw it." She sounded sad now, and her whole mood changed from fear to an odd hollowness. "Dave asked me what happened. I told him, but he didn't believe me. He didn't believe me, Sasha. My husband didn't believe me."

"I'm sorry." I felt horrible for her, and her voice had risen to an alarming pitch. "But I'm still confused. Why would Cal Bloom hurt you? And show you Cissy's photo."

"I told you, he was nasty," she snapped, and then stumbled to the doorway. "I gotta calm down. My hands. I can't do anything unless I have a drink."

"I'll make you coffee," I offered, but Leah shook her head.

She weaved her way around the caskets to a small storage room near the locked elevator. I followed, curious about what she meant by a drink. Alcohol, apparently, since several bottles lined a shelf unit inside. They resembled the ones hotels put in guest rooms. Leah stripped off her gown and gloves, slid one bottle into her pants' pocket, and plucked two more from the shelf. She shoved aside shrink-wrapped paper plates on a shelf and grabbed a stack of plastic cups. After sloshing clear liquid into two of them, she added a dash of salt.

"Tequila, minus the worm, but no lime." Leah waved me over, picked up one cup, and swallowed half the contents. "Bottoms up, Sasha."

I shook my head. "Sorry. I do like infused vodka, but I prefer tea."

"No stove or microwave down here, sorry. There's one in the lounge upstairs."

"That's okay. I'm not thirsty."

"This stuff is what keeps me sane," she said and waved at the shelf. "I hid it down here so nobody would find out."

"But someone did, right? Is that how you got that bruise?"

Leah whirled around, a deer-in-the-headlights expression plastered on her face. "Cal found my stash three weeks ago. Guess I didn't hide it very well."

"But it's not an excuse to hurt anyone."

"I know. It hurt a lot." After finishing off the first little bottle, she poured a second into her cup. "I've been using makeup to hide it. I forgot one day. That's when Alison noticed. She asked me what happened, so I told her. I told her Cal grabbed me. You should have seen the look on her face." Leah cackled and then gulped more tequila.

I raised an eyebrow. "I can imagine she was shocked."

"Ha. She denied it, of course. Her husband wouldn't hurt anyone, yadda yadda. Sure, right. Cal Bloom was perfect. And Alison was practically perfect in every way."

Her bold, singsong voice changed her entire outlook. I wondered when Dave would return. Maybe he could explain what had been going on between Bloom and his wife. The real story about working conditions at the funeral home. But Leah continued rambling.

"She got everything. Whatever she wanted. Alison demanded a new kitchen, new floor, cabinets, appliances. Second floor, their living quarters. Top of the line stove, forty-eight inches wide, with a microwave warming drawer. A Sub-Zero refrigerator. She was relentless. Designer clothes, shoes, phones, cars. New everything."

I remembered what the mayor said the day of the parade. "New furniture, too."

"Oh, yes. Whatever it took to keep her off his back. Cost him over forty grand, with the furniture and kitchen. Alison never cooked dinner in that new kitchen, either, not once! She always ordered carryout. That's what Cal complained about, anyway. Endlessly. I felt sorry for him. He didn't deserve such a witch. She was bona fide, too."

"Wow." I found it odd that Leah's rage had tapered off and been displaced by a deep-seated jealousy. "Alison spent a lot of time at the Silver Birches."

"Yeah. I figured she wouldn't bother visiting her mom once she got all that inheritance money. I mean, you told me she upped Cal's insurance policy, right? So I asked Dave. Over a million bucks! Unbelievable." Leah finished her drink, eyed the cup with sorrow, but sounded steadier than I'd expected. "They were both crazy."

That was the second time she referred to Alison in the past tense. As if she were dead. Another red flag that signaled strange behavior to me. My stomach knotted.

"So what happened? Were you and Dave both here when the mayor came to change into the costume?" I worded the next question with care. "Then Cal had a heart attack."

Leah paused so long, I wondered if she'd heard me. "Yeah. He clutched his chest and everything. Keeled over, boom. Just like that."

"Then what happened?"

She shrugged. "Nothing. He was dead."

I folded my arms across my chest. "The

preliminary autopsy report showed a skull fracture. That he hit his head."

"Oh. Yeah, that's right." Leah tossed the empty cup and both bottles into the wastebasket. "Dave said it was an accident."

That didn't answer all my questions, however. "Why did you drive him all the way to the bench by the Quick Mix Factory? Why not call 9-1-1, or the police? If you explained all about what happened, they'd have believed you."

"No. They wouldn't believe me. Dave didn't."

I cleared my throat. "When we found the mayor, his gloves were soaking wet. I saw burns on his hands and chest, too. Like he'd been electrocuted."

"He did that to himself. Wanna see? Come on, I'll show you."

Leah pulled off her face mask, tossed it as well, and led the way upstairs. I was glad to leave the basement. We passed the side parlor with the Victorian hearse, the office, and the main parlors. The lounge was tucked away near the restrooms, behind two glass doors, with shirred curtains blocking the interior. I recognized the alcove and its antique phone stand, near the back doors that led outside. A red light blinked above. Probably an alarm.

Uneasy, I dug out my cell phone. I didn't have time to text Mason or my dad, however. Leah stood inside the lounge, the doors open. Watching me. I slipped the phone into my coat pocket. Shivered, since it felt colder here than in the basement.

"I'll make you that tea." Leah smiled. "We only turn up the heat right before a showing. Around five o'clock, a few hours before Mr. Cullen tonight. Dave says keeping it at sixty-four degrees saves money. That's another thing Cal didn't give us credit for, keeping the utility bills down. Penny pinching. But, oh, Alison never went without."

"I take it you don't like her."

"Why should I? She asked for the world, he gave it to her. He always made excuses for her greediness. Poor Alison suffered during the divorce, when Joyce made trouble, on and on. But then he'd complain. Every time he opened his wallet."

"What kind of trouble did Joyce make?"

"That's old news. Someone slashed Alison's tires, threw a rock and smashed her car window. Prank phone calls. That kind of thing." Leah held up a basket with a dozen foil packets. "I have mint, or orange spice, or regular black tea."

"Mint is good."

"Sugar?"

"Yes, please." My throat was dry. Maybe I was thirsty after all. "Things must have settled down, though. Between Cal's wives."

"He had to pay alimony to Joyce, but not child support after she dumped Kristen on him. Now that cash cow's ended."

Leah walked over to the counter and filled a mug with water. She set it in the microwave, punched the panel buttons, and then pushed aside a small coffee maker. While she was busy with the tea, fetching a canister of sugar, I sat down and texted my dad.

At the funeral home. Help.

The microwave beeped. I didn't get a chance to forward the message to Mason before Leah stood beside me, holding my steaming tea mug. She set it before me.

"Who are you calling?" Suspicion tainted her words.

"I was going to call Maddie," I said. Truthful enough, since I always did at some point every day. "Remember, you said you'd show me what happened to the mayor."

Leah waved at the sink. "Cal was washing his hands over there. And then he suddenly fell backward. Hit his head, I guess."

"You said he clutched his chest. Did he mention having chest pains before that?" I asked. "Or numbness in his arm or shoulder? Most people have warning signs."

"Nope, he didn't say anything. Just fell backward. Dead."

"But you said he electrocuted himself."

"I guess that's right." Her evasiveness was stranger yet. "Drink your tea."

"Why didn't you call 9-1-1? Or check for a pulse."

"He was dead. Dave said it had to be an accident. We couldn't do anything." Leah waved at the mug, frantic. "You said you wanted tea! Drink it."

Her savage tone was another red flag. Since she watched me so close, I brought the cup's edge to my lips, pretended to swallow a big gulp, and then set it down. "Great. Thanks."

"Good, I'm glad you like it." She broke into a wide smile.

"Back to Cal Bloom. There had to be some source of electricity for him to get shocked. Bad enough to bring on a heart attack."

"He was washing his hands." Leah blew out a long breath, clearly frustrated. "Why are you asking so many questions! He died. End of story."

"But —"

"Drink your tea, Sasha. All of it."

"I'm not thirsty anymore." I pushed the cup halfway across the table. Her story had flaws and was jumbled together, wrong in parts. And I didn't trust her now.

"It probably won't matter. You drank enough."

I froze at her smug tone. "You put something in the tea, didn't you? Like the wine. In that gift basket Dave took over to Alison Bloom."

"How clever of you." Leah pursed her lips, eyes narrowed. "Alison's dead, too bad. She deserved it. Like Cal Bloom. He wouldn't sign those papers, and neither would she. Said she'd never sell, even if we begged her a hundred times. Now you know. And you'll be sick in a few minutes, too bad. You didn't need to drink much. I put in extra, to make sure you'll die."

"What did you put in it?" I stared at the mug, wishing I hadn't touched it at all.

"It only takes an ounce to kill." She drew out a small bottle from her pocket. The third one from the shelf downstairs, except the label was missing. "It's formalin. A mixture of water, menthol, and thirty-seven percent formaldehyde. We use it for embalming."

Shock hit me like a cold blast of wind. I pushed my chair back and stood, praying that the mug's rim had no toxic residue. Could it be absorbed through the skin? My lips burned. Was that real or only my imagination? I scrubbed my mouth with my coat sleeve. If only I could get to the sink and wash, but no. That was where she electrocuted the mayor.

She'd fry me the same way.

Leah blocked any escape to the door, and squinted, studying me. As if waiting for me to drop dead. My legs felt wooden, paralyzed. My whole body, in fact. I had to get out of there. Before she had any chance of forcing the rest of that tea down my throat.

"How did you put the formalin into the wine bottle?"

"A syringe through the cork. Too bad I couldn't put in more than an ounce. Otherwise it would have looked suspicious, being too full." She leaned forward with a sly smile. "You feeling any nausea yet? Maybe disoriented? This time I'll get to witness the effects in person. That's gonna be really cool for me. Too bad for you, though."

I hated how she kept repeating "too bad."

"But, Leah. I thought we were friends."

"Sorry, friend. I can't have you telling the cops what we did. We have to make sure you don't, that's all. Just like Alison."

"I won't tell anyone."

"That's what Cal said, too. He always lied," Leah said. "He told me that he'd never cheat on Alison, not after he cheated on Joyce. But why did he show me that photo of Cissy? Want to see it? Cal left it here, you know."

She pulled a wrinkled photo from her pocket and held it up, although the bright ceiling light added a glare to the shiny surface. That and the creases didn't hide much of Cissy, with her blond locks falling over one eye, lips pouting. She sprawled across a rumpled bed in crimson Victoria's Secret bra and panties, a garter belt, black stockings. One red high heel shoe lay on the floor. The other dangled off her arched foot.

"Cissy Davison thinks she's so hot, like a movie star." Leah crushed the photo in her fist. "I told Cal I'd wear an outfit like this, and he could take a photo. All he had to do was sign the papers. But he laughed at me. That was so stupid of him."

I forced myself to sound calm, although every nerve inside me screamed. "Yes, that was. He shouldn't have laughed."

"Right! All guys like seeing women half-naked, or totally naked. Even Dave."

I sensed Dave had no clue about any of this. Maybe he didn't want to accept that Cal Bloom's death was anything but an accident. I couldn't see him conspiring with Leah to murder the mayor. And I prayed that Dad had gotten my text.

"Cal washed his hands, right over there, and put on his gloves. He kept laughing. I got mad. So I pushed the coffee pot into the sink. Too bad it was still plugged in."

"What did Dave do?" I asked.

"He wasn't here," Leah said impatiently. "Dave really was sick at home, so I took care of everything myself. I didn't need him."

"So the shock brought on Cal's heart attack."

"Uh-huh. Too bad it didn't kill him. I did check, you know." She sounded matter of fact, with a hint of pride. "He gasped for air, and squirmed like a pig. He was a pig. Always winking at me. At lots of women around the village, including you. Putting us down like we couldn't do anything right. Cal fired me, did you know?"

"He fired you?"

"He wanted to hire someone else to do makeup," Leah said, shoulders shaking, half-sobbing. "Someone he could trust! After all the classes I've taken, all the people I took pains to make beautiful again. It wasn't fair, Sasha. I couldn't let him do that to me."

I didn't know what to say to that, but knew losing her job had definitely pushed her over the edge. Cal Bloom must not have realized the danger he'd put himself in. He'd made the same mistake with Gina Lawson, dismissing her, and most women. Assuming they'd accept whatever he decided. Gina took steps to claim payment. Leah's actions went beyond the pale.

"Cal said he'd tell Dave, too, about me offering to pose for him. What a jerk!" Leah yelled that, her face flushed red. "So I hit him. Hard as I could, on the back of his head. With that pewter urn, the most expensive one that he always pushed people into buying for cremation. Wasn't that poetic justice? He was good and dead after that."

Now I knew the truth. "How did you get him all the way out to the van, though? Cal must have weighed almost three hundred pounds."

"And he called me fat!" She huffed, warming to her story. "I got the big rolling cart we use to bring the caskets from the basement. It took a lot, I was sweating by the time I got Cal on it. Then I pushed him out to the van."

"Nobody saw you?"

"It was dark by then. That was the easy part. Now Kristen will sell the funeral home to Dave, and I'll get what I want for a change. Beautiful clothes, instead of wearing black all the time. And a vacation! We never go anywhere, or get anything new for the house."

Dave Richardson suddenly appeared in the lounge's doorway. "Leah. I told you, we don't need any of that to be happy."

She whirled around at the sound of his voice. He sounded calm. Too calm. Shivers raced through me again, and my skin tingled. Was that another effect of formalin poisoning? My head ached. I blinked, trying to clear my vision.

"You promised we'd go to Hawaii for our anniversary. Did we? No —"

"We couldn't leave after Dad came down sick."

"There's always an excuse! Next month, next year, we have to save more money."

Dave heaved a deep sigh. "You said Cal hit his head. Why did you lie to me?"

I didn't want to be here, listening to their exchange, but I was trapped. Maybe I'd be able to slink past them while they argued. Leah shoved the table against me, furious, her strength fueled by adrenaline. A wave of tea splashed over the cup's rim.

"You're not going anywhere, Sasha. You're going to die."

"No, Leah. You need help," Dave said softly. I felt sick, but she ignored him.

"You weren't here! There was blood, all over the floor, so I cleaned it up. Bleached it, too. I couldn't let you find out what happened." When Dave inched closer to her, she held out a hand. "You never believe me, no matter what I tell you —"

"Cal never told you jokes. He swore he never made a pass at you."

This time she screamed at her husband. "He didn't have to! I caught him looking at that photo of Cissy, the slut. Cal Bloom was a lying, cheating, dirty old man."

I stole a glance at Dave, fearing what would happen next. Would he turn her in to the cops, or protect his wife from being caught? If so, I was doomed. They could work together to get rid of me. Finish the job Leah had started with the formalin.

"Everything will work out, but you have to trust me," Dave said.

"No." Her fear vanished — replaced by confidence. "Sasha drank the tea. If it wasn't enough to kill her, I've got more. Right here."

Leah held up a syringe. I backed against the wall while Dave froze, fists clenched. Was he going to play the hero, and take it by force? She could stick him and then use the rest on me. We'd both end up dead. I reached across the table, since she warily watched Dave.

"You can't stop me. Sasha will die —"

"Wrong."

The instant Leah turned her head, I sloshed the tea toward her face. With a screech, she clawed at her eyes but then blindly threw the syringe. It clattered against the wall, inches from my head. I crunched it under my shoe in satisfaction.

Sirens roared in the distance. Before I dashed to the foyer and out into the cold, panting in relief, I saw Dave wiping Leah's face, neck, and hands with paper towels. I didn't care if she suffered. Or what would happen to her, not after she tried to poison me.

I was so done with crazy killers. Murder, too.

CHAPTER 26

My alarm beeped again. I rolled over in bed, wishing I could stay there all day. Reaching a hand over, I snoozed the button for the third time. Closed my eyes, cherished the last inkling of a sweet dream. Jay's arms around me, his kisses sweet. And wet.

"Rosie!" I swiped my mouth. "I love you, too, but ugh. You want to go out already?"

I checked the clock. Nine o'clock, although the Silver Bear Shop was closed Christmas Eve and Christmas Day. A nice two-day stretch to relax — before our after-Christmas sale, with fifteen to twenty-five percent off holiday accessories and teddy bears. Some customers hadn't picked up their Beary Potter Keepsake wizard bears yet. But we'd met the deadline, thankfully. Except the Child's Play Toy Box Co. sent dozens of last-minute orders.

That meant we'd be producing and shipping bears through January.

"Sasha," Maddie called from downstairs. "Breakfast!"

Leaving the cozy warmth of my down comforter wasn't easy. I threw on a pair of fleece pajama pants and a hoodie, then brushed my hair and teeth. The formalin in that mug of tea had chafed my lips and the skin below my mouth. It could have been far worse, though. I had minor abrasions, compared to poor Alison Bloom.

Sighing, I applied the prescription ointment and hoped it would fade before Jay returned today. I wished I'd gone shopping for something else. Maybe my gift for Jay wasn't as perfect as I first thought.

It's almost Christmas. The magic will soon begin.

"Okay, Grandpa T. R." Hearing his voice in my head cheered my spirits. Rosie waited by the stairs, so I rubbed her curly ears. "Santa Paws is coming tonight! Let's go."

In the kitchen, my parents sat with Aunt Eve and Uncle Ross, coffee mugs in hand, and the remains of eggs, bacon, and waffles on their plates. Falling snow obliterated the view through the window of everything but white-coated trees. Rosie shot outside without her sweater or coat. She didn't linger, however. I caught her before she could shake herself. Ice caked her paw pads, which I gently loosened with a soft towel.

"— sure to get a plea deal," Dad was saying. "Premeditated murder, plus poisoning. The last is a fifteen-year felony. But I haven't heard much yet."

The awful memory of the funeral home rushed back. I had fled from the lounge to find Dad rushing from his car, but he whisked me to the hospital before I finished explaining. After receiving my text, he'd sent Dave Richardson while he hunted down Chief Russell.

Dad also explained that Dave had shared his fears of losing everything at the pub. His self-respect, the business, family honor — and he'd kept a close watch on Leah, hoping his suspicions were wrong. He'd sensed Cal Bloom's death hadn't been an accident, but chose to be passive.

That decision nearly cost my life.

The doctors had examined my inflamed skin and proclaimed me lucky that I'd evaded a more severe injury. After I explained a gazillion times, to the hospital staff, Chief Russell, and my family once Dad drove me home, I remained numb to it all for several days.

I'd trusted Leah. While not a close friend, she seemed so vulnerable and I felt drawn to help her. Little did I suspect that she'd cracked. I also felt betrayed by Dave, who chose to bury his head in the sand. Leah could easily have added two more murders, mine and Alison Bloom's. I shuddered, remembering that tea. How sly she'd looked, how self-satisfied until Dave arrived and interfered. At least I'd survived without being poisoned.

Maddie waved a hand in front of my face. "Wakey, wakey! Feeling better?"

"Thank God you didn't swallow that stuff." Uncle Ross slapped the table. "They'll put Leah Richardson away for life, since she admitted her guilt."

"Alison's inflammation in her stomach and throat won't heal for a long time," Mom said. "I'm so angry at Dave. The truth was staring him in the face. No one in Silver Hollow will ever let him or the whole clan forget this."

"People won't hold it against them," Dad said. "Even if they won't forget, they will forgive Dave for being blindsided. It's Christmas Eve, so let's count our blessings."

I couldn't help feeling apathetic, though. Dad had called Jay and told him everything, and I knew he'd be upset. Especially since we'd both nearly been killed a few months ago. Jay had warned me to avoid sleuthing. So did Detective Mason. I'd ignored them both and plodded on to confront another close brush with death. Mom felt guilty, and swore she'd never ask me again to prove anyone's innocence. Not even Dad's, and that made me laugh.

But I had some serious thinking to do.

Rosie jumped up, surprising everyone by her frantic barking by the door. I covered my face with my hands, praying Jay hadn't arrived. I wasn't emotionally ready to face him. Hearing Detective Mason's voice, I sagged in relief. He remained by the door, refusing to sit.

"Sasha." Slowly I raised my eyes and met his gaze. Mason gave a wry smile. "I'm not gonna say 'I told you so,' but don't beat yourself up. I missed the boat, like you did."

"By an ocean. And you did say 'I told you so.'"

"How's Mrs. Richardson?" Dad asked the detective. "Still in the hospital?"

He nodded. "Dave flushed her eyes before any permanent damage was done, but she inhaled it and that affected her lungs. She's changed her story half a dozen times, but it doesn't matter. I have to say this town's getting a bad rep."

"Not our fault," I said. He laughed.

"I hope I won't have to come back for a long time. If ever."

Before departing, Mason brought out a package for Rosie. "Hope this doesn't drive you nuts, but she's a sweet dog. Have a wonderful holiday, folks. A safe one."

"Same to you and your family." Dad shook his hand.

Rosie squeaked the new toy, a soft gingerbread man, over and over. That would get old fast, but I didn't mind. She'd get a few new toys tomorrow as well. She'd been too bored lately. Maddie rushed off to the mall with Dad for last-minute shopping. My aunt and uncle also left, and Mom made me promise to call if I needed anything before she headed home. I agreed.

Anything for peace and quiet.

Huddled under a blanket on the sofa, I picked up a book. Rosie jumped up with her toy, circled three times beside me, and lay down. *Squeak, squeak.* I closed my eyes. An ear-splitting bark woke me, and I nearly slid off the sofa when Rosie jumped across my chest and raced to the back door. Tail wagging, she scratched and whined. I caught sight of Jay on the porch outside, bundled in his thick coat and scarf, shifting from one foot to the other.

"Calm down, Rosie." I opened the door wide. "Merry Christmas!"

He hugged me, snowy coat and all, and I

heard an odd muffled sound. Jay sported light brown stubble on his jaw and upper lip, and he showered me with more snowflakes when he unwound his wool scarf.

"Merry, merry. I've got another surprise for you. Hope you like it."

"How about this?" I pointed to my mouth, my cheeks burning. "Dad told you, right?"

"Hey, don't blame yourself. I should have been here, but I'm home for good."

"Promise?"

"As long as you promise never to sleuth again without me."

Squeak, squeak, squeak. Rosie had brought her gingerbread toy over, hoping to play, but we ignored her. Jay hugged me again, tighter. This time I felt something wriggle beneath his coat, and found the zipper. Before I tugged it down far, a tiny pointed muzzle appeared.

"Aww!" I drew the small, adorable, black and tan toy poodle into my arms.

Rosie jumped against my legs, sniffing like mad. "She's not a puppy," he said. "She had a litter before she was rescued by Wags and Whiskers. She's two years old, seven pounds." Jay peeled off his coat, boots, and then stooped to give Rosie a hug and rub her ears. "My sister Lauren took her, but she couldn't keep her with work and studying. Thought I'd bring Sugar Bear down here, see if they'd get along. I hope you'd like her."

"Sugar Bear! What a darling name."

I cuddled her against my cheek, which she licked over and over again. Her dark eyes blinked, and the little dog wriggled so hard, I knelt to introduce Rosie. High-pitched yips from Sugar Bear melted my older dog's heart. Rosie whined in excitement and crouched, her butt in the air, tail wagging, clearly wanting to play.

I figured we'd better take it slow and kept close watch on them both. Sugar Bear soon rushed off to explore the kitchen and other rooms, Rosie tagging after her. I had to laugh.

"I love her! I've been worried about Rosie lately, that she's been lonely. But I know that Nyx will have a major hissy fit. Whoops. There she is now."

We rushed to find the cat snarling and spitting, her black tail as fat as a hairbrush. Sugar Bear ignored her, sniffing around, oblivious. Rosie avoided Onyx, shrinking from her anger. Jay and I laughed so hard, the weight of everything that had happened since the staff party faded.

"Thank you." I kissed him. "I bet you're tired."

"I left at six this morning, can you believe it? Lots of accidents." Jay fetched a bag he'd brought in when he arrived, which I hadn't noticed. "This is for you. Open it now. Why wait till tomorrow morning?"

"You don't have to convince me."

I ripped the paper away to reveal a cardboard box, stripped the packing tape, and then dove through a drift of foam peanuts to draw out an intricate wood carving, about a foot and a half high. The detailed teddy bear stood on a square base, one arm outstretched. The face and fur looked incredibly realistic, Jay's specialty.

"Keep going. The rest is in the box's bottom." He ducked when I tossed a few peanuts his way. "Better watch out, or Sugar Bear might eat them. Rosie, too."

"True, and we don't want doggie tummy trouble." My hand finally struck a smaller box, so I opened it to find a small brass lantern. "Wow."

"See, the bear holds the lantern's handle." He threaded it through and then showed me the bottom. "It's like those clip lamps. Uses an LED bulb, so reading should be easy."

"So cool! Thanks, so much." I kissed him in appreciation, and then beckoned him to the kitchen. Sugar Bear lapped water from

Rosie's dish. I handed him the square box wrapped in gold foil paper. "It's your new studio."

He snickered. "Not very heavy for a building. Feels empty, in fact." Jay ripped aside the wrapping, flipped the lid, and stared at the folded square of paper inside. "A blueprint?"

"I told you. Your studio."

"You're giving me a studio." Jay stared at the smoothed out paper. "For real."

"Not technically. I'm paying for the soundproofing. That way Maddie won't have to hear your chainsaw, although she claims it wouldn't bother her." I snatched up Sugar Bear before Onyx scratched her eyes out. My sister's cat slunk toward the cat tower, climbed to the highest level, and settled herself. Wary, and watching. "Guess who's the dominant girl?"

"Sugar Bear takes a dare, from what Lauren told me." He ruffled the dog's fluffy topknot and then returned to study the heavy sheet. "So where is this?"

"What used to be Flambé. The whole back half of the building can be your studio, unless you want to make changes," I added. "Or you could pick somewhere else. But you'd better let my dad know. He's already hired a crew."

"Wow!" Jay kissed me. "I don't know what to say."

"Dad bought it, and said he'll give you a good rental price for the back half. Maddie pays him for Silver Moon, but Mom's buying out Maggie Davison's shop in the village. That will give her street cred when she runs for mayor, but if you'd prefer that location —"

"No, I like this idea better," Jay interrupted. "Too much noise and people on Main Street for me to work. So what are her plans for that?"

I couldn't help my excitement. "I talked her into the idea, because vintage is really popular right now. She's opening a combination shop and art gallery, so you can display your carvings there. Maddie will, too, Zoe Fisher, even Maggie Davison."

He still looked stunned. "Wow."

"You said that already."

Jay caught me and Sugar Bear in a hug, and then scooped up Rosie as well. She licked his nose and one eye. "I'd say this is the best holiday ever, being here with you."

"I agree." I kissed him, too, grateful I'd lived to see Christmas.

ABOUT THE AUTHOR

Meg Macy is an award-winning author and artist. Her first published book, *Double Crossing,* won the 2012 Spur Award for Best First Novel from Western Writers of America. Meg is also one-half of the writing team of D. E. Ireland, authors of the Eliza and Henry Higgins Mystery series — of which two titles have been Agatha Award finalists. Meg lives in Southeastern Michigan, the setting for her Shamelessly Adorable Teddy Bear mysteries. Visit the author online at megmacy.com, Facebook.com/MegMacyTeddyBearCozies/, Twitter.com/megmims, and Pinterest.com/meg_macy.

The employees of Thorndike Press hope you have enjoyed this Large Print book. All our Thorndike, Wheeler, and Kennebec Large Print titles are designed for easy reading, and all our books are made to last. Other Thorndike Press Large Print books are available at your library, through selected bookstores, or directly from us.

For information about titles, please call:
(800) 223-1244

or visit our website at:
gale.com/thorndike

To share your comments, please write:
Publisher
Thorndike Press
10 Water St., Suite 310
Waterville, ME 04901